THE MISSIONARY

THE MISSIONARY:
AN INDIAN TALE

SYDNEY OWENSON

(Lady Morgan)

edited by Julia M. Wright

broadview literary texts

National Library of Canada Cataloguing in Publication Data

Morgan, Lady (Sydney), 1783-1859
  The missionary : an Indian tale

(Broadview literary texts)
Includes bibliographical references.
ISBN 1-55111-263-9

1. Missions, Portuguese—India—History—Fiction.
2. Inquisition—Fiction. I. Wright, Julia M. (Julia Margaret), 1964-
II. Title. III. Series.

PR5059.M3M5 2002   823'.7   C2001-904249-3

Broadview Press Ltd. is an independent, international publishing house, incorporated in 1985

North America
Post Office Box 1243, Peterborough, Ontario, Canada K9J 7H5
3576 California Road, Orchard Park, NY 14127
Tel: (705) 743-8990; Fax: (705) 743-8353;
e-mail: customerservice@broadviewpress.com

United Kingdom:
Thomas Lyster, Ltd.,
Unit 9, Ormskirk Industrial Park, Old Boundary Way, Burscough Rd,
Ormskirk, Lancashire L39 2YW Tel: (1695) 575112; Fax: (1695) 570120;
E-Mail: books@tlyster.co.uk

Australia:
St. Clair Press, P.O. Box 287, Rozelle, NSW 2039
Tel: (02) 818-1942; Fax: (02) 418-1923

www.broadviewpress.com

Broadview Press gratefully acknowledges the financial support of the Book Publishing Industry Development Program, Ministry of Canadian Heritage, Government of Canada.

Typesetting and assembly: True to Type Inc., Mississauga, Canada.
PRINTED IN CANADA

Contents

Appendix B: Reviews of and Responses to Owenson's Writing

Appendix C: A Selection of Owenson's Poetry from *Poems* (1801)
and *The Lay of an Irish Harp* (1807)

Acknowledgments

I would like to thank the Social Sciences and Humanities Research Council of Canada for its generous support of my research. To Professor Balachandra Rajan I owe a considerable debt: his graduate course on representations of India in English literature was intellectually energizing, and first led me to Owenson's work. The British Library and its very helpful staff provided me with essential access to editions of Owenson's work as well as the orientalist texts cited in the pages of *The Missionary*. The anonymous readers of my proposal for this edition and Jason Haslam offered useful advice that helped in particular with the introduction. Throughout this project, James Allard provided invaluable research assistance; he, along with Jacqueline Howse, also helped with the proofreading of the text.

Introduction

"It is," said he, "from the harmonies and conformities of nature, that man should borrow his political and moral adaptions, and learn from the Legislature of the Universe those beneficent laws, which should form the social compact of mankind. Whenever the institutions of government shall tend to excite and develope the natural sensibility of man, the happiness of the state will be affected, for virtue itself is but composed of the affections; and the maxim of wisdom, or the exertion of art, proceeds only from that secret impulse by which nature urges man to enlighten and cherish his brother man."
—Sydney Owenson, *Woman; Or, Ida of Athens* (2: 14-15)

The Author's Life and Writing

Sydney Owenson, Lady Morgan after 1812, was one of the most successful writers of her day. Publishing novels, travelogues, essays, and poetry for over half a century, she had a reputation that extended beyond Ireland and Britain to North America and continental Europe, where her work was frequently translated.[1] Byron, Caroline Lamb, Charles Robert Maturin, Thomas Moore, Walter Scott, Mary Wollstonecraft Shelley, and Percy Bysshe Shelley were among her diverse array of admirers and imitators. Her influence extended beyond the Romantic period to include the Victorian; one of her Victorian reviewers asserts, she has "been almost as much ours as our fathers'" (Rev. of *Luxima*). She was always controversial. Writing in defence of Irish nationalist aspirations, she found opponents among conservative British reviewers, and supporters among liberals who favoured a moderation of British colonial domination in Ireland. In continental Europe, her writings often marked a similar divide in other nationalist debates—so much so that they were sometimes banned and even burned. She was also controversial because she acknowledged the exclusion of women from political debate and activity but then foregrounded politics in her writing;

---

1   Chorley and Redding ("Lady Morgan") note the success of Owenson's writings in continental Europe. There was an American edition of *The Missionary* in 1811 and a French translation in 1812 (Dean ix-x).

many of the conservative reviews chastized her as a bluestocking (a derogatory term for a woman intellectual) and made such strong remarks that they were rebuked in return for speaking inappropriately about a woman.[1] Always near the centre of cultural and political power, she was the friend of Thomas Campbell, Lamb, Moore, Mary Shelley, and vast numbers of aristocrats.[2] The Austrian emperor barred her from entering his territory, the British government made her the first woman recipient of a government pension for contributions to literature, and through it all her books sold extremely well, many of them appearing in multiple editions in a variety of countries.[3]

Owenson's early work is dominated by the sentimental tradition which held such ascendance in the latter decades of the long eighteenth century. Her first published volume, *Poems* (1801), is full of tears, sighs, and lyres, but also of specifically nationalist sentiment and not a little of the irony that would characterize much of her later writing. In her first decade as a published author, Owenson produced three volumes of verse, five novels, the libretto for an operetta, and an essay on contemporary Irish theatre. *The Mission-*

---

1   Byron writes, "what cruel work you make with Lady Morgan—you should recollect that she is a woman—though to be sure they are now & then very provoking—still as authoresses they can do no great harm—and I think it a pity so much good invective should have been laid out upon her—when there is such a fine field of us Jacobin Gentlemen for you to work on" (*Letters* 6:12-13). Chorley perhaps made the most biting attack, suggesting that those who wished to sustain gender proprieties should "for consistency's sake" treat women more politely (see Appendix B).

2   Mary Shelley requested Owenson's address as early as 1825 (1: 486), and gave Owenson a precious lock of Byron's hair, writing, "I send you the *relic* & you may say that I have never parted with *one* hair to any one else" (2:294). Owenson's friendship with Lamb and Moore spanned decades as well, and she went with Thomas Campbell to Byron's funeral (Stevenson 253). A full list of Owenson's political and cultural acquaintances would be a veritable "Who's Who" of the first half of the nineteenth century.

3   Stevenson writes, "In 1824 the Emperor published a decree specifically prohibiting Lady Morgan, Lord Holland, and three other well-known liberals from setting foot within the bounds of" the Austrian Empire (229); see also Redding ("Lady Morgan" 206). On Owenson's pension and the argument that she is the "first professional woman writer," see Colin B. Atkinson and Jo Atkinson.

ary: An Indian Tale, completed in 1810 and published in 1811, is the last work and, in many senses, the culmination, of this era. Like *The Novice of St. Dominick* (1805) and *The Wild Irish Girl* (1806), the novel imagines a personal and sentimental solution to institutionalized religious intolerance. And, like *The Wild Irish Girl*, *Woman; Or, Ida of Athens* (1809), her poetry, and *Patriotic Sketches of Ireland* (1807), it deals with colonial domination in terms drawn from Enlightenment notions of sensibility and their literary expressions, particularly the Della Cruscan school of sentimental poetry. Like Della Crusca, most notably in his poetry in favour of the abolition of the slave trade and the aspirations of the French Revolution, Owenson uses the conventions of literary sensibility to add emotional force to her political points.

Most of Owenson's novels, including *The Missionary*, were widely read and became sufficiently well known that the term "Owensonian school" was coined (Dean vii; Campbell 109). But *The Wild Irish Girl* in particular was an overwhelming success, running through numerous editions and influencing many of Owenson's contemporaries, including Maturin, author of *The Wild Irish Boy*, and Scott, whose first *Waverley* novel is much indebted to Owenson's national tale.[1] And it put Owenson herself into the spotlight. Friends and enemies alike began calling her "Glorvina," after the heroine of the novel, and Owenson began to perform the role at society parties. Dressed in a mock-antique Irish costume, she would play the harp and sing plaintive Irish airs, a performance about which Owenson had few illusions. She condemns being "forced for tasteless crowds to sing" in Fragment XXIV of *Lay of an Irish Harp* (1807), and would later recall,

> it became the fashion to ask that other [Owenson, as Glorvina] and her Irish harp to Dublin parties. This (*par parenthèse*), not because she wrote novels, and was an honest, pains-taking little person, leaving no calling for the idle trade, and turning to account the *petit bout de talent*, given her, by Him, from whom all is derived, to lighten the burden, which misfortune had heaped on her family;—but because she was the *enfant gâté* of a particular faction, and lived with the Lady Harringtons, Asgills, and all sorts of great official English ladies. (*Book* 1:62-63)

---

1 See, for instance, Ferris (*Achievement* 122-33).

On her introduction to high society in England, the theatricality of her presentation was deemed of more importance to her hostess than her comfort as a guest: "I too was treated *en princesse*, (the Princess of *Coolavin*), and denied the civilized privileges of sofa or chair, which were not in character with the habits of a 'Wild Irish Girl.' So, there I sat, *'patience per force with wilful choler meeting,'* the lioness of the night! exhibited and shewn off like 'the beautiful hyena that never was tamed,' of Exeter Change,—looking almost as wild, and feeling quite as savage!" (*Book* 1:105). Like her actor-father, she exhibited the Irishness that the English aristocrats expected—an Irishness with which she was not particularly comfortable, politically or personally.

Some of her aristocratic friends, the Abercorns, had an English physician, Dr. T. Charles Morgan. Morgan and Owenson began a courtship, and the Abercorns encouraged it, arranging for the knighting of Dr. Morgan in the hopes of making him more attractive to Owenson. Owenson kept stalling (as she had done in the past with other suitors) but she was, early one morning, called to a wedding by Lady Abercorn: "Glorvina, come upstairs directly, and be married; there must be no more trifling!" (Stevenson 155).[1] So, on 20 January 1812, Sydney Owenson became Lady Morgan.[2] There is something of a lull in her literary output during the second decade of her career as a writer, perhaps in part because the newly married couple travelled extensively in Europe. While "Miss Owenson" produced at least nine volumes in the years 1801-11, "Lady Morgan" produced only four volumes between 1812 and 1821: two novels and two travelogues. The novels, *O'Donnel* (1814) and *Florence Macarthy* (1818), are two national tales in the style which Owenson helped to set in *The Wild Irish Girl*. *O'Donnel*, however, marks a turn away from the sentimental heroine—innocent, naive, and loving, if always, in Owenson's formulation, very intelligent—towards a more active and skeptical heroine who works in the background. As Mary Campbell puts it, the Duchess

---

1 Campbell follows Stevenson's account (118).
2 Whether to call the author "Owenson" or "Morgan" is a perennial problem for students of her work, particularly since she published about a third of her works under the first name and significant works under both names. Since *The Missionary* was published under "Owenson," and that novel is obviously the focus here, I will refer to her as "Owenson" throughout except when following quotations and titles that refer to her as "Morgan."

of Belmont is not, like Glorvina, "a princess of Celtic myth, but a woman of the world, clever, witty and sensible" (130). Like many of Owenson's later heroines, she "weaves in and out of the plot sorting it all out" (Campbell 129).[1] *O'Donnel* also marks an increasing turn towards satirical representations of the British and Anglo-Irish elites, particularly those who accepted Irish stereotypes that served colonial interests by infantilizing the Irish or representing them as merely entertaining.

She also participated more directly in public debate by contributing to the journals and magazines of the day, including the *Athenaeum* and the *New Monthly Magazine*. But it was her travelogues, *France* (1817) and *Italy* (1821), which attracted the most attention. Under the guise of a travel narrative, she addressed contemporary political issues in terms with powerful implications for Irish politics, as Jeanne Moskal has argued, and in terms that generally horrified conservatives. A lengthy review of *France* in the *Quarterly* charged her with a catalogue of sins, including "Jacobinism" (that is, supporting the French Revolution's political aims), "impiety," and "licentiousness"; the review reveals the depth of hostility to Owenson's political writings, while also casting light on the conservative alignment of sexual impropriety, French culture, political radicalism, and impiety. *Italy* was arguably even more controversial. Mary Shelley was among its many admirers (3:129), and Byron praised it in a letter to Moore: "By the way, when you write to Lady Morgan, will you thank her for her handsome speeches in her book about *my* books? I do not know her address. Her work is fearless and excellent on the subject of Italy—pray tell her so—and I know the country. I wish she had fallen in with *me*, I could have told her a thing or two that would have confirmed her positions" (*Letters* 8:189).

But *Italy* brought conservatives' hostility to Owenson to a head. Since *Woman*, she had been regularly attacked by such notable conservative reviewers as William Gifford and John Wilson Croker, with all the sexist vitriol and personal insults that too often mars early nineteenth-century literary criticism.[2] Just months after the publication of *Italy*, Croker approached the legal authorities to have

---

1 For a useful discussion of such heroines, see Ferris, "Writing on the Border." The male hero of *Woman* anticipates these heroines in many regards.

2 See Ferris for an excellent survey of gender-focussed reviews of Owenson's work (*Achievement* 46-52), and the excerpts from reviews of *Woman* and *France* in Appendix B for some striking examples.

the titles of Owenson's husband and brother-in-law declared "null and void" (Campbell 180). But this was mere peevishness in comparison with continental responses. The "Papal and Austrian governments banned *Italy* in all countries of the Empire, and Lady Morgan was prohibited from travelling there" (Atkinson 84); copies of her work "had been seized and burned at Turin" (Stevenson 229), and Byron feared a copy of an (unnamed) Owenson volume being sent to him in Italy would be seized by the authorities (*Letters* 10: 55–56). People in Austrian territory were especially vulnerable: in 1823, Henry Edward Fox wrote, "Lady Morgan's book has done incalculable harm, especially to those she praises for having liberal opinions; and for that many have been banished, imprisoned or watched" (158; Campbell 181).[1] Austria's actions against Owenson were sufficiently striking to be remembered thirty-five years later (Redding, "Lady Morgan" 206).

Owenson, however, continued to publish politically engaged materials. While the controversy over *Italy* raged, she published a biography of painter Salvator Rosa, not because of his contributions to art, she provocatively remarks, but because of his "qualities" as an "Italian patriot, who, stepping boldly in advance of a degraded age, stood in the foreground of his times, like one of his own spirited and graceful figures, when all around him was timid mannerism and grovelling subserviency!" (1:iii–iv). In 1825, a series of essays that she had written for the *New Monthly Magazine* appeared as a volume, *Absenteeism*. She also published responses to her critics and autobiographical materials such as *The Book of the Boudoir* (1829). Owenson thus expanded her generic horizons while continuing to work with travelogues and novels and, by co-writing *The Mohawks* (1822) with her husband, briefly returning to verse.

In 1827, Owenson published *The O'Briens and the O'Flahertys*, the novel widely regarded as her best. *The O'Briens* brings together Irish politics, Owenson's wittily satirical representations of high society, and her new sort of heroine. Beavoin O'Flaherty not only "weaves in and out of the plot sorting it all out," but also voices the growing political pessimism of Owenson's work. The novel ends on a fatalistic note, with the Irish hero and heroine in exile in Napoleonic France, and on the verge of being exiled even from

---

1 On the rigorous censorship in this period of the Austrian empire, see Sked (44–52).

that haven, victims of a series of political environments that condemn the idealistic and exile the loyal. Owenson writes in the Preface, "To live in Ireland and to write for it, is to live and write *poignard sur la gorge*; for there is no country where it is less possible to be useful with impunity, or where the penalty on patriotism is levied with a more tyrannous exaction" (xv).[1] In *The O'Briens*, Owenson also turns from the idealization of the Irish past with which she became so strongly identified after *The Wild Irish Girl* and her performances as "Glorvina"; the idealization of the Irish past and radicalism are both, she suggests, ideological traps.

The O'Briens was Owenson's last Irish novel.[2] Most of Owenson's later volumes are political essays or memoirs of society life. In *Book of the Boudoir*, published in the year of Catholic Emancipation, she explains the shift in the focus of her writing:

> But the day is now fast approaching, when all that is Irish will fall into its natural position; when fair play will be given to national tendencies, and when the sarcastic author of the O'Donnels and the O'Briens, having nothing to find fault with, will be reduced to write, "*à l'eau rose*," both for boudoirs, or albums for ladies' dressing rooms. Among the multitudinous effects of catholic emancipation, I do not hesitate to predict a change in the character of Irish authorship. (1:vii)

---

1 Dennis makes light of such claims, asking, "What indeed were the hazards and dangers, especially for a female writer?" (183). The dangers for Owenson may have been relatively slight—as long as she did not set foot in Austrian territory, of course. But, by referring to such fears, Owenson draws attention to the ways in which implicit threats served to suppress political dissent in Ireland after the many trials and executions of the 1790s (including, perhaps most notably, the hanging of satirist Rev. James Porter in 1798 and the 1794 prosecution for sedition of Dr. William Drennan who, like Owenson, was both a nationalist writer and a favourite of the Dublin elite). When Owenson published *The Wild Irish Girl*, prosecutions for political writings were very much within recent memory; in *The O'Briens*, those prosecutions are explicitly addressed, and the hero must flee the authorities because of a pamphlet he had written.

2 Most criticism of Owenson's fiction has focussed on *The Wild Irish Girl* in particular and Owenson's Irish novels in general. On Owenson's Irish novels, see, for instance, Flanagan (109-64), Tracy, Dunne (especially "Fiction"), Ferris (especially "Writing"), and Leerssen's essays.

At the start of Queen Victoria's reign, she became the first woman writer to receive a government pension for her literary work. She also left Dublin and moved to London with her husband. In London, she was at the centre of a social whirl, holding parties memorable for her anecdotes and witty remarks. William John Fitzpatrick, for instance, writes, when "Hawthorne's *Scarlet Letter* was praised" at one of her social gatherings, Owenson replied, "Well, I cannot concur with you. The story is perfectly monstrous. I cannot understand making a lady who has committed some peccadillo, wear a great scarlet patch on her chest. Why, if we were all obliged to wear scarlet patches in consequence of our peccadillos, we could never venture out of doors, and there would soon be an end to all society" (130-31). But she also continued to deal with contemporary political issues. In 1840, for instance, she published a negative review of Thomas Carlyle's *Chartism* in the *Athenaeum* that well-known journalist Harriet Martineau asked to see (Arbuckle 29*n*). Owenson remained very much in the public eye as a writer even though the popularity of her novels began to decline.

While Owenson published steadily over six decades, and was frequently at the centre of public debate because of her controversial political positions, the early years of her life are comparatively unknown. Owenson's biographers must rely heavily on Owenson's autobiographical material—most of it produced in the latter years of her life. Owenson could tell a good tale, and it is hard to tell how far her autobiographical accounts are shaped by literary imperatives rather than historical fact. Biographies of Owenson published shortly after her death, including Fitzpatrick's *The Friends, Foes, and Adventures of Lady Morgan* (1859) and W. H. Dixon's *Lady Morgan's Memoirs* (1862), are sometimes unreliable. According to Fitzpatrick, for instance, *The Missionary* was published after Owenson's marriage to Morgan, is subtitled "An Italian Tale," with Hilarion re-cast as an Italian priest, and Luxima dies of "an epidemic fever" (72); in fact, in the page he spends on the novel, he gets very little right. Dixon is much better, drawing extensively on Owenson's unpublished autobiographical narrative and letters, but he still indicates, for instance, that *St. Clair* (1803) was in print in 1801 (1:205) and occasionally gives incorrect titles for her works. Similar errors, particularly with dates, appear in other nineteenth-century accounts of Owenson's life. According to an obituary which appeared the month after her death, *The Wild Irish Girl* was "published in 1801" and Owenson had published two novels by 1800 ("Obituary: Lady Sydney Morgan" 538).

It is clear that her father was Robert Owenson, an Irish actor and theatre manager who had changed his name from MacOwen to the anglicized "Owenson" to avoid anti-Irish prejudice; Catholic and bilingual, speaking both Irish and English, he often performed the "stage Irishman" (a comic stereotype) for theatre-goers but appeared in a variety of other roles. He was also a close friend of many Irish nationalists of the late eighteenth century. One of Robert Owenson's better-known friends, Edward Lysaght, a poet and nationalist politician, was the godfather of his first child, Sydney.[1] It is also clear that her mother was Jane Hill, an English Protestant, whom Owenson describes as quite proper and religious but tolerant of other views. In one autobiographical account, Owenson writes, "Father Farer became a frequent guest at [mother's] tea-table, to the entire satisfaction of my father, who was much pleased to set him at the Rev. Mr. Macklin, particularly as my mother greatly enjoyed their controversial synod ... [where] points of faith were freely discussed" (Dixon 1:76-77). Owenson and her only sibling, Olivia (later Lady Clarke), spent their early years in Dublin, in a bilingual, binational, and bireligious household, whose guests included many of the most prominent writers, politicians, and musicians of the day. They were tutored for a time by Thomas Dermody, who was recognized as a prodigy in the classical languages and as a talented poet while still in his teens; he published half-a-dozen volumes of verse in his short lifetime, and Owenson praised his poetry in such works as "Retrospection" and "The Minstrel Boy" (see Appendix C). After their mother's death, the sisters were sent to a Huguenot school in Clontarf in which the language of instruction was primarily French. When her father's theatre fell on hard times, Owenson began to work as a governess for the Featherstones and also worked in that capacity for the Crawfords, but quickly became able to support herself and assist her family through her writing.

It is not clear when Owenson was born, or where. On the first subject, she was famously coy. Her biographers have cited dates

---

1 Lysaght is perhaps best known as the author of "The Man Who Led the Van of Irish Volunteers," a poem in praise of the important nationalist politician, Henry Grattan. Grattan "moved addresses in favour of Irish legislative independence, unsuccessfully 1780-81, successfully 1782" (Foster 171n); he also fought for Catholic relief, and against the Act of Union.

from 1776 to 1783.[1] However, a date of 1783 is consistent with what we know of Dermody's life and his relationship with the Owenson family as well as the remarks that Owenson made about her early life.[2] It is common to note the story that she was born in the Irish Sea, between Ireland and Britain. Fitzpatrick offers it as fact (6) but, in the autobiographical account published by Dixon, Owenson offers a different narrative of her birth: at home in Ireland, on Christmas Eve, during a party in which Lysaght was among the guests. The first tale of her birth recalls her parentage, the daughter of an Irish Catholic and an English Protestant in a nation divided along sectarian lines by the anti-Catholic Penal

---

1 Fitzpatrick gives the year of her birth as 1778 (6), but twentieth-century scholars often follow Stevenson (3, 12) and cite 1776 (Campbell 1; Kirkpatrick xxii). 1783 is given as her birthdate in Owenson's obituary in *The Gentleman's Magazine* and in some twentieth-century works, including Seamus Deane's *Field Day Anthology* (2:948). Owenson's friend Redding tacitly supports the date of 1783, writing that Owenson "says she began her known authorship in the regular way at seventeen" ("Lady Morgan" 214); if she were born in December 1783, she would have been seventeen when her first known volume, *Poems* (1801), was published.

2 Dermody was born in 1775 and, "When he was about fifteen, he ran away to Dublin" (Boylan 83). According to a number of sources, Dermody joined the Owenson household after a short time in Dublin and became the family tutor; he "enlisted in the British army" "shortly" after 1792 (Boylan 83) and published a poem addressed to the Owenson sisters in 1792. He thus must have become the Owensons' tutor between 1790 and 1792, and left the family by 1793. If Sydney was born in 1783 and Olivia two or three years later, the sisters would have been in the early years of their schooling during Dermody's tuition, and at ages consistent with Owenson's claim that Dermody was given the task of teaching the sisters "to read and write" (Dixon 1:90). According to her autobiographical account in Dixon's *Memoirs*, Owenson was barely nine years old when her mother died; she and her sister were then sent to school in Clontarf, where they saw Dermody and found out that he had joined the army, claims again consistent with a birthdate for Sydney of 1783. A birthdate of 1776 would have Owenson being tutored, by someone just a year older than her, at an age when most of her contemporaries would have been completing their educations.

Laws,[1] and her life as a spokesperson for Ireland who was favoured, at least superficially, by the British liberal elite. The second version emphasizes her nationalist roots and associations: having been subjected to British colonial rule for centuries, Ireland was the site of nationalist, anti-imperialist movements throughout Owenson's lifetime.

The Missionary and Sites of Conquest: Ireland, India and Portugal

As Balachandra Rajan suggests, India in *The Missionary* is "not a real country but a contrivance, seen through the spectacles of Orientalist books" (137). It is specifically a contrivance for addressing colonialism and the attendant issue of religious intolerance while apparently dislocating them from Owenson's main sphere of interest, nineteenth-century Ireland, by nominally rooting them in seventeenth-century Portugal and India.[2] These three conquered spaces—Ireland, India, and Portugal—had all been at the forefront of public debate in the years leading up to *The Missionary*'s publication. In 1798, Ireland was the site of a major uprising against British colonial rule, an uprising ended by armed force and the Act of Union (1800) which abolished the Irish Parliament and brought Ireland under the direct rule of the British Parliament; in 1803, there had been another uprising, albeit a smaller and more poorly organized one, resurrecting the spectre of Irish dissent despite the Union rhetoric of sisterhood

1   The Penal Laws, moderated throughout the eighteenth century, were a repressive set of statutes that limited Catholics' access to the political, educational, and economic spheres. Being Catholic in eighteenth-century Ireland meant not being able to vote, hold political office, or get a university degree, and suffering what Owenson terms "insecurity of property" (*O'Briens* 50); various legal measures were in place to allow seizures of land and other property from practicing Catholics. Foster suggests that "by the 1730s the worst was over. But *de facto* toleration could not be taken for granted; several *causes célèbres* indicate there were always those ready to use legal formalities" (205), and so the Penal Laws remained a significant factor in Ireland throughout the eighteenth century.

2   Owenson was not the first, or the last, to use India to address Ireland's situation indirectly. See, for instance, McLoughlin's argument that Edmund Burke wrote extensively on India because he was silenced on Ireland but could freely address colonial questions when referring to India (178-81), and discussions of Moore's *Lalla Rookh* by, for instance, Majeed (93-100) and Sharafuddin (171-82).

between Britain and Ireland. India, colonized by the Portuguese in the sixteenth century but increasingly under British rule during Owenson's lifetime, was the site of the so-called "Vellore Mutiny" of 1806, an uprising against British rule which shook government complacency and brought the question of managing cultural difference back into public debate. Portugal, claimed by Spain in 1580 and treated much like a Spanish colony until the Revolution of 1640, was invaded again by Spain in 1801; in 1807, as Napoleon marched towards Portugal's capital, the Portuguese royal family fled to one of Portugal's colonial possessions, Brazil, while the British government rallied its military to Portugal's support. Arthur Wellesley (later Duke of Wellington) fought campaigns against Napoleon in Portugal (1808-10), leading to a French retreat in 1811 (within weeks of *The Missionary*'s publication). In *The Missionary*, these sites of European domination are paralleled and mapped onto each other, revealing broad lessons about the cultural, and specifically religious, intolerance that validates and energizes the imperial drive to conquer.

Ireland's colonial condition was, until Catholic Emancipation in 1829, always first and foremost in Owenson's writing, if sometimes coded through discussions of religious intolerance or colonial oppression in other nations, such as France, Greece, and Portugal. Owenson's life spans some of the most heated political debate over the imperial project in general, and Ireland's position in relation to Britain in particular. In 1782, Henry Grattan, in a famous speech to the Irish Parliament, demanded greater political autonomy for Ireland, alluding to the American Revolution to obliquely threaten the British authorities who effectively controlled the Irish Parliament. Some concessions were offered, but the newly won powers were gradually eroded during Owenson's childhood, leading to the rise of various nationalist groups in Ireland, including the Volunteers in the 1780s and the United Irishmen in the 1790s. Political tensions culminated in a series of uprisings and the further erosion of Irish political sovereignty. The United Irishmen Uprising of 1798 was brutally suppressed, and formed the excuse for the Act of Union which ended all semblance of Irish political autonomy by formally bringing Ireland under the rule of the British Parliament. A pause in widespread nationalist activity followed the suppression of the '98 uprising, but nationalist energies soon found a new focus in Daniel O'Connell's fight for Catholic Emancipation. When Emancipation was finally achieved in 1829, it symbolically (and, to a degree, practically) brought to an end over a century of institutionalized and wide-ranging discrimination against Catholics:

Catholics could finally hold political, government, and military offices, and thus have a say in the governance of a country in which they constituted the majority.

But the social realities of middle- and upper-class Dublin were less polarized. Owenson could hobnob with the British elite and the Anglo-Irish Ascendancy (the mediators and beneficiaries of British colonial rule in Ireland) while writing novels, poems, and travelogues which espoused a liberal, anti-imperial, and pro-Irish political position. Such apparent contradictions were not unusual for the day. Lord Castlereagh, one of the leading military figures in the suppression of the 1798 United Irishmen uprising and other repressive actions on behalf of British Empire, was among those "Whigs and Tories" Owenson recalls seeing "united" and "innocently playing their 'small games,' after having played, through the preceding week, their great game, on the opposite sides of the two houses" (*Book* 1:127). It is easy to forget, in a time when cities regularly number in the tens of millions, how much more contracted were urban environments in the early years of the Industrial Revolution—and how much more contracted were the circles of the literati and the social elite in those cities. In Ireland, there was another factor at play: the English had maintained a colonial presence in Ireland for over half a millennium by the time of Owenson's writing, and intermarriages and cultural exchanges had complicated any facile ethnic distinctions, particularly among the middle and upper classes. This informs the government's emphasis on religion as a means of distinguishing between the empowered and the disempowered, and the United Irishmen's vision of an Irish nation which includes all of its inhabitants, regardless of language, religion, or class—a vision forged after heated debate within the United Irishmen leadership over whether their group, predominantly Presbyterian at first, would support Catholic Emancipation and reach out to Catholic nationalist organizations.

Throughout the history of English colonization, the Irish were periodically invaded, economically and legally oppressed, subjected to a racist discourse, and barred from ethnically specific cultural practices such as language and religion. Pre-1800 Ireland was, in effect, the testing ground for the British imperial practices that would be used outside Europe in the nineteenth and early twentieth centuries. But the imperialist classificatory system consolidated during the Victorian Empire repeatedly trips over Ireland. In the physical, cultural, and technological terms of that system, Ireland was not that different from Britain. The Irish people were white and Christian (though infrequently Anglican). Many Irish people were educated in the same body of cultural knowledge as their colonizers, and Ireland contributed a number of writers to the "English" literary canon, including Jonathan Swift, Laurence Sterne, Edmund Burke, Frances Sheridan and R. B. Sheridan. The Irish economy also entered the industrial and capitalist era, one of the acid tests of modernity during the heyday of British Empire, at around the same time as the British. In broad terms, as the British Empire turned from Ireland towards Asia, North America, Australia, and then Africa, it became increasingly dependent on a discourse of "the Other" (defined as non-white, non-Christian, non-English-speaking, and non-technological) in which Ireland, England's oldest colony, posed something of a conundrum. English Renaissance texts almost uniformly represent the Irish as primitive, violent, uncivilized, and unassimilable. But, by the end of the eighteenth century, "savage" Ireland was countered by an Ireland represented as Britain's "sister." In 1800, the Act of Union took away "savage" Ireland's Parliament, and then gave "sister" Ireland some seats in the British Parliament—one of the many signs of uncertainty over how to fit Ireland into the British Empire, as the outer rim of the imperial centre, or as the inner rim of the colonial periphery. Throughout the nineteenth century, Ireland teeters on the brink of both.

The Missionary's opening and closing pages refer to a time in Portugal's history when that nation, like Ireland, was dominated by its neighbour. Spain took control of Portugal in 1580, and maintained its power until the Portuguese Revolution and Restoration in 1640. Most of the action in *The Missionary* takes place in the late 1630s, thus spanning the final years of Spain's rule of Portugal.[1] The most probable source of Owenson's information about seventeenth-century Portugal is *The History of the Revolutions of Portugal* by Abbé Vertot (1655-1735); the *History* was republished throughout the eighteenth century, and had appeared in a new edition, with a supplementary piece on Brazil, in 1809. Vertot argues that Spanish rule of Portugal was broadly colonial in its strategies, weak-

---

1 See Note 1 in "Explanatory Notes," below, for further dates and details. Hilarion's mission to India is approved in 1635, probably near the end of the year (if Owenson is using October 21st as Saint Hilarion's feastday), and he likely arrives in India in the middle of 1636. The "Conclusion" alone takes place after the "Revolution of Portugal"; it is set in 1664, the year of Bernier's visit to Cashmire.

ening or circumventing indigenous power structures and economically disabling and exploiting the population at large. Philip II of Spain "regarded the right of conquest as his securest title, and both he and his successors regulated their conduct on the same principle, since Philip the IIId, and Philip the IVth, his son and grandson always treated the Portugueze much more as a conquered people, than as natural subjects" (Vertot 21). Olivares, cited by name in Owenson's novel, "proposed to denationalize the Portuguese nobility by calling it to serve in Madrid and by intermarriage with the houses of Castile, to impose new taxation in Portugal ... and to enforce a general military service" (Livermore 170). The parallels between Spain's domination of Portugal and Britain's domination of Ireland would not have been lost on Owenson or her readers. The British denationalized the Irish aristocracy through a program of disinheriting indigenous landowners and replacing them with Protestant settlers. During Owenson's day, there was a growing Irish diaspora: successful writers and politicians, among them Burke and R. B. Sheridan, went to England, and many of the well-to-do Catholic families sent their children overseas for their education.

In her description of Portugal, Owenson unmistakably echoes the factionalization of Ireland which the United Irishmen and others hoped to supersede, in part through the de-politicization of religion. Having "sunk into a Spanish province,"

> Portugal became divided into two powerful factions, and the Spanish partizans, and Portuguese patriots, openly expressed their mutual abhorrence, and secretly planned their respective destruction. Even Religion forfeited her dove-like character of peace, and enrolled herself beneath the banners of civil discord and factious commotion. The Jesuits governed with the Spaniards; the Franciscans resisted with the Portuguese; and each accused the other of promulgating heretical tenets, in support of that cause, to which each was respectively attached. (71)

Owenson places her protagonist, Hilarion, in the thick of Portuguese resistance to Spanish domination. In *The Missionary*, Hilarion's paternal uncle is the Archbishop of Lisbon; according to Vertot, a member of the Acugna family was Archbishop of Lisbon at the time of the Portuguese Revolution, and he "was unanimously declared president of the council, and lieutenant-general for the king" (95) after the overthrow of the Spanish vice-reine and her minister, Vasconcellas. Don Lewis d'Acugna, another revolutionary conspirator, is named as the Archbishop's nephew in Vertot's history (40). In Owenson's novel, "Don Lewis, Duke d'Acugna," is Hilarion's elder brother. By connecting Hilarion explicitly to these Acugnas, Owenson makes him recognizable to her contemporaries as a member of one of the most important families in the Portuguese Revolution and Restoration. The many references to Portugal have been almost completely overlooked in studies of *The Missionary*. But Hilarion's family connections inform many of the novel's details, from Hilarion's decision to join the Franciscans, the Goan authorities' hostility towards him in India, and his use of the name "Count of Acugna" at the time of his arrest. He is, by association, an opponent of Spanish rule in Portugal and, from a nationalist perspective, a close relative of the rightful rulers of Portugal and the Portuguese colony of Goa in which the Spanish condemn Hilarion, Count d'Acugna, to death.

On his mother's side, Hilarion is even more closely identified with the rightful rulers of Portugal. Hilarion's mother is a member of the Bragança family (73); the Duke of Bragança became King John IV of Portugal after the Revolution of 1640. By allying her protagonist with the Bragança family as well, Owenson links him to a key moment in the history of Britain's presence in India. In 1662, Britain's King Charles II married John IV's daughter, Catherine of Bragança. Portugal and Britain, at the time, were competitors in Indian trade, but Portugal needed assistance in defending itself from Holland, another trade competitor, and from Spain, which did not yet recognize Portugal's independence. In exchange for such assistance from Charles II, Portugal gave, as Catherine's dowry, "2 m. *cruzados*, the cession of Tangier and the right to trade with the Portuguese colonies: Bombay was added later" (Livermore 190). By giving Britain access to Tangier (in Africa) and Bombay (in India), the marriage greatly contributed to Britain's strength as a European trading power in the large region known as "the East," and gave the nation an important toehold in India specifically.

India, of course, is the primary setting for *The Missionary* and though, in Rajan's phrase, "a contrivance," one that is not uninformed by Owenson's awareness of its colonial history in general, and the 1806 "Vellore Mutiny" in particular. In the eighteenth century, India became both an important source of British revenue and the site of an administrative tangle that generations of Britons would try to sort through and morally justify. At the turn of the century, much of the disarray emerged from the variety of positions on Britain's presence in India and debate over the terms on which

Anglo-Indian relationships should be framed. Europeans had had an official presence in India since the sixteenth century, starting primarily with Portugal's conquest of Goa, a city and island on the western coast of India and thus a useful port for European traders. Trade was the keynote rather than colonial domination in the sense of general control over the population at large. Portugal's interest was primarily in trade routes and convenient ports, and Portugal was followed by a number of other European countries also in pursuit of trading profits. England's "East India Company" (EIC) was founded in 1600; its Dutch counterpart was founded in 1602, and a French company in 1664. But, while beginning with ports and coastal regions, these traders moved increasingly inland, forging a link between profit and territorial control that went beyond simply securing trade routes.

In the middle of the eighteenth century, Britain's competitors for the subcontinent began to fall away and aggressive leaders of the EIC decided that they could better protect their commercial interests by acting like a state. Robert Clive is usually credited with taking the EIC in this direction, forging alliances with local governments, supporting sympathetic administrations, and using military force against unsupportive administrations in order to achieve dominance in Bengal (a region in the northeastern part of the subcontinent). Clive's actions made the EIC even more profitable to its agents by releasing them from various economic controls. Before Clive, they had to compete "on the same terms as Indian merchants"; after Clive, they enjoyed "duty-free" status and began to imagine ways of making money that extended beyond "normal trading" (Spear 199). The next decades saw the rise of the "nabobs," EIC agents who returned to England with fabulous wealth taken out of the Indian economy.[1] Pitt's India Act (1784) brought the EIC more clearly under the control of the British Parliament, devolving the EIC's political powers to the British state. The Act thus "forbade the governor general [of the EIC] to declare war on any Indian state without the express authority of the directors, and declared [that] 'to pursue schemes of conquest and extension of dominion in India are measures repugnant to the wish, the honor, and the policy of this nation'" (Spear 211). The India Act laid the groundwork for the impeachment of Warren Hastings, the

---

1 See Chatterjee for an excellent survey of literary representations of the nabob (31-48).

Governor General of the EIC. Hastings was charged with abusing his powers in India; the trial was held in the British Parliament and lasted from 1788 to 1795. Although it ended with Hastings' acquittal, the lengthy trial revealed to the British public the extent of the EIC's exploitative practices.

Hastings, however, also presided over a relatively culturally sensitive EIC. Under his administration, Sir William Jones founded the Asiatick Society of Bengal. (British power in India in the late eighteenth century was limited to Bengal, in northeastern India, and a handful of smaller regions, mostly in the south and east.) During the final years of the eighteenth century, Jones and other EIC agents published dozens of volumes on Indian history, languages, and literatures. While Victorian administrators would insist on a thoroughly anglicized education for their agents and the Indian population at large, Hastings, Jones, and others of their generation supported schools which taught Sanskrit and Arabic as well as financed translations that would help to make English-speaking readers acquainted with the cultural wealth of the region. Late eighteenth-century British orientalist scholarship is hardly free of the problems that Edward Said has identified in orientalism as a whole, including, for instance, feminized or primitivized characterizations of the peoples of the "East" (a loose term for all regions east of Europe, including Asia and what we now term the "middle east"), Eurocentric terms of reference, and the use of ostensibly neutral scholarship to justify and further imperial activities. But much of the scholarship produced by EIC agents during Jones' tenure was at least not programmatically and unapologetically geared towards trivializing the merits and the relevance of the cultures it claimed to describe—a position that would begin to dominate soon after Jones' tenure had ended. As Sara Suleri notes, "An astonishing development in the narratives of Anglo-India is the rapidity with which the British understanding of the dynamics of Indian civilization atrophied into a static and mistrustful interpretation of India as a locus of all things ancient" (33). While Jones' successors sought to assimilate the peoples of the subcontinent by anglicizing them, Jones and many of his contemporaries assimilated them by stressing parallels among diverse cultures.

Such an assimilatory program was consistent with Enlightenment thought in positing a cultural diversity within a universal humanity. Enlightenment notions of "universal humanity" are generally predicated on notions of white, European, literate, Christian male identity: in sum, to be universal is to be like the European philosophers who defined what was universal (a bias that often becomes clear when such philosophers as David Hume and Adam Smith address non-British cultures). But, in the late eighteenth century, the concept of a universal humanity facilitated a limited form of cultural pluralism that mitigated, or at least potentially countered, rising imperialist pressures to essentialize difference through, for instance, J.F. Blumenbach's division of humanity into "races" in which biology and character are deterministically linked. Colonial administrators at the turn of the century, however, were often more concerned with the dynamics of popular opinion in the centre of imperial power and in the colonized space. As the "Extract from the Minutes of the Court of Directors, 25th July, 1809" included in Lord Bentinck's *Memorial* suggests (see Appendix A), administrators believed it important to endorse, at least publicly, religious tolerance in order to maintain support in Britain, and to avoid stirring up resentments among the Indians increasingly important as a source of labour to the Company's military, governmental, and trading enterprises.

In her many footnotes, Owenson makes only one reference to events in post-seventeenth-century India: in Chapter XVI, she writes, "An insurrection of a fatal consequence took place in *Vellore* so late as 1806, and a mutiny at Nundydrag and Benglore, occurred about the same period: both were supposed to have originated in the religious bigotry of the natives, suddenly kindled by the supposed threatened violation of their faith from the Christian settlers." On 9 July 1806, a number of "Sepoys" (Indian soldiers in a British-run regiment) rose up against their officers in Vellore. The uprising was brief, but bloody, and sent shockwaves through the EIC and the British populace, who could still remember the Hastings Impeachment of the previous decade. The "Report of the Commission" (9 August 1806) charged with investigating events at Vellore represents the uprising as, in large degree, the consequence of a Muslim conspiracy. Their theory was consistent with the general position of the EIC at the time, particularly in the wake of the Rohilla war (see Perkins and Russell 26-28), in demonizing the Muslim population of India and infantilizing the Hindus. Thus, in the "Report," the Hindu soldiers are represented as naturally loyal and subservient, and so "the outrages on the late occasion were of foreign growth, and could only have been inspired by a barbarous Enemy" (71); the "barbarous Enem[ies]" deemed responsible for inciting rebellion among the loyal troops at Vellore are the sons of Sultan Tipu, who had, in effect, been exiled to Vellore after their father's defeat at Seringapatam.

But while the Commission could argue about who was responsible for this conspiracy, they could not dismiss what many, including Lord Bentinck, Governor of Vellore during the uprising, deemed the predominant, if not the sole, cause:

> By a late Order of his Excellency the Commander in Chief, of the 13th March 1806, Section XI. paragraph 10—"It is ordered by the Regulations, that a Native Soldier shall not mark his face to denote his Cast, nor wear Earrings, when dressed in his Uniform; and it is further directed, that at all Parades, and upon all Duties, every Soldier of the Battalion shall be clean shaved on the chin. It is directed also, that uniformity shall be preserved in regard to the quantity and shape of the hair upon the upper lip, as far as may be practicable." ("Report" 67)

There was also a new uniform turban, to be issued to all troops after enough had been made. One officer, Colonel M'Kerras, "had resolved not to communicate [the order] to his Sepoys, as he was convinced that it would be the cause of great dissatisfaction," but knowledge of the order circulated by unofficial means ("Report" 67). The Commission writes,

> The article of Dress is, both with the Hindoos and the Mahommedans, an indication of their cast, and a badge of their respective distinctions and places in society; and when it is recollected how obstinately the Indians of all descriptions adhere to their Customs, and with what difficulty the Natives were brought to adopt many parts of their present Military Dress, it will not appear surprising that some of the late innovations in that respect were offensive to their feelings.
> The Sepoys appear to have felt, that the wearing of the new Tarband [sic] would make them come to be considered as Europeans, and would have removed them from society and intercourse of their own Casts. (70)

This, as the 1809 Minutes from the Court of Directors suggest, became the more famous cause of the uprising. But soon afterwards religious and cultural toleration—that is, the official policy of disallowing discriminatory practices—would start to disappear from the EIC in favour of a program of education that stressed anglicization and conformity, a program for which James Mill notoriously argued barely a decade after Vellore in his *History of British India* (1817). This is not to suggest that there was a sudden and radical turn in British popular opinion, or among EIC officials. Many, including Bentinck, continued to argue for toleration, and such pleas were renewed after the 1857 uprising against British rule in India; and positions like Mill's are to be found in writing on India long before 1817.[1] But there was a sea-change, as general opinion and official policy set aside toleration in place of programmatic anglicization.

In the context of an ongoing debate about religious tolerance and colonial policy in India, Owenson's choice of location is particularly apt: in 1810, a decade after the Act of Union, and before O'Connell re-energized the fight for Catholic Emancipation, Ireland was largely considered a settled matter by the British. India, however, was the new field of imperial debate: economic ethics, administrative policies, official toleration, and the advisability of allowing missionaries unfettered access were all being hotly debated. Owenson's temporal setting is as carefully selected: by choosing the early seventeenth century, Owenson can address both Spanish-Portuguese colonial policy at Goa and Spain's domination of the Portuguese. Her representation of these interlocking repressive regimes is less comparative than iterative: each imperialistic administration generates only nationalist opposition, as resentment boils up into revolution in Portugal and India, just as in 1798 Ireland. India's Mughal Empire occasionally hovers on the edge of Owenson's narrative, but she focusses on European regimes; as in her other novels, her focus is on Christian intolerance, and the false civility of Europeans. Owenson suggests that, in parts of the region untouched by European rule, different ethnic and religious groups live side by side. In Owenson's Cashmire (Kashmir is a mountainous region on the northern edge of India), a Muslim army camps for days without any apparent disruption to the lives of the Hindu population. In various gatherings—at Lahore, the caravan travelling south from Cashmire—devotees of different religions, including Muslims, Hindus, Sikhs, and Catholics, meet with little, if any, hostility. It is only among Europeans that religious difference is made the excuse for physical violence.

---

1   See, for instance, Grant in Appendix A.

Literary Contexts: Sensibility, Irish Nationalist Literature, and Travel Writing

Sensibility provides the general moral framework for Owenson's early work, especially the fiction and poetry up to and including *The Missionary*.[1] She avowed herself an admirer of the Della Cruscans (Stevenson 42, 95), a school of poetry in which sensibility was often directed towards radical political aims. As Nicola J. Watson notes, Owenson's "novels were frequently indicted for their endorsement of the sentimental heroine, an endorsement that was recognized as 'Jacobinical'" (117). But Owenson continued to situate her early novels in precisely this context, though clearly aware of the growing need to defend sentimental fiction on political and literary terms. Owenson's first novel, *St. Clair*, is addressed to "Children of passion and sentiment" (iii), and its title page includes a lengthy quotation from the work of Henry Home (Lord Kames), a prominent writer on sensibility. In her introduction to *Woman*, Owenson writes,

> The stoicism of a philosophy which establishes its doctrine by mathematical demonstration, will smile at an enthusiasm which seduces the fancy and the heart to scenes so sacred to the visions and the sentiments of both; but surely to that high feeling of the soul called sensibility, to that high faculty of the mind termed genius, Athens, in the recollection of what it once was, and in the consideration of what it now is, must ever present an object of touching, of lively, and profound interest. (1:xv)

The literature of sensibility can seem maudlin to postmodern eyes, and overly contemplative when it pauses to linger on a character's emotional state or an evocative scene; it is often dismissed, much too quickly, by readers trained in realist fiction or the self-reflexive novels of the twentieth century. The literature of sensibility cannot be evaluated in terms of these later variants of the novel form. Its aims and values are neither plot-centered nor formal. Its focus is

---

1 My use of these terms follows Todd's characterization of eighteenth-century usage; that is, "A 'sentiment' is a moral reflection, a rational opinion usually about the rights and wrongs of human conduct," while "sensibility" "came to denote a faculty of feeling, the capacity for extremely refined emotion and a quickness to display compassion for suffering" (7) or, in other words, the capacity for sentiment.

rather on the development and contemplation of moral feeling, a pre-psychoanalytic examination of emotion in the context of the needs of society and of the individual. Plot is important insofar as it enables spectacular scenes of intense emotion—as in the dramatic auto-da-fè scene near the end of *The Missionary*—but not in and of itself.

Sensibility provided the terms for many eighteenth-century discussions of morality in literature, philosophy, ethics, and political thought. With the rising middle class, the industrial revolution, a growing dependence on commerce, and nervousness over empire, Britons had to deal with a variety of new moral questions—and Enlightenment notions of sensibility provided a much-needed lexicon. Sensibility, for instance, was not obviously religion-specific and so did not raise the spectre of the religion-based civil conflicts of the seventeenth century. It helped to lay the foundation for a more inclusive view of the social body, including all those who feel for others in that social body. In sentimental theory of the eighteenth century, "mankind's societal nature was analysed as based on 'sympathy' or—in more contemporary terms—as a kind of formative and pre-political bonding" (Nairn 80).[1] Most importantly for authors trying to counter the commerce-driven arguments of those favouring the expansion of empire, sensibility offered a way of talking about a dimension of human experience and relations that exceeded the utilitarian, addressing "a sociability not explicable in terms of political or material necessity" (Mullan 30).

Four precepts of sensibility are important here: first, that feelings of sympathy or disgust are determined by the virtue of the person who is the object of sympathy; second, that the more virtuous are more susceptible to these feelings of sympathy or disgust, but that everyone is susceptible in some degree; third, that a rational awareness of the public good informs our sympathy and that this is the basis of justice; fourth, that an individual's sensibility can be strengthened and refined by experiencing sympathy for others in life and literature. The fourth precept offers the lever by which literature can achieve political effect. One of Owenson's admirers, P. B. Shelley, writes, "The great secret of morals is Love; or a going out of our own nature, and an identification of ourselves with the beautiful which exists in thought, action, or

---

1   For a more detailed exposition of the function of sympathy in eighteenth-century notions of social cohesion, see Mullan, especially chapter 1.

person, not our own. A man, to be greatly good, must imagine intensely and comprehensively; he must put himself in the place of another and of many others" ("Defence" 487-88). The task of the literature of sensibility is to provide the opportunity for such morally refining imaginings. As Janet Todd puts it in her excellent introduction to sensibility,

> In all forms of sentimental literature, there is an assumption that life and literature are directly linked, not through any notion of a mimetic depiction of reality but through the belief that the literary experience can intimately affect the living one.... Sentimental literature is exemplary of emotion, teaching its consumers to produce a response equivalent to the one presented in its episodes. It is a kind of pedagogy of seeing and of the physical reaction that this seeing should produce, clarifying when uncontrolled sobs or a single tear should be the rule, or when the inexpressible nature of the feeling should be stressed.
>
> A sentimental work moralizes more than it analyzes and emphasis is not on the subtleties of a particular emotional state but on the communication of common feeling from sufferer or watcher to reader or audience. (4)

The literature of sensibility operated within a philosophical framework in which literature *acted* upon the reader with morally improving effects, so many of the writers who fought slavery, sexual oppression, colonial oppression, poverty, and other social ills relied on its terms to further as well as express their agenda, from Della Crusca in the late eighteenth century to American abolitionist writings almost a century later. Sensibility made it possible to explain the error, and arouse the reader's compassion, by intensifying a moral social bond. In his discussion of *Patriotic Sketches*, Richard C. Sha argues that Owenson's "habitual stimulation of her viewers' sensibility is designed to encourage them to do what they can to end oppression of the Irish poor" (205): there is a clear causal chain linking literary representation, the reader's emotional response, and the reader's actions in the world.

While Owenson draws broadly on philosophical and literary notions of sensibility in *The Missionary*, she also attends to particular strands of that discourse, particularly those which define national feeling and the genre of sentimental travel writing. In his section on "Patriotism" in *Sketches of the History of Man* (1774), Home considers the implications of sensibility for Enlightenment notions of nationhood and national feeling. Home argues, "Patriotism is enflamed by a struggle for liberty, by a civil war, by resisting a potent invader, or by any incident that forcibly draws the members of a state into strict union for the common interest" (2:317-18). Moreover, "patriotism is connected with every social virtue; and when it vanishes, every virtue vanishes with it" (2:246); patriotism "triumphs over every social motive, and is a firm support to every virtue. In fact, where ever it prevails, the morals of the people are found to be pure and correct" (2:314-15). Home's notion of patriotism presumes both a moral nation and a moral people; patriotism is both the consequence and the cause of moral action at the personal and the political levels, and is promoted better by suffering than by plenty. Thus, "A continual influx of wealth into the capital, generates show, luxury, avarice, which are all selfish vices; and selfishness, enslaving the mind, eradicates every fibre of patriotism" (2:326). The moral and social dimension of sensibility examined by Home in relation to patriotism made it especially useful for anti-colonial nationalist discourse.

The United Irishmen, active for most of the 1790s, repeatedly drew on the conventions of literary and philosophical sensibility in their writing. Sentimental nationalism offered a means by which to turn the negative impact of colonialism to national advantage. Because definitions of sympathy emphasize responses towards those who suffer, suffering itself, instituted by the colonial administration, becomes a catalyst by which to forge the sympathetic bonds that will unite the people into a nation. Such a formulation of "fellow-feeling," in Adam Smith's phrase (4), lays the basis for a nationalism that is not merely a love of country, but a moral engagement with a sympathetic community from which the nation and its morality derive. United Irishman William Drennan suggests that national sentiment makes "a man ... capable of every thing good and great," and that, without a nation, the people "become a mere number ... without any inherent principle of motive of common action, unattached to each other" (212). The model was pervasive enough to survive the suppression of the United Irishmen. In the anonymous novel, *The Matron of Erin* (1816), for instance, a character asserts, "the common sufferings of Irishmen unite us, however differing in religious persuasion, for the general good" (1: 21). In such formulations of national coherence, the action of sympathy itself forms the bond that unites all in the national cause, and can only be compromised by artificial social structures or political violence. In *Sketches of the Philosophy of Life* (1818), Owenson's husband,

T. Charles Morgan, addresses these issues in terms that recall the crises of *The Missionary*:

> Among the causes which modify reaction should be mentioned those which act through the social affections. The human animal is born with the strongest instinctive tendencies to be moved through the accidents and suffering of the species.... The tendency of reason is ... too frequently opposed to the natural sympathies. The simple and uncultivated man, provided his feelings are not stifled, and his heart narrowed by an excessive difficulty in procuring the first wants of his existence, and by a consequent life of penury and distress, is open to all the kindlier feelings of nature, and sympathizes readily with the stranger.... While the creature of high wrought civilization, whose multiplied necessities and artificial passions oblige him to reason at every step, and to calculate every action, is, too frequently, self-centred, cold, and indifferent, and he extracts the materials of individual gratification, even from the failure of friends, the misfortunes of his country.... With such men disinterestedness is folly, and patriotism a pretence. (299-300)

It is consequently suggestive that Hilarion, the only Acugna of the novel who is not actively working for Portugal's independence, is frequently represented as a man of "stifled" and "artificial" feelings:

> The complexional springs of passion in the character of the Missionary had been regulated and restrained by the habits of his temperate and solitary life; the natural impetuosity and ardour of his feelings had been tranquillized and subdued, by the principles of his pure and spiritual religion; and though his perceptions were quick and rapid in their exercise, yet he had so accustomed his mind to distrust its first impulse, that, all enthusiast as he was, he was yet less so from the vivacity of a first impression than from the mental operation which succeeded to it. (100)

While Ian Dennis suggests that the novel "makes clear that the tyranny of passionate desire is suffered equally by both partners" (48), passion in Owenson's novel is more broadly defined than simple erotic desire. It is consistently aligned with the natural social feelings in general and national sentiment in particular.

National feeling, though, can complicate international relations—a frequent subject of travelogues. Owenson's *Missionary* is framed as a travel narrative: in the first volume, Hilarion travels thousands of miles, from Portugal to the Indian port of Goa, then north to Tatta, and, by boat along the Indus, east to Lahore and finally north to Cashmire; in the third volume, expelled from Cashmire, Hilarion and Luxima travel overland back to Tatta and then oversea to Goa. Owenson draws heavily on travel narratives by Bernier, Thèvenot, and Hamilton and, like many travel writers, lingers over the flora and fauna of the region with a specificity unusual in English narratives set in Europe. But, more importantly, Owenson draws on the genre's conventional use as a vehicle for addressing cultural contact. In her influential study, *Imperial Eyes: Travel Writing and Transculturation*, Mary Louise Pratt considers the ways in which European travelogues were used to represent and negotiate cultural difference in what she terms "contact zones," spaces in which peoples "previously separated by geographic and historical disjunctures" (7) meet. The sentimental variant of the travelogue, argues Pratt, presents feeling, particularly "conjugal love," "as an alternative to enslavement and colonial domination, or as newly legitimated versions of them" (86). Sensibility in these texts conceals the violent relations of the colonial project, turning the (male) European colonizer into an object of admiration, loyalty, and love for the (feminine) colonized.

There are a number of parallels between such texts and Owenson's *The Missionary*. Owenson follows the basic plot: a European travels in colonized and not-yet-colonized spaces, is admired and loved by someone native to one of those spaces, and gathers information on "unknown" (to Europeans) peoples and regions that is, through the travelogue itself, conveyed to European readers. Like many non-European heroines in colonial texts, Luxima is given an elevated social status that distinguishes her "from the stereotypic portraits of slaves and savages" (Pratt 100). The ending of the novel, in some respects, follows the texts considered by Pratt, particularly European-written narratives set in the Americas in which "'cultural harmony through romance' always breaks down. Whether love turns out to be requited or not, whether the colonized lover is female or male, outcomes seem to be roughly the same: the lovers are separated, the European is reabsorbed by Europe, and the non-European dies an early death" (97).

But there are some key differences. Luxima, for instance, though of high birth, does not fit the pattern in having "European affiliations" or royal status (Pratt 100). She is a priestess, elevated by her virtues, and her husband's untimely death, above her peers. More compellingly, the lovers are not separated while alive, despite the Inquisition's attempts, but only through Luxima's death, and Hilarion is not "reabsorbed by Europe"—he lives out his days in Cashmire, separated from all society. More to the point, colonial activity is not moderated by sensibility, but is the very sign of a faulty sensibility: as Hilarion falls in love with Luxima and rediscovers human feeling, he qualifies, then halts, and finally argues against the missionary project. Arguing against proselytization gives the Inquisition the excuse it needs to arrest him—and the Inquisition is clearly not only a supporter but also a symbol of colonial activity in Goa. Sensibility alienates Hilarion first from the missionary project and then from the religious and political authorities of Spain as Owenson reworks the conventions of the sentimental travelogue to make a very different case. If endings convey the moral of a narrative, Hilarion's decision to live alone in a cave rather than return to Europe is especially provocative.

Part of the context for Owenson's departure from convention lies in the fact that, unlike the European writers discussed by Pratt, Owenson is herself a colonized subject. *The Wild Irish Girl*, like the sentimental travelogue, represents a colonizing subject travelling through a colonial space and falling in love with a colonized subject who is (unlike Luxima) really a princess. As in *The Missionary*, Owenson departs from the conventional ending: the colonized princess marries the colonizing hero, and so the conciliatory "national tale" is born from the ashes of the sentimental travelogue.[1] While, as Rajan notes, Glorvina and Luxima are very different as characters (137), they are not very different in terms of their pedagogical-sentimental function. In both texts, the heroine educates the colonizing hero on her culture while refining, through her sentimental attraction and intelligence, his sensibility so far as to supersede his prejudices against her people and culture. But the colonized heroine of *The Wild Irish Girl* is, of course, Irish, and so strongly identified with Owenson herself that "Glorvina" became the author's nickname. It is consequently not such an easy matter to identify the author's position with that of the European travelling hero in *The Wild Irish Girl* and, by extension, that of the *Missionary*. Unlike *The Wild Irish Girl*, *Novice*, and *Woman*, the

---

1   The conciliatory marriage between colonized and colonizer is a hallmark of the national tale, particularly in its early versions. For a useful discussion of the national tale in relation to the marriage plot, colonialism, and cultural difference, see Trumpener, especially chapter 3.

Missionary does not end in a marriage, perhaps registering contemporary anxieties about marriages between peoples who are, according to post-Blumenbach European thought, of different "races." But the Irish novel, *St. Clair*, like *The Missionary*, ends in tragedy, with one lover killed by a military figure and the other left to languish.[1] Moreover, the impossibility of marriage is used to reinforce Owenson's point about the disciplinary pressure of cultural habit. In the opening paragraphs of Chapter XII, Hilarion considers the prohibitions in both of their cultures against religious devotees breaking vows of chastity.

But, at the same time, Owenson does draw heavily on an orientalist discourse that tacitly sanctions the imperial project. Hilarion's part in the ending of the novel departs radically from convention, but not Luxima's: she does die at the novel's end. Owenson, in her gendering of her primary representatives of East and West, complies thoroughly with the orientalist feminizing of the East and corollary masculinizing of the West. This gendering serves Owenson's purpose in facilitating a recognizable sentimental arrangement—a female victim is always the most sympathetic. Moreover, as Joseph Lew remarks, the structural similarities in the plots of some of Owenson's early novels, including *The Missionary*, "suggests that Owenson thought ... that the relationships of colonizer to colonized always retain structural similarities, and that these relationships had important continuities with those of men to women in the early nineteenth century" (64). But while choosing a woman to represent the East can productively introduce a critique of patriarchy and heighten the emotional impact of the work's arguments, it does so at a price—that is, at the cost of appearing to reinforce sexist and imperialist claims. Rajan, comparing representations of Hilarion to those of Luxima, concludes that "All of the epithets surrounding Hilarion are evocative of a natural right to dominance, and all of the epithets surrounding Luxima evoke a natural propensity to subjection" (130-31).

Luxima, moreover, is often represented in terms of orientalist clichés: she is frequently described as "languid," for instance, in body and spirit, and her religion is consistently aligned with "error." The description of Cashmire also falls into the common European representation of it as the lost Eden (adding special

---

1 Campbell notes that the two texts are also similar in addressing "the psychological states of two idealistic young people who fall in love, without being aware of it" (108).

weight to Owenson's Miltonic allusions) rather than as a real place inhabited by real people. Goa has workers, a government, an urban environment—but not Cashmire. Owenson's Cashmire seems to have only a handful of inhabitants and a couple of religious buildings; the rest is an exotic and idealized wilderness. The Pundit is arguably a moderate instance of the stereotype of the deceptive colonized subject. The scene of Luxima's excommunication in Chapter XII anticipates dozens of scenes in imperial Gothic narratives from adventure fiction to television and film (for instance, *Indiana Jones and the Temple of Doom*) in which horrified Europeans secretly watch elaborate and frightening religious rituals while fearing for their own bodily safety.

Owenson's text is ideologically and representationally hybrid. It uses orientalist clichés that align the East with the passive, emotional and feminine, and the West with the active, rational and masculine. It uses sentimental clichés that posit a universal sensibility that cuts across cultural difference, and privileges emotion over reason. And it has a heroine who thinks and acts on her own, retaining her commitment to her religion and arguing with the man she loves instead of submitting to his strong desire for her conversion. Rajan argues,

> Read metafictionally, Owenson's narrative can be seen as tracking with extraordinary accuracy the narrative of the breakdown of the imperial statement. The novel's rhetorical self-entrapment, its growing anxiety with itself, its reluctance to relinquish its own inauguration, and even the use of Milton for invocations that are consistently critiques suggest more than a superficial allegory of empire. Viewed in relation to the undermining forces within imperial discourse, many of the novel's self-perplexities that might be evaluated as literary shortcomings become eloquent in mapping the disarticulation of the metafiction that they both resist and sustain. (138)

This "tracking" follows the narrative line of the novel, and Hilarion's changing attitudes—and, in the logic of literary sensibility, the imagined (British) reader's changing attitudes. The orientalist clichés are most frequent and emphatic in the first volume of the novel, when Hilarion is fully committed to the missionary project and contemptuous of other religious and cultural beliefs, but they begin to fall away in Volume II as Luxima's arguments for religious tolerance and fundamental similarity are expressed. By Volume III,

Hilarion's residual hostility to other religions is often set against Luxima's call for tolerance, and Hilarion does not benefit by the comparison. That Hilarion does not, as Luxima asks with her dying breath, preach religious tolerance adds a sour note to the novel's tragic ending.

Rajan's remarks not only offer a useful perspective on the complexities in the politics and shifting tone of *The Missionary*, but also suggestively recall postcolonialist discussions of Irish writing in general. David Lloyd writes,

> the experience of colonized cultures such as Ireland's, with differing but increasing degrees of intensity, is to be subjected to an uneven process of assimilation. What is produced, accordingly, is not a self-sustaining and autonomous organism capable of appropriating other cultures to itself, as imperial and postmodern cultures alike conceive themselves to be, but rather, at the individual and national-cultural level, a hybridization ... in which antagonism mixes with dependence and autonomy is constantly undermined by the perceived influence of alien powers. (111-12)

As a consequence of this "uneven process of assimilation," argues Lloyd, the nineteenth-century Irish novel operates disjunctively in relation to the contemporary British novel, apparently failing to meet its criteria for coherence:

> Far from being simply an intrinsically benign and democratic form, the novel enacts the violence that underlies the constitution of identity, diffusing it in the eliciting of identification.
>
> In certain contexts, like that of Ireland, that process of identification breaks down ... because no cultural space is offered for representations which are not already apparently partisan. (In this respect Edgeworth and Lady Morgan may have been sharper critical observers of their practice than Carleton.) At the moment of the nation's emergence, of the various attempts to gain hegemony over self-representation in every sphere, the novel, like other cultural forms, is engaged with unusual self-consciousness in the activity of social transformation. The necessary myth of the novel, its formal transcendence of or aesthetic disinterest in social conflicts, is unusually difficult to maintain. (154-55)

Owenson's text thus not only reveals the "breakdown of the imperial statement" in general, but also echoes the as-yet-unconsolidat-
ed national statement in Ireland. The scene of Owenson reading
aloud sections of *The Missionary* to "distinguished guests" and asking for their suggestions (Campbell 108), discussed by Rajan (131),
dramatizes the larger cultural problem in which Irish voices regularly consulted and absorbed the colonizers' "suggestions" but, as
Lloyd notes, unevenly. Such uneven absorption is figured through
Luxima, who follows some of the forms of Hilarion's faith but is
never really converted (that is, assimilated) despite all of the missionary's efforts and attractiveness.

The Missionary: Reception, Romantic Orientalism, and Religious Toleration

The publication of Owenson's *The Missionary* was well-timed. Portugal was a hot news item, Vellore was still fresh in the public mind,
and there was a newly energized vogue for orientalist narratives.
While the 1780s and 1790s had seen a flurry of novels, tales and
plays set in the East, orientalist literature became especially popular
in the 1810s. Byron famously advised Moore, "Stick to the East;—
the oracle Staël told me it was only poetical policy. The North,
South, and West, have all been exhausted" (*Letters* 3:101). Byron's
justification aside, there were other reasons for British readers' fas-
cination with the East. Besides Vellore, there was the French occupation of Egypt and fears that Napoleon would invade India, as well
as popular interest in Greece's struggle for independence from the
Ottoman Empire (a subject Owenson had directly engaged in
Woman). The Lake Poets and later Romantic poets alike produced
oriental tales in verse. Of the Lake Poets, S.T. Coleridge, with
Byron's encouragement, published "Kubla Khan" (1816) and
Robert Southey published the epics, *The Curse of Kehama* (1810)
and *Thalaba the Destroyer* (1801). Of the younger Romantics, Byron
published a great deal of verse set in the East, from sections
of *Childe Harold's Pilgrimage* (1812-18) to his "Eastern Tales"
(1813-14), P.B. Shelley published *Alastor* (1816), *The Revolt of Islam*
(1818), and *Prometheus Unbound* (1820), and Thomas Moore
received a record advance for his prose-verse hybrid, *Lalla Rookh*
(1817).

While *The Missionary*'s importance is sometimes dismissed by
modern critics, it was very successful in its day. It went through
seven editions between 1811 and 1834, and "brought its author

four hundred pounds" (Dean vii)—no mean sum in early nine-teenth-century publishing. It was published in England, France (in translation), and the United States. It did so well that Owenson's English publisher, Stockdale, published an enlarged edition of her first novel, *St. Clair*, in late 1811—with "By Miss Owenson, Author of *The Missionary*" on the title page. It was also noticed in the reviews. In the *British Critic*, the reviewer paused to admire the energy of Owenson's prose—dubbing her a "lively lady"—before complaining that the plot of her "Indian Tale" was too complex and intense, and the action too improbable. The reviewer was especial-ly incredulous over Hilarion's decision to leave aristocratic comfort for monastic life and then "volunteer" to go to India as a mission-ary. In a substantial and more positive piece in the *Critical Review*, Owenson is praised for her delineation of character. The reviewer writes, "We must in justice say that in painting the missionary's feel-ings, his virtuous struggles, his remorse, his love, and the delicacy of his conduct and behaviour to the beloved object of his affections, Miss Owenson has displayed great force of expression, and a strong glow of rich colouring" (195). While reviewers sometimes com-plained of excess, it is Owenson's "force of expression" that readers tended to remember. In 1838, Henry F. Chorley argues that Owen-son's early novels, including *The Missionary*, "belong to a past dynasty of fiction" in terms of characterization and form, but adds that they "have still something of their own which distinguishes them among their contemporaries. Their scenery, their passion, their enthusiasm is eminently national; and, being dashed off with all the fervour and self-confidence of youth, it is not wonderful that they speedily made their way to distinguished success" (52-53). When the novel was republished in revised form, as *Luxima, the Prophetess* (1859), its political significance was more fully acknowl-edged; a review of *Luxima* in the *Literary Gazette* lauds Owenson's "powers of discernment half a century since" and echoes the pref-ace to *Luxima* in recognizing the novel's importance in the wake of the 1857 Indian uprising.[1]

Modern critics are finding other terms in which to evaluate the novel's merits and significance. For instance, Rajan traces some of Owenson's engagements with Milton's work in *The Missionary* and concludes that "Few writers remember Milton as vividly and

---

1 See Appendix B for fuller excerpts from these reviews; reviews of the day were usually published anonymously.

thoughtfully as Owenson" (134). Most recent scholarship on the novel addresses the wide-ranging impact of *The Missionary* on authors whose works were sometimes less successful than Owenson's at the time, but are now considered canonical. The Lake Poets' circle, predictably, did not care for Owenson's work. She was too firmly identified with the Jacobin stream of literature from which they were trying to disengage themselves. Southey disapproved of her "opinions" (Stevenson 189), and William Hazlitt is credited with a somewhat negative article on her biography of Salvator Rosa for the *Edinburgh Review*. William Wordsworth openly, and rather rudely, snubbed her at a party. He was mocked in return with typical Owensonian irony: Henry Crabb Robinson writes, "I was told she asked her neighbour, Has not Mr. Wordsworth written some poems?" (qtd. Stevenson 253). The second-generation Romantic poets and their circles, however, responded quite differently. In Owenson, they found a literary and political precursor; Byron, Moore, and the Shelleys in particular often praised Owenson's work, and were clearly indebted to her writings.

The influence of *The Missionary* on P.B. Shelley is especially well-established, and critics have long traced his debts to and interest in the novel.[1] The poet made no secret of his admiration of *The Missionary* and especially its heroine. Between mid-June and late July in 1811, P. B. Shelley repeatedly asked Thomas Jefferson Hogg to read *The Missionary*:

> The only thing that has interested me, if I except your letters has been one novel. It is Miss Owenson's *Missionary* an Indian tale. Will you read it, it is really a divine thing. Luxima the Indian is an Angel. What pity that we cannot incorporate these creations of Fancy; the very thought of them thrills the soul. Since I have read this book I have read no other—but I have thought strangely. (*Letters* 1: 107)

> Have you read a new novel, the Missionary by Miss Owenson. It is a divine thing, Luxima the Indian Priestess, were it possible to embody such a character, is *perfect*. The Missionary has been my companion for some time. I advise you to read it. (*Letters* 1:112)

---

1   See, for instance, Dean (vii-ix), Dennis (48), Drew (258-82), Leask (126-29), Lew (40), Rajan (159), and Viswanathan (27).

Have you read the Missionary it is a beautiful thing. It is here &
I cd. not help reading it again—. or do you not read novels. (*Letters* 1:130)

As Leask observes, Luxima was "a character-type to which he
returned obsessively in his oriental poems" (102). In Byron's oriental tales, *The Missionary* is a less obvious presence, though there are
echoes of Owenson's *Woman*—a work which Byron addresses at
length in a note to *Childe Harold's Pilgrimage* (*Poetical Works* 881).
Recently, critics such as D.S. Neff, Joseph Lew, and William D.
Brewer have addressed Mary Shelley's debts to Owenson, finding
echoes of *The Missionary* in *Frankenstein* (1818), *Mathilda* (written in
1819), and *Falkner* (1837).

Thomas Moore also knew the novel (*Letters* 1: 304), and his popular *Lalla Rookh*, reprinted throughout the nineteenth century,
shows considerable debts to Owenson. Dean suggests that "Moore
prepared himself for *Lalla Rookh* ... by actually studying *The Missionary*" (vii).[1] Moore's frame narrative is, for instance, set in the
same period, includes members of Aurangzeb's family, and involves
a long journey to Cashmire; as Dean notes, his "imagined" Cashmire is "substantially derived" from Owenson's (vii).[2] Like Owenson's novel, Moore's text is nominally secured in an "authentic" East
by footnotes; the two friends cite many of the same sources, including Bernier, Dow, Thévenot, Grose, and Jones, using the East, as
Mohammed Sharafuddin suggests of Romantic orientalist verse, "as
a mask either concealing, or making it easier to develop, ideas too
radical or too alien for the average literary opinion of the time"
(136).

Discussions of such authors' debts to Owenson emerge in concert with a larger critical emphasis on the novel's engagement with
orientalism. The novel is frequently mentioned in passing in studies of nineteenth-century orientalist discourse and imperialism. In
Owenson's only "Indian tale," however, her focus is rather unique-
ly on religious intolerance in relation to cultural difference. She had
dealt with it before. In *The Wild Irish Girl*, an English protagonist
overcomes his prejudice against the Irish in part by witnessing their
own religious tolerance. But, perhaps because religion was so

---

1   As Majeed notes, Moore first mentions *Lalla Rookh* in September 1811
    (93), just a few months after *The Missionary's* publication.
2   The title character of Moore's work is Aurangzeb's daughter; in *The Mis-
    sionary*, Aurangzeb's nephew, Solyman, courts Luxima.

thoroughly politicized in Ireland, she makes her strongest statements against religious intolerance in her non-Irish novels. In *The Novice*, de Sorville, the novel's voice of moral authority, declares,

> My dear count, we too often take up our religious and political opinions by inheritance, and defend them as we should our estates, merely because they descend to us from our forefathers.... [T]each her [Imogen], that true virtue and true religion are confined to no sect, to no party, to no country, and to no age; that, like the dew of heaven, their influence is universal and impartial, and when unopposed by prejudices, their vital principles are to be equally found in the heart of the catholic and protestant, the Jew and the mussulman, the Christian divine and the Indian bramin. (3:52-53)

In *Woman*, Owenson's statements on religious tolerance became so overt that she was attacked by her own publisher. In an 1809 letter, responding to her publisher's charges of religious unorthodoxy, she writes, "of *human virtue*, I do not believe that any particular faith is to be considered, as it must be admitted that a Brahmin or Mussulman, a Catholic or Protestant, may all be perfectly virtuous men, though they differ in points of faith" (qtd. in Dixon 1:348). In *The Missionary*, Owenson fleshes out this defense, representing "virtuous men" of the Hindu, Islamic, and Christian faiths sentimentally overcoming the religious intolerance of their cultures through love for someone of another faith.

While Owenson's anti-Catholic publisher, Stockdale, might have thought *The Missionary* likeminded because of its critique of the Inquisition and Catholic officials,[1] the novel contests his pho-

---

1 One of the great ironies of the book's production is that, after a deal with her previous publisher, Phillips, fell through in 1810, Owenson signed a contract with J. J. Stockdale as Castlereagh looked on approvingly (Dixon 1:424). Castlereagh helped to suppress the 1798 uprising, and handled some of the arrests which preceded it (including author Charles Hamilton Teeling's); Stockdale is the publisher, and possibly the author, of *The History of the Inquisitions* (1810), an anti-Catholic work that begins with a heated diatribe against Catholic Emancipation (see Appendix A). Owenson repeatedly cites the *History* in the final pages of her novel, but not elsewhere, raising the question of whether the notes were added when she changed publishers.

bic views by envisioning the reform of Hilarion, the exemplary monk, from evangelism to tolerance, and then to a personal, unarticulated religion with features of different faiths. Owenson does pepper her novel with references to Christianity as the "true" faith and Hindu beliefs as "superstition," though usually when providing Hilarion's perspective. For the reader who looks beyond the clichéd epithets, Owenson represents both religions as furthering, at their best, the "general or social good" and the happiness of others. The relative merits of the two religions are largely beside Owenson's point.

Home writes, "It is lamentable to observe, that religious sects resemble neighbouring states; the nearer they are to one another, the greater is their mutual rancour and animosity" (2: 200). In Romantic-era Ireland, "Catholic" and "Protestant" functioned as ethnic markers as much as religious ones, in large part because hostilities between the two groups were fostered by a colonial policy that favoured Protestantism (and especially Anglicanism) in an attempt to convert the Catholic majority and so assimilate them on terms that would supposedly reduce political conflict.[1] Thus, in *The Missionary*, as in such contemporary Irish works as Moore's *Memoirs of Captain Rock* (1824), proselytization serves as a synecdoche for colonial policy, and religious intolerance for the various means by which the colonized are abjected.[2] The target of such texts is not religious belief, but the use of religion to validate and facilitate the stifling of the rights of the colonized. As Owenson puts it in *The Missionary*, the Inquisition "silenced the feelings of patriotism, and stilled the impulse of humanity" (240). For Owenson, as for many other nationalists of the day, "patriotism" and "the impulse of humanity" are closely linked. If proselytization is a synecdoche for colonial policy, "feeling"—for religion, for family, for community—is at once a metonym for and the moral validation of nationalist resistance. And it is this complex feeling that sparks the uprising at the end of Owenson's novel.

In *The Missionary*, religious difference melts away as Owenson either establishes broad similarities or sets aside differences as culturally arbitrary and immaterial to the essence, and best part, of reli-

---

1   The policy was not very effective: "Conversions actually *increased* after the [Penal] laws were moderated in the 1770s" (Foster 206).

2   In Moore's satiric *Memoirs*, an English missionary travels to Ireland to convert Catholics, but, after hearing the details of colonial history, he decides that his first priority is to return home and convert the English.

gious feeling. A key strategy in this regard is the use of Christian terms—such as "excommunication" and "rosary"—to denote elements of the Hindu religion, and provide a basis for collapsing the apparent distance between the religious precepts of the two main characters. There are, for instance, a number of references to Hilarion's Catholic rosary and Luxima's "Brahminical rosary"; in one scene, Luxima wears Hilarion's rosary, and in others her rosary is explicitly contrasted to the cross she wears after her baptism. The rosaries become focal points through which Owenson addresses and then collapses the religious differences of the lovers. Owenson expands the rosary's significance by identifying it with personal affections as well as religious practice. Luxima asks Hilarion, "This rosary was fastened on my arm by a parent's tender hand, and bathed in Nature's holiest dew—a parent's tender tears; hold not the Christians relics, such as these, precious and sacred? Thou hast called thy religion the religion of the heart; will it not then respect the heart's best feelings?" (194). Similarly, Owenson overtly links Luxima's expulsion from her religion and community with the scene of Hilarion's execution: "It was on such an evening as this, that the Indian Priestess witnessed the dreadful act of her excommunication; the heavens smiled then, as now; and man, the minister of error, was then, as now, cruel and unjust,—substituting malevolence for mercy, and the horrors of a fanatical superstition for the blessed peace and loving kindness of true religion" (247). As Gauri Viswanathan notes in her discussion of *Luxima, the Prophetess*, "the double focus provides the occasion for a penetrating critique of religious absolutism as the source of both colonial and patriarchal oppression" (31).

But perhaps the most compelling "double focus" lies in Owenson's identification of sati with the Inquisition's auto-da-fè (a Portuguese phrase meaning "act of the faith"), a public spectacle in which the condemned were tied to stakes with wood at their feet that was then set on fire. Sati (or "suttee"), a ritual in which Hindu widows immolated themselves on their husband's funeral pyres, was infamous in Romantic-era Britain although the extent of its use was disputed. Sati functioned as a touchstone in a larger debate about the missionary project. In general, the EIC position at the turn of the century (in keeping with arguments by such British orientalists as Dow and Jones) held, for mostly pragmatic reasons, that Europeans should not interfere with Indian religious practices. In the dominant EIC view, making Christian texts available was fine; condemning other religions, actively trying to convert people, and trying to interfere with religion-related practices could only threaten British interests by deeply offending the populace and so intensifying resistance to British rule. This put the EIC and the missionaries on opposing sides, and at a time when the missionary movement was gaining momentum in Britain as well as in the empire.[1]

In 1807, after the Society of Missionaries published some anti-Islamic and anti-Hindu tracts in India, the Governor General sought the right to review Society publications and limit any increase in the number of missionaries, complaining specifically that the Society's tracts maligned Hindu deities and the principles of Islam ("Copy of a Letter" 41, 42, 46). EIC officials declared sati "unbannable" because it was "part of Hindu tradition" (Chatterjee 111), and argued that it was rarely practiced. In "On the Duties of a Faithful Widow" (1795), for instance, EIC agent Henry Colebrooke argues, "happily the Martyrs of this superstition have never been numerous. It is certain, that the instances of the widows' sacrifice are now rare: on this it is only necessary to appeal to the recollection of every person residing in *India*, how few instances have actually occurred within his knowledge" (219). But sati became, to those who favoured the expansion of British domination in India, a useful symbol and justification: if women were being burned alive, the argument went, the practice had to be stopped by British law and the Christian religion.[2] Imperial expansion thus had a moral validation—it was, in a sense, a new Crusade, and one with the chivalric motive of rescuing innocent women. Consequently, they relied heavily on dramatic representations of beautiful young women being forced to the pyre.

In *The Widow of Malabar* (1791), an imitation of a French play, Mariana Starke offers such a representation. The play opens with a "Young Bramin" referring to sati as "A sacrifice which all nature shudders at" (2) while a "Chief Bramin" defends it; Indamora, the widow in question, is initially willing to participate in the ritual, but changes her mind after she discovers the Young Bramin is her long-lost brother. At the end of Act II, in a startlingly violent speech, a

---

1   For instance, the London Society for Promoting Christianity amongst the Jews was established in 1809; see Ragussis for an excellent discussion of such groups.

2   Sati was also used, as Nussbaum argues, in a feminist discourse which, in sum, lamented the subjection of women everywhere while praising European culture as the least oppressive.

British officer, Raymond, threatens to "sweep their bloody Race from earth / Their friends, their altars, nay, their very Idols" and make "the whole city one huge Funeral Pyre" (32) if Indamora commits sati. British troops arrive as Indamora is about to "cast herself on the Pile" (43) and they halt the proceedings. After Raymond gives a speech on Christian mildness, claiming that "Christians conquer / To save and humanize Mankind," Indamora declares, "Who wou'd not be a Christian?" (45). The Chief Bramin commits suicide and Raymond directs his successor, the Young Bramin, "There, in yon Temple, henceforth reign supreme, / And, on its altars, fix the Christian Cross" (47). Starke's polemical play aligns sati with the uncivilized past of India, and represents British military force as the pressure necessary to bring to fruition the Indian potential for civilization and proper sensibility, a potential represented by the Young Bramin.

Given the common identification of sati as a form of spectacle that serves Indian hegemonic interests (embodied by the Chief Bramin in Starke's play), an identification reinforced by the widespread use of wedding imagery in representations of sati (Chatterjee 111–16), Owenson's dramatic description of an auto-da-fè offers a subtle counterpoint to contemporary descriptions of sati. Felicity Nussbaum argues that William Hodges, in *Travels in India During the Years 1780, 1781, & 1783* (1793), "mystifies sati and makes the widow heroic" (185); the "fearless widow ... is portrayed as heroically unperturbed by the approaching specter of pain and death" (184). This, of course, is Hilarion's attitude as he faces death at the hands of the Inquisition. Moreover, in Hodges' account, "the Asians' disengagement is fully distinguished from the emotion of the European observer" (Nussbaum 184), a pattern repeated in Starke's play as Raymond responds to Indamora's imminent sacrifice with genocidal rage. In Owenson's description of the auto-da-fè, however, the Indian audience is emotional and the European agents of the Inquisition impassive. In Chapter XVI of *The Missionary*, gender and national polarities are reversed: the Portuguese Count, rather than the Cashmirian widow, is compelled by the narrow interests of the elite to participate in a spectacle that will end with his death; and the Indian spectators, rather than the European spectators, rise up in horror at a practice they find barbaric.

Reinforcing the implications of this scene, Owenson represents Luxima as an ambivalent sign to the assembled crowd. The Christians see the cross around her neck, while the Hindus see the tellertum on her forehead. Each group views Luxima as a supernatural figure of justice in the face of religious persecution. For the Christians, she is a "miracle, wrought for the salvation of a persecuted martyr," that is, Hilarion; for the Hindus, she heralds an avatar, "announcing vengeance to the enemies of their religion" (249). Luxima's significance is not only doubled, but links one form of intolerance to the other: the violence of the Inquisition is linked to the colonial suppression of indigenous religions. The Inquisition, briefly brought to England in the sixteenth century by Mary I ("Bloody Mary"), still had a powerful resonance in British culture and frequently played a role in Gothic fiction; the Inquisition was as powerful a symbol to opponents of Catholic toleration in Britain as sati was to opponents of religious toleration in India. With Luxima's declaration, "My beloved, I come!—*Brahma* receive and eternally unite our spirits!" (249), Owenson suggests that belief and desire, not armed officers, draw her to the flames, and emphatically breaks from the usual pattern in European texts on sati. Luxima is not tugged towards the pyre by her parents, or pressured by the elders of her community; since she is not married, or even engaged, to Hilarion, there is not even any clear cultural directive. Sati in Owenson's text is a "voluntary immolation" (249). Luxima chooses according to her religious beliefs and her feelings for Hilarion— but Hilarion and the others condemned by the Inquisition are marched under guard to the same flames.

There is another form of violence here, and it is done to the mind rather than the body. In the words of the epigraph to Owenson's first novel, *St. Clair,* "Where *manners* and *refined sentiments* prevail, the *mind* is susceptible of more grievous wounds than the body" (title page). As Owenson implies throughout *The Missionary,* the mind is governed by cultural practice as well as personal emotion. Suffering and trauma are generated when the two are opposed to each other, but clarity and direction emerge when they work in concert. Katie Trumpener argues that, as Luxima's "thoughts are pulled back and forth between old cultural alliances and new emotional ties," her "self-alienation" "suggests a sociohistorical genesis of mental illness" (146). Luxima's decision to commit sati is represented as a moment in which emotional and cultural pressures are again harmonious: "she rushed to the pile in all the enthusiasm of love and of devotion" (251). Hilarion, similarly, is willing to die at the hands of the Inquisition because of "holy resignation and religious hope" (247), resisting only when Luxima is at risk and religion is once again at odds with love. But the ex-converts about to be executed by the Inquisition are still in the throes of "self-alienation": "The timid Indians, who, in the zeal and enthusiasm of their own religion, might have joyously and voluntarily sought the death, they now met with horror, hung back, shuddering and weeping in agony and despair" (248).Viswanathan argues that *Luxima* (in which these passages are substantially the same as in *The Missionary*) "presents the experience of spiritual change as an experience of social disruption, threatening to dislodge the convert as the subject of her own spiritual narrative. Nor is excommunication merely a metaphor for alienation or metaphysical abstraction, for the social isolation of Christian converts is carefully grounded in an elaborately drawn historical reality" (28-29), thus leaving the implications for the post-Vellore British administration of India unsugared. Conversion puts affection and belief at odds, alienating the convert from family and friends, as well as familiar cultural artifacts and practices, creating vulnerable, suffering subjects. Conversion, in other words, creates only "grievous wounds."

Luxima's conversion to Christianity proves to be superficial; Hilarion cannot wrest her from a faith she associates with family ties. She accepts some Christian forms, including baptism, and expresses respect for Hilarion's beliefs, but makes it clear that her religious beliefs have not actually changed. But the European missionary ceases to be a missionary. He becomes a hermit "whose religion was unknown" but bears Hindu features; like Luxima, for instance, he "prayed at the confluence of rivers, at the rising and the setting of the sun" (260). If, as Viswanathan's larger argument affirms, conversion narratives were complicit in an imperialist drive to incorporate "the Other" into the growing empire, then the failure to convert Luxima, Hilarion's discarding of the conversion project, and Hilarion's partial conversion to Luxima's faith suggest that Owenson's novel offers a sustained critique of such narratives. Conversion, in Owenson's text, cannot assimilate to any meaningful degree; it can only dissociate individuals from their families and communities, thwarting "natural" sentiments. As partial converts, Luxima is exiled from her homeland and Hilarion becomes a hermit far from his.

Historical Locations: From *The Missionary* to *Luxima*

Owenson goes to considerable lengths to maintain the historicity of *The Missionary*, and to use authoritative accounts. Her novel opens in the mid-1630s, on the verge of the Revolution of Portugal, and, in the final pages, jumps ahead to Bernier's visit to

Cashmire in 1664. In her narrative, Owenson cites only literary texts produced by the end of the 1660s: she quotes the Bible, Shakespeare's plays, Milton's *Paradise Lost*, and medieval Persian poetry. In her many footnotes, she clearly chooses her sources carefully.[1] *The Missionary* is set during the internecine conflicts associated with Aurangzeb. But, instead of quoting Dryden's famous play, *Aureng-Zebe*, she favours eyewitness accounts from the period she is describing and translations of Indian and Persian texts.

Her selection of sources is also interesting in another regard. In her footnotes, she cites seventeen sources on Indian culture and history as well as the Portuguese presence in India. Eleven of those seventeen sources were originally written in languages other than English: Thévenot's travelogue, Anquetil Duperron's treatise, Guyon's history, a French translation of a "Shaster," Sonnerat's travelogue, Voltaire's world history, two versions of Bernier's travelogue, Colebrooke's and Jones's translations of Indian legal texts, and Dow's translation of a Persian history. Of the sources originally written in English, half are travelogues (Grose, Forster, Hamilton) and one is a history of the Inquisition only partly interested in India. Besides Dow's prefatory materials, Owenson cites only two English orientalist works—Kindersley's and Craufurd's. While John Drew has traced echoes of Jones's work in Owenson's narrative and many of Owenson's mythological identifications are taken, unacknowledged but almost word for word, from Kindersley's work, the footnotes direct the reader elsewhere—away from England.[2] If, as Pamela Perkins and Shannon Russell suggest, Elizabeth Hamilton's use of predominantly English sources in her *Translation of the Letters of a Hindoo Rajah* (1796) establishes an "anglocentric version of India" (31), Owenson's version of India is de(anglo)centered. Owenson directs her audience to an overtly cosmopolitan body of scholarship in which firsthand accounts from a variety of national perspectives, rather than British scholarship, are given priority.

Owenson's reference to Vellore is a singular rupture in her careful situating of her narrative in the seventeenth century and in parts of India untouched by British rule. It is a highly suggestive one, not only bringing the novel's call for religious tolerance into the con-

---

1　Owenson uses footnotes extensively in most of her prose works; on this subject see, for instance, Leerssen ("How *The Wild Irish Girl*") and Moskal.

2　On Owenson's debts to Jones, see Drew (241-54); others have addressed this aspect of Owenson's work, including Leask (102).

text of a contemporary controversy, but also explaining Owenson's decision to revisit the novel after another Indian "mutiny" in 1857. The reasons for the 1857 uprising are complex, and subject to debate among historians. But the catalyst for the uprising was quickly and generally understood to be the introduction of a new rifle which required that soldiers bite off the ends of greased cartridges before loading them; reports that the cartridges were greased in cow and pig fat caused alarm among Hindu and Muslim soldiers who did not wish to break religious dietary laws that prohibited such contact with these materials. When soldiers who refused to use the cartridges were sentenced to long prison terms, tensions escalated and the uprising followed, starting in May 1857 and ending only in July 1858, after heavy casualties on both sides.

The controversy over the uprising quickly turned to the EIC's governance of India. In 1857, a friend of Owenson's, Cyrus Redding, argued,

> India is ours by conquest; the people are not dissatisfied; they have not risen against our rule. The India Company may have been guilty of avarice, and of crime in obtaining a position of which their acts show the unworthiness; but that is past. The people of England cannot heal the wounds in honour and humanity the Company has inflicted. India—and the opinion is pretty general as well as just—India must be ruled directly by the crown as British territory. We must no longer be taxed that India may be misruled, and that the people of England may be insulted by the agents of a mercenary company. ("Indian Affairs" 497)

In "The Company's Raj," an anonymous article published in *Blackwood's* that same year, the author responds derisively to such positions as Redding's:

> It was a sin to permit a company of merchants to invade a distant continent, and go on adding province to province in the British name. This national offence must now be repaired by at once transferring the natives to the protection of the Crown, so allowing free scope for the intelligence and energy of Parliament to ameliorate their condition, and consolidate our power in the interests and affections of the indigenous races. Such is the language not unfrequently heard in circles that ought to be ashamed of the dense ignorance on which it is based. (616)

The "circles" condemned here eventually won out, however, and control of India was transferred from the EIC to the British government soon after the uprising. The "real" causes of the uprising are less important here than the immediate popular perception that, as in Vellore, the English had pushed the Indian people too far by failing to show due regard for their religious feelings. In the opening pages of his article, Redding cites personal letters from the first decade of the century to refute reports of the Vellore Mutiny published by the *Times* and the *Examiner* in the wake of the 1857 uprising, concluding,

> We should not have dwelt so long on this subject, but the massacre of Vellore is denominated "anti-Christian" in the *Examiner*, and a conspiracy against our faith! Little did the writer of the article know the intense attachment of the native of the East to his religious rites, and that to them he will sacrifice even life itself. He has inherited for twenty-five hundred years those doctrines and rites which he professes, and which missionary labours have nowhere shaken to any extent worthy of mention. ("Indian Affairs" 493-94)

Given the frequently cited connection between Vellore and the 1857 uprising in early responses to the events of 1857 and 1858, it is less surprising that, of all of the novels to which she could have returned, Owenson chose *The Missionary*, spending the final months of her life revising the novel and preparing it for the press under the title, *Luxima, the Prophetess: A Tale of India*. The author of the unsigned preface to *Luxima* made the connection between the novel and the 1857 uprising almost explicit:

> Vividly portraying as it does the gorgeous Scenery, the Manners, Customs, and, above all, the RELIGION of that portion of the great Indian Empire to which it relates—and these have been subject to little, if any change—the story of "Luxima," will, it is presumed, prefer no ordinary claims to public attention, and the more particularly on account of the recent melancholy occurrences which have distracted a country with which we have so long had extensive commercial relations. (iii-iv)

While the preface-writer claims that the novel "has been greatly altered, and re-modelled" (iii), the text of *Luxima* is little different from *The Missionary*: the plot is the same, the sequence of paragraphs is the same as in the 1811 novel, and most of the notes are identical. Many of the changes are mechanical. For instance, she excises a garbled passage and corrects the French (something she could not do from Dublin when *The Missionary* was being published in London).[1] She also pruned some of the more sentimental sections, deleting such passages as the following:

> His eloquence was irresistible: it was the language of fearless genius, of enthusiastic zeal; vehement and impassioned, it ever aspired at the pathetic, or reached the sublime; and if it were, sometimes, more dazzling than judicious, more affecting than correct, still it persuaded when it failed to convince, still it was distinguished by those touches of tenderness, by those visions of enthusiasm, which blend and assimilate, so intimately, with human feeling, which ever address themselves, with such invariable success, to human passion! (83-84)

then pausing, she drew aside her veil, lest the almost impalpable web should intercept the fancied sound which expectation hung on. Thus, as she stood animated by suspenseful love, glowing with the hues of heaven, her up-held veil floating, like a sun-tinged vapour, round her; she looked like the tender vision which descends upon Passion's dream, like the splendid image, to whose creation Genius entrusts its own immortality.

O woman! Nature, which made you fair, made you fairest in the expression of this her best feeling; and the most perfect loveliness of a cold insensibility becomes revolting and deformed, compared to that intelligence of beauty which rushes upon the countenance from the heart that is filled with a pure and ardent affection: then thought breathes upon the lip, independent of

---

1   Owenson frequently lamented being unable to correct proofs when she lived in Dublin and her works were being published in England. In an 1809 note "To the Public," Owenson writes, "my little works have been always printed (from an illegible MS.) in one country while their author was the resident of another," adding the footnote, "It is a fact that can be attested by my publishers that I never corrected a proof sheet of any one of my works, nor ever resided in England during their printing or publication" (*Woman* 1: vi). She was mocked by the *Quarterly* for her pains, but included a similar prefatory defense in *O'Donnel.*

sound; and the eye images in a glance, all that the soul could feel in an age! (162)

She thus revises the text for a Victorian audience trained in the realist novel by omitting those passages most indebted to the literary conventions of sensibility (as well as, perhaps, heeding critics who argued that her early work was marred by overwrought language).

Some of her changes, however, go beyond this general pattern. In *Luxima*, for instance, she increases the attention to nonhegemonic religions. She names her revised novel after the Hindu priestess instead of the Catholic missionary, adds a lengthy note on Buddhism, and supplements her note on quietism. She also adds a paragraph in which the Pundit suggests that a show of power could be counter-productive in Hilarion's attempts to convert the Hindus. After a passage which appears in both versions of the novel, in which the Pundit advises Hilarion, "it is at this period, that you may seize on an opportunity of advancing your doctrines, as, by throwing off your European habit, and undergoing purification in the consecrated tanks of the temple, you become qualified to enter its vestibule" (89), she inserts the sentence, "The Pundit looked earnestly on his listening auditor, and then added emphatically, 'but you must go alone, an ostentatious mission would destroy all hope of success and perhaps risk your life'" (*Luxima* 34). In *Luxima*, it is "this proposal" to which "the Missionary made no reply" (34), rather than the earlier one of "throwing off [his] European habit" and "undergoing purification" according to Hindu practice.

Perhaps the most significant alterations appear in the opening pages of *Luxima*. Owenson adds new details about Hilarion's early life and preparation for India, giving him a strong female relative and a teacher who is rumoured to be from India:

> To this solitary and deserted castle, Hilarion, Count d'Acugna, had been sent in early boyhood by his uncle and the Archbishop of Lisbon, at the request of his grandmother, the Duchess of Acugna—the St. Helena of her time and country—when he had scarcely attained his tenth year. His sole companion was his preceptor, an old brother of the order of St. Francis, whom tradition reported to be a converted Hindoo, a Brahmin by descent, and long a professor of Indian learners. (4)

The Duchess of Acugna thus becomes another in a long line of powerful religious women who appear or are discussed in

Owenson's later fiction (most notably *The O'Briens*), and Hilarion, like O'Brien, O'Donnel, and other Owenson heroes, reaps the benefits of such a woman's influence. The new characterization of the preceptor, however, is arguably the most provocative alteration to the novel. When Owenson was writing *The Missionary* in 1810, those who valued Indian culture were still very much in the ascendancy. Thus Mill complains in 1817 that Jones's positive view of Indian culture was so powerful that it was difficult to "obtain a hearing" for the opposite position (1: 431). By the middle of the nineteenth century, however, Mill's views had superseded Jones's, bolstered by a developing racist discourse in which physical and intellectual features were deterministically linked, and emerging notions of "racial degeneracy." While she later refers to the teacher without qualification as a "Hindoo," her original implication that the preceptor's origins are subject to rumour rather than immediately ascertainable from his appearance or cultural knowledge calls into question racial determinism—and the determinability of race. More significantly, to put an Indian into a seventeenth-century European monastery as a highly regarded scholar and the teacher of a son of the powerful houses of Bragança and Acugna is to undermine the prevailing assumption that culture and knowledge pass from "enlightened" Europe to its "benighted" colonies. On a more practical note, this also makes it possible for Owenson to explain the rapidity with which Hilarion learns Luxima's language:

> In a few days, therefore, his mission to India was determined on for the following spring. He passed the interim in profound study of the Hindoo language and the Sanscrit, and placed himself under the tuition of the learned converted Hindoo. Permission too, from the Governor of the Order to leave the convent was obtained, and he repaired to Lisbon to procure the necessary credentials for his perilous enterprise. (*Luxima* 11-12)

By giving him an Indian teacher in Portugal, in addition to the tutelage of the Pundit in India, Owenson makes her missionary Indian-educated and thus further authorizes his conclusions about the futility and immorality of proselytization while also complicating his status as European by making his education more cosmopolitan.

The Missionary was not only influential on Romantic orientalist literature, and part of a considerable body of work by one of the most popular and controversial authors of the first half of the nineteenth century. The novel does more than reveal a broadly liberal, though still largely Eurocentric, view of Indian culture and colonial practices. It also registers the complex imbrication of political discourses in a particular historical moment. In *The Missionary*, Portugal's domination by Spain overlaps India's colonization, with Ireland's colonization hovering implicitly on the margins of both; the feminization of the orient becomes the opportunity for an emotional plea for tolerance and tacit regard, veering into Jacobin sentimentality and feminism while still dragging sexist and racist stereotypes behind it; calls for religious tolerance in India are supported by anti-Catholic representations of the Inquisition; expertise on India is decentered, distanced from British scholarship and the East India Company but never fully separated from them. The basic plot of *The Missionary* is a familiar one; as in *Romeo and Juliet*, two "star-cross'd" lovers meet, fall in love, and are tragically separated by factional hostilities. But the details of its setting, footnotes, and historical framing embed that basic plot in interrelated but distinct Romantic-era debates over the imperial project, religious and cultural difference, gender, and the sociopolitical force of sensibility.

Sydney Owenson (Lady Morgan): A Brief Chronology

1783   Born 25 December, the first child of Robert and Jane Owenson (formerly Robert MacOwen and Jane Mill).

1784   Owenson's only sibling, Olivia, is born c. 1784-85. William Jones establishes the Asiatick Society of Bengal.

1786   Edmund Burke initiates impeachment proceedings against Warren Hastings, governor of the East India Company until 1785.

1788   The Asiatick Society begins publishing *Asiatick Researches*; Hastings' impeachment trial begins in the British Parliament.

1790-91   About this time, Thomas Dermody, poet and linguistic prodigy, joins the Owenson household in Dublin and begins to tutor the Owenson sisters. The Society of United Irishmen is founded in Belfast (14 Oct. 1791); a sister organization is founded in Dublin later in 1791.

1792   Dermody publishes *Poems, Consisting of Essays, Lyric, Elegiac, &c.* (1792), which includes "To Miss Sidney and Miss Olivia Owenson."

c.1793   Jane Owenson dies, and the Owenson sisters are sent away to school in Clontarf.

1794   Robert Owenson opens a theatre in Kilkenny. Dr. William Drennan, a popular Dublin physician, is tried, and acquitted, on charges of sedition arising from his involvement with the United Irishmen.

1795   Impeachment proceedings conclude against Hastings; he is acquitted.

1796   In Ireland, tension increases between government and nationalist forces: in March, the Insurrection Act is passed, allowing curfews, searches for arms, and the death penalty for taking oaths (that is, to the United Irishmen); in October, Habeas Corpus is suspended; in December, the French fleet, with United Irishmen leader Wolfe

Tone, approaches Bantry Bay, but is held back by inclement weather.

1798   In March, a number of United Irishmen leaders, including the popular Lord Edward Fitzgerald, are arrested; martial law is imposed. In May and June, the United Irishmen uprising takes place, with significant conflicts in Wexford (in the south of Ireland) and Ulster (in the north). The uprising is largely suppressed by the end of the summer. Trials and executions follow; Wolfe Tone commits suicide while in prison awaiting execution.

1799   Sir William Jones's collected *Works* are published.

1800   Owenson begins working as a governess, but dislikes the job and leaves it after a year or so. Act of Union is passed, to take effect 1 Jan. 1801; it abolishes the Irish Parliament and brings Ireland under the direct jurisdiction of the British Parliament.

1801   Owenson publishes her first volume, *Poems*.

1802   Dermody dies, at the age of twenty-seven.

1803   Owenson publishes her first novel, *St. Clair: Or, the Heiress of Desmond*. The Emmett Uprising takes place in Ireland; the leader, Robert Emmet, is executed.

1804   Owenson publishes *A Few Reflections, Occasioned by the Perusal of a Work, Entitled, "Familiar Epistles to Frederick J——s Esq., On the Present State of the Irish Stage."*

1805   Owenson publishes *The Novice of Saint Dominick* and *Twelve Original Hibernian Melodies*.

1806   Owenson publishes her most famous novel, *The Wild Irish Girl: A National Tale*; she soon becomes known by the name of the novel's heroine, "Glorvina." "Vellore Mutiny" against British rule in India takes place on 9 July.

1807   Owenson writes the words for an operetta, *The First Attempt, or Whim of a Moment*; she also publishes *The Lay of an Irish Harp; Or, Metrical Fragments* and *Patriotic Sketches of Ireland*. Thomas Moore publishes the first number of the immensely popular *Irish Melodies* (1807-34).

1808   Owenson's sister Olivia marries Arthur Clarke.

1809   Owenson publishes *Woman: Or, Ida of Athens*; the *Quarterly Review* begins publication, including a negative review of *Woman* in its first number.

1810   Owenson finishes writing *The Missionary: An Indian Tale*; Phillips prints a volume, and then halts the presses because of a dispute with Owenson over royalties. Owenson goes to London to find another publisher. Unlawful Oaths Act passed to inhibit "secret" societies, in effect, further suppressing organized political dissent in Ireland.

1811   Owenson publishes *The Missionary: An Indian Tale* with Stockdale. She meets the author, Lady Caroline Lamb, and becomes engaged to Dr. T. Charles Morgan. Edward Lysaght, Owenson's godfather, dies; his *Poems* are published. Daniel O'Connell establishes Catholic Board.

1812   Owenson and the recently knighted Morgan are married on January 20th; Owenson thus becomes "Lady Morgan." Owenson's father dies in the spring.

1813   The Morgans begin living at 35 Kildare Street, Dublin; it becomes a political and literary salon of note.

1814   Owenson publishes *O'Donnel: A National Tale. New Monthly Magazine* begins publication; Owenson and her husband later become contributors to the journal.

1816   Owenson's friend, Lamb, publishes *Glenarvon*, a novel set in Ireland about the time of the United Irishmen uprising.

1817   Owenson publishes *France*. Moore publishes *Lalla Rookh*.

1818   Owenson publishes *Florence Macarthy: An Irish Tale*. Sir Charles Morgan publishes *Sketches of the Philosophy of Life*.

1821   Owenson publishes *Italy* (with notes and appendix by Sir Charles Morgan), and *A Letter to the Reviewers of "Italy," including an answer to a pamphlet entitled, "Observations upon the calumnies and misrepresentations of Lady Morgan's Italy."*

1822   Owenson and her husband publish another co-authored work, *The Mohawks: A Satirical Poem*.

1823   O'Connell founds the Catholic Association.

1824   Owenson publishes *The Life and Times of Salvator Rosa*. She is barred, by decree of the Emperor, from entering Austria.

1825   Owenson publishes *Absenteeism*, an essay which had previously appeared, serially, in *New Monthly Magazine*. Catholic Association dissolved under Unlawful Societies Act, and then resurrected under different terms. Catholic Emancipation Bill defeated in the House of Lords.

1827   Owenson publishes a novel about the 1798 uprising, *The O'Briens and the O'Flahertys: A National Tale*.

1828   *Athenaeum* begins publication; Owenson later contributes to the journal. O'Connell is elected to Parliament, increasing the pressure for Catholic Emancipation because, as a Catholic, he is not eligible under the Penal Laws to hold elected office.

1829   Owenson publishes an autobiographical work, *The Book of the Boudoir*. Catholic Emancipation is passed.

1830   Owenson publishes *France in 1829-1830*.

1832   First Reform Bill passed by the British Parliament; the Irish Reform Bill includes more parliamentary seats for Ireland and adjustments to the Irish franchise.

1833   Owenson publishes *Dramatic Scenes from Real Life*.

1835   Owenson publishes *The Princess, Or the Beguine*.

1837   Lord Melbourne, on behalf of the British government, grants Owenson a literary pension of £300 per year. She and her husband leave Dublin and move to London, England.

1840   Owenson publishes *Woman and her Master*.

1841   Owenson and her husband publish *The Book Without a Name*.

1843   Sir Charles Morgan dies.

1845   Owenson's sister Olivia (Lady Clarke) dies. The potato blight appears in Ireland, and famine quickly follows; the population of Ireland falls from over eight million in 1841 to less than six million by 1861.

1851   Owenson publishes *Letter to Cardinal Wiseman, in answer to his "Remarks on Lady Morgan's statements regarding St. Peter's Chair."*

1852   Moore dies.

1857-58   Indian uprising against British rule known at the time as the "Indian Mutiny" takes place from May 1857 to July 1858. In August 1858, the British government assumes direct control of India, ending the East India Company's administration.

1859   Owenson publishes *Passages from my Autobiography*; it covers the years 1818-1819. She dies in mid-April, while seeing *Luxima, the Prophetess: A Tale of India* through the press.

A Note on the Text

The copy text for this edition is the second edition of 1811, printed in London by J. J. Stockdale (the third edition is identical to the second). Living in Dublin at the time, Owenson was unable to correct the proofs for *The Missionary*, and the text has a number of printer's errors; French passages are particularly poorly typeset. Many of the errors and inconsistencies may have arisen from a change of printers. The first two volumes were printed by S. Gosnell of Little Queen Street, London, and are virtually error-free. The final volume was printed by J. Brittell of Marshall-Street, Golden-Square, and it contains twice as many errors as the other two volumes combined, including such mechanical errors as the occasional use of numbers rather than asterisks in footnotes and faulty chapter numbers (Chapter XVII, for example, is designated Chapter IV). Some spelling conventions were also altered between the first two volumes and the last.

I have silently corrected obvious errors and superficial inconsistencies after consultation with a later version of the novel, *Luxima, the Prophetess* (1859), which Owenson was correcting in the final weeks of her life. Because English-language writers of this period had no standard spelling for terms related to India and its cultures, the variant spellings of such terms have usually been preserved; spellings have only been regularized if there is a single variant spelling of a word that is otherwise consistently spelled, and, to avoid confusion, in the case of Sirinigar, a placename that appears frequently but in a variety of forms.

As in many Romantic-era texts, quotations are usually slight misquotations. This is clearest when Owenson is quoting literary sources, but errors also appear in her quotations from documentary sources. Such errors have not been corrected, since to do so might interfere with Owenson's sense. Her reference style has also been preserved (including her occasional use of French abbreviations, such as "tom." or "T." for "tome").

All footnotes to the novel and the material in the appendices are taken from the original publications; all editorial notes are listed under "Explanatory Notes."

THE MISSIONARY:
AN INDIAN TALE

TO THE MOST NOBLE
ANN JANE,
MARCHIONESS OF ABERCORN,
THE FOLLOWING
TALE
IS RESPECTFULLY INSCRIBED,
BY
THE AUTHOR.

VOLUME I

CHAPTER I.

In the beginning of the seventeenth century, Portugal, bereft of her natural sovereigns, had become an object of contention, to various powers in Europe. The houses of Braganza and of Parma, of Savoy and Medici, alike published their pretensions, and alike submitted to that decision, which the arms of Spain finally made in its own favour. Under the goading oppression of Philip the Second, and of his two immediate successors, the national independence of a brave people faded gradually away, and Portugal, wholly losing its rank in the scale of nations, sunk into a Spanish province. From the torpid dream of slavish dependence, the victims of a mild oppression were suddenly awakened, by the rapacious cruelties of Olivarez, the gloomy minister of Philip the Fourth; and the spring of national liberty, receiving its impulse from the very pressure of the tyranny which crushed it, already recovered something of that tone of force and elasticity which finally produced one of the most singular and perfect revolutions, which the history of nations has recorded.[1] It was at this period, that Portugal became divided into two powerful factions, and the Spanish partizans, and Portuguese patriots, openly expressed their mutual abhorrence, and secretly planned their respective destruction. Even Religion forfeited her dove-like character of peace, and enrolled herself beneath the banners of civil discord and factious commotion. The Jesuits governed with the Spaniards; the Franciscans resisted with the Portuguese; and each accused the other of promulgating heretical tenets, in support of that cause, to which each was respectively attached.[*]

It was in the midst of these religious and political feuds, that the Order of St. Francis became distinguished in Portugal, by the sanctity and genius of one of its members; and the monastery, into which the holy enthusiast had retired from the splendour of opulence and rank, from the pleasures of youth and the pursuits of life, became the shrine of pilgrimage, to many pious votarists, who sought Heaven through the mediation of him, who, on earth, had already obtained the title of "the man without a fault."

---

[*] The Jesuits, being charged with fraudulent practices, in endeavouring to persuade the Indians that the Brahminical and Christian doctrines differed not essentially, were openly condemned by the Franciscans; which laid the foundation of those long and violent contests, decided by Innocent the Tenth, in favour of the Franciscans.[2]

The monastery of St. Francis stands at the foot of that mighty chain of mountains, which partially divides the province of Alentejo from the sea-beat shores of Algarva.[3] Excavated from a pile of rocks, its cells are little better than rude caverns; and its heavy portico, and gloomy chapel, are composed of the fragments of a Moorish castle,[4] whose mouldering turrets mingle, in the haze of distance, with the lofty spires of the Christian sanctuary, while both are reflected, by the bosom of one of those lakes so peculiar to Portugal, whose subterraneous thunder rolls with an incessant uproar, even when the waves of the ocean are still, and the air breathes of peace. Celebrated, in the natural history of the country, for its absorbent and sanative qualities, Superstition had wrested the phænomenon to her own mystic purposes; and the roaring lake, which added so fine and awful a feature to the gloomy scenery of the convent, brought to its altars the grateful tributes of those, who piously believed that they obtained, from the consecrated waters, health in this world, and salvation in the world to come.

To the left of the monastery, some traces of a Roman fortress, similar to that of Coimbra,[5] were still visible: to the north, the mighty hills of Alentejo terminated the prospect: while to the south, the view seemed extended to infinitude by the mightier ocean, beyond whose horizon fancy sought the coast of Carthage; and memory, awakening to her magic, dwelt on the altar of Hannibal, or hovered round the victor standard of Scipio Africanus.[6] The mountains; the ocean; the lake of subterraneous thunder; the ruins of Moorish splendour; the vestiges of Roman prowess; the pile of monastic gloom:—magnificent assemblages of great and discordant images! What various epochas in time; what various states of human power and human intellect, did not ye blend and harmonize, in one great picture! What a powerful influence were not your wilderness and your solemnity, your grandeur and your gloom, calculated to produce upon the mind of religious enthusiasm, upon the spirit of genius and melancholy; upon a character, formed of all the higher elements of human nature, upon such a mind, upon such a genius, upon such a character as thine, Hilarion!

Amidst the hanging woods which shaded the southern side of the mountains of Algarva, rose the turrets of the castle of Acugna; and the moon-beams which fell upon its ramparts, were reflected back by the glittering spires of St. Francis.

To this solitary and deserted castle, Hilarion, Count d'Acugna, had been sent, by his uncle and guardian, the Archbishop of Lisbon, in 1620. The young Hilarion had scarcely attained his tenth year. His sole companion was his preceptor, an old brother of the order of St. Francis. History attests the antiquity and splendour of the House d'Acugna. The royal blood of Portugal flowed in the veins of Hilarion, for his mother was a daughter of the House of Braganza.[7] His elder, and only brother, Don Lewis, Duke d'Acugna, was one of the most powerful grandees in the state; his uncle, the Archbishop of Lisbon, was considered as the leader of the disaffected nobles, whom the Spanish tyranny had almost driven to desperation; and, while the Duke and the Prelate were involved in all the political commotions of the day, the young Hilarion, impressed by the grand solemnity of the images by which he was surrounded; inflamed by the visionary nature of his religious studies; borne away by the complexional enthusiasm of his character, and influenced by the eloquence and example of his preceptor, emulated the ascetic life of his patron saint, sighed to retire to some boundless desert, to live superior to nature, and to nature's laws, beyond the power of temptation, and the possibility of error; to subdue, alike, the human weaknesses and the human passion, and, wholly devoted to Heaven, to give himself up to such spiritual communions and celestial visions, as visit the souls of the pure in spirit, even during their probation on earth, until, his unregulated mind becoming the victim of his ardent imagination, he lost sight of the true object of human existence, a life acceptable to the Creator by being serviceable to his creatures. Endowed with that complexional enthusiasm, which disdains the ordinary business of life, with that profound sensibility which unfits for its pursuits, wrapt in holy dreams and pious ecstacies, all external circumstances gradually faded from his view, and, in his eighteenth year, believing himself, by the sudden death of his preceptor, to be the "inheritor of his sacred mantle," he offered up the sacrifice of his worldly honours, of his human possessions, to Heaven, and became a monk of the order of St. Francis.

The Archbishop, and the Duke d'Acugna, received the intelligence of his profession with less emotion than surprise. Absence had loosened the tie of natural affection. The political state of Portugal rendered an adequate provision for the younger brother of so illustrious an house, difficult and precarious; and the Patriarch of Lisbon well knew that, to enter the portals of the church was not to close, for ever, the gate of temporal preferment. The uncle and the brother wrote to felicitate the young monk on his heavenly vocation, presented a considerable donation to the monastery of

St. Francis, and soon lost sight of their enthusiast-relative in the public commotions and private factions of the day.

CHAPTER II.

There is a dear and precious period in the life of man, which, brief as sweet, is best appreciated in recollection; when but to exist is to enjoy; when the rapid pulse throbs, wildly, with the vague delight which fills the careless heart, and when it may be truly said, "that nothing is, but what is not."[8]

While this rainbow hour lasted, the thorny wreath, which faith had plaited round Hilarion's brow, was worn as cheerily, as if the rose of pleasure had glowed upon his temple. The vows he had made were ever present to his mind. The ceremonies of his religion occupied his imagination; and its forms, no less than its spirit, engaged his whole existence. He had taken holy orders, and was frequently engaged in the interesting offices of the priesthood. He studied, with unwearied ardour, the sacred legends and records of the convent library, and, during six years of monastic seclusion, his pure and sinless life had been so distinguished by religious discipline and pious austerity; by devotional zeal and fervid enthusiasm; by charitable exertion and rigid self-denial; and by an eloquence in the cause of religion, so profound, so brilliant, and so touching, that, even envy, which, in a cloister's gloom, survives the death of better passions, flung not its venom on his sacred character; and the celebrity of the *man without a fault* had extended far beyond the confines of his own secluded monastery.

The monks conceived, that his illustrious birth, not less than his eminent genius and unrivalled piety, threw a splendour on their order, and they daily looked forward to the hour when the Father Hilarion should wave the banner of successful controversy over the prostrate necks of the fallen Jesuits. Yet the brotherhood had hitherto but remotely hinted their wishes, or suggested their expectations. The familiar ease of the novice had faded away with the purple bloom of the youth; and the reserved dignity of the man threw, at an hopeless distance, those whom the monk, indeed, in the meekness of religious phraseology, called his superiors; but whom the saint and the nobleman equally felt unworthy to be classed with him, as beings of the same species; he stood alone, lofty and aspiring, self-wrapt and dignified; and no external discipline, no internal humiliation, had so crucified the human weakness in his bosom, as wholly to exclude the leaven of mortality from the perfection of religious excellence.

Hitherto the life of the young monk resembled the pure and holy dream of saintly slumbers, for it was still a dream; splendid indeed, but visionary; pure, but useless; bright, but unsubstantial. Dead to all those ties, which, at once, constitute the charm and the anxiety of existence, which agitate while they bless the life of man, the spring of human affection lay untouched within his bosom, and the faculty of human reason unused within his mind. Hitherto, his genius had alone betrayed its powers, in deceiving others, or himself, by those imposing creations, by which faith was secured through the medium of imagination; and the ardour of his tender feelings wasted, in visions of holy illusion, or dreams of pious fraud. Yet these feelings, though unexercised, were not extinct; they betrayed their existence even in the torpid life he had chosen; for the true source of his religion, enveloped as it was in mysteries and dogmas, was but a divine and tender impulse of gratitude towards the First Cause; and his benevolent charity, which he coldly called his duty, but the extension of that impulse towards his fellow-creature! His habits, though they had tended to calm the impetuosity of his complexional character, and to purify and strengthen his moral principles, had added to his enthusiasm, what they had subtracted from his passions, and had given to his zeal, all that they had taken from his heart: but when the animated fervour of adolescence subsided in the dignified tranquillity of manhood, when the reiteration of the same images denied the same vivacity of sensation as had distinguished their original impression, then the visions, which had entranced his dreaming youth, ceased to people and to cheer his unbroken solitude; then, even Religion, though she lost nothing of her influence, lost much of her charm. While the faith which occupied his soul was not sufficient, in its pure but passive effects, to engage his life; the active vital principle, which dictates to man, the sphere for which he was created, preyed on its own existence, and he turned upon himself those exertions, which were intended to benefit the species to which he belonged: his religious discipline became more severe; his mortifications more numerous; his prayers and penance more rigid and more frequent; and that which was but the result of the weakness of human nature, conscious of its frailty, added new lustre to the reputation of the saint, and excited a warmer reverence for the virtues of the man. Accustomed to pursue the bold wanderings of the human mind, upon subjects whose awful mystery escapes all human research, intense study finally gave place to ceaseless meditation. Connecting, or endeavouring to connect, his incongruous ideas, by abstract principles, he lost sight of fact, in pursuit of inference; and, excluded from all social intercourse, from all active engagement, his ardent imagination became his ruling faculty, while the wild magnificence of the scenes by which he was surrounded, threw its correspondent influence on his disordered mind; and all within, and all without his monastery, contributed to cherish and to perpetuate the religious melancholy and gloomy enthusiasm of his character. More zealous in his faith at twenty-six than he had been at eighteen, it yet no longer opened to his view the heaven which smiled upon his head; but, beneath his feet, an abyss which seemed ready to ingulf him. He sometimes wildly talked of evil deeds which crossed his brain; of evil passions which shook his frame; and doubted if the mercy of his Redeemer extended to him, whose sinless life was not a sufficient propitiation for sinful thoughts: and this sensitive delicacy of a morbid conscience plunged him into habitual sadness, while it added to his holy fame, and excited a still higher veneration for his character, in those who were the witnesses of its perfection.

He frequently spent days, devoted to religious exercises, in the gloomy woods of the monastery; and the monk, who, from kindness or from curiosity, pursued his wanderings, sometimes found him cradled on a beetling cliff, rocked by the rising storm; sometimes buried amidst the ruins of the Moorish castle, the companion of the solitary bittern; and sometimes hanging over the lake, whose subterraneous thunder scared all ears but his.

The change which had gradually taken place in the character and manners of the monk had long awakened the attention of the Prior and the brotherhood of St. Francis; but such was the veneration he had established for his character, by the austerity of his life, and the superiority of his genius, by the rank he had sacrificed, and the dignity he had retained, that his associates sought not in natural or moral causes for the source of effects so striking and so extraordinary: they said, "It is the mysterious workings of divine grace; it is a vocation from Heaven; a miracle is about to be wrought, and it is reserved for a member of the order of St. Francis to perform it."

These observations had reached the ears of the Father Hilarion, when those who pronounced them believed him lost in spiritual meditation; they became imprinted on his mind; they fastened on his imagination; they occupied his waking thought, and influenced his broken dream. It was in one of those suspensions of the senses, when a doubtful sleep unlinks the ideas, without wholly subduing the powers of the mind, that he fancied a favourite dove had flown from his bosom, where it was wont to nestle, towards the east; that, suddenly endowed with the power of flight, he pursued the bird of peace through regions of air, till he beheld its delicate form absorbed in the effulgence of the rising sun, whose splendour shone so intensely on him, that, even when he awoke, he still felt its warmth, and shrank beneath its brightness. He perceived, also, that the dove, which had been the subject of his vision, and which had drooped and pined during the preceding day, lay dead upon his bosom. This dream made a strong impression on his mind. The effects of that impression were betrayed in a discourse which he delivered on the eve of the festival of St. Hilarion.[9] He took for his subject the life of Paul, whom he called the first missionary. He spoke of the faith of the apostle, not as it touched himself only, but as to its beneficent relations towards others.

In the picture which he had drawn, the monks perceived the state of his own mind. They said, "It is not of St. Paul alone he speaks, but of himself; he is consumed with an insatiable thirst for the conversion of souls; for the dilatation and honour of the kingdom of Christ. It is through him that the heretical tenets of the Jesuits will be confounded and exposed. Let us honour ourselves and our order, by promoting his inspired views." In a few days, therefore, his mission to India was determined on. Arrangements for his departure were effected, permission from the Governor of the order to leave the convent was obtained, and he repaired to Lisbon, to procure the necessary credentials for his perilous enterprise.[10]

After a separation of fifteen years, the Father Hilarion appeared before his guardian uncle, and his brother, the Duke d'Acugna; and never did a mortal form present a finer image of what man was, when God first created him after his own likeness, and sin had not yet effaced the glorious impress of the Divinity. Nature stood honoured in this most perfect model of her power; and the expression of the best and highest of the human passions would have marred that pure and splendid character of look, which seemed to belong to something beyond the high perfection of human power or of human genius. Lofty and dignified in his air, there was an aspiring grandeur in the figure of the Monk, which resembled the transfiguration of mortal into heavenly greatness: and, though his eagle-eye, when raised from earth, flashed all the fire of inspiration; yet, when again it sunk in holy meekness, the softer excellence of heavenly mercy hung its tender traits upon his pensive brow; his up-turned glance beaming the heroic fortitude of the martyr; his down-cast look, the tender sympathies of the saint; each, respectively, marking the heroism of a great soul, prepared to suffer and to resist; the sensibility of a feeling heart, created to pity and to relieve; indicating a character, formed upon that bright model, which so intimately associated the attributes of the God with the feelings of the man.

The Duke and the Archbishop stood awed in the presence of this extraordinary being. They secretly smiled at what they deemed the romance of his intentions; but they had not the courage to oppose them: they were rich in worldly arguments, against an enterprise so full of danger, and so destitute of recompense; but how could they offer them to one, who breathed not of this world; to whom earthly passions, and earthly views, were alike unknown; who already seemed to belong to that heaven, to which he was about to lead millions of erring creatures: all, therefore, that was reserved for them to effect, was, to throw a splendour over his mission, correspondent to his illustrious rank; and, in spite of the intrigues of the Jesuits, the reluctance of the Spanish vice-reine, and the wishes of the minister, Miguel Vasconcellas, the united influence of the houses of Braganza and Acugna procured a brief from the Pope's legate, then resident in Lisbon, constituting a Franciscan monk apostolic nuncio in India, and appointing Goa, then deemed the bulwark of Christianity, in Hindostan, the centre of his mission.[11]

Followed to the shore by a multitude of persons, who beheld in the apostolic nuncio another Francis Xaverius,[12] the Father Hilarion embarked with the Indian fleet, on board the admiral's ship, which also carried the governor-general, recently appointed to the government of Goa. The Nuncio was accompanied by a coadjutor, a young man strongly recommended by the Archbishop of Braga, a Jesuit, and the professed enemy of the Franciscans, who had obtained the appointment of his protegé by his influence with the minister.

During the voyage, the rank and character of the Missionary procured him the particular attentions of the Viceroy; but the man of God was not to be tempted to mingle with the profane crowd which surrounded the man of the world. Devoted to a higher communion, his soul only stooped from heaven to earth, to relieve the sufferings he pitied, or to correct the errors he condemned; to substitute peace for animosity; to restrain the blasphemies of the profane; to dispel the darkness of the ignorant; to support the sick; to solace the wretched; to strengthen the weak, and to encourage the timid; to watch, to pray, to fast, and to suffer for all. Such was the occupation of a life, active as it was sinless.

Such was the tenour of a conduct, which raised him, in the estimation of those who witnessed its excellence, to the character of a saint; but endeared him still more to their hearts, as a man who mingled sympathy with relief, and who added to the awful sentiment of veneration he inspired, the tender feeling of gratitude his mild benevolence was calculated to awaken.

Yet, over this bright display of virtues, scarcely human, one trait of conduct, something less than saintly, threw a transient shadow. He had disgraced the coadjutor from his appointment, for an irregularity of conduct almost venial from the circumstances connected with it. With him, virtue was not a relative, but an abstract quality, referable only to love of Deity, and independent of human temptation and mortal events; he, therefore, publicly rebuked the coadjutor as a person unworthy to belong to the congregation of the mission. He said, "Let us be merciful to all but to ourselves; it is not by our preaching alone we can promote the sacred cause in which we have embarked—it is also by our example." Even the mediation of the Viceroy was urged in vain. Firm of purpose, rigid, inflexible, he acted only from conviction, the purest and the strongest; but once resolved, his decree was immutable as the law of the God he served. His severe justice added to the veneration he inspired; but as he wept while he condemned, it detracted nothing from the general sentiment of affection he excited.

The voyage had been far from prosperous. The fleet had suffered much from repeated storms; and danger the most imminent, accompanied by all those awful appearances, with which conflicting elements strike terror into the boldest heart, had betrayed in the sufferers exposed to their rage, all the symptoms of human weakness, reduced to a feeling sense of its own insignificance, by impending destruction, under the most terrific and awful forms of divine power. The Missionary, alone, seemed uninfluenced by the threatened approach of that dreadful and untimely death, to which he stood exposed, in common with others. Calm and firm, his counsel and exertions alike displayed the soul incapable of fear; to whom life was indifferent, and for whom death had no terrors while his frame, as if partaking the immortality of his soul, resisted the influence of fatigue, and the vicissitudes of the elements. He met, unappalled, the midnight storm; he beheld, unmoved, the tumultuous billows, which rushed loudly on, pouring destruction in their course, and bore, with uncomplaining firmness, the chilling cold of Cape Verd, the burning heats of Guinea, and the pestilential vapours of the line.[13]

It was on the first day of the sixth month of the voyage, that the fleet sailed up the Indian seas, and, through the clear bright atmosphere, the shores and mighty regions of the East presented themselves to the view, while the imagination of the Missionary, escaping beyond the limits of human vision, stretched over those various and wondrous tracts, so diversified by clime and soil, by government and by religion, and which present to the contemplation of philosophy a boundless variety in form and spirit. Towards the west, it rested on the Arochosian mountains, which divide the territories of Persia from those of India—primæval mountains! whose wondrous formation preceded that of all organic matter, coequal with the globe which bears them! and which still embosom, in their stupendous shades, a nest of warlike states, rude as the aspects of their native regions, and wild as the storms that visit them; the descendants of those warrior hordes, which once spread desolation over the eastern hemisphere, till the powerful genius of an individual triumphed over the combined forces of nations, and the Affgans found, that the natural bulwark of their mountains was alone a sufficient barrier against the victorious arms of Tamerlane.[14]

From the recollection of the character and prowess of the Tartar hero, the mind of the Missionary turned towards the shores, which were rather imagined than perceived in so great an interval of distance; and the Impostor of Mecca occurred to his recollection, with the scenes of his nativity and success.[15] Bold in error, dauntless in imposition, enslaving the moral freedom while he subverted the natural liberty of mankind, and spreading, by the force of his single and singular genius, the wild doctrines he had invented, over the greatest empires of the earth, from the shores of the Atlantic to the walls of China; his success appeared even more wondrous, and his genius more powerful, than that of the Tartar conqueror. The soul of the Missionary swelled in the contemplation of scenes so calculated to elevate the ideas, to inflame the imagination, and to recall the memory to those æras in time, to those events in human history, which stimulate, by their example, the powers of latent genius, rouse the dormant passions into action, and excite man to sow the seeds of great and distant events, to found empires, or to destroy them.

His spirit, awakening to a new impulse, partook, for a moment, the sublimity of the objects he contemplated, the force of the characters he reflected on, and, expanding with its elevation, mingled with the universe. He remembered, that he, too, might have been an hero; he, too, might have founded states, and given birth to doctrines; for what had Timur boasted, or Mahomet possessed, that nature had denied to him? A frame of Herculean mould; a soul of fire; a mind of infinite resource; energy to impel; genius to execute; an arm to strike; a tongue to persuade; and a vital activity of spirit to give impulse and motion to the whole:—such were the endowments, which, coming from God himself, give to man so dangerous an ascendant over his species; and such were his. For the first time, his energy of feeling, his enthusiasm of fancy, received a new object for its exercise. He pursued, with an eagle glance, the sun's majestic course: "To-day," he said, "it rose upon the Pagoda of Brahma; it hastens to gild, with equal rays, the temple once dedicated to its own divinity, in the deserts of Palmyra; to illumine the Caaba of Mecca; and to shine upon the tabernacle of Jerusalem!"[16] He started at the climax. The empires of the earth, and the genius of man, suddenly faded from his mind; he thought of Him, in whose eye empire was a speck, and man an atom; he stood self-accused, humbled, awed; and invoked the protection of Him, who reigns only in perfect love in that heart, where worldly ambition has ceased to linger, and from whence human passions have long been exterminated.

The vessel in which he had embarked, was among the last to reach the port of Goa; and the reputation of his sanctity, and the history of his rank, his genius, and his mission, had preceded his arrival. The places under the civil and ecclesiastical government of Goa, were filled by Spaniards, but the Portuguese constituted the mass of the people.* They groaned under the tyranny of the Spanish Jesuits, and they heard, with a rapture which their policy should have taught them to conceal, that an apostolic nuncio, of the royal line of Portugal, and of the order of St. Francis, was come to visit their settlements, to correct the abuses of the church, and to pursue the task of conversion, by means more consonant to the evangelical principles of a mild and pure religion. An enthusiast multi-

---

* The misfortune of Portugal being united to the kingdom of Spain after the death of Cardinal Henry, uncle to the King Sebastian, gave a terrible blow to the Portuguese power in the Indies.—GUYON, Histoire des Indes Orientales.[17]

tude rushed to the shore, to hail his arrival: the splendid train of the Viceroy was scarcely observed; and the man of God, who disclaimed the pomp of all worldly glory, exclusively received it. He moved slowly on, in all the majesty of religious meekness: awful in his humility—commanding in his subjection; his finely formed head, unshaded, even by his cowl; his naked feet unshrinking from the sharpness of the stony pavement; the peace of Heaven stamped on his countenance; and the cross he had taken up, pressed to his bosom. All that could touch in the saint, or impose in the man, breathed around him: the sublimity of religion, and the splendour of beauty, the purity of faith, and the dignity of manhood; grace and majesty, holiness and simplicity, diffusing their combined influence over his form and motions, his look and air.

He passed before the residence of the Grand Inquisitor, who stood, surrounded by his ecclesiastical court, at a balcony, and witnessed this singular procession. At the moment when the Missionary reached the portals of a Carmelite monastery, where he was to take up his residence, the monks approached to receive him; the multitude called for his benediction: ere he retired from its view he bestowed it; and never had the sacred ceremony been performed with a zeal so touching, with an enthusiasm so devout, with a look, an attitude, an air so pure, so tender, so holy, and so inspired. The portals closed upon the saint; and those who had touched the hem of his garment, believed themselves peculiarly favoured by Heaven.

The next day he received an audience from the Bishop and Grand Inquisitor of Goa; marked by a distinction due to his rank; but characterized by a coldness, and by some invidious observations, little consonant to the enthusiasm of his own character, and unbefitting an enterprise so laudable and magnanimous as that in which he had engaged.—The Missionary, disgusted with all he saw and all he heard, with the luxury and pomp of the ecclesiastical court, and with the chilling haughtiness and illiberal sentiments of those who presided over it, and who openly condemned the tenets of the order to which he belonged;* quickly resolved on an immediate departure from Goa. A few days, however, were requisite to arrange the circumstances necessary for the promotion of his mis-

---

* The power of that formidable ecclesiastic, the Inquisitor General, is very terrible; and extends to persons of all ranks—the Viceroy, Archbishop, and his vicar, excepted.—See HAMILTON's New Account of the East Indies.[18]

sion. His vow of poverty related only to himself; but his mission required worldly means, as well as divine inspiration, to effect its beneficent purpose; and the charity which became a duty towards persons of his own order in Christendom, must, in a country where his religion was not known, depend upon the casualty of natural feeling: something, therefore, which belonged to earth, entered into an enterprise which referred ultimately to heaven; and the saint was obliged to provide for the contingencies of the prelate and the man.

The route which he laid out for his mission, was from Tatta to Lahore, by the course of the Indus, and from Lahore to the province of Cashmire.[19] To fix upon this remote and little known province, as the peculiar object of his mission, was an idea belonging to that higher order of genius, which grasps, by a single view, what mediocrity contemplates in detail, or considers impracticable in accomplishment. To penetrate into those regions, which the spirit of invasion, or the enterprise of commerce, had never yet reached; to pass that boundary, which the hallowed footstep of Christianity had never yet consecrated; to preach the doctrine of a self-denying faith, in the land of perpetual enjoyment; and, amidst the luxurious shades, which the Indian fancy contemplates as the model of its own heavenly Indra, to attack, in the birthplace of Brahma, the vital soul of a religion, supposed to have existed by its enthusiast votary beyond all æra of human record, beyond all reach of human tradition, which had so long survived the vicissitudes of time, the shock of conquest, and the persecution of intolerance: this was a view of a bold and an enthusiastic mind, confident in the powers of a genius which would rise with the occasion, and superior to all earthly obstacles, which might oppose its efforts; of a mind, to be incited, rather than to be repelled, by difficulties; to be animated, rather than subdued, by danger.

The person, the character, the life, the eloquence of the Missionary, were all calculated to awaken a popular feeling in his favour; and, during the few weeks he remained at Goa, the confessional from which he absolved, and the pulpit from whence he preached, became the shrines of popular devotion.

His eloquence was irresistible: it was the language of fearless genius, of enthusiastic zeal; vehement and impassioned, it ever aspired at the pathetic, or reached the sublime; and if it were, sometimes, more dazzling than judicious, more affecting than correct, still it persuaded when it failed to convince, still it was distinguished by those touches of tenderness, by those visions of enthusiasm, which blend and assimilate, so intimately, with human feeling, which ever address themselves, with such invariable success, to human passion!

The departure of the Nuncio from Goa was attended by circumstances which accorded not with the character of the apostle of Him, who, in approaching the spot whence he was to announce his divine mission to the rulers of the people, "came riding on an ass;"[20] for the departure of the Missionary was triumphant and splendid. The most illustrious of the Portuguese families in Goa attended in his train, and the homage of the multitude pursued him to the shore, whence he was to embark for Tatta. He moved meekly on in the midst of the crowd; but through the profound humility of his countenance shone such magnanimity of soul, such perfect consciousness of a genius and a zeal equal to the sacred enterprise in which he had embarked, that the most favourable presages were formed of the success of a man, who seemed to blend, in his character, the piety of the saint with the energy of the hero. He embarked:—the anchor was raised; a favourable breeze swelled the sails. The Missionary stood on the deck, dignified, but not unmoved: the triumph of religion, softened by its meekness, sat on his brow! The happy auspices under which he had left the centre of his mission, promised him a return still more triumphant: his soul swelled with emotions, which diffused themselves over his countenance; and as the vessel receded from the shore, his ear still caught the murmured homage offered to his unrivalled excellence. The humility of the monk rejected the unmerited tribute; but the heart of the man throbbed with an ardour, not all saintly, as he received it; and the pious visionary, who attempted, by an abstraction of mind, to love God, without enjoying the pleasure which accompanies that love, now, with a natural feeling, superior to the influence of a stoical zeal, unconsciously rejoiced, even in the suffrages of man.

CHAPTER III.

On the evening of the day in which the apostolic Nuncio arrived at Tatta, he embarked on the Indus, in a bungalow of twelve oars, for Lahore.[21] He beheld, not without emotion, the second mightiest stream of the East; sacred in the religious traditions of the regions through which it flows, and memorable from its connexion with the most striking events in the history of the world;

whose course became a guide to the spirit of fearless enterprise, and first opened to the conqueror of Asia a glimpse of those climes which have since been so intimately connected with the interests of Europe, which have so materially contributed to the wealth and luxury of modern states, and so obviously influenced the manners and habits of western nations. The scenery of the shores of the Indus changed its character with each succeeding day; its devious waters bathed, in their progress, the trackless deserts of Sivii, whose burning winds are never refreshed by the dews of happier regions; or fertilized the mango-groves of the Moultan; or poured through the wild unprofitable jungle, glittering amidst its long and verdant tresses, which so often shelter the wary tiger, or give asylum to the wild boar, when pursued to its entangled grass by the spear of the Indian huntsman. Sometimes its expansive bosom reflected images of rural beauty, or warlike splendour; and Hindu villages, surrounded by luxuriant sugar-canes and rice-grounds, rich in plenteous harvest, and diversified by all the brilliant hues of a florid vegetation, were frequently succeeded by the lofty towers of a Mogul fortress, or the mouldering ramparts of a Rajah castle; by the minarets of a mosque, peering amidst the shades of the mourning cypress; or the cupolas of a pagoda, shining through the luxurious foliage of the maringo, or plantain-tree; while the porpoise, tossing on the surface of the stream, basked in the setting sunbeam; or the hideous gurreal, voracious after prey, chased the affrighted fisherman, who, urging his canoe before the terrific monster, gave to a scene, wrapt in the solemn stillness of evening, an awful animation. Sometimes, when the innoxious shores awakened confidence, groups of simple Indians were seen, in the cool of those delicious evenings which succeed to burning days, offering their devotions on the banks of the stream, or plunging eagerly into its wave; the refreshing pleasure derived from the act, communicating itself to the soul and the frame, and both, in the belief of the enthusiast votarist, becoming purified by the immersion.

As the vessel glided down that branch of the Indus called the Ravii, every object, to the imagination of the Missionary, became consecrated to the memory of the enterprise of Alexander; and, while the same scenes, the same forms, habits, dress, and manners, met his view, as had two thousand years before struck the minds of the Macedonians with amazement, his historic knowledge enabled him to trace, with accuracy, and his reflecting mind, with interest, those particular spots, where Alexander fought, where Alexander conquered![22]

Arrived at Lahore, he entered one of the most magnificent cities of the East, at a period when the unfortunate and royal Dara had sought it as an asylum, while he waited for the forces, led by his heroic son, Solyman, previously to the renewal of their exertions for the recovery of an empire, wrested from them by the successful genius of Aurengzebe.[*]

Lahore, at that period, formed the boundary of Christian enterprise in India; and the Jesuits had not only founded a convent there, but were permitted, by the tolerant Gentiles,[24] publicly to perform their sacred functions, and to enjoy, with unrestrained freedom, the exercises of their religion.[†] The Missionary was received by the order, with the respect due to his sacred diploma and royal briefs; but neither his principles, nor the rigid discipline of his life, would permit him to reside with men, whose relaxed manners, and disorderly conduct, flung an odium on the purity of the religion, to which they were supposed to have devoted themselves. It was his ambition to make for himself a distinct and distinguished character; and, like the missionaries of old, or those pious sancassees so highly venerated in India,[26] he pitched his tent on the skirts of a neighbouring forest, and interested the attentions of the Indians, by the purity of a life, which shocked neither their ancient usages nor popular opinions; and which, from its self-denial and abstemious virtue, harmonized with their best and highest ideas of human excellence.[‡]

At Lahore he was determined to remain until he had made himself master of the dialects of Upper India, where the pure Hindu was deemed primeval; and his previous knowledge of the

---

[*] Dara having advanced beyond the river Bea, took possession of Lahore; giving his army time to breathe; in that city, he employed himself in levying troops and in collecting the imperial revenue.—DOW's *History of Hindostan*, vol. iii. p. 274.[23]

[†] "Autre fois les Jésuites avaient un établissement dans cette ville, et remplissaient leurs fonctions sacrés, et offraient aux yeux des Mahométans et des Gentiles, la pomp de leurs fêtes."—BERNIER.[25]

[‡] Monsieur de Thevenot speaks of a convent of religious Hindus, at Lahore: they have a general, provincial, and other superiors; they make vows of obedience, chastity, and poverty; they live on alms, and have lay brothers to beg for them; they eat but once a day; the chief tenet of their order is, to avoid doing to others, what they would not themselves wish to endure; they suffer injuries with patience, and do not return a blow; and they are forbidden even to *look* on women.

Hebrew and Arabic tongues, soon enabled him to conquer the difficulties of the task to which he devoted himself, with an ardour, proportioned to the enthusiasm of his genius and the zeal of his enterprise. He had placed himself under the tuition of a learned Pundit,[27] who was devoted to secular business, and had travelled into various countries of the East, as a secretary and interpreter. A follower of the Musnavi sect, or "worship of the Invisible," the religion of the philosophers of Hindostan, he yet gave his public sanction to doctrines which he secretly despised. To him, the wildest fictions and most rational tenets of the Brahminical theology appeared equally puerile; but the apprehension of "loss of cast" (an excommunication which involves every worldly evil) restrained the avowal of his sentiments, and secured his attention to forms and ceremonies, which were the objects of his secret derision. A Cashmirian by birth, he was endowed with all the acuteness of mind which peculiarly distinguishes his country; and equally indifferent to all religions, he was yet anxious to forward the Christian's views, whose doctrines he estimated, by the character of him who preached them.

Although Cashmire was the principal object of Hilarion's mission, his zeal, no longer impeded by his ignorance of the language of those whom he was to address, already broke forth, accompanied by that brilliant enthusiasm, by that powerful eloquence, whose influence is invariable on popular feelings: he resorted to places of public meetings, to consecrated tanks, and to the courts of a pagoda. The tolerance of the followers of Brahma evinced itself, in the indulgence with which the innovating tenets of the Christian were received. They molested not a man, who thus daringly appeared among them, openly to dispute the doctrines of a faith, interwoven with the very existence of its professors: but a few of the lower casts only assembled around him, and even they listened to him with less conviction than curiosity,* and indolently rejected what they took not the trouble to examine or to dispute.

---

* A Hindu considers all the distinctions and privileges of his cast, as belonging to him by an incommunicable right; and to convert, or be converted, are ideas equally repugnant to the principles, most deeply rooted in his mind; nor can either the Catholic or Protestant Missionaries in India, boast of having overcome those prejudices, except among a few of the lower casts, or of such as have lost their casts altogether.— Voyages aux Indes par M. SONNERAT, tom. i. p. 58.

It was in vain, that the apostolic Nuncio sought an opportunity to converse with the learned and distinguished Brahmins of the province: his Pundit, whose confirmed deism set all hope of conversion at defiance, assured his pupil, that the highest class of that sacred order, who always adopt the sacerdotal stole, were seldom to be seen by Europeans, or by persons of any nation but their own. Acting as high-priests, devoted to religious discipline, in private families of distinction, or shut up in their colleges, when not engaged in the offices of their religion, they gave themselves up, exclusively, to the cultivation of literature, and to the study of logic and metaphysics, so prevalent in their schools, resembling, in the simplicity and virtue of their lives, the ascetics of the middle ages; except when they became elevated to some high dignity in their ancient and sacred hierarchy, and were then called upon, during certain seasons, to appear in the world, with all the imposing splendour and religious pomp, which peculiarly belongs to their distinguished rank and venerated profession.

While he spoke, the Pundit drew from his breast a gazette of the court of Delhi;* and read, from what might be deemed a literary curiosity, the following paragraph: "The holy and celebrated Brahmin, Rah-Singh, the incarnation of Brahma upon earth, and the light of all knowledge, has been lately engaged in performing the Upaseyda† through the provinces of Agra and Delhi, from whence he returns by Lahore to Cashmire, the resemblance of paradise, by the attraction of the favour of Heaven. The Guru is accompanied by the daughter of his daughter, who has adopted the sacerdotal stole, and has become a Brachmachira. The reputation of her holiness has spread itself over the earth, and her prophecies are rays of light from Heaven."

The Pundit, then putting aside the gazette, said, "This Guru, or bishop, who holds an high jurisdiction over all which relates to his cast, has long survived those powers of intellect, from which his brilliant reputation arose; and his influence must have wholly declined, had it not been supported by the merited celebrity of his grand-daughter: he has brought her up in the Vedanti sect, which he himself professes, the religion of mystic love: a creed finely

---

* Gazettes de la cour de Delhi, des nouvelles publiques qui marquent, jour par jour, et non dans ce stile ampoullé qu'on reproche aux Orientaux, ce qui se passe d'importante à la cour et dans les provinces—ces sont des gazettes répandues dans toute l'empire.—ANQUETIL DU PERRON, p. 47.[28]

† A ceremony similar to that of confirmation in the Catholic church.

adapted to the warm imagination, the tender feelings, and pure principles of an Indian woman; and which, sublime and abstracted, harmonizes with every idea of human loveliness and human grace."

"And what," demanded the Missionary, "are its leading tenets?"

"That matter has no essence, independent of mental perception; and that external sensation would vanish into nothing, if the divine energy for a moment subsided: that the soul differs in degree, but not in kind, from the creative spirit of which it is a particle, and into which it will be finally absorbed: that nothing has a pure and absolute existence, but spirit: and that a passionate and exclusive love of Heaven is that feeling only, which offers no illusion to the soul, and secures its eternal felicity."

"This doctrine, so pure, and so sublime," replied the Missionary, "wants but the holy impress of revelation, to stamp it as divine."

The Pundit answered: "The religion of Brahma, under all its various sects and forms, is peculiarly distinguished by sublimity, and even the utmost extravagance of its apparent polytheism is resolvable into the unity of deity; while the mythological fables it offers to the credence of the multitude are splendid and poetical, like the forms and ceremonies of its religious duties. Of those you will be able to judge to-morrow, as the Guru of Cashmire enters Lahore, to perform the ceremony of the Upaseyda, in the Pagoda of Crishna; where, after having distributed the holy waters, he will hear the learned men of the province dispute on theological subjects. As this is considered the grand field for acquiring distinguished reputation among the Brahmins and literati of India, it is at this period, that you may seize on an opportunity of advancing your doctrines, as, by throwing off your European habit, and undergoing purification in the consecrated tanks of the temple, you become qualified to enter its vestibule."

To the proposal, the Missionary made no reply. He seemed lost in profound thought, but it was thought animated by some new and powerful excitement. His eye flashed fire, his countenance brightened, his whole frame betrayed the agitations of a mind roused to extraordinary exertion; the ambition of genius, and the enthusiasm of religious zeal, mingled in his look. The Pundit secretly observed the effects of his proposal, and withdrew. The Missionary, during the rest of the night, gave himself up to meditation and to prayer. Visions of a victorious zeal poured on his mind, and pious supplications offered to Heaven, for their accomplishment, breathed on his lips.

CHAPTER IV.

The day on which the Guru of Cashmire made his entrance into Lahore, was a day of public festivity and joyous agitation to its inhabitants. The higher casts, the Brahmins and Chitterries,[29] went out by the gate of Agra to meet him, some mounted on camels splendidly caparisoned; others reposing in palanquins, luxuriously adorned. At sunrise, the sacred procession appeared descending an eminence towards the town. The religious attendants of the Guru, mounted on Arabian horses, led the van; followed by the Ramganny, or dancing priestesses of the temple, who sung, as they proceeded, the histories of their gods, while incarnate upon earth. Their movements were slow, languid, and graceful; and their hymns, accompanied by the tamboora, the seringa, and other instruments, whose deep, soft, and solemn tones, seem consecrated to the purposes of a tender and fanciful religion, excited in the soul of their auditors, emotions which belonged not all to Heaven.

This group, which resembled, in form and movement, the personification of the first hours of Love and Youth, was succeeded by the Guru, mounted on an elephant, which moved with a majestic pace; his howdah, of pure gold, sparkling to the radiance of the rising day. Disciples of the Brahmin surrounded his elephant, and were immediately followed by a palanquin, which from its simplicity formed a striking contrast to the splendid objects that had preceded it. Its drapery, composed of the snowy muslin of the country, shone like the fleecy vapour on which the sun's first light reposes: its delicate shafts were entwined with the caressing fibres of the camalata, the flower of the Indian heaven, dedicated to Camdeo, the god of "mystic love,"[30] whose crimson blossoms breathed of odours which soothed, rather than intoxicated, the senses.

The acclamations which had rent the air on the appearance of the Guru, died softly away as the palanquin approached. An awe more profound, a feeling more pure, more sublimated, seemed to take possession of the multitude; for, indistinctly seen through the transparent veil of the palanquin, appeared the most sacred of vestals, the Prophetess and Brachmachira of Cashmire. Her perfect form, thus shrouded, caught, from the circumstance, a mysterious charm, and seemed, like one of the splendid illusions, with which the enthusiasm of religion brightens the holy dream of its votarist, like the spirit which descends amidst the shadows of night upon the slumbers of the blessed. Considered as the offspring of Brahma, as a ray of the divine excellence, the Indians of the most distinguished rank drew back as she approached, lest their very breath should pollute that region of purity her respiration consecrated; and the odour of the sacred flowers, by which she was adorned, was inhaled with an eager devotion, as if it purified the soul it almost seemed to penetrate. The venerated palanquin was guarded by a number of pilgrim women, and the chief casts of the inhabitants of Lahore; while a band of the native troops closed the procession, which proceeded to the Pagoda of Crishna.

From the contemplation of a spectacle so new, so unexpected, the Missionary retired within his solitary tent, with that feeling of horror and disgust, which a profanation of the sentiment and purposes of religion might be supposed to excite, in a mind so pure, so zealous, so far above all the pomp and passions of life, and hitherto so ignorant of all the images connected with their representation. The music, the perfumes, the women, the luxury, and the splendour of the extraordinary procession, offended his piety, and almost disordered his imagination. He thought, for a moment, of the perils of an enterprise, undertaken in a country where the very air was unfavourable to virtue, and where all breathed a character of enjoyment, even over the awful sanctity of religion; a species of enjoyment, to whose very existence he had been, hitherto, almost a stranger; but the genius of his zeal warmed in proportion to the obstacles he found he had to encounter, and he waited impatiently for the arrival of the Pundit, who was to lead him to the vestibule of the pagoda.

They proceeded, before mid-day, to the temple, which was approached through several avenues of lofty trees. On every side marble basins, filled with consecrated water, reflected from their brilliant surfaces, the domes and galleries of the pagoda. On every side the golden flowers of the assoca, the tree of religious rites, shed their rich and intoxicating odours.

In submission to those prejudices, which he could only hope finally to vanquish by previously respecting, he suffered himself to be led to a consecrated tank, and, having bathed, he assumed the Indian jama.[31] As he passed the portals of the pagoda, he was struck by the grotesque figure of an idol, before whose shrine a crowd of deluded votarists lay prostrate: he turned away his eyes in horror, kissed the crucifix which was concealed within the folds of his dress, and proceeded to the vestibule of the temple. The ceremony of the day was concluded; the priestesses had performed their religious dances before Crishna, the Indian Apollo, and idol of the temple; the usual offerings of fruit and flowers, of gold and precious odours, had been made at his shrine; and the learned of the various sects of the Brahminical faith had assembled, at an awful distance round the Guru, to hold their religious disputation and controversial arguments.

In the centre of the vestibule, and on an elevated cushion, reposed the venerable form of the Brahmin. His beard of snow fell beneath his girdle; an air, still, calm, and motionless, diffused itself over his aged figure; a mild and holy abstraction involved his tranquil countenance; no trace of human passions furrowed his expansive brow; all was the repose of nature, the absence of mortality; and he presented to the fancy and the mind, a fine and noble image that venerated God, an incarnation of whose excellence he believed himself to be. A railing of gold and ebony marked the hallowed boundary, which none were permitted to pass, save the Prophetess of Cashmire. *She* sat near him, veiled only by that religious mystery of air and look, which involved her person, as though a cloud of evening mists threw its soft shadows round her. Forbidden the use of ornaments, by her profession, except that of consecrated flowers, the scarlet berries of the sweet sumbal, the flower of the Ganges, alone enwreathed her brow; a string of mogrees, whose odour exceeded the ottar of the rose, encircled her neck, with the dsandam, or three Brahminical threads, the distinguishing insignia of her distinguished cast.* Her downcast eyes were fixed upon the muntras, the Indian rosary, which were twined round her wrist; and o'er whose beads she softly murmured the Gayatras, or text of the Shaster.[32] And when, with a slight motion of the head, she threw back the dark shining tresses which shaded her brow, in the centre of her forehead appeared the small consecrated mark of the tallertum.[33] So finely was her form and attitude contrasted by the venerable figure of her aged grandsire, that the spring of eternal youth seemed to diffuse its immortal bloom and freshness round her, and she looked like the tutelar intelligence of the Hindu mythology, newly descended on earth, from the radiant sphere assigned to her in the Indian zodiac.

At a little distance from the railing, stood the pilgrim-women who attended on the chief Priestess, fanning the air with peacock's feathers, and diffusing around an atmosphere of roses, from the

---

* From the time that they assume the dsandam, they are called the Brahmasaris, or children of Brahma.

musky tresses and fragrant flowers of the Brachmachira. On either side of the vestibule stood groups of the various sects of Brahma and of Bhudda, while pilgrims and faquirs, with the chief casts of Lahore, filled the bottom of the vast and mighty hall.[34]

The religious disputants spoke in orderly succession, without appearing to feel or to excite enthusiasm, contented to detail their own doctrines, rather than anxious to controvert the doctrines of others. A devotee of the Musnavi sect took the lead; he praised the mysteries of the Bhagavat, and explained the profound allegory of the six Ragas,[*] who, wedded to immortal nymphs, and fathers of lovely genii, presided in the Brahminical mythology over the seasons. A disciple of the Vedanti school spoke of the transports of mystic love, and maintained the existence of spirit only; while a follower of Bhudda supported the doctrine of matter, as the only system void of all illusion. One spoke of the fifth element, or subtle spirit, which causes universal attraction, so that the most minute particle is impelled to some particular object; and another, of the great soul which attended the birth of all embodied creatures, connecting it with the divine essence which pervades the universe; while all, involved in mysteries beyond the comprehension of human reason, or lost in the intricacies of metaphysical theories, betrayed, in their respective doctrines, the wreck of that abstract learning, which, too little connected with the true happiness of society, was anciently borrowed, even by the Greeks themselves, from the sages of India, and by the partial revival of which, even the philosophers of modern Europe once made a false, but distinguished reputation.

It was during a pause which followed the declaration of the last-mentioned tenets, that the apostolic Nuncio suddenly appeared in the midst of the vestibule. His lofty and towering figure, the kindling lustre of his countenance, the high command which sat upon his brow, the bright enthusiasm which beamed within his eye, and the dignified and religious meekness which distinguished his air and attitude, all formed a fine and striking contrast to the slight diminutive forms, the sallow hues, and timid sadness, of the Indians who surrounded him. Clad in a white robe, his fine-formed head and feet uncovered, he looked like the spirit of Truth descended from heaven, to spread on earth its pure and radiant

---

[*] The "Raga Mala," or Necklace of Melody, contains a highly poetical description of the Ragas and their attendant nymphs.

light. The impression of his appearance was decisive: it sank at once to the soul; and he imposed conviction on the senses, ere he made his claim on the understanding. He spoke, and the multitude pressed near him—he spoke of the religion of Brahma, of the Avaratas, or incarnations of its founder,[35] and of those symbolic images of the divine attributes, beneath whose mysterious veil a pure system of natural religion was visible, which, though inevitably dark, uncertain, and obscure, was not unworthy to receive upon its gloom the light of a divine revelation: then, raising his hands and eyes to heaven, and touching the earth with his bended knee, he invoked the protection of the God of Christians, even in the temple of Brahma, and, surrounded by idols and by idolaters, boldly unfolded the object of his mission, and preached that word, whose divinity he was ready to attest with his blood.

His eloquence resembled, in its progress, those great elementary conflicts, whose sounds of awe come rolling grandly, deeply on, breathing the mandate of Omnipotence, and evincing its force and power; till touched, rapt, inspired by his theme, the tears of holy zeal which filled his eyes, the glow of warm enthusiasm which illuminated his countenance, the strong, but pure emotions, which shook his frame, kindled around him a correspondent ardour. Some *believed*, who sought not to *comprehend*; others were persuaded, who could not be convinced; and many admired, who had not been influenced; while all sought to conceal the effects his eloquence and his doctrine produced: for their hearts and their imaginations were still the victims of that dreadful fear, which *loss of cast* inspired; and the truths, so bright and new, now offered to their reason, were not sufficient in their effects to vanquish prejudices so dark and old, as those by which the Indian mind was held in thraldom. He ceased to speak, and all was still as death. His hands were folded on his bosom, to which his crucifix was pressed; his eyes were cast in meekness on the earth; but the fire of his zeal still played, like a ray from heaven, on his brow.

The Guru of Cashmire, who had listened to the wild mysteries of the Indian sophists, and the pure truths of the Christian Missionary, with equal composure, and, perhaps, with equal indifference, now arose to speak, and a new impulse was given to the attention of the multitude. Prejudice and habit resumed their influence, and all hung with veneration on the incoherent words pronounced by the tremulous and aged voice of a Brahmin, to whom his votarists almost paid divine honours, and who, with a motionless air and look, exclaimed: "I set my heart on the foot of Brahma, gaining knowledge only of him: it is by devotion alone, that we are enabled to see the three worlds, celestial, terrestrial, and ethereal; let us, then, meditate eternally within our minds, and remember, that the natural duties of the children of Brahma are peace, self-restraint, patience, rectitude, and wisdom. Praise be unto Vishnu!"

He ceased:—the dome of the temple was rent with acclamations: the oracle of the north of India, his words were deemed rays of light. The rhapsody, which made no claim on the understanding, accorded with the indolence of the Indian mind:—the eloquence of the Missionary was no longer remembered; and the disciples of the Guru hastened to conduct him to the college prepared for his reception. The procession resumed its order. Incense was flung upon the air; the choral hymn was raised by the priestesses, and the imposing splendour of the most powerful of all human superstitions, resumed its influence over minds which sought not to resist its magic force.

The apostolic Nuncio remained alone in the temple. He inhaled the fragrance of the atmosphere, he caught the languid strains of the religious women, and he beheld the splendid processions winding through the arches of the temple, and disappearing among the trees which screened its approach. At his feet lay some flowers, which fell from the palanquin of the Prophetess, as she passed him. He stood, not confounded, but yet not unmoved. The rapid vicissitude of feeling, of emotion, which he had undergone, was so new to a mind so firm, to a soul so abstracted, that for a moment he felt as though his whole being had suffered a supernatural change. But this distraction was but momentary: the man of genius soon rallied those high unconquerable powers, which, for an instant, had bent to the impression of novel and extraordinary incidents, and had been diverted from their aspiring bias by circumstances of mere external influence. The man of God soon recovered that sacred calm, which a breast that reflected Heaven's own peace had, till now, never forfeited. He cast round his eyes, and beheld on every side disgustful images of the darkest idolatry: he shuddered, and hastened from the Pagoda. In one of its avenues he was met by the Pundit. The Cashmirian complimented him in all the hyperbole of Eastern phrase, on the power of his unrivalled eloquence, and the force of his unanswered arguments: he said, "that it rather resembled the inspiration of Heaven, than the ability of man;" and declared, "that he believed its influence, though

not general, was in some individual instances strong and decisive."
The Missionary turned his eyes on him with a religious solicitude
of look. "I allude," replied the Pundit, "to the Brachmachira, *the
Priestess of Cashmire*, whose conversion, if once effected, might
prove the redemption of her whole nation."

A deep blush crimsoned the face of the Missionary, and he
involuntarily drew his hand across his eyes, though unconscious
that any look beamed there which Heaven should not meet. "You
are silent," said the Pundit, "and, doubtless, deem the task impracticable; and I confess it to be nearly so. This may be the last pilgrimage the Priestess will undertake, and, consequently, the last
time she will ever publicly show herself; for, except when engaged
in the offices of their religion, as sacerdotal women, all the females
of her cast, in India, are guarded in the retirement of their zenanas,
with a vigilance unknown in other countries. Habituated to this
sacred privacy,[36] the fairest Hindus sigh not after a world, of which
they are wholly ignorant. Devoted to their husbands and their
gods, religion and love make up the business of their lives. Such
were they, when Alexander first invaded their country—such are
they now. Pure and tender, faithful and pious, zealous alike in their
fondness and their faith, they immolate themselves as martyrs to
both, and expire on the pile which consumes the objects of their
affection, to inherit the promise which religion holds out to their
hopes; for the heaven of an Indian woman is the eternal society of
him whom she loved on earth. In all the religions of the East,
woman has held a decided influence, either as priestess or as victim; but the women of India seem particularly adapted to the
offices and influence of their faith, and in the religion of Brahma
they take a considerable part. The Ramgannies, or officiating
priestesses, are of an inferior rank and class, in every respect, and
are much more distinguished for their zeal than for their purity;
but the Brachmachira is of an order the most austere and most
venerated, which can only be professed by a woman who is at once
a widow* and vestal: a seeming paradox, but illustrated by the history of Luxima, the Prophetess of Cashmire.

"Born in the most distinguished cast of India, she was
betrothed, in childhood, to a young Brahmin of superior rank; but,
from the morning she received the golden girdle of marriage, she

---

* See "Duties of a faithful Widow," translated from the Shanscrit, by H.
Colebrook, Esq.[37]

beheld him no more. He had devoted himself to the Tupaseya, or sacred pilgrimage, until the age of his bride should permit him to claim her. He went to the sacred Caves of Elora, he visited the Temple of Jaggarnauth, and died on his return to Cashmire, at Nurdwar, while engaged in performing penance near the source of the Ganges.[38]

"Tender, pious, and ambitious, Luxima would have ascended the funeral pile. The tears and infirmities of her grandsire prevailed. Childless but for her, she consented for his sake to live, and embraced the alternative held out to women in her situation of becoming a Brachmachira, being the only child of an only child. The riches of her opulent family, according to the laws of Menu,[39] centre in herself, and are expended in such acts of public and private beneficence as are calculated to increase the popular veneration, which her extraordinary zeal, and the austere purity of her life, have awakened. To make pilgrimages, frequently to repeat the worship of her sect, and to lead a life of vestal purity, are the peculiar duties of her order. To be endowed with the spirit of prophecy is its peculiar gift. Multitudes, from every part of India, come to consult her on future events; and her vague answers are looked upon as decisions, which, sometimes verified by chance, are seldom suffered by prepossession to be considered as false.

"There are a few of this order now existing in India, and Luxima is the most celebrated. But it is not to her zeal only she owes her unrivalled distinction: she is, by birth, a sacerdotal woman and a Cashmirian; the ascendency of her beauty, therefore, is sometimes mistaken for the influence of the zeal which belongs to her profession; and perhaps the Priestess too often receives an homage which the woman only excites.* She is a disciple of the Vedanti school: the delicate ardour of her imagination finds a happy vehicle in the doctrines of her pure but fervid faith; and the sublime but impassioned tenets of religious love flow with peculiar grace from lips which seem equally consecrated to human tenderness. Every thing adds to the mystic charm which breathes o'er her character and person. Abstracted in her brilliant error, absorbed in the splendid illusion of her religious dreams, believing herself the

---

* "Certainly," says De Bernier, "if one may judge of the beauty of the sacred women by that of the common people, met with in the streets, they must be very beautiful." P. 96. "The beauties of Cashmire, being born in a more northern climate, and in a purer air, retain their charms as long, at least, as any European women."—GROSE, p. 239.[40]

purest incarnation of the purest spirit, her elevated soul dwells not on the sensible images by which she is surrounded, but is wholly fixed upon the heaven of her own creation; and her beauty, her enthusiasm, her graces, and her genius, alike capacitate her to propagate and support the errors of which she herself is the victim.

"Such is the proselyte I propose to your zeal. Once converted, her example would operate like a spell on her compatriots, and the follower of Brahma would fly from the altar of his ancient gods, to worship in that temple in which she would become a votarist."

The Pundit paused, and the Nuncio was still silent. At last he asked, "if the Pundit had not observed, that an interview with an Indian woman of the Braminical cast was next to impossible?"

"It is nearly so with all Indian women of distinction," he replied; "but a Brachmachira, from being more sacred than other women, excites more confidence in her friends.* To approach her would be deemed sacrilege in any cast but her own; but her obligation to perform worship to the morning and evening sun, on the banks of consecrated rivers, exposes her to the view of those who are withheld by no prejudices, or restrained by no law, from approaching her."

They had now reached the Missionary's tent. The Pundit took his leave, and the Christian retired, to give himself up to the usual religious exercise of the evening.

CHAPTER V.

The institutes of a religion which form a regular system of superstitious rites, sanctioned by all that can secure the devotion of the multitude, are rigidly observed by the followers of Brahma; and among the many splendid festivals held in honour of their gods, there is none so picturesque, and none so imposing, as that instituted in honour of Durga, the goddess of nature, whose festival is ushered in by rural sounds and rural games. "It is thus," say the

---

* The women are so sacred in India, that even the common soldiery leave them unmolested in the midst of slaughter and desolation.—DOW, History of Hindoostan, vol. iii. p. 10.[41]

Puranas, or holy text, "she was awakened by Brahma, during the night of the gods."

The dawn had yet but faintly silvered the plantain-trees which thatched the Christian's hut, when the distant strains of sylvan music stole on his ear, as he knelt engaged in the exercise of his morning devotions. The sounds approached: he arose, and observed a religious procession moving near his tent towards a pagoda, which lay embosomed in the dark shades of the forest. The band was led by faquirs and pilgrims. The idol was carried by women, underneath a canopy of flowers. A troop of officiating priestesses danced before its triumphal car: the splendour of their ornaments almost concealed their charms, and they moved with languid grace, to the strains of pastoral instruments, while small golden bells, fastened round their wrists and ancles, played with the motion of their feet, and kept time to the melody of their hymns. They were succeeded by the Guru of Cashmire, reposing on a palanquin, and the Brahmins of the temple followed. The Prophet-ess led the band of tributary votaries; *her* eyes, with a celestial meekness, threw their soft and dewy beams on the offerings which she carried in a small golden vase; and her cheek seemed rather to reflect the tint of the scarlet berries of the mullaca, which twined her dark hair, than to glow with the blush of a human emotion. The folds of her pure drapery, soft and fleecy as it was, but faintly defined the perfect forms of her perfect figure, of which an exquis-ite modesty, a mysterious reserve, were the distinguishing charac-teristics. Her thought seemed to belong to Heaven, and her glance to the offering she was about to make at its shrine. A train of reli-gious women surrounded her, and the procession was filled up with votaries of every description, and of every class, from the princely Chittery to the humble Soodar, all laden with their vari-ous offerings of rice and oil, of fruit and flowers, of precious stones and exquisite odours.

As they proceeded, they reached an altar erected to *Camdeo, the god of mystic love.* At the sight of this object, every eye turned with devotion on his consecrated Priestess. The procession stopped. The sibyl Priestess stood at the foot of the shrine of her tutelar deity, and the superstitious multitude fell prostrate at the feet of the Prophetess. They invoked her intercession with the god she served: mothers held up their infants to her view; fathers inquired from her the fate of their absent sons; and many addressed her on the future events of their lives; while she, not more deceiving than deceived, became the victim of her own imposition, and stood in the midst of her votarists, in all the imposing charm of holy illusion. Her enthusiasm once kindled, her imagination became disordered: believing herself inspired, she looked the immortality she fancied, and uttered rhapsodies in accents so impressive and so tender, and with emotions so wild, and yet so touching, that the mind no longer struggled against the imposition of the senses, and the spirit of fanatical zeal confirmed the influence of human loveliness.

Hitherto, curiosity had induced the Missionary to follow the procession; but he now turned back, horror-struck. Too long had the apostle of Christianity been the witness of those impious rites, offered by the idolaters to the idolatress; and the indignation he felt at all he had seen, at all he had heard, produced an irritability of feeling, new to a mind so tranquil, and but little consonant to a character so regulated, so subdued, so far above even the laudable weakness of human nature. He considered the false Prophetess as the most fatal opponent to his intentions, and he looked to her conversion as the most effectual means to accomplish the success of his enterprise. He shuddered to reflect on the weakness and frailty of man, who is so often led to truth by the allurements which belong to error; and he devoted the remainder of the day to the consideration of those pious plans, by which he hoped, one day, to shade the brow of the Heathen Priestess with the sacred veil of the Christian Nun.

The complexional springs of passion in the character of the Missionary had been regulated and restrained by the habits of his temperate and solitary life; the natural impetuosity and ardour of his feelings had been tranquillized and subdued, by the principles of his pure and spiritual religion; and though his perceptions were quick and rapid in their exercise, yet he had so accustomed his mind to distrust its first impulse, that, all enthusiast as he was, he was yet less so from the vivacity of a first impression than from the mental operation which succeeded to it. The idea which was cooly admitted into his mind, gradually possessed itself of his imagination, and there gave birth to a series of impressions and emotions, which, in their combined force, finally mastered every thought and act of his life. Thus he became zealous in any pursuit, not because it had, in the first instance, struck him powerfully, nor that he had suffered himself to be borne away by its immediate impression, but because that, suspicious of himself, he had examined it, in all its points of view, considered it in all its references, and studied it in all its relations, till it exclusively occupied his reveries, received the glow of his powerful fancy, and engaged all the force of his intellectual being. It was thus that he frequently meditated himself into passion, and that the habits of his artificial character produced an effect on his conduct similar to that which the indulgence of his natural impulses would eventually have given birth to.

When the description of the Priestess of Cashmire first met his ear, it made no impression on his mind: when he beheld her receiving the homage of a deity, all lovely as she was, she awakened no other sentiment in his breast than a pious indignation, natural to his religious zeal, at beholding human reason so subdued by human imposition. When her story had been related to him, and her influence described, he then considered her as the powerful rival of his influence, and the most fatal obstacle to the success of the enterprise he had engaged in; but when the Pundit had awakened the hope of her conversion, and asserted the possibility of her influence becoming the instrument of divine grace to her nation, then the Indian gradually became the sole and incessant subject of his thoughts; and her idea was so mingled with his religious hopes, so blended with his sacred mission, so intimately connected with all his best, his brightest views and purest feelings, that, even in prayer, she crossed his imagination; and when he sued from Heaven a blessing on his enterprise, the name of the idolatress of Cashmire was included in the orison.

The Guru and his train had left Lahore, on the evening of the festival of the goddess Durga, for his native province; and, a few weeks after his departure, the Missionary commenced his pilgrimage towards Upper India. He was now equal to his undertaking; for he spoke the pure Hindu with the fluency of an educated native, and read the Shanscrit with ease and even with facility. He had made himself master of the topography of the country—the valley of Cashmire, its villages, its capital, its pagodas, and the temple and Brahminical college, in which the Guru presided; and already furnished with the means of providing for the few contingencies of his pilgrimage, the most necessary luxury of which is afforded by the numerous tanks and springs, whose construction is considered a religious duty, the apostolic Nuncio left Lahore, and commenced his journey to Cashmire.

The black robe of his order flung over his lighter Indian vestment, his brow shaded by the monastic cowl, his hand grasping the pastoral crosier, wearing on his breast the sacred crucifix, and nourished only by the fruits and nutritious grains, with which a bounteous nature supplied him. His, resembled the saintly progress of the Apostles of old; a fine image of that pure, tender, and self-denying faith, whose divine doctrines he best illustrated by the example of his own sinless life; but he observed, with an acute feeling of disappointment, that the harvest bore no proportion to the exertions of the labourer. In whatever direction he turned his steps, the zeal of Hindu devotion met his view, while every where the religion of the Hindus gave him the strongest idea of the wild extravagance which superstition is capable of producing, or the acute sufferings which religious fortitude is equal to sustain. Every where he found new reason to observe, how perfectly the human mind could bend its plastic powers to those restraints, which the law of society, the prejudices of country, or the institutes of religion, imposed. He felt, how arbitrary was the law of human opinion; how little resorted to were the principles of human nature; how difficult to eradicate those principles impressed on the character without any operation of the reason, received in the first era of existence, expanding with the years, and associating with all the feelings, the passions, and the habits of life. But these reflections, equally applicable to human character in the West and in the East, were now first made under the new impressions formed by the observation of novel prejudices in others, not stronger, perhaps, but different from his own; and he whose life had been governed by a dream, was struck by the imbecility of those who submitted their reason to the tyranny of a baseless illusion.

Amidst the tissue of prejudices, however, which disfigure the faith of the Hindus, he sometimes perceived the force of their mild and benevolent natures bearing away the barriers of artificial distinctions; and though it is deemed infamous, and hazards loss of cast, for a follower of Brahma to partake of the same meal with the professor of any other faith, yet the Missionary found in India the true region of hospitality; choulteries, or public asylums for travellers, frequently occurred in the course of his route; while the master of every simple hut was ready to spread the mat beneath the stranger's feet, and to weave the branches of his plantain-tree above the stranger's head; to present to the parched lip of the wanderer the milk of his cocoa-nut, and to his aching brow the shade of his humble roof. Happy are they who preserve, amidst the wreck of human reason, the dear and precious vestiges of human tenderness!

As the Missionary proceeded towards the north, he was still hailed with the pensive welcome of the Indian smile. Some few of the simple and patriarchal people, who had heard of Europe, knew him by his complexion for a native of the West; but the greater number believed him to be a wandering Arab, from the lofty dignity of his stature, from the brilliant expression of his countenance; and then would ask him to speak of the Genii of his religion, or to relate to them those splendid tales for which his nation is so celebrated: but when he sought to undeceive them, when he declared that he came, not to amuse by fiction, but to enlighten by truth; when he openly avowed to them the nature and object of his sacred mission, they fled him in fear, or heard him with incredulity.

It was in vain that he invoked from Heaven some part of that miraculous power granted to those who had preceded him; that he might be able, with Francis Xavier, to cure the sick by a touch, or raise the dead by a look.* He could, indeed, watch with the saint, pray with the saint, and suffer with the saint, perhaps even far beyond those who had succeeded him: he could overwhelm by his eloquence, command by his dignity, attach by his address, and awe by his example; but he could not subvert a single law of nature, nor, by any miraculous power, change the immutable decree of the First Will:—for, to him it was still denied to convert those from error, through the medium of astonishment, whom he could not subdue by the influence of truth.

In less than a fortnight from his departure from Lahore, he reached the upper region, those dreadful and desolate plains, which stretched towards the base of the great and black rock of Bimbhar. Alone in the dreary waste, the Missionary felt all the value of an enterprise, marked by perils so terrific; but he felt it unsubdued. The dry and hot air† parched his lip; his feet trod in the channel of a torrent, dried up, whose bed seemed strewed with burning lava; a fever preyed upon the springs of being, and a parching thirst consumed his vitals; death, in the most dreadful form, met his view, but found him unappalled; and the tide of life was almost exhausted in his veins, when, worn out and feeble, he reached the foot of the rock of the pass of Bimbhar, denominated *The Mouth of the Vale of Cashmire*. High, sharp, and rude, it held a menacing aspect. Weak

---

* "The process of the saint's canonization," says the biographer of Xavier, "makes mention of four dead persons, to whom God restored life at this time by the ministry of his servant."[42]

† "Cet excès de chaleur vient de la situation de ces hautes montagnes qui se trouvent au nord de la route, arrêtent les vents frais, réfléchissent les rayons du soleil sur les voyageurs, et laissent dans la campagne un ardeur brulante."—BERNIER.[43]

and enfeebled, the Missionary with difficulty ascended its savage acclivities. Nature seemed almost to have made her last effort when he reached its summit; his strength was wholly exhausted. Supported by his crosier, he paused, and cast one look behind him. He beheld the terrific wastes he had passed, and shuddered: he turned round, and flung his glance on the scene which opened at his feet; and the heaven which receives the soul of the blessed, met his view.[*]

Confined within the majestic girdle of the Indian Caucasus,[45] Cashmire, the birth-place of Brahma, the scene of his avatars, came at once under his observation. The brilliant scene, the balmy atmosphere, renovated his spirits and his frame. He rapidly descended the rock, now no longer bleak, no longer rude, but embossed with odoriferous plants, and shaded by lofty shrubs. His vital powers, his mental faculties, seemed to dilate to the influence of the pure and subtil air, which circulated with a genial softness through his frame, and gave to his whole being a sense of vague but pure felicity, which made even life itself enjoyment. The cusa-grass, which shrunk elastically beneath his steps, emitted a delicious odour; the golden fruit of the assoca-tree offered a luscious refreshment to his parched lip, and countless streams of liquid silver meeting, in natural basins, under the shade of the seringata, whose beauty has given it a place in the lunar constellations, offered to his weary frame the most necessary luxury that he could now enjoy.

It was evening when he reached the vale of Cashmire.[†] Purple mists hung upon the lustre of its enchanting scenes, and gave them, in fairy forms, to the stranger's eye. The fluttering plumage of the peacocks and lories fanned the air, as they sought repose among the luxuriant foliage of the trees: the silence of the delicious hour knew no interruption, but from the soothing murmurs of innumerable cascades. All breathed a tranquil but luxurious enjoyment;

---

[*] "Il (Bernier) n'eut plutôt monté ce qu'il nomme l'affreuse muraille du monde (parce qu'il regarde Cashmire un paradis terrestre), c'est-à-dire une haute montagne noire et pelée, qu'en descendant sur l'autre face il sentoit un air plus frais et plus temperé: mais rien ne le surprit tant, dans ces montagnes, que de se trouver, tout d'un coup, transporté des Indes en Europe."—Histoire Générale des Voyages, livre ii. p. 301.[44]

[†] According to Forster, the utmost extent of this delicious vale from S. E. to N. W. is scarcely 90 miles; other travellers assert it to be but 40 miles from east to west, and 25 from north to south.

all invited to a repose which resembled a waking dream. The Missionary had no power to resist the soft and new emotions which possessed themselves of his whole being; it seemed as if sensation had survived all power of perception; and, throwing himself on the odorous moss, which was shaded by the magnificent branches of the pamelo, the oak of the East, he slept.

CHAPTER VI.

The morning dawn, as it silvered the snows on the summits of the vast chain of the Indian Caucasus, and shed its light along the lower declivities of the hills of Cashmire, which swell at their base, awakened the Christian wanderer from a dream, pure and bright as a prophet's vision. In sleep he had believed himself to be in the abodes of the just, and he awakened in the regions of the blessed. Refreshed, invigorated, he arose, and offered the incense of the heart to Him, of whose power and beneficence his soul now received such new and splendid images.

Taking the broad stream of the Behat as his guide, he proceeded along its winding shores, towards the district of Sirinagar.[46] Surrounded by those mighty mountains whose summits appear tranquil and luminous, above the regions of clouds which float on their brow; whose grotesque forms are brightened by innumerable rills, and dashed by foaming torrents, the valley of Cashmire presented to the wandering eye scenes of picturesque and glowing beauty, whose character varied with each succeeding hour. Sometimes the mango-groves, with their golden oblong fruit and gigantic leaves, were mingled with plantations of mulberry, which, rising in luxuriant foliage, give sustenance to myriads of industrious insects, spinning from tree to tree their golden threads, which float like fairy banners, or brilliant particles of light, upon the fragrant gale; while, as emulous of their exertions, the Indian weaver seated at his loom beneath the shade of his plantain-tree, plied his slender fingers amidst the almost impalpable threads of his transparent web. Sometimes the ruins of a pagoda appeared through the boles of a distant forest, or the picturesque view of a Hindu village, formed of the slender bamboo, thatched with the brilliant leaves of the water-melon, appeared amidst the surrounding cotton-grounds, glowing with that tinted lustre of colouring, falsely deemed exclusively peculiar to the scenery of tropical climes; while herdsmen tending their snowy flocks on the brow of the surrounding hill, or youthful women carrying on their veiled heads vases of consecrated waters from the holy springs of the valley, recalled to the mind of the Missionary the venerable and touching simplicity of the patriarchal age.

Wherever the Christian wanderer appeared, he was beheld with curiosity and admiration. The dignity of his form commanded respect, and the meekness of his manner inspired confidence. They said, "It is a sanaissee, or pilgrim, of some distant nation, performing tupesya in a strange land;" and, with the same benevolent kindness with which they relieved the pilgrims of their own religion, did they administer to his comforts: but when, availing himself of the interest he excited, he endeavoured to unfold to them the nature and object of a mission, to accomplish which he had come from distant regions, they turned coldly from him, saying, "God has appointed to each tribe its own faith and, to each sect its own religion: let each obey the appointment of God, and live in peace with his neighbour."

This decided disappointment of all his holy views, grieved, without discouraging him. The perseverance of a genius not to be subdued, was the grand feature of his character; and a religious hope still hurried him towards that point, which was the object of his pious ambition. He deemed the conversion of the Prophetess a task reserved for him alone: the conversion of her nation a miracle which *she* only could accomplish.

He now proceeded to Sirinagar, and, within a few leagues of the capital,[*] he was struck by the appearance of a cave, in which he resolved to fix his abode. It was evening when the Missionary reached the base of a lofty mountain, which seemed a monument of the first day of creation. It was a solemn and sequestered spot, where an eternal spring seemed to reign, and which looked like the cradle of infant Nature, where she first awoke, in all her primeval bloom of beauty. It was a glen, skreened by a mighty mass of rocks, over whose bold fantastic forms and variegated hues dashed the silvery foam of the mountain torrent, flinging its dewy sprays around, till, breaking into fairy rills, it stole into a branch of the Behat, whose overflowing, at some distant period, had worn its way into the heart of the rock, and produced a small sparry cavern

---

[*] So called by the Hindus and by the ancient annals of India; but Bernier and Forster denominate the capital and its district by the same name as the kingdom or province.

which, from the splendour of the stalactites that hung like glittering icicles from its shining roof, had been named by the people of the country, *the grotto of congelations*. Wild and sequestered as was this romantic place, it yet, by its vicinity to the huts of some goalas, or Indian shepherds, left not its inhabitant wholly destitute of such assistance as even his simple and frugal life might still require; while, on every side, the luscious milk of the cocoa-nut, the fruit of the bread-tree, the nutritious grains of the wild rice plant, the luxurious produce of innumerable fruit-trees, and the pure bath of the mountain spring, were luxuries, supplied by Nature, in these, her loveliest and favourite regions.

The Missionary employed himself, during the evening, in erecting at the most remote extremity of the grotto, a rude altar, on which he placed the golden crucifix he usually carried suspended from his girdle; and, having formed what might be even deemed a luxurious couch of mosses and dried leaves, a night of calm repose passed swiftly away. The dawn, as it shone through the crevices of his asylum grotto, was reflected by the golden crucifix suspended over his altar. The heart of the Christian throbbed with an holy rapture, as he observed the ray of consecrated light. He arose, and prostrated himself before the first shrine ever raised to his Redeemer, in the most distant and most idolatrous of the provinces of Hindoostan: he then took his crosier, and issued forth, looking like the tutelar spirit of the magnificent region he was going to explore. A goala who was descending the rocks with his dogs, gave him as he passed a look of homage, such as the mind instinctively sends to the eye when its glance rests upon a being whom Providence seemed to have formed in all the beneficence and prodigality of its creative power.

The Missionary, taking the path towards Sirinagar, emerged from the deep shade of his glen, into a scene of picturesque beauty, which burst, in all the radiance of the rising day, upon his view, terminated by the cultivated hills of Sirinagar, and the snowy mountains of Thibet, rising like a magnificent amphitheatre to the east; but a grove of mangoostin-trees, still wrapt in the soft mists of dawn, became an object peculiarly attractive, in proportion to the retiring mystery of its gloomy shade. The Missionary struck off from the high road, to pierce into its almost impenetrable recesses. He proceeded through a path, which, from the long cusa-grass netted over it, and the entangled creepers of the parasite plants, seemed to have been rarely, if ever, explored. The trees, thick and umbrageous, were wedded, in their towering branches, above his head, and knitted, in their spreading roots, beneath his feet. The sound of a cascade became his sole guide through the leafy labyrinth. He at last reached the pile of rocks whence the torrent flowed, pouring its tributary flood into a broad river, formed of the confluence of the Behat and a branch of the Indus: the spot, therefore, was sacred;* and a shrine, erected on the banks of the river, opposite to the rising sun, already reflected the first ray of the effulgent orb, as it rose in all its majesty from behind the snowy points of the mountains of Thibet. Before the altar, and near the consecrated shrine, appeared a human form, if human it might be called, which stood so bright and so ethereal in its look, that it seemed but a transient incorporation of the brilliant mists of morning; so light and so aspiring in its attitude, that it appeared already ascending from the earth it scarcely touched, to mingle with its kindred air. The resplendent locks of the seeming sprite were enwreathed with beams, and sparkled with the waters of the holy stream, whence it appeared recently to have emerged. A drapery of snow shone round a form perfect in grace and symmetry. One arm, decorated with a rosary, was pointed to the rising sun; the other, at intervals, was thrice applied to the brow, and the following incantation from the Brahminical scriptures was then lowly and solemnly pronounced: "O pure waters! since you afford delight, grant me a rapturous view of heaven; and as he who plunges into thy wave is freed from all impurity, so may my soul live, free from all pollution." Thrice again bowing to the sun, the suppliant thus continued: "On that effulgent power, which is Brahma, do I meditate: governed by that mysterious light which exists internally within my breast, externally in the orb of the sun, being one and the same with that effulgent power, since I myself am an irradiated manifestation of the supreme Brahma."†

This being of spiritual mystery seemed then given up to a silent and religious rapture; and the Missionary, by a slight movement, changing his position, beheld the rapt countenance of the votarist, who had so sublimely assimilated herself to the orb she worshipped, and the God she served. It was Luxima! At the rustling of his robe among the trees, she started, turned round, and her eyes fell upon his figure, while her own was still fixed in the graceful

---

* The confluence of streams is sacred to the followers of Brahma.

† "L'Eternel, absorbé dans la contemplation de son essence, résolut dans la plénitude des temps de former des êtres participants de son essence et de sa béatitude."—SHASTAR, traduit en Français.[47]

attitude of devotion. Silently gazing, in wonder, upon each other, they stood finely opposed, the noblest specimens of the human species, as it appears in the most opposite regions of the earth; she, like the East, lovely and luxuriant; he, like the West, lofty and commanding: the one, radiant in all the lustre, attractive in all the softness which distinguishes her native regions; the other, towering in all the energy, imposing in all the vigour, which marks his ruder latitudes: she, looking like a creature formed to feel and to submit; he, like a being created to resist and to command: while both appeared as the ministers and representatives of the two most powerful religions of the earth; the one no less enthusiastic in her brilliant errors, than the other confident in his immutable truth.

The Christian Saint and Heathen Priestess remained for some time motionless, in look as in attitude: till Luxima, from a sudden impulse, withdrawing her eyes, the sensation of amazement depicted in her countenance, was rapidly succeeded by a bashful and timid emotion, which rosed her cheek with crimson hues, and threw round her an air of shrinking modesty, which softened the inspired dignity of the offspring of Brahma. But when the Priestess disappeared, the woman stood too much confessed; and a feminine reserve, a lovely timidity, so characteristic of her sex, overwhelmed the Missionary with confusion: he remained, leaning on his crosier, his eyes cast down upon his beads, his lips motionless.

Luxima, who resembled as she stood, the flower which contracts and folds upon itself, even to the influence of the evening air, was the first to interrupt this unexpected and mysterious interview; with a sudden movement she glided by the stranger, but with an air of chill reserve, of majestic distance, as though she feared the unhallowed vestment of infidelity should pollute the consecrated garb of vestal sanctity. He addressed her not, nor by a movement attempted to oppose her intention. He saw her proceed up an avenue of asoca-trees, which received the glittering form of the Priestess into their impervious shade. As she disappeared amidst the deepening gloom, she seemed, to the eye of her sole spectator, like the ray which darts its sunny lustre through the dark vapours gathered, by evening, on the brow of night. Still was his glance directed to the path she had taken; still did the brilliant vision float on his imagination, till the sun, as it deepened the shadows of the trees around him, told how long a reverie, so new and singular in its object, had stolen him from himself. He started, and moved unconsciously towards the bank of the stream, where traces of her idolatrous rites were still visible. Some unctuous clay, mingled with the ottar of the rose, strewed its perfume on the earth; and near it lay a wreath of the buchampaca, the flower of the dawn, whose vestal buds blow with the sun's first ray, and fade and die beneath his meridian beam, leaving only their odour to survive their transient blooms.

This wreath, so emblematic of the fragile loveliness of her who wore it, lay glistening in the sun. The Missionary took it up. A prejudice, or a pious delicacy, urged him to let it drop: he knew that it had made a part of an idolatrous ceremony; that it had been twined by idolatrous hands; but he could not forget, that those hands had looked so lovely and so pure, that they almost consecrated the act they had been engaged in: he wished also to believe, that those hands would yet adjust the monastic veil upon the Christian vestal's brow; he blamed, therefore, a fastidiousness, which almost resembled bigotry, and again took up the wreath. It breathed of the musky odours which had effused themselves from the tresses of the Indian as she passed him; and thus awakened to the recollection of their interview, he wandered back to his grotto, forgetful of his intention to visit Sirinagar, and occupied only in reflecting on the accident which had thus rendered him a resident in the neighbourhood of the Priestess of Cashmire.

CHAPTER VII.

The day was bright and ardent, the grotto was cool and shady; and the Missionary felt no inclination to leave a retreat, so adapted to the season and his tone of mind. He engaged in the perusal of the Scriptures, an abridged translation of which he had made into the Hindu dialect, and in devotional exercises and pious meditations: yet, for the first time, he found his thoughts not always obedient to his will; but he perceived that they had not changed their character, but their object; and that, in reverting to the interview of the morning, they still took into the scale of their reflection, the subject of his mission.

When he had finished the holy offices of the evening, he walked forth to enjoy its coolness and its beauty. He bent his steps involuntarily towards the altar erected at the confluence of the streams. The whole scene had changed its aspect with the sun's course: it was still and gloomy, and formed a strong relief to the luxuriancy of the avenue of asoca-trees, on whose summit the western sky poured its flood of crimson light. He wandered through its illuminated shades, till he suddenly found himself in a little valley, almost surrounded by hills, and opening, by a rocky defile, towards the mountains of Sirinagar, which formed a termination to the vista. In the centre of the valley, a stream, dividing into two branches, nearly surrounded a sloping mound, which swelled from their banks. The mound was covered with flowering shrubs, through whose entwining branches the shafts of a Verandah were partially seen, while the Pavilion to which it belonged, was wholly concealed. The eye of the Missionary was fascinated by the romantic beauty of this fairy scene, softened in all its lovely features by the declining light, which was throwing its last red beams upon the face of the waters. All breathed the mystery of a consecrated spot, and every tree seemed sacred to religious rites. The bilva, the shrub of the goddess Durga;* the high flowering murva, whose nectarous pores emit a scented beverage, and whose elastic fibres form the sacrificial threads of the Brahmins; the bacula, the lovely tree of the Indian Eden; and the lofty cadamba, which, dedicated to the third incarnation, is at once the most elegant and holy of Indian trees; all spoke, that the ground whereon he trod was consecrated; all gave a secret intimation to his heart, that his eyes then dwelt upon the secluded retreat of the vestal Priestess of Cashmire.

At the moment that he was struck by the conviction, a light and rustling noise seemed to proceed from the summit of the mound. He drew back, and casting up his eyes, perceived Luxima descending amidst the trees. She came darting lightly forward, like an evening iris; no less brilliant in hue, no less rapid in descent. She passed without observing the Missionary, and her dark and flowing tresses left an odour on the air, which penetrated his senses. He had not the power to follow, nor to address her: he crossed himself, and prayed. He, who in the temple of the idol had preached against idolatry to a superstitious multitude, bold and intrepid as a self-devoted martyr, now, in a lovely solitude, where all was calculated to soothe the feelings of his mind, and to harmonize with the tender mildness of his mission, trembled to address a young, a solitary, and timid woman. It seemed as if Heaven had withdrawn its favour; as if the spirit of his zeal had passed away. While he hesitated, Luxima had approached the stream, and the light of the setting

---

* The Goddess of Nature in the Indian mythology.

sun fell warmly round her. Thrice she bowed to the earth the brow irradiated with his beams, and then raising her hands to the west, while all the enthusiasm of a false, but ardent devotion, sparkled in her upturned eye, and diffused itself over her seraphic countenance, she repeated the vesper worship of her religion.

It was then that a zeal no less enthusiastic, a devotion no less fervid, animated the Christian Priest. He darted forward, and seized an arm thus raised in impious homage. He discarded the usual mildness of his evangelic feelings; with vehemence he exclaimed, "Mistaken being! know you what you do? that profanely you offer to the Created, that which belongs to the Creator only!"

The Indian, silent from amazement, stood trembling in his grasp; but she gazed for a moment on the Missionary, and, to an evident emotion of apprehension and astonishment, succeeded feelings still more profound. A resentful blush crimsoned her cheek, and her dark brows knit angrily above the languid orbs they shaded. The touch of the stranger was sacrilege. He had seized a hand, which the royal cast of her country would have trembled to have approached: he had equally shocked the national prejudice and natural delicacy of the woman, and violated the sacred character and holy office of the Priestess; she withdrew, therefore, from his clasp, shuddering and indignant, and looking imperiously on him, exclaimed, "Depart hence:—that, by an instant ablution in these consecrated waters, I may efface the pollution of thy touch; leave me, that I may expiate a crime, for which I must else innocently suffer."[48]

The Missionary, with an air of dignified meekness, letting fall his arms and casting down his eyes to the earth, replied: "Daughter, in approaching thee, I obey a will higher than thy command; I obey a Power, which bids me tell thee, that the prejudice to which thy mind submits, is false alike to happiness and to reason; and that a religion which creates distinction between the species, cannot be the religion of truth; for He who alike made thee and me, knows no distinction: He who died to redeem my sins, died also for thy salvation. Children of different regions, we are yet children of the same Parent, created by the same Hand, and inheritors of the same immortality."

He ceased. Luxima gazed timidly on him, and expressions strongly marked, and of a varying character, diffused themselves over her countenance. At last she exclaimed, "Stranger, thou sayest we are of the same *cast*. Art thou, then, an irradiation of the Deity, and, like me, wilt thou finally be absorbed in his divine effulgence?

Ah, no! thou wouldst deceive me, and cannot. Thou art *he*, the daring Infidel, who, in the temple at Lahore, denied all faith in the triple God, the holy Treemoortee; Brahma, Vishna, and Shiven: thou art he, who boldly dared to imitate the sixth avatar, in which Brahma, as a priest, did come to destroy the religions of nations, and to diffuse his own: yes, thou art he, who would seem a god among us, and, by seducing our minds from the true faith, deprive us of our *cast* on earth, and plunge us, hereafter, into the dark Nerekah, the abode of evil spirits. I know thee well, and thy power is great and dreadful; for in the midst of the shrines of the Gods I worship, thy image only fixed my eye; and when Brahma spoke by the lips of his Guru, thy voice only left its accents on my ear. Ere thou didst speak, I took thee for the tenth avatar, which is yet to come; and when I listened to thee, I deemed thee one of the Genii of the Arab's faith, whose words are false though sweet. But they say thou art a Christian, and a sorcerer; and punishment, with a *black aspect* and a *red eye*, waits on the souls of them who listen to, and who believe thee."

With these words, rapidly pronounced, blushing at her own temerity, in thus addressing a stranger of another sex, and involved in the confusion of her own new and powerful feelings, she would have glided away; but the Missionary following, caught the drapery of her robe, and said, with impressive dignity, "I command thee, in the name of Him who sent me, to stay and hear."

Luxima turned round. Her cheek was pale, she trembled, and raised her hands in the attitude of supplication. Shrinking back upon herself, fear, mingled with a sense of the profanation she endured, seemed to be the leading emotion of her soul. The Missionary, struck by the pleading softness of her air, and apprehensive of forfeiting all chance of another interview, by a perseverance in now detaining her, drew back a few paces, and crossing his hands on his bosom, and casting his eyes to earth, he sighed, and said, "Go! thou art free; but take with thee the prayers and blessings of him, who, to procure thy eternal happiness, would joy to sacrifice his mortal life." He spoke with enthusiasm and feeling:—Luxima heard him in amazement and emotion. Free to go, she yet lingered for a moment; then raising her eyes to heaven, as if she invoked the protection of some tutelary deity, she turned abruptly away, and gliding up the mount, disappeared amidst the umbrage of its trees.

The Missionary remained motionless. The result of this interview convinced him, that in the same light as the infidel appeared to him, in such had he appeared to her; alike beyond the pale of salvation, alike dark in error. Her prejudices, indeed, extended even beyond the abstract sentiment; for his words were not only deemed sacrilegious, but his very presence was considered as pollution: and her opinions seemed so animated by her enthusiasm, her religious faith so blended with her human ambition, that he believed he might well deem the conversion of her nation possible, could hers be once effected. But to those obstacles were opposed the success, which had even already crowned his progressive efforts: either by a fortunate chance, or by a divine providence, he had established himself near her residence; he was acquainted with the places of her morning and evening worship; he had addressed her, and she had replied to him. She had, indeed, confessed she feared his presence, and she had endeavoured to fly him; but had she not also avowed the deep impressions he had made on her mind? that she had mistaken him for an incarnation of her worshipped god; and, in the consecrated temple of her faith, where she stood, not more adoring than adored, that *his* image only rested on her imagination, *his* accents only dwelt upon her ear?

The Missionary moved rapidly away, as this conviction came home to his heart. He believed he felt it all, as a religious should only feel, through the medium of his mission, and not as a man through the agency of his feelings; and he returned thanks to Heaven, that the grace of conversion was already working in the pure, but erring, soul of the innocent infidel, slowly indeed, and under the influence of the senses; but the ear which had been charmed, the eye which had been fixed, were organs of intellect, the powerful sources of mind itself.

Another day rose on the cave of the apostolic Nuncio; but he extended not his wanderings beyond the huts of the neighbouring Goalas: when he approached them, he was hailed with smiles; but when he attempted to preach to them, they listened to him with indifference, or heard with incredulity. He sighed, and believing his hour was not yet come, looked forward, with religious patience, to the moment, when he should present, to the worshippers of Brahma, a Neophyte, whose conversion would be the sole miracle which graced his mission: but what miracle could better evince the divinity of the doctrine he advanced, than that a Priestess of Brahma, a Prophetess, a Brachmachira, should believe in, and receive it? He beheld, therefore, from the summit of his asylum, towns and villages, the palaces of Rajahs, and the cottages of the Ryots;[49] but he approached them not. The charms of a solitude, so lovely and so profound, grew with an increasing and hourly influence on his heart and imagination. Pure light and pure air, the softest sounds and sweetest odours, skies for ever sunny, and shades for ever cool, the song of birds and murmur of cascades, all, in a residence so enchanting, rendered life itself an innocent enjoyment. The goalas called him "The Hermit of the Grotto of Congelations;" and believing him to be an harmless fanatic, and a holy man of some unknown faith, they respected his solitude, and never intruded on it, but to furnish him with the simple necessaries his simple life required.*

For some time he forbore approaching the consecrated grove of the Priestess: he wished to awaken confidence, and feared to banish it by importunity. On the evening of the third day, he directed his steps towards the pavilion of Luxima, always concealing himself amidst the trees, lest he should be observed by any of the few attendants who resided with her. At a little distance from the confluence of the streams, his ear was struck by a moan of suffering. He flew to the spot whence it proceeded, and beheld a young fawn in the fangs of a wolf; an animal rarely seen in the innoxious shades of Cashmire, but which is sometimes driven, by hunger, from the mountain wilds of Thibet into the valley. The animal, fierce in want, now suddenly dropt his bleeding prey, and turned on the man. The bright glare of his distended eyes, the discovery of his fang-teeth, his inclined head, the sure presages of destruction, all spoke the attack he meditated. The Missionary, firm and motionless, met his advance with the spear of his crosier; and though the wolf rushed upon its point, the slight wound it inflicted only served to whet his rage. He gained upon his opponent. The Missionary threw away the crosier. He had no alternative: he rushed upon the animal; he struggled with its strength: the contest was unequal; but it was but of a moment's duration: the animal lay strangled at his feet, and the Missionary returned his acknowledgments to that Power, which had thus nerved his arm, and preserved his life. He then turned to the fawn. It was but slightly wounded; and as it lay trembling on the grass, its preserver could not but admire its singular beauty. Its form was perfect, its velvet coat was smooth and polished, and its delicate neck was encircled by a sil-

---

* "Il ne faut à ces nations que des nourritures rafraîchissantes, et mère la nature leur a prodigué des forêts de citroniers, d'oranges, de figuiers, de palmiers, de cocotiers, et des campagnes couverte de riz."—Essai sur les Mœurs et l'Esprit des Nations. VOLTAIRE.[50]

ver collar, clasped with the mountain gem of Cashmire. Some Shanscrit characters were engraven on this collar, but the Missionary paused not to peruse them. The suppliant looks of the gentle and familiar fawn excited his pity: it seemed no stranger to human attentions, and caressed the hand of the Missionary, when he took it in his arms to bear it to his cave; for it was unable to move, and his benevolent nature would not permit him to leave it to perish. It was also evident, that it was the favourite of some person of distinction, to whom he would take pleasure in restoring it; for though he had conquered all human affections in himself, and had lived alone for Heaven, neither loving nor beloved on earth, yet sometimes he remotely guessed at the happiness such a feeling might bestow on others less anxious for perfection; and a vague wish would sometimes escape his heart, that *he* too might love: but when that wish grew with indulgence, and extended itself to a higher object; when the possible existence of a dearer, warmer, feeling, filled his enthusiast soul, and vibrated through all his sensible being, then the blood flowed like a burning torrent in his veins, his heart quickened in its throb to a feverish pulsation—he trembled, he shuddered, he prayed, and was resigned.

When he had reached the grotto, he placed his helpless burden on some moss. He bathed its wound, and applying to it some sanative herbs, was about to bind it with the long fibres of the cusagrass, when the light which flowed in upon his task was suddenly obscured. He was on his knees at the moment: he turned round his head, and perceived that the shadow fell from a form which hovered at the entrance of his grotto. The form was Luxima's: it was the Priestess of Brahma who presented herself at the entrance of the Christian's cave: it was the zealous Brachmachira, who stood within a few steps of the Christian's altar. The Missionary remained in the motionless attitude of surprise. He could not be deceived: it was no vision of ethereal mildness, such as descends upon the abodes of holy men; for, all pale, and spiritual, and heaven-born as it looked, it was still all woman: it was still the Idolatress. With eyes of languid softness, with looks so wild, so timid in their glance, as if she trembled at the shade her figure pictured on the sunny earth; before the Monk had power to rise, she advanced into the centre of the grotto, and kneeling opposite to him, and beside the fawn, she said, "Almora, my dear and faithful animal; thou whom I have fostered, as thy mother would have fostered thee; thou dost, then, still live! and the innocent spirit thy lovely form embodies, has not yet fled to some less pure receptacle." At the sound of her caressing voice, the favourite raised her languid eyes, and fawned upon her hands. "It lives!" she said joyfully; and turning her look upon the Missionary, added, in a softer voice, "And thou hast saved its life?"

As she spoke, her eyes fell in bashful disorder, beneath the fixed look of the Missionary; and again gently raising their dewy light, threw around the cavern, a glance of wonder and curiosity. The sun was setting radiantly opposite to its entrance, and the spars of its vaulted roof shone with the hue and lustre of vivid rubies: pure rays of refracted light fell from the golden crucifix on the surface of the marble altar; and the figure of the Monk, habited only in the white jama, finely harmonized with the scene, and gave to the grotto that air of enchantment, which the Indian fancy delights to dwell on. The mind of Luxima seemed rapt in the wondrous imagery by which she was surrounded. She again turned her eyes on the Monk, and suddenly starting from her position, the head of the fawn fell from her bosom. "Thou art wounded!" she exclaimed, with a voice of pity and of terror. The Monk perceived that the breast of his jama was stained with blood. "Thou wilt bleed to death!" she continued, trembling, and approaching him: "thou, who, unlike other infidels, art so tender towards a suffering animal, art thou to suffer unassisted?"

"My religion teaches me to assist and to relieve all who live and suffer," said the Missionary; "but here, who is there to assist me?"— Luxima changed colour; she flew out of the grotto, and in a moment returned. "Here," she said eagerly, "here is a lotos-leaf filled with water, bathe thy wound: and here is an herb, sovereign in fresh wounds; apply it to thy bosom: and to-morrow an Arab physician from Sirinagar shall attend thee."—"The wound lies not in my bosom," replied the Monk: "it is my right arm which has been torn by the fangs of the wolf, and I cannot assist myself; yet I thank thee for thy charitable attentions."

Luxima stood suspenseful and agitated. Natural benevolence, confirmed prejudice, the impulse of pity, and the restraint of religion, all were seen to struggle in the expression of a countenance, which faithfully indicated every movement of the soul. At last nature was victorious, and raising her eyes and hands to heaven, she exclaimed, "Praise be to Vishnu! who still protects those who are pure in heart, even though their hands be polluted!" Then gently, timidly, approaching the Missionary, she knelt beside him, and raising the sleeve of his jama, she bathed the wound, which was slight, applied to it the sanative herbs, and, tearing off part of her veil, bound his arm with the consecrated fragment. Thus engaged, the colour frequently visited and retired from her cheek. When her hand met the Missionary's, she shuddered and shrank from the touch; and when his eye dwelt on hers, she suddenly averted their glance. They fell at last upon her own faded wreath of the buchamhaca, which was suspended from a point of the rock: she blushed, and cast them down on the rosary of the Christian Hermit, which, at that moment, encircled her own arm. She perceived that his eyes also rested on them. "I found them," she said, replying to his look; "for having missed a fawn, who had followed me to the stream of evening worship, I implored the assistance of Moodaivee, the Goddess of Misfortune, and she conducted me to a spot, where I perceived the shining hairs of my favourite, lying scattered around the body of a wolf, who lay, grim and terrific, even in death. I said, 'Who is he, powerful as the flaming column, in which Shiven did manifest his strength—who is he, bold and terrible, who thus destroys the destroyer?' Thy beads told the tale; and the red drops which fell from the wound of the fawn, tracked the path to this cave of wonders, where I have found thee, kind infidel, acting as an Hindu would have acted; who shudders as he moves, lest, beneath his incautious steps, some viewless insect bleeds. Receive, then, into thy care, this wounded animal; and when it can be removed, lead it, at sunrise, to the confluence of the streams; there I will receive it."

As she spoke, she advanced to the entrance of the cave, and performing the salaam, the graceful salutation of the East, disappeared. Had a celestial visitant irradiated with its brightness the gloom of his cavern, the Missionary would not have been more overwhelmed by emotions of surprise and admiration; but, in recovering from his confusion, he recollected, with a strong feeling of self-reproach, that he had suffered her to depart, without availing himself of so singular an opportunity of increasing her confidence, and extending their intercourse. He arose—and resuming his monkish robe, followed her with a rapid step. He perceived her, like a vapour which a sunbeam lights, floating amidst the dark shadows of the surrounding trees. The echo of his footsteps caught her ear: she turned round, and the flush of quick surprise mantled even to her brow; yet a smile of bashful pleasure played round her lips. The Missionary turned away his eyes, and secretly wished she might not thus smile again; for the pearl, whose snowy lustre the chunam had not yet dimmed, marked by contrast the ruby brightness of those lips, which, when they smiled, lost all their usual character of seraph meekness, and chased from the playful countenance of the woman, the dignified tranquility which sat upon the holy look of the Priestess.

The Missionary was now beside her. "The dew of evening," he said, "falls heavy, the sun is about to withdraw its last beam from the horizon, and the cause which drove a ferocious animal into these harmless shades may still exist, and send another from the heights of Thibet; therefore, daughter, have I followed thee!" The Indian looked not insensible, nor yet displeased by his attention; but when he called her *daughter*, she raised her eyes in wonder to the form of him, who thus assumed the sacred rights of paternity: but she read not there his claim, and repeated in a low voice—"*Daughter!*"—"Yes," he replied, as a vague sense of pleasure thrilled through his heart, when she repeated the word; "yes, I would look upon thee as a daughter, I would be unto thee as a father, I would guide the wanderings of thy mind, as now I guide thy steps, and I would protect thee from evil and from error, as I now protect thee from danger and from accident."

The countenance of Luxima softened as he spoke. He now addressed himself, not to her prejudices, which were unvanquishable, but to her feelings, which were susceptible: he addressed her, not as the priest of a religion she feared, but as a man, whom it was impossible to listen to, or to behold, without interest; and the Missionary, observing the means most likely to fascinate her attention and to win her confidence, now dropt the language of his mission, and spoke to her with an eloquence, never before exerted but in the cause of religion. He spoke to her of the lovely wonders of her native region; of the impression which the venerable figure of her grandsire had made on his mind, in the temple of Lahore; and of her own story, which, he confessed, had deeply interested him: he spoke to her of the loss of affectionate parents, of the untimely fate of a youthful bridegroom, and of the nature of the austere life she herself led; of the tender ties she had relinquished, of the precious feelings she had sacrificed. In adverting thus to her life, he was governed by an acute consciousness of all the privations of his own; he spoke of the subjection of the passions, like one constituted to know their tyranny, and capable of opposing it; and he applauded the fortitude of virtue, like one who estimated the difficulty of resistance by the force of the external temptation and the internal impulse: he spoke a language not usually his own—the *language of sentiment*: but if it wanted something of the force, it wanted nothing of the pathos which distinguished the eloquence of his religion.

Luxima heard him with emotion. Her heart was eloquent, but

the nature of her religion, and feminine reserve, alike sealed her lips. She replied to his observation by looks, and to his questions by monosyllables. He only understood, from her timid and brief answers, that her grandsire was then residing at his college at Siri-nagar, and that she lived in religious retirement, in her pavilion, with only two female attendants, wholly devoted to the discipline and exercises of her profession. But though her words were few, reserved, and guarded; yet the warm blush of sudden emotion, the playful smile of unrepressed pleasure, the low sigh of involuntary sadness, and all those simple and obvious expressions of strong and tender feelings, which, in an advanced state of society, are obscured by ceremony, or concealed by affectation, betrayed, to the Monk, a character, in which tenderness and enthusiasm, and genius and sensibility, mingled their attributes.

When she had reached the base of the mound, the Missionary sought not to proceed. "Daughter," he said, "thou art now within the safe asylum of thy home. Peace be unto thee! and may He, who gave us equally hearts to feel his goodness, guard and protect thee!" As he spoke, he raised his illumined eyes to heaven, and clasped his hands in the suppliant attitude of prayer. The dovelike eyes and innocent hands of the Indian were raised in the same direction; for, gazing on the glories of the firmament, a feeling of rapturous devotion, awakened and exalted by the enthusiasm of the Missionary, filled her soul.

In this sacred communion, the Christian Saint and Heathen Priestess felt in common and together; and their eyes were only withdrawn from heaven, to become fixed on each other. The beams of both were humid, and both secretly felt the sympathy by which they were united. Luxima withdrew in silence; and the Missionary, as he caught the last glimpse of her form, sighed, and said, "How worthy she is to be saved! how obviously does a dawning grace shed its pure light over the dark prejudices of her wandering mind!" Then he recalled her looks, her blushes, her words: all alike breathed of a soul, formed for the highest purposes of devotion; a heart endowed with the most exquisite feelings of nature: and, in meditating on the character of his future proselyte, he remained wandering about the shades of her dwelling, until the rays of a midnight moon silvered their foliage; then a strain of soft and solemn music faintly stole on his ear, and powerfully awakened his attention. This mysterious sound proceeded from the summit of the mound; and led by strains which harmonized with the hour, the place, and with the peculiar tone of his feelings and his mind, he ascended the acclivity; but it was with slow and doubtful steps, as if he were impelled to act by some secret impulse, which he did not approve, and could not resist. As he reached the summit of the mound, he perceived, by the peculiar odours which breathed around him, that it was planted with the rarest and richest shrubs. A spring, gushing from its brow, shed a light dew on every side, which bestowed an eternal freshness on the balmy air, and on those fragrant flowers, which opened now their choicest sweets.

A pavilion, surrounded by a light and elegant verandah, rose, like a fairy structure, from the midst of the surrounding shades; and, from one of the lattices, proceeded those aërial sounds, which,

"Sweet as from blest voices uttering joy,"[51]

had first allured his attention. It seemed to inclose a particular apartment. Its lattices were composed of the aromatic verani, whose property it is, to allay a feverish heat; and which, by being dashed by the waters of an artificial fountain, bestowed a fragrant coolness on the air. A light gleamed through one of the lattices, and the Missionary found no difficulty in penetrating, with his eye, into the interior of the room. He perceived that the light proceeded from a lamp, suspended from the centre of the ceiling, which was painted with figures taken from the Indian mythology. Beneath the lamp stood a small altar, whose ivory steps were strewed with flowers and with odours.

The idol, to whom the offerings were made, wore the form and air of a child: by his cany bow, his arrows tipt with Indian blossoms, the Missionary recognised him as the lovely twin of the Grecian Cupid; while, before her tutelar deity, knelt Luxima, playing on the Indian lyre, which she accompanied with a hymn to Camdeo.[52] The sounds, wild and tender, died upon her lips, and she seemed to

"Feed on thoughts,
Which voluntary mov'd harmonious numbers."[53]

She then arose, and poured incense into a small vase, in which the leaves of the sacred sami-tree burnt with a blue phosphoric light: then bowing to the altar, she said, "Glory be to Camdeo; him by whom Brahma and Vishnu are filled with rapturous delight; for the true object of glory is an union with our beloved: that object really exists; but, without it, both heart and soul would have no existence."

As she pronounced this impassioned invocation, a tender and ardent enthusiasm diffused itself over her countenance: her eyelids gently closed, and soft and delightful visions seemed to absorb her soul and feelings.

The Missionary hastened away, and rapidly descended the mound. He had seen, he had heard, too much: even the very air he breathed communicated its fatal softness to his imagination, and tended to enervate his mind. A short time back, and the Indian had shared with him a feeling as pure and as devotional as it was sublime and awful: he found her now involved in idolatrous worship. Hitherto a chaste and vestal reserve had consecrated her look, and guarded her words; now a tender and impassioned languor was distinguished in both: and the virgin priestess, the widowed bride, who had hitherto appeared exclusively consecrated to the service of that Heaven she imaged upon earth, seemed now only alive to the existence of feelings in which Heaven could have no share.

For whose sake was this tender invocation made? lived there an object worthy to steal between the vestal Prophetess and her paradise of Indra? He recalled her look and air, and thought that as he had last beheld her in all the grace and blandishment of beauty and emotion, she resembled less the future foundress of a religious order, than one of the lovely Rajini, or female Passions, which, in the poetical mythology of her religion, were supposed to preside over the harmony of the spheres, and to steal their power over the hearts of men by sounds which breathed of heaven. But he discarded the seducing image, as little consonant to the tone of his mind, while he involuntarily repeated, "The true object of soul and mind is the glory of a union with our beloved;" until, suddenly recollecting the doctrines of mystic love, and that, even in his own pure faith, there were sects who addressed their homage to Heaven in terms of human passion,[*] Luxima stood redeemed in his mind: for, whatever glow of imagination warms the worship of colder regions, he was aware that, in India, the ardent gratitude of created spirits was wont to ascend to the Creator in expressions of the most fervid devotion; that the tender eloquence of mystic piety too frequently assumed the character of human feelings; and that the faint line, which sometimes separated the language of love from that of religion, was too delicate to be perceptible but to the pure in spirit and devout in mind. He was himself of a rigid principle and a stoical order, and the language of his piety, like its sentiment,

---

[*] It is unnecessary to mention the well-known doctrine of quietism, embraced by the Archbishop of Cambray.[54]

was lofty and sublime. Yet he was not intolerant towards the soft and pious weaknesses of others; and he now believed that the ardent enthusiasm of the lovely Heathen was a sure presage of the zeal and faith of the future Christian.

The little hills which encircled the vale where chance had fixed the residence of the Nuncio, seemed now to him as a magic boundary, whose line it was impossible to pass; and during the day which succeeded to that of Luxima's visit, he wandered near the path which led to her pavilion, or returned to his grotto, to caress the fawn she had committed to his care; but always with a feeling of doubt and anxiety, as if expectation and disappointment divided his mind; for he thought it probable, that the humanity of Luxima might lead her, now her first prejudices were vanished, again to visit him, to inquire into the state of his own slight wound, or to see her convalescent favourite. Once he believed he heard her voice; he flew to the mouth of the grotto, but it was only the sweet soft whistle of the packimar, the Indian bird-catcher, as he hung, almost suspended, from the projection of a neighbouring rock, pointing his long and slender lines tipped with lime to the gaudy plumage of the pungola, who builds her nest in the recesses of the highest cliffs; or lured to his nets, with imitative note, the lovely and social magana, the red-breast of the East. Again he heard a light and feathery foot-fall: he thought it must be Luxima's, but he only perceived at a distance, a slender youth bending his rapid way, assisted by a slight and brilliant spear; and by his jama of snowy white, and crimson sash and turban, he recognised the useful and swift Hircarah, the faithful courier of some Indian rajah or Mogul omrah.

The sun, as it faded from the horizon, withdrew with it, hopes scarcely understood by him who indulged them. Hitherto his mind had received every impression, and combined every idea, through a religious influence; and even the Indian, in all the splendour of her beauty, her youth, and her enthusiasm, had stolen on his imagination solely through the medium of his zeal. Until this moment, woman was to him a thing unguessed at and unthought of. In Europe and in India, the few who had met his eye were of that class in society to whom delicacy of form was so seldom given, by whom the graces of the mind were so seldom possessed. Hitherto he had only stood between them and Heaven: they had approached him penitent and contrite, faded by time, or chilled by remorse; and he had felt towards them as saints are supposed to feel, who see the errors from which they are themselves exempt. His experience, therefore, afforded him no parallel for the character and form of the Priestess. A rapturous vision had, indeed, given him such forms of heaven to gaze on; but on earth he had seen nothing to which he could assimilate, or by which compare her.

Yet, in reflecting on her charms, he only considered them as rendering her more worthy to be converted, and more capable of converting. He remembered that the pure light of Christianity owed its first diffusion to the influence of woman; and that the blood of martyred vestals had flowed to attest their zeal and faith, with no inadequate effect. This consideration, therefore, sanctified the solicitude which Luxima awakened in his mind; and anxiously to expect her presence, and profoundly to feel her absence, were, he believed, sentiments which emanated from her religious zeal, and not emotions belonging to his selfish feeling.

On the evening of the following day, he repaired to the altar at the confluence of the streams, accompanied by the fawn, which was now sufficiently recovered to be restored to its mistress. His heart throbbed with a violence new to its sober pulse, when he perceived Luxima standing beneath the shadowy branches of a cannella-alba, or cinnamon-tree, looking like the deity of the stream, in whose lucid wave her elegant and picturesque form was reflected. The bright buds of the water-loving lotos were twined round her arms and bosom: she seemed fresh from her morning worship, and the enthusiasm of devotion still threw its light upon her features; but when the Missionary stood before her, this devotional expression was lost in the splendour of her illuminated countenance. The pure blood mantling to her cheek gradually suffused her whole face with radiant blushes: a tender shyness hung upon her downcast eyes; and a smiling softness, a bashful pleasure, finely blended with a religious dignity, involved her whole person. There was so much of the lustre of beauty, the freshness of youth, the charm of sentiment, the mystery of devotion, and the spell of grace, in her look, her air, her attitude, that the Missionary stood rapt in silent contemplation of her person, and wondering that one so fit for heaven should yet remain on earth.

The fawn, which had burst from the string of twisted grass by which the Missionary led it, now sprung to the feet of her mistress, who lavished on her favourite the most infantile caresses; and this little scene of re-union gave time to the Missionary to recover the reserved dignity of the apostolic Nuncio, which the abruptly awakened feelings of the man had put to flight. "Daughter," he said, "health and peace to thee and thine! May the light of the true religion effuse its lustre o'er thy soul, as the light of the sun now irradiates thy form!"

As he spoke a language so similar to that in which the devotions of the heathen were wont to flow, he touched, by a natural association of ideas, on the chord of her enthusiasm; and thrice bowing to the sun, she replied, "I adore that effulgent power, in whose lustre I now shine, and of which I am myself an irradiated manifestation."

The Missionary started; his blood ran cold as he thus found himself so intimately associated in the worship of an infidel; while, as if suddenly inspired, he raised his hands and eyes to heaven, and, prostrate on the earth, prayed aloud, and with the eloquence of angels, for her conversion.

Luxima, gazing and listening, stood rapt in wonder and amazement, in awe and admiration. She heard her name tenderly pronounced, and inseparably connected with supplication to Heaven in her behalf: she beheld tears, and listened to sighs, of which she alone was the object, and which were made as offerings to the suppliant's God, that she might embrace a mode of belief, to whose existence, until now, she was almost a stranger. Professing, herself, a religion which unites the most boundless toleration to the most obstinate faith; the most perfect indifference to proselytism, to the most unvanquishable conviction of its own supreme excellence; she could not, even remotely, comprehend the pious solicitude for her conversion, which the words and emotion of the Christian betrayed; but from his prayer, and the exhortations he addressed to her, she understood, that she had been the principal object of his visiting Cashmire, and that her happiness, temporal and eternal, was the subject of his ardent hopes and eloquent supplications.

This conviction sunk deep into her sensible and grateful heart, which was formed for the exercise of all those feelings which raise and purify humanity; and it softened, without conquering, the profound and firm-rooted prejudices of her mind; and when the Monk arose, she seated herself on a shelving bank, and motioned to him to place himself beside her. He obeyed, and a short pause ensued, which the eloquent and fixed looks of the Indian alone filled up; at last, she said, in accent of emotion, "Christian, thou hast named me an idolatress; what means that term, which must sure be evil, since, when thou speakest it, methinks thou dost almost seem to shudder."

"I call thee idolatress," he replied, "because even now, thou didst offer to the sun that worship, which belongs alone to Him who said, 'Let there be light; and there was light.'"—"I adore the sun," said Luxima, with enthusiasm, "as the great visible luminary; the emblem of that incomparably greater Light, which can alone illumine our souls."—"Ah!" he replied, "at least encourage this first principle of the true faith, this pure idea of an essential Cause, this sentiment of the existence of a God, which is the sole idea innate to the mind of man."—"I would adore Him in his works," replied the Priestess; "but when I would contemplate him in his essence, I am dazzled; I am overwhelmed; my soul shrinks back, affrighted at its own presumption. I feel only the mighty interval which separates us from the Deity; overpowered, I sink to the earth, abashed and humbled in my conscious insignificance."

"Such," said the Missionary, "are the timid feelings of a soul, struggling with error, and lost in darkness. It is by the operation of divine grace only, that we are enabled to contemplate the Creator in himself; it is by becoming a Christian that the divine grace only can be obtained!"

Luxima shuddered as he spoke. "No," she said; "the feeling which would prompt me to meet the presence of my Creator; to image his nature to my mind; to form a distinct idea of his being, power, and attributes, would overpower me with fear and with confusion."

As she spoke, a religious awe seemed to take possession of her soul. She trembled; her countenance was agitated; and she repeated rapidly the creed of the faith she professed, prostrating herself on the earth, in sign of the profound submission and humility of her heart. The Missionary was touched by a devotion so pure and so ardent; and, when she had ceased to pray, he would have raised her from the earth; but, warm in all the revived feelings of her religion, her prejudices rekindled with her zeal; she shrunk from an assistance she would have now deemed it sacrilegious to accept, and, with a crimson blush, she haughtily exclaimed, "As the shadow of the pariah defiles the bosom of the stream over which it hangs its gloom, so is the descendant of Brahma profaned by the touch of one who is neither of the same cast nor of the same sex."[55]

The Missionary stood confused and overwhelmed by sentiments so incongruous, and by principles so discordant, as those which seemed to blend and to unite themselves in the character and mind of this extraordinary enthusiast. At one moment, the purest adoration of the Supreme Being, and the most sublime conceptions of his attributes, betrayed themselves in her eloquent words; in the next, she appeared wholly involved in the wildest superstitions of her idolatrous nation. Now she hung upon his words with an obvious delight, which seemed mingled with conviction; and now she shrunk from his approach, as if he belonged to some species condemned of Heaven. To argue with her was impossible: for there was an incoherence in her ideas, which was not to be reconciled, or replied to. To listen to her was dangerous; for the eloquence of genius and feeling, and the peculiar tenets of her sect, gave a force to her errors, and a charm to her look, which weakened even the zeal of conversion in the priest, in proportion as it excited the admiration of the man. Determined, therefore, no longer to confide in himself, nor to trust to human influence on a soul so bewildered, so deep in error, the Missionary drew from his bosom the scriptural volume, translated into the dialect of the country, and, presenting it to her, said, "Daughter, thou seest before thee a man, who has subdued the passions incidental to his nature; a man, who has trampled beneath his feet the joys of youth, of rank, of wealth; who has abandoned his country and his friends, his ease and his pleasure, and crossed perilous seas, and visited distant regions, and endured pain, and vanquished obstacles, that others might share with him that bright futurity, reserved for those who believe, and follow the divine precepts which this sacred volume contains. Judge, then, of its purity and influence, by the sacrifices it enables man to make. Take it; and may Heaven pour into thy heart its celestial grace, that, as thou readest, thou mayst edify and believe!"

Luxima took the book, gazing silently on him who presented it. His countenance, the tone of his voice, seemed no less to affect her senses, than the solemnity of his address to impress and touch her mind. The Missionary moved slowly away; he had restored his mind to its wonted holy calm; he wished not again to encounter the eyes, or listen to the accents of the Indian. If she were not influenced by the inspired writings he had put into her hand, "neither would she by one who should descend from heaven."[56]

He proceeded on, nor glanced one look behind him; and, though he heard a light foot-fall near him, yet his eyes were still fixed upon his rosary. At last a sweet and low voice pronounced the name of "Father!" The tender epithet sunk to his heart: he paused, and Luxima stood beside him. He turned his eyes on her for a moment, but suddenly withdrawing them, he fastened their

glances on the earth. "Daughter," he said, "what wouldst thou?"—
"Thy forgiveness!" she replied timidly: "I shrunk from thy
approach, and therefore I fear to have offended thee; for haply the
women of thy nation offend not their gods, when men of other
casts approach them, and they forbid it not."

"The God whom they adore," he said, "judges not by the act
alone, but by the motive. The pure in heart commit no evil deeds;
and, perhaps, there are women, even of thy nation, daughter, who
would deem the presence of a Christian minister no profanation to
their purity."

"But I," she returned, with majesty, "I am a sacerdotal woman!
a consecrated vestal, and a guarded Priestess! And know, Christian,
that the life of a vestal should resemble the snow buds of the
ipomea, when, hid in their virgin calix, the sun's ray has never
kissed their leaves. Yet, lest thou part from me in anger, accept this
sacrifice."

As she spoke, she averted her eyes. A deep blush coloured her
cheek; and, trembling between an habitual prejudice and a natural
feeling, she extended to the Missionary hands of a pure and exquisite beauty, which never before had known a human pressure. The
Missionary took them in silence. He believed that the rapid pulsation of his heart arose from the triumphant feeling excited by the
conquest of a fatal prejudice; but when he recollected also, that this
was the first time the hands of a woman were ever folded in his
own, he started, and suddenly dropt them; while Luxima, animated by a devotional fervour, clasped them on her bosom, and said,
in a low and tender voice, "Father, thou who art thyself pure, and
holy as a Brahmin's thought, pray for me to thy gods; I will pray
for thee to mine!" Then turning her eyes for a moment on him,
she pronounced the Indian salaam, and, with a soft sigh and pensive look, moved slowly away.

The Missionary pursued her with his glance, until the thicken-
ing shade of a group of mangoostan-trees concealed her from his
view. Her sigh seemed still to breathe on his ear, with a deathless
echo: at last, he abruptly started, and walked rapidly away, as if, in
leaving a spot where all breathed of her, he should leave the idea
of her beauty and her softness behind him. He endeavoured to
form an abstract idea of her character, independent of her person;
to consider the mind distinct from the woman; to remember only
the prejudice he had vanquished, and not the hands he had
touched; but still he felt them in his own, soft and trembling; and
still he sought to lose, in the subject of his mission, the object of

his imagination. He endeavoured to banish her look and her sigh from his memory; and to recall the last short, but extraordinary conversation he had held with her. He perceived that a pure system of natural religion was innate in her sublime and contemplative mind; but the images which personified the attributes of Deity, in her national faith, had powerfully fastened on her ardent imagination, and blended their influence with all the habits, the feelings, and the expressions of her life. The splendid mythology of the Brahminical religion was eminently calculated to seduce a fancy so warm; and the tenets of her sect, to harmonize with the tenderness of a heart so sensible. But a life so innocent as that she led, and a mind so pure as that she possessed, rendered her equally capable to feel and to cherish that abstract and awful sense of a First Cause, without which all religion must be cold and baseless.

This consciousness of a predisposition to truth on her part, with the daily conquest of those prejudices which might prevent its promulgation on his, gave new vigour to his hopes, and, in the anticipation of so illustrious a convert, he already found the sacrifices and labours of his enterprise repaid.

THE END OF VOL. I.

VOLUME II

Revolution of the Mind.

CHAPTER VIII.

It was the season of visitation of the Guru of Cashmire to his granddaughter. The Missionary beheld him with his train approach her abode of peace, and felt the necessity of absenting himself from the consecrated grove, where he might risk a discovery of his intentions unfavourable to their success. He knew that the conversion of the Brachmachira was only to be effected by the frequent habit of seeing and conversing with her, and that a discovery of their interviews would be equally fatal to both. Yet he submitted to the necessity which separated them, with an impatience, new to a mind, whose firm tenour was, hitherto, equal to stand the shock of the severest disappointment. Still did his steps involuntarily bend to the skirts of the grove, and still did he return sad, without any immediate cause of sorrow, and disappointed, without any previous expectation. To contemplate the frailty, to witness the errors of the species to which we belong, is to mortify that self-love, which is inherent in our natures; yet to be dissatisfied with others, is to be convinced of our own superiority. It is to triumph, while we condemn—it is to pity, while we sympathize. But, when we become dissatisfied with ourselves; when a proud consciousness of former strength unites itself with a sense of existing weakness; when the heart has no feeling to turn to for solace; when the mind has no principle to resort to for support; when suffering is unalleviated by self-esteem, and no feeling of internal approbation soothes the irritation of the discontented spirit; then all is hopeless, cold, and gloomy, and misery becomes aggravated by the necessity which our pride dictates, of concealing it almost from ourselves. Days listlessly passed, duties neglected, energies subdued, zeal weakened; these were circumstances in the life of the apostolic Nuncio, whose effects he rather felt than understood. He was stunned by the revolution which had taken place in his mind and feeling, by the novelty of the images which occupied his fancy, by the association of ideas which linked themselves in his mind. He would not submit to the analysis of his feelings, and he was determined to conquer, without understanding their nature or tendency. Entombed and chained within the most remote depths of his heart, he was deaf to their murmurs, and resisted their pleadings, with all the despotism of a great and lofty mind, created equally to command others and itself. With the dawn, therefore, of the morning, he issued from his cave, intending to proceed to Sirinagar, determined no longer to confine his views to the conversion of the solitary infidel; but to change, at once, the scene and object, which had lately engrossed all the powers of his being, and to bestow upon a multitude, those sacred exertions, which he had, of late, wholly confined to an individual.

His route to Sirinagar lay near the dwelling of the Priestess. He perceived, at a considerable distance, the train of the Guru returning to his college; Luxima, therefore, was again mistress of her own delicious solitude. The impulse of the man was to return to the grotto, but the decision of the Priest was to proceed, to effect his original intention. As he advanced, the glittering shafts of Luxima's verandahs met his eye, and he abruptly found himself under the cannella-alba tree, beneath whose shade he had last beheld her. He paused, as he believed, to contemplate its luxuriancy and its beauty, which had before escaped his observation. He admired its majestic height, crowned by branches, which drooped with their own abundance, and hung in fantastic wreaths of green and brilliant foliage, mingling with their verdure, blossoms of purple and scarlet, and berries bright and richly clustered. But an admiration so coldly directed, was succeeded by a feeling of amazement and delight, when he observed the date of the day his last interview with Luxima carved on its bark; when he observed, hanging near it, a wreath of the may-hya, whose snowy blossoms breathe no fragrance, and to which an oly-leaf was attached, bearing the following inscription from the Persian of Saddi: "The rose withers, when she no longer hears the song of the nightingale."[57]

The lovely elegance of mind, which thus so delicately conveyed its secret feeling, received a tribute, which the votarist trembled as he presented; and pure and holy lips, which had hitherto only pressed the saintly shrine, or consecrated relic, now sealed a kiss, no longer cold, upon an object devotion had not sanctified. But the chill hand of religion checked the human feeling as it rose; and the blood ran coldly back to the heart, from which, a moment before, it had been impelled, with a force and violence he shuddered to recollect.

Suddenly assuming a look of severity, as if even to awe, or to deceive himself, he hurried on, nor once turned his eye towards the sunny heights which Luxima's pavilion crowned. He now proceeded through the rocky defile, which formed the mouth of the valley, and advanced into an avenue, which extended for a league, and led to various towns, and different pagodas. This avenue, grand and extensive as it was, was yet composed of a single tree; but it was the banyan-tree, the mighty monarch of Eastern forests; at once the most stupendous and most beautiful production of the vegetable world. The symbol of eternity, from its perpetual verdure and perpetual spring, independent of revolving seasons, and defying the decay of time, it stands alone and bold, reproducing its own existence, and multiplying its own form, fresh and unfaded amidst the endless generation it propagates; while every branch, as emulous of the parent greatness, throws out its fibrous roots, and, fastening in the earth, becomes independent, without being disunited from the ancient and original stem. Thus, in various directions, proceeds the living arcade, whose great and splendid order the Architect of the universe himself designed; while above the leafy canopy descend festoons of sprays and fibres, which, progressively maturing, branch off in lighter arches, extending the growing fabric from season to season, and supplying, at once, shade, fruit, and odour, sometimes to mighty legions, encamped beneath its arms; sometimes to pilgrim troops, who make its shade the temple of their worship, and celebrate, beneath its gigantic foliage, their holy festivals and mystic rites. This tree, which belongs alone to those mighty regions, where God created man, and man beheld his Creator, excited a powerful emotion in the bosom of the Missionary as he gazed on it.

✳ It was through the arcades of the wondrous banyan, that a scene finely appropriate struck his view—an Eastern armament in motion, descending the brow of one of the majestic mountains of Sirinagar: the arms of the troops glittering to the sun-beam, flashed like lightning through the dark shade of the intervening woods, while, in their approach, were more visibly seen, elephants surmounted with towers; camels, bearing on their arched necks the gaudy trappings of war; the crescent of Mahomet beaming on the standard of the Mogul legions; and bright spears, and feathery arrows, distinguishing the corps of Hindu native troops; the van breaking from the line to guard the passes, and detachments hanging back in the rear to protect the equipage; while the main body, as if by an electric impulse, halted, as it gradually reached the valley where it was to encamp. This spectacle, so grand, so new, and so imposing, struck on the governing faculty of the Missionary's character—his strong and powerful imagination. He approached with rapid steps the spot where the troops had halted; he observed the commander-in-chief descend from a Tartar horse; he was distinguished by the imperial turban of the Mogul princes, but still more by the youthful majesty of his look, and by the velocity of his movements. Darting from rank to rank, he appeared like a flashing beam of light, while his deep voice, as it pronounced the word of command, was re-echoed from hill to hill with endless vibration. Already a camp arose, as if by magic, among the luxuriant shrubs of the glen. The white flags of the royal pavilion waved over a cascade of living water, and tents of snowy whiteness, in various lines, intersected each other amidst the rich shades of the mango and cocoa-tree; the thirsty elephants, divested of their ponderous loads, steeped their trunks in the fountains; and the weary camel reposed his limbs on banks of odorous grasses. All now breathed shade, refreshment, and repose, after heat, fatigue, and action. Faquirs, and pilgrims, and jugglers, and dancers, were seen mingling among the disarmed troops; and the roll of drums, the tinkling of bells, the hum of men, and the noise of cattle, with the deep tone of the Tublea, and the shrill blast of the war-horn, bestowed appropriate sounds upon the magic scene. As the Missionary gazed on the animated spectacle, a straggler from the camp approached to gather fruit from the tree under which he stood, and the Missionary inquired if the troops he beheld were those of Aurengzebe? "No," replied the soldier; "we do not fight under the banners of an usurper, and a fratricide; we are the troops of his eldest brother, and rightful sovereign, Daara, whom we are going to join at Lahore, led on by his gallant son, the 'lion of war,' Solyman Sheko. Harassed by fatigue, and worn out by want and heat, after crossing the wild and savage mountains of Sirinagar, Solyman has obtained the protection of the Rajah of Cashmire, who permits him to encamp his troops in yonder glen, until he receives intelligence from the Emperor, his father, whose fate is at present doubtful."*

The soldier, having then filled his turban with fruit, returned to his camp.

He who truly loves, will still seek, or find, a reference, in every object, to the state and nature of his own feelings; and that the fate of a mighty empire should be connected with the secret emotions of a solitary heart, and that "the pomp and circumstance of war"[59] should associate itself with the hopes and fears, with the happiness and misery of a religious recluse living in remote wilds, devoted to

---

* The new Emperor Aurengzebe had scarcely mounted his throne near Delhi, when he was alarmed with intelligence of the march of Solyman Sheko, by the skirts of the northern mountains, to join his father, Daara, at Lahore.—DOW, 286.[58]

the service of Heaven, and lost to all the passions of the world, was an event at once incredible—and true!

A new sense of suffering, a new feeling of anxiety, had seized the Missionary, when he understood the gallant son of Daara, the idol of the empire, had come to fix himself in the vicinage of the consecrated groves of the Cashmirian Priestess. He knew that, in India, the person of a woman was deemed so sacred, that, even in all the tumult of warfare, the sex was equally respected by the conqueror and the conquered; but he also knew in what extraordinary estimation the beauty of the Cashmirian women was held by the Mogul princes; and though Luxima was guarded equally by her sacred character and holy vows, yet Solyman was a hero and a prince! and the fame of her charms might meet his ear, and the lonely solitude of her residence lure his steps. This idea grew so powerful on his imagination, that he already believed some rude straggler from the camp might have violated, by his presence, the consecrated groves of her devotion, and, unable to dismiss the thought, he hurried back, forgetful of his intention to visit Sirinagar, and believing that his presence only could afford safeguard and protection to her, who, but a short time back, shrunk in horror from his approach. So slow and thoughtful had been his movements, and so long had he suffered himself to be attracted by a spectacle so novel as the one he had lately contemplated, that, notwithstanding the rapidity of his return, it was evening when he reached the sacred grove; he advanced within view of the verandah, he darted like lightning through every alley or deep-entangled glen; but no unhallowed footstep disturbed the silence, which was only animated by the sweet, wild chirp of the mayana; no human form, save his own, peopled the lovely solitude; all breathed of peace, and of repose. In the clear blue vault of heaven the moon had risen with a bright and radiant lustre, known only in those pure regions, where clouds are deemed phenomena. The Missionary paused for a moment to gaze on Luxima's verandah, and thought that, haply, even then, with that strange mixture of natural faith and idolatrous superstition, which distinguished the character of her devotion, she was worshipping, at the shrine of Camdeo, in the almost inspired language of religious sublimity. This thought disturbed him much; and he asked himself what sacrifice he would not make, to behold that pure but wandering soul, imbued with the spirit of Christian truth; but what sacrifice on earth was reserved for him to make, who had no earthly enjoyment to relinquish? "Yes," he exclaimed, "there is yet one: to relinquish, for ever, all communion with Luxima!" As this thought escaped his mind, he shuddered: had she then become so necessary to his existence, that to relinquish her society, would be deemed a sacrifice? He dismissed the terrific idea, and hurried from a place where all breathed of her, whom he endeavoured to banish from his recollection. As he approached his cave, he was struck by the singular spectacle it exhibited: a fracture in the central part of the roof admitted the light of the moon, which rose immediately above it; and its cloudless rays, concentrated as to a focus, within the narrow limits of the grotto, shone with a dazzling lustre, which was increased and reflected by the pendent spars, and surrounding congelations; while a fine relief was afforded by the more remote cavities of the grotto, and the deep shadow of the œcynum, whose dusky flowers and mourning leaves drooped round its entrance. But it was on the altar, from its peculiar position, that the beams fell with brightest lustre; and the Missionary, as he approached, thought that he beheld on its rude steps, a vision brighter than his holiest trance had e'er been blessed with; for nothing human ever looked so fair, so motionless, or so seraphic. His eye was dazzled; his imagination was bewildered; he invoked his patron saint, and crossed himself; he approached, and gazed, and yet he doubted; but it was no spirit of an higher sphere; no bright creation of religious ecstasy:—it was Luxima! it was the pagan! seated on the steps of the Christian altar; her brow shaded by her veil; her hands clasped upon the Bible which lay open on her knee, and a faint glory playing round her head, reflected from the golden crucifix suspended above it. She slept; but yet so young was her repose, so much it seemed the stealing dawn of doubtful slumber, that her humid eyes still glistened beneath the deep shadow of her scarce-closed lashes: the hue of light which fell upon her features, was blue and faint; and the air diffused around her figure, harmonized with the soft and solemn character of the moonlight cave. The Monk stood gazing, every sense bound up in one; his soul was in his glance, and his look was such as beams in the eye when it snatches its last look from the object dearest to the doting heart, till an involuntary sigh, as it burst from his lips, chased by its echo, the soft and stealing sleep of Luxima. She started, and looked round her, as if almost doubtful of her identity. She beheld the Missionary standing near her, and arose in confusion, yet with a confusion tinctured by pleasurable surprise.

"Luxima!" he exclaimed, in a voice full of softness, and for the first time addressing her by her name. "Father!" she timidly returned, casting down her eyes; then, after a short but touching pause, she added, "Thou wonderest much to see me here, at such an hour as this!"

"Much," he returned: "but, dearest daughter, seeing thee as I have seen thee, I rejoice much more."

"Many days," she said, in a low voice, "many days have fled since I beheld thee; and I prophesied, from the vision of my last night's dream, that thy wound would gangrene, were it not speedily touched by the three sacrificial threads of a Brahmin; therefore came I hither to seek thee, and brought with me thy Christian Shaster, but I found thee not; thinking thou wast performing poojah,[60] near some sacred tank, I sat me down upon thy altar steps, to wait thy coming, and to read thy Shaster; till weariness, the darkness, and the silence of the place, stole upon my senses, the doubtful slumber in which thou didst find me wrapt."

"And dost thou regret," said the Missionary, with a pensive smile, "that the spirit of thy prophecy is false? Or dost thou rejoice, that my wound, which awakened thy anxiety, is healed?" Luxima made no reply—the feeling of the woman, and the pride of the Prophetess, seemed to struggle in her bosom; yet a smile from lips, which on *her* had never smiled before, seemed to excite some emotion in her countenance. And after a short pause, she arose, and presenting him the Scriptures, said, "Christian, take back thy Shaster, for it should belong to thee alone. 'Tis a wondrous book! and full of holy love; worthy to be ranked with the sacred *Veidam*, which the great Spirit presented to Brahma to promote the happiness and wisdom of his creatures." The Missionary had not yet recovered from the confusion into which the unexpected appearance of Luxima, in his grotto, had thrown him; he was, therefore, but ill prepared to address her on a subject so awfully interesting, as that to which her simple, but sacrilegious commentary, led. He stood, for a moment, confounded; but, observing that Luxima was about to depart, he said, "Thou camest hither to seek and to do me a kindness, and yet my presence banishes thee: at least, suffer me to give thee my protection on thy return." As he spoke, they left the grotto together; and, after a long silence, during which, both seemed engaged with their own thoughts, the Missionary said, "Thou hast observed truly, that the inspired work I have put into thy hands is full of holy love; for the Christian doctrine is the doctrine of the heart, and, true to all its purest feelings, is full of that tender-loving mercy, which blends and unites the various selfish interests of

Fear for his well-being

doubting super-natural powers BUT still finding a reasonable explanation for them.

mankind, in one great sentiment of brotherly affection and religious love!"

"Such," said Luxima, with enthusiasm, "is that doctrine of mystic love, by which our true religion unites its followers to each other, and to the Source of all good; for we cannot cling to the hope of infinite felicity, without rejoicing in the first daughter of love to God, which is charity towards man. Even here," she continued, raising her eyes in transport, "in a dark forlorn state of separation from our beloved, we live solely in him, in contemplating the moment when we shall be reunited to him in endless beatitude!"

"Luxima! Luxima!" exclaimed the Missionary, with emotion, "this rhapsody, glowing and tender as it is, is not the language of religion, but the eloquence of an ardent enthusiasm; it bears not the pure and sacred stamp of holy truth, but the gloss and colouring of human feeling. O my daughter! true religion, pure and simple as it is, is yet awful and sublime—to be approached with fear and trembling, and to be cultivated, not in fanciful and tender intimacy, but in spirit and in truth; by sacrifices of the earthly passions, and the human feeling; by tears which sue for mercy, and by sufferings which obtain it." As he spoke, his voice rose; his agitation increased. Luxima looked timidly in his eyes and sighed profoundly: the severity of his manner awed her gentle nature; the rigid doctrines he preached, subdued her enthusiasm. She was silent: and the Monk, touched by her softness and trembling, lest, in scaring her imagination or wounding her feelings, he might counteract the effects he had already, and with such difficulty, produced; or, by personally estranging her from himself, loosen those fragile ties which were slowly drawing her to Heaven; he addressed her in a softened and tender voice: "Luxima, forgive me! if to thy gentle nature, the manners of a man, unused to any intercourse with thy sex, and wholly devoted to the cause for which he sacrifices every selfish feeling; if, my daughter, I say, they appear cold, rigid, and severe; judge not of the *motive*, by the *manner*, nor think that aught, but the most powerful interest in thy temporal and eternal welfare, could move him to a zeal so ardent, as he has now betrayed. Forgive him, then, who, to recall thy wandering mind to truth, would risk a thousand lives. Forgive him, whose thoughts, and hopes, and views, are now, all, all engrossed by thee; who makes no prayer to Heaven, which calls not blessing on thy head; whose life is scarcely more than one long thought of Luxima!" The Missionary stopt, abruptly: never had his zeal for conversion led him before to such excess of enthusiasm, as that he now betrayed; while Luxima, touched and animated by a display of tender and ardent feeling, so sympathetic to her own, exclaimed, with softness and with energy, "O father, thus I also feel towards thee; and yet, to see thee prostrate at the shrine of Brahma, *I* would not see thee changed from what thou art—for thou belongest to thy sublime and pure religion; and thy religion to thee, who art thyself so noble and so true, that, much as I do stand in awe of thee, yet more do I delight to hear, and to behold thee, than any earthly good beside!"

The Missionary pressed his hand to his forehead as she spoke, and drew his cowl over his face. He returned no answer, to a speech, every word of which had reached his inmost heart. Thoughts of a various nature crossed each other in his mind; and those he endeavoured to suppress, were still more dominant than those he sought to encourage. At last a glimmering light fell from the summit of the mound which was crowned by Luxima's pavilion; and denoted that the moment of separation was near. To conceal from Luxima, that Solyman and his army were encamped in her neighbourhood—and yet to warn her of the danger of wandering alone in the consecrated shades of her dwelling; were points, in his opinion, necessary, but difficult, to reconcile. He, therefore, slightly observed, that, as the scattered troops of Daara were proceeding through Cashmire to Lahore, he would, in future, become the guardian of her wanderings, and hover round her path, at sunset, until the absence of the intruders should banish all apprehension of intrusion. Luxima replied to him only by a sigh half suppressed, and by a look, timid, tender, and doubtful; in which a lingering prejudice, mingled with a growing confidence, and feeling, and opinion, fading into each other, still seemed faintly opposed. She half-extended to him a hand which instinctively recoiled from the touch of his; and when he *almost* pressed it, trembled, and hastily withdrew.

Hilarion, as he wandered back, alone, to his grotto, recalled his last conversation with Luxima; and gave himself up to a train of reflection, new as the feelings by which it was inspired. Hitherto he had considered pleasure and sin as inseparably connected, since, to suffer and to resist, was the natural destiny of man: but the Indian Priestess, so pure, though mistaken in her piety; so innocent, and yet so pleasurable in her life; so wholly devoted to Heaven, yet so enjoying upon earth, convinced him that his doctrine was too exclusive; and that there were, in this world, sources of blameless pleasure, which it were, perhaps, more culpable to neglect than to embrace.

"It is impious," he said, "to suppose that God created man to taste bitterness only; it is also folly; since, formed as we are, the existence of evil presupposes that of good: for the suffering we endure is but the loss of happiness we have enjoyed, or the privation of that we sigh for: and, though the pride of human virtue may resist the conviction, yet the energy of intellect, the fortitude of virtue, or the zeal of faith, can have no value in our eyes, but as they lead to the happiness of others, or to our own. The object, even of religion itself, points out to us, a good to be attained, and an evil to be avoided; it prescribes to us as the end of our actions, eternal felicity; nor can a rational being be supposed to act voluntarily, but with a view to his own immediate or distant happiness. That good can indeed alone be termed happiness, which is the most lasting, the most pure; and is not that 'the good which "faith preferreth?"'" At this conclusion he sighed profoundly, and added, "Providence has indeed also placed within our reach, many lesser intermediate enjoyments, and endowed us with strong and almost indestructible propensities to obtain them; but are they intended as objects of our pursuit and acquirement, or as tests by which our imperfect and frail natures are to be tried, purified, and strengthened? Alas! it is instinct to desire; it is reason to *resist!* The struggle is sometimes too much for the imperfection of humanity. Man, to be greatly good, must be supremely miserable; man, to secure his future happiness, must sustain his existing evil; and, to enjoy the felicity of the world to come, he must trample beneath his feet the pleasures of that which is." It was thus that his new mode of feeling was still opposed by his ancient habit of thinking; and that a mind, struggling between a natural bias and a religious principle of resistance, between a passionate sentiment and an habitual self-command, became a scene of conflict and agitation. His restless days passed slowly away, in endless cogitations, equally unproductive of any influence upon his feelings or his life. But when evening came, in all the mildness of her softened glories, peace and joy came with her; for then the form of his Neophyte rose upon his view: her smile of languid pleasure met his eye, her accent of tender softness sighed upon his ear: sometimes moving beside him, sometimes seated at his feet—he spoke, and she listened—he looked on her, and she believed: while he trembled from a twofold cause—to observe, that her mind seemed more engaged with the object who spoke, than with the subject discussed; and that she too frequently appeared to attend to the doctrine, for the sake of him only who preached it. But if in one hour her pure soul expanded to the reception of truth; in the next, it gave up its faculties to a superstition the most idolatrous: if now she pressed to her vestal lips the consecrated beads of the Christian rosary—again she knelt at the shrine of her tutelar idol: when her spiritual guide, affecting a severity foreign to his feelings, reproved the inconsistency of her principles, exposed the folly and incongruity of a faith so vacillating, and urged her openly to embrace, and publicly to profess the Christian doctrine, she fell at his feet—she trembled—she wept. The feelings of the woman, and the prejudices of the idolatress, equally at variance in her tender and erring mind; fearing equally to banish from her sight the preacher, or to embrace the tenets he proposed to her belief; she said, "It were better to die, than to live under the curse of my nation; it were better to suffer the tortures of Narekah,* than on earth to *lose cast*, and become a wretched Chancalas!"[61] As she pronounced these words, so dreadful to an Indian ear, her whole frame became convulsed and agitated. And the Missionary, endeavouring to soothe the emotions he had excited, sought only to recall that mild and melting loveliness of look and air, his admonitions had chased away, or his severity discomposed; while, frequently, to vary the tone of their intercourse, and to give it a home-felt attraction in the eyes of his Neophyte, he led her to speak of the domestic circumstances of her life, of the poetical mysteries of her religion, and the singular usages and manners of her nation. It was in such moments as these, that the native genius of her ardent character betrayed itself; and that she poured on his listening ear, that tender strain of feeling, or impassioned eloquence, which, brightened with all the sublimity of Eastern style, was characterized by all that fluent softness and spirited delicacy, which belongs to woman, in whatever region she exist, when animated by the desire of pleasing *him*, the object of her preference. "And while looks intervened, or smiles,"[62] the pleasure which these interesting conversations conferred on a mind so new to such enjoyments, was secretly and unconsciously cherished by the Missionary, and obviously betrayed, by the soft tranquillity and increasing languor of his manner; by the long and ardent gaze of his fixed eyes; by the low-drawn sigh, which so often lingered on the top of his breath; and by all those traits of pleasurable sensation, which spoke a man, in whose strong mind, rigid principles, and tranquil heart, human feeling, even under the pure and sacred veil

---

* The Brahminical hell.

of religion, was making an unconscious and insidious inroad. Confirmed by the opinion of others, and by his own experience, into a belief of his infallibility, he dared not even to *suspect* himself: yet there were moments when a look of ineffable tenderness, a ringlet wafted by the wind over his cheek, or eyes drawn in sudden confusion from his face, awakened him from his illusionary dream—and then he flew to prayers and penance, for the indulgence of feelings, which had not yet stained his spotless life, by any thought or deed of evil; and, though the sudden consciousness sometimes struck him, that temptation only was the test of virtue, and that nature could not be said to be subdued, till she had been tried—yet he seldom suffered himself to analyze feelings, which perhaps would have ceased to exist, had they been perfectly understood. It was thus, the innate purity of the mind betrayed the unconscious sensibility of the heart, while the passions became so intimately incorporated with the spirit, as to leave their influence and agency almost equal. Frequently seeking, in the sophistry of the heart, an excuse for its weakness, he said, "It is Heaven which has implanted in our nature the seeds of all affection, and the love we bear to an individual is but a modification of that sentiment we are commanded to cherish for the species; and surely that love must be pure, which we cherish, without the wish or hope of gathering any fruit from its existence, but that of the pleasure of loving: the disinterestedness of a Christian may go thus far, but can go no further; the purest of all canonized spirits* has said, "The wicked are miserable, because they are incapable of loving. Love, therefore, is solely referable to virtue; it is by the corruption of passion that it ceases to be love. May we then continue to love, that we may continue to be guiltless!"

CHAPTER IX.

Peace had fled the breast of the man of God! It had deserted him in wilds, which the tumults of society had not reached; it had abandoned him in shades, where the ravages of passion were unknown; and left him exposed to affliction and remorse, in scenes, whose tranquil loveliness resembled that heaven his faith had promised to his hope. He had brought with him into deserts, the virtues and the

---

* Saint Catherine de Gênes.[63]

prejudices which belong to social life, in a certain stage of its progress; and in deserts, Nature, reclaiming her rights, unopposed by the immediate influence of the world, now taught him to feel her power, through the medium of the most omnipotent of her passions. Hitherto, forming his principles and regulating his feelings, by an artificial standard of excellence, which admitted of no application to the actual relations of life; governed by doctrines, whose fundamental tenets militated against the intentions of Providence, by doctrines, which created a fatal distinction between the species, substituted a passive submission for an active exercise of reason, and replaced a positive, with an ideal virtue—he resembled the enthusiast of experimental philosophy, who shuts out the light and breath of heaven, to inhale an artificial atmosphere, and to enjoy an ideal existence.

But Nature had now breathed upon his feelings her vivifying spirit: and as some pleasurable and local sensation, which, at first, quivers in the lip, and mantles on the cheek, gradually diffuses itself through the frame, and communicates a vibratory emotion to every nerve and fibre; so the sentiment, which had, at first, imperceptibly stolen on his heart, now mastered and absorbed his life. He now lived in a world of newly connected and newly modified ideas; every sense and every feeling was increased in its power and acuteness—thoughts passed more rapidly through his mind, and he felt himself hurried away by new and powerful emotions, which he sought not to oppose, and yet trembled to indulge. He had not, indeed, relinquished a single principle of his moral feeling—he had not yet vanquished a single prejudice of his monastic education; to feel, was still with him to be weak—to love, a crime—and to resist, perfection; but the doctrines which religion inculcated and habit cherished, the vows which bigotry exacted, and prejudice observed; while they scrupulously guarded the inviolable conduct of the priest, had lost their influence over the passions of the man. And the painful vibration, between the natural feeling and conscientious principle, left him a prey to those internal and harassing conflicts, which rose and increased, in proportion to the respective exercise and action of a passionate impulse, and a rigid sense of duty.

Thus, among the privations of a week, peculiarly holy in his church, and exclusively devoted to religious exercises, he imposed on himself the most difficult of all restraints, that of abstaining from the society of his dangerous Neophyte; but the restless impatience with which he submitted to the severe and voluntary penance, enhanced every pleasure, and exaggerated every enjoyment, he had relinquished. It more sweetly melodized the voice he languished again to hear. It heightened the lustre of those eyes he sighed again to meet; it endeared those innocent attentions which habit had made so necessary to his happiness; and, by rendering the Indian more dangerous to his imagination than to his senses, invested her with that splendid, that touching ideal charm, which love, operating upon genius, in the absence of its object, can alone bestow.

Dearer to his heart, as she became more powerful to his imagination, her idea grew upon his mind with a terrific influence, disputing with Heaven his nightly vigil and daily meditation. It was in vain that he imposed on himself the law not to behold, or to commune with her for six tedious days: his steps, involuntarily faithful to his feelings, still led him against his better reason to those places, in whose fragrant shades she appeared to him a celestial visitant: sometimes he beheld her at a distance at the confluence of the streams, engaged in the idolatrous, but graceful rites of her half-resigned religion—and then he believed himself commanded by duty to fly to her redemption, and to rescue her from the ancient errors into which his absence again had plunged her; till, suddenly distrusting the impulse which led him towards her presence, he fled from the sight of the dangerous Heathen, and almost wished, that infidelity could assume an appearance more appropriate to its own deformity. Sometimes, when the ardour of the meridian sun obliged her to seek the impervious shades of her consecrated grove, he beheld her reclined on flowers, engaged in the perusal of the religious fables of her poetic faith; and then a recollection of a genius which shone bright and luminous even through the errors which clouded its lustre, mingled itself with the actual impression of her beauty; and he believed a communion with a mind so pure, would counteract the influence, while it added to the charm, of a form so lovely.

But when, from the summit of his rocks, when the moonlight silvered their abrupt points, he beheld her, gliding like a pure and disembodied spirit, through the shades of her native paradise, and, with a timid and uncertain step, moving near the woody path which led to his grotto; her countenance and person characterized by the solicitude of anxious tenderness, and the sadness of disappointed hope; then she appeared to him a creature loving as beloved; then he admitted the blessed conviction, that he had inspired another with that feeling, which had given to him a new sense of being; then he was tempted to throw himself at her feet, and to avow the existence of that passion which he now believed, with a mingled emotion of rapture and remorse, was shared and returned by her who had inspired it. Yet still, habits of religious restraint, even more, perhaps, than religion itself, checked the dangerous impulse; and that ardent sentiment which resisted the force of his reason and the influence of his faith, submitted to the dictates of what might be deemed rather his prejudice than his principle. Shuddering and trembling, he fled from her view, and sought, in the recollection of the infidelity of the Brahminical Priestess, a resource against the tenderness and the charms of the lovely woman. But when, at last, this insupportable absence finally and irresistibly "urged a sweet return;"[64] when the stated exercises of devotion no longer opposed the more active duties of conversion; then love, consecrated by the offices of religion, pursued the object of its secret desire; and, the week of self-denial past, the evening of the seventh day became, to him, the sabbath of the heart. He left the cave of his solitude and his penance, and, with a rapid but unequal step, proceeded towards the fatal stream, on whose flowery shores the Priestess of Brahma still offered up her vesper homage to the luminary, whose fading beam was reflected in the up-turned eyes of its votarist.

As he approached the Priestess and the shrine, his heart throbbed with a feverish wildness unknown to its former sober pulse. Pleasure, enhanced by its recent privation; love, warming as it passed through the medium of an ardent imagination; a consciousness of weakness, cherished by self-distrust; and an apprehension of frailty proportioned to the exaggerated force of the temptation—all mingled a sensation of suffering with the sentiment of pleasure; and the visitation of happiness, to a heart which had of late studiously avoided its enjoyment, resembled that rapid return of health, which is so frequently attended with pain to the exhausted organs; while conscience, awakened by the excess of emotion, dictated a reserve and coldness to the studied manners, to which the ardour of unpractised and impetuous feelings with difficulty submitted. At last, through the branches of a spreading palm-tree, he beheld, at a distance, the object who had thus agitated and disturbed the calmest mind which Heaven's grace had ever visited. She was leaning on the ruins of a Brahminical altar, habited in her sacerdotal vestments, which were rich but fantastic. Her brow was crowned with consecrated flowers; her long dark hair floated on the wind; and she appeared a splendid image of the religion she professed—bright, wild, and illusory; captivating to the senses, fatal to the reason, and powerful and tyrannic to both.

The Missionary paused and gazed—and advanced, and paused, again; till, on a nearer approach, he observed that her eager look seemed to pursue some receding object; that her cheek was flushed, and that her veil, which had fallen over her bosom, heaved to its rapid palpitation. Never before had he observed such disorder in her air, such emotion in her countenance, while the abstraction of her mind was so profound, that she perceived not his approach, till he stood before her: then she started as from the involvement of some embarrassing dream; a soft and unrepressed transport beamed in her eyes, which at once expressed joy, surprise, and apprehension; and the changeful hues of her complexion resembled the dissolving tints of an iris, as they melt and mingle into each other, blending their pale and ruby rays till the vivid lustre fades slowly away upon the colourless air. Pale and smiling as one who was at the same time sad and pleased, she extended her hand to the Missionary, and said, in a voice replete with tenderness and emotion, "My father, thou art then come at last!" While, suddenly starting at the faint rustling of the trees as the wind crept among their leaves, she cast round an anxious and inquiring glance. The Missionary let fall her hand, and, folding his own, he remained silent, and fixed on her a look equally penetrating and melancholy; for the rapture of a re-union so wished for, was now disturbed by doubts, whose object was vague, and embittered by suspicions, whose existence was agony. Luxima, timid and pensive, cast her eyes to the earth, as if unable to support the piercing severity of his gaze; a transient blush mantled on her cheek, and again left it colourless.

"Luxima," said the Missionary, in emotion, "we meet not now, as we were wont to meet, hailing each other with the smile of peace." With eyes which spoke the heart in every glance, and all the precious confidence of innocence and truth, "I would say," he continued, looking earnestly on her, "that, since we parted, something of thy mind's angelic calmness was forfeited, or lost; something of thy bosom's sunshine was shadowed, or o'ercast."

"But thou art here," she returned, eagerly, "and all again is peace and brightness." The Missionary withdrew his eyes from her blushing and eloquent countenance, and cast them on the earth. Her looks made too dangerous a comment on the words her lips had uttered, which he felt were too delightful, and feared were too evasive; which his heart led him to believe, and his reason to distrust;

and, seating himself beside her on the bank where she now
reposed, after a silent pause, which the half-breathed sighs of the
Indian only interrupted, he said,

"Well! be it so, my daughter; be still the guardian of thy bosom's
secret; pure it must be, being thine. I have no right to wrench it
from thee. If it be a human feeling, belonging only to mortality, to
hopes which this world bounds, or thoughts which this life limits,
I, who am not thy temporal, but thy spiritual friend, can have no
claim upon thy confidence. Oh, no! believe me, Luxima, that,
between thee and me, nothing can now, or ever will, exist, but the
sacred cause which first led me to thee."

This he said with a vehemence but little corresponding to the
character he had assumed, and with an air so cold and so severe,
that Luxima, timid and afflicted, had no force to reply, and no
power to restrain her emotions. Drooping her head on her bosom,
she wept. Touched by her unresisting softness, moved by a sadness,
his severity had caused, and gazing with secret admiration on the
grace and loveliness of her looks and attitude, as she chased away
the tears which fell on her bosom, with her long hair, "Luxima,"
he said, in a tone which struggled between his secret emotion, and
assumed coldness, "Luxima, why do you weep? I am not used to
see a woman's tears, save when they fall from hearts which penitence, or grief, has touched; but yours, Luxima—they fall in such
tender softness: dearest daughter, have I offended you?"

"'Tis true," said Luxima, cheered by the increasing tenderness
of his manner, "thou art so grandly good, so awful in thy excellence, that, little used to wisdom or to virtue so severe, I fear thee
most, even when most I—" She paused abruptly, and blushed; then
raising her eyes to his, a soft confidence seemed to grow upon their
gaze, and, with that fatal smile that so changed the character of her
countenance, from the sedate tranquillity of the Priestess to the
bashful fondness of the woman, she said, "Father, with us the divine
wisdom is not personified, as cold, severe, and rigid; but as the
infant twin of love, floating in gay simplicity in the perfumed dews
which fill the crimson buds of young camala-flowers."*

"Luxima," he returned, seduced into softness by her tender
air, "if I am in look and word severe, such are my habits; but my
heart, dear daughter, at least I fear to thee, is too, too weak; and,
when I see thee sad, and am denied thy confidence—" He paused;

---

* It is thus Brahma is represented in his avatar of divine wisdom.

and the rainbow-look of Luxima changing as she spoke, she replied:

"I am, indeed, not quite so happy as I have been. Once my lip knew no mystery, my heart no care, my brow no cloud; but, of late, I strive to hide my thoughts even from myself. I oft am sad, and oft regret the glorious death they robbed me of; for, oh! had I expired upon my husband's pyre, in celestial happiness with him I should have enjoyed the bliss of Heaven while fourteen Indras reign."[65]

The Missionary started as she pronounced this rhapsody; a new pang seized his heart, and made him feel as if the deadly drop, which lurks beneath the adder's fang, had been distilled into a vital artery: for Luxima had loved, since Luxima lamented even that dreadful death itself, which, in her own belief, would have united her eternally to the object for whom her passion still seemed to survive.

"Luxima," he said coldly, "till now I never knew you loved; but though you had, a woe so idle and so causeless, as that you cherish for a long-lost object, is sanctioned neither by sentiment nor duty, by reason nor religion."

"Had he lived," said Luxima, with simplicity, "it would then have been no sin to love."

"Bound to a vestal life," returned the Missionary, changing colour, "like me devoted to eternal celibacy, can *you* lament an object who would have loved you with a *human passion*; with such a love as should not even be dreamed of in a vestal's thoughts?"

"He was my husband," said Luxima, turning away her eyes, and sighing.

"Not by religion's holy law," replied the Missionary, in a hurried tone of voice; "for forms idolatrous and wild but mock the sacred name; not by the law of sentiment, for no endearing intercourse of heart and soul blended your affections in one indissoluble union, for ye were almost strangers to each other; he saw thee but in childhood, and not, as now, a woman!—and so lovely!" He paused, and a deep scarlet suffused even his brow.

"He was at least," said Luxima, with mild firmness, "*my husband* according to the law and the religion of my country."

"But if you have abandoned that religion," returned the Missionary, "the ties it formed are broken, and with them should their memory decay."

"Abandoned it!" repeated Luxima, shuddering, and raising her eyes to heaven. "O Brahma!!"

"Luxima," said the Missionary, sternly, "there is no medium; either thou art a Pagan or a Christian; either I give thee up to thy idols, and behold thee no more, or thou wilt believe and follow me."

"Then I will believe and follow thee," she replied quickly, yet trembling as she spoke.

"O Luxima! would I could confide in that promise! for, through thee alone, I count upon the redemption of thy nation."

"Father," she returned, "a miracle like *that*, can only be performed by thee. Look as I have seen thee look—speak as I have heard thee speak;—give to others that new sense of truth, which thou hast given to me:—and then—"

"Luxima," interrupted the Missionary, in great emotion, "you are misled, my daughter; misled by the ardour of your gratitude, by an exaggerated sense of powers which belong not to man, but to Heaven, whose agent he is. The power of conversion rests not exclusively with me; in you it might effect more miracles than I have ever manifested."

Luxima waved her head incredulously. "Never," said she, "shall I become the partner of thy pious labours! and should I even appear as thy proselyte, if I were not looked on with horror, I should at least be considered with indifference."

"With indifference!" he repeated, throwing his eyes over the perfect loveliness of her form and countenance: "Luxima, is there on earth a being so divested of all human feeling, as to behold, to hear thee with indifference?"

"Art thou not such a one?" demanded Luxima, with a timid and trembling anxiety of look and voice.

"I, Luxima!—I—" he faltered, and changed colour; then, after a momentary pause, casting down his eyes, he resumed, "To be divested of all faculty of sense, were it possible, would be a state of organization so fatal and so imperfect, as to leave the being thus formed equally without the wish and without the power of becoming virtuous; for virtue, the purest, the most severe, and, O Luxima! by much the most difficult to attain, is that virtue which consists in the conquest over the impulses of a frail and perverse nature, by religion and by reason. Thinkest thou then, dearest daughter, that it belongs to *my* nature, being man, to live divested of all human feeling, of all human passion; to behold, with perfect insensibility, forms created to delight; to listen with perfect indifference to sounds breathed to enchant; and that when, upon thy cheek, the crimson hues of modesty and pleasure mantle and mix their soft suffusion; when in thy eyes, rays of languid light—Luxima! Luxima!" he continued vehemently, and in confusion, "I repeat to thee, that there can be no virtue where there is no temptation; no merit, but in resistance; but in an entire subjection, through religion, of those feelings which, by a sweet but dread compulsion, drag us towards perdition. And, oh! if trial be indeed the test of virtue, I at least may hope to find some favour in the sight of Heaven, for my trials have not been few." As he spoke, his whole frame trembled with uncontrollable emotion, and the paleness of death overspread his face.

Luxima, moved by an agitation in one, who had hitherto appeared to her eyes superior to human feeling, and to human weakness, was touched by an emotion so accordant to the tender softness and ardent sensibility of her own character; and timidly taking his hand, and looking with an half-repressed fondness in his eyes, she said, "Art thou then also human? Art thou not all-perfect by thy nature? I thought thee one absorbed in views of heaven, resembling the pure spirit of some holy Saneasse, when, having passed the troubled ocean of mortal existence, it reaches the Paradise of Kylausum, and reposes in eternal beatitude, at the foot of *Him* who is clothed with the *fourteen worlds*."[*]

The Missionary withdrew his hand, and reposing on it his head, remained for some time lost in thought; at last he said, "Luxima, have you then among your people such men as you have now described; who, by a perfect abstraction of mind, live divested of all human feeling, and who, walking through life in a state of rigid self-denial, renounce all its enjoyments, from a conviction of their vanity? Can a religion so false as theirs produce an effect so perfect? And can the most powerful sensations, the most tyrannic passions incident to the very constitution of our natures, making an inseparable part of our structure, connected and interwoven with all the powers of existence—can they submit and bend to the influence of *opinion*; to an idea of excellence originating in, and governed by, a fatal and fanatic superstition; but worthy, from its purity and elevation, to be the offspring of that *grace*, which comes alone from Heaven?"

Luxima replied, "It is written in the Vaides and Shastries, whose light illuminates the earth, that '*the resignation of all pleasure is better than its enjoyment*;' and that he who resists the passions of his nature shall be planted in the world of *daivers*, or pure spirits; there to enjoy eternal bliss. And *one such* person I knew; who having abandoned all

---

[*] Paraubahzah Vushtoo, or First Cause.

earthly attachments, and broken all earthly ties, lived remote from man, absorbed in the contemplation of the *Divine Essence:* never had his lip imbibed the refreshing beverage of the delicious *caulor,* or the juice of newly-gathered fruits; never had he inhaled the odour of morning blossoms, nor bathed in the cool wave which smiles to the light of the night-flower-loving god; never had he pillowed his sacred brow with the downy leaves of the *mashucca,* nor pressed the hand of affection, nor listened to the voice of fondness; and his eye, fixed on earth or raised to heaven, still met no objects but such as tended to chasten his thoughts, or to elevate his soul;— till one day a *holy woman,* devoted to the service of her religion, ascended the high hill, where the hermit dwelt in peace. She came, with others, in faith and sanctity, to ask his meditation with Heaven, according to the custom of her nation. The woman departed edified from his presence, for she had communed with him on the subject of the nine great luminaries, which influence all human events;—but the soul of the hermit pursued her in secret; *he* whose infant hand grasps the lightning's flash,* the god of the flowery bow, had touched the cold, pure thought of the recluse with a beam of his celestial fire:—*he loved!*—but he loved a *vestal priestess,* and therefore was forbidden all hope. The Faquir pined in sadness, and sought to wash away his secret fault in the holiest wave which purifies the erring soul from sin; and the *goddess* of the *eight virgins* received him in her consecrated bosom.† Doubtless he is now one of the *daivers,* the saints, who, by the voluntary sacrifice of moral life, obtain instant admittance to the heavenly regions." Luxima sighed as she concluded her little tale.

The Missionary echoed her sigh, and raising a look of sadness to her pensive countenance, he demanded, "And knew the vestal priestess the secret of the hermit's love?"

"Not until he had passed into the world of spirits; and then a wandering yogi, who had received his last words ere he plunged into the Ganges, brought her, at his desire, a wreath of faded flowers:‡ the red rose of passion was twined with the ocynum, the

---

* The Indian Cupid is frequently represented armed with a flash of lightning.

† Gungee, the presiding deity of the Ganges: she has eight vestal attendants, which personify the eight principal rivers in Hindoostan.

‡ Flowers have always been the tasteful medium for the eloquence of Eastern love: like the Peruvian quipas, a wreath, in India, is frequently the record of a life.[66]

flower of despondency; and the fragile mayhya, the emblem of mortality, drooped on the camalata, the blossom of heaven. The faded wreath thus told the love and fate of him who wove it."

"And this fatal priestess, Luxima?" said the Missionary, with an increased emotion, showing there was a nerve in his heart, which vibrated in sympathy to the tale she told. Luxima made no reply to the doubtful interrogatory; and the Missionary, raising his eyes to her face, perceived it crimsoned with blushes, while her tearful eyes were fixed on the earth. He started—grew pale; and, covering his face with his hands, after a long silence, he said, "Luxima! thy Hermit was a virtuous though a most misguided man; his temptation to error was powerful; the virtue of resistance was his, and the crime of self-destruction was the crime of his dark and inhuman superstition—terrific and fatal superstition! in all its views injurious to society, and pernicious to the mortal nature of man, which thus offers a soothing but impious alternative to the human suffering, and the human woe; which thus, between infamy and an almost impossible resistance to a clear and fatal temptation, offers a final resource beyond all which reason can bestow, or time effect; beyond all, save that which religion proffereth; and thus alluring the worn, the weary, and long-enduring life to its own wished-for *immolation*, crowns and conceals the fatal act beneath a host of bright illusions, and offers to the suicide rewards, which should belong to him alone who dares to *live* and *suffer*, who feels and who resists; and who, though impelled by passion, or seduced by sentiment, still restrains the wish, corrects the impulse, and rules and breaks the stubborn feeling nature breathed into his soul when it was first quickened, that, by this daily death, he might ensure that life which is eternal. If, Luxima, there lived such a man, thus enduring and thus resisting, would you not give him your applause?"

"I would give him my pity," said Luxima, raising her hands and eyes in great emotion.

The Missionary replied with a deep sigh, "You would do well, my daughter; it is pity only he deserves." Then, after a long pause, he said firmly, "Luxima, I came hither this evening to commune with thee upon that great subject, which should alone unite us; but the mysterious emotion in which I found thee wrapt, distracted thoughts, which are not yet, I fear, all Heaven's; nor did thy little story, dearest daughter, serve to tranquillize or soothe them; for, in the mirror of another's faults, man, weak and erring, may still expect to see the sad reflection of his own. But now the dews of evening fall heavily, the light declines, and it is time we part; and, O Luxima! so long as we continue thus to meet, thus may we ever part, in the perfect confidence of each other's virtue, and each other's truth." He arose as he spoke.

Luxima also arose; she moved a few paces, and then paused, and raised her timid eyes to his, with the look of one who languishes to repose some confidence, yet who stands awed by the severity of the elected confidant.

The Missionary, who now studiously avoided those eloquent looks of timid fondness, whose modesty and sensibility so sweetly blended their lovely expressions, withdrew his eyes, and fixed them on the rosary he had taken from his breast, with the abstracted air of one wrapt in holy meditation. Thus they walked on in silence, until they had reached the vicinage of Luxima's habitation. There, as was his custom, the Missionary paused, and Luxima turning to him said, "Father, wilt thou not bless me, ere we part?" The Missionary extended his pastoral hands above her seraph head; the blessing was registered in his eyes, but he spoke not, for his heart was full. Luxima withdrew, and he stood pursuing, with admiring eyes, her perfect form, as she slowly ascended to her pavilion: then turning away as she disappeared, he sighed convulsively, as one who gives breath to emotion after a long and painful struggle to suppress or to conceal it. His thoughts, unshackled by the presence of her to whom they pointed, now flowed with rapidity and in confusion; sometimes resting on the mysterious emotion he had observed in the countenance and air of the ingenuous Indian; sometimes on the suicide Hermit; and sometimes on himself, on his past life, his former vows, and existing feelings; but these recollections, conjured up to soothe and to confirm, served but to disquiet and to agitate; and thus involved in cogitation, slow and lingering in his step, he involuntarily paused as he reached the bank, whose elastic moss still bore the impression of Luxima's light form. He paused and gazed on the altar of her worship; it was to him as some sad memorial, whose view touches on the spring of painful recollection; and the pang which had shot through his heart, when for a moment he had believed her false as the religion at whose mouldering shrine she stood, again revived its painful sensation, like the memory of some terrific vision, which long leaves its shade of horror upon the awakened mind, when the dream which gave it has long passed away from the imagination. There is no love where there is no cause for solicitude; and the first moment when hope and fear slumber in the perfect consciousness of exclusive and unalienable possession, is perhaps the first moment when the calm of indifference dawns upon the declining ardour of passion. To the eye of philosophy it would have been a curious analysis of the human heart, to have observed the workings of a strong and solitary feeling, in a character unsophisticated and unpractised; to have observed a passion, neither cherished nor opposed by any external object, feeding on its own vitals, and seeking instinctively to maintain its own vivacity, by fancying doubts for which it had no cause, and forming suspicions for which it had no subject. Still in search of some hidden reason for the restless conflicts of his unhappy mind, the Missionary stood musing and gazing on the spot where the mysterious emotion of Luxima had excited that painful, suspicious, and indefinite sentiment, of whose nature and tendency he was himself ignorant. He could fear no rival in that consecrated solitude, which his presence alone violated; but he was afflicted to believe that Luxima could muse, when he was not the subject of her reverie; that Luxima could weep, when he caused not her tears to flow; that Luxima could be moved, touched, agitated, and he not be the sole, the powerful cause of her emotion. It is this exacting, tyrannic, and exclusive principle which forms the generic character of a true and unmixed passion: it is this feeling by which we seek and expect to master and possess the whole existence of the object beloved, which distinguishes a strong, ardent, and overwhelming sentiment, from those faint modifications of the vital feeling, which serve rather to amuse than to occupy life; to interest rather than absorb existence. It is thus that love, operating upon genius, is assisted by the imagination, which creates a thousand collateral causes of hope and fear, of transport and despair; which, in moderate characters, find no existence, and which, at once fatal and delightful, are the unalienable inheritance of natural and exquisite sensibility, of a peculiar delicacy of organization, and of those refined habits of thought and feeling to which it gives birth.

While thus occupied, creating for himself ideal sources of pain and pleasure, the twilight of evening was slowly illumined by the silver rising of a cloudless moon; which threw upon the shining earth the shadow of his lofty figure; it tinged with living light the crystal bosom of the consecrated waters; it scattered its rays upon the motionless foliage of the night-loving sephalica, and found a bright reflection in some object which lay glittering amidst the fragments of the ruined altar. When the heart is deeply involved, every sense allies itself to its feelings, and the eye beholds no object, and the ear receives no sound, which, in their first impression, awakens not the master pulse of emotion. The Missionary saw, in the beaming fragment, some ornament of the sacerdotal vestments of the Brahminical Priestess. Considering it as more consecrated by her touch than by the purposes to which it had been devoted, he stooped, and blushed as he did it, to rescue and preserve it;— but it was no gem sacred to religious ornament; it made no part of the insignia worn by the children of Brahma; it was the *silver crescent* of Islamism; it was the device of the disciples of Mahomet; the ornament worn in the centre of the turban of the Mogul officers; and deeply impressed on its silvery surface, obvious even to a passing glance, and engraven in Arabic characters, was the name of the heroic and imperial Prince Solyman Sheko.

The Missionary saw this, and saw no more; a tension in his brow, a sense of suffocation, as though life were about to submit to annihilation; a pulse feeble and almost still, limbs trembling, and eyes which no longer received the light, left him no other voluntary power than to throw himself on the earth; while the strong previous excitement produced, for a few seconds, a general diminution of the vital action; and he lay as though death had given peace to those feelings which nothing in life could at the moment soothe or assuage. From this temporary suspension of existence he was roused by the sound of horses' feet: he startled; he arose, and sprung forward in that direction whence the sound proceeded: he perceived (himself unseen, amidst the trees) a person on horseback, who, standing in his stirrup, and shading his eyes from the lustre of the moonlight, cast round an anxious and inquiring glance, then approached within the hallowed circle of the Brahminical altar.

The Missionary rushed from his concealment—the paleness of his countenance rendered more livid by the moonlight which fell on it, and by the dark relief of his black cowl and flowing robe. He stood, amidst the ruins of the heathen shrine, resembling the spirit of some departed minister of its idolatrous rites, the terrific guardian of the awful site of ancient superstition. Whatever was the impression of his abrupt and wild appearance, the effect was instantaneous: ere he had uttered a sound, the stranger suddenly disappeared, as if borne on the wings of the wind. The Missionary in vain pursued his flight. After having followed the sounds of the horse's feet, till a deathlike silence hung upon their faded echo, the sole result of his observation was, that the mysterious intruder had fled towards the Mogul camp, which still lay in the plains of

Sirinagar; and the sole inference to be drawn from the singular adventure was, that Luxima was beloved by the son of the imperial Daara—that Luxima was false—and that he was most deceived! This conviction fell on him like a thunderbolt. Thoughts of a new and gloomy aspect now rushed on each other, as if they had been accelerated by the bursting of some barrier of the mind, which, till that moment, had retained them in their natural course. He could not comprehend the nature of those frightful sensations which quivered through his frame—that deadly sickness of the soul with which the most dreadful of all human passions first seizes on its victim. His mind's fever infected his whole frame—his head raged—his heart beat strongly; and all the vital motions seemed hurried on, as if their harmony had been suddenly destroyed by some fearful visitation of divine wrath. He threw himself on the dewy earth, and felt something like a horrible enjoyment, in giving himself up, without reservation, to pangs of love betrayed, of faith violated, of a jealousy, whose fury rose in proportion to the loveliness of its object, and to the force and ardour of the character on which it operated. His memory, faithful only to the events which aimed at his peace, gave back to his imagination Luxima in all her bewitching tenderness, in all the seduction of her seeming innocence: he felt the touch of her hand, he met the fondness of her look; his heart kindled at her blush of love, and melted at her voice of passion. He beheld her, bright and fresh, at the rising sun—tender and languid at its setting; but by him these delights of a first and true love were now only remembered to be resigned—these joys, which he had almost purchased with the loss of heaven, could now no longer live for him. Another would gaze upon her look, and meet her caress, and answer to her tenderness; another would send his hopes forth, with the rising and the setting sun: but for him there was no longer a morning, there was no longer an evening! all was the sad gloom of endless night. In a mind, however, such as his, to doubt one moment, was to decide the next—his sole, his solitary, his tyrannic passion, becoming its own retribution, would, he believed, accompany him to the grave; its object, he determined to resign for ever. To strengthen him in his intention, he opposed the holy calm, the sacred peace, the heavenly hopes and solemn joys of his past and sinless life, to the sufferings, the conflicts, the conscious self-debasement of his late and present existence. He remembered that he was the minister of Heaven; devoted, by vows the most awful and the most binding, to its cause alone; and that he had come into perilous and distant regions, to preach its truths, not by precept only, but by example, and to substitute, in the land of idolatry, the religion of the Spirit, for that of the senses. He sought pertinaciously to deceive himself, and to mistake the feelings which rose from the pangs of jealousy, for the visitation of conscience, suddenly awakened from its long and death-like slumber, by the fatal consequences of that intoxicating evil, which had so long entranced and "steeped it in forgetfulness."[67] He sought to believe that his guardian angel had not yet abandoned him, and that Heaven itself, by miraculous interposition, had snatched him from an abyss of crime, towards which, an ardent and unguarded zeal for its sacred cause had insensibly seduced him. Struck by the conviction, he prayed fervently, and vowed solemnly; but his prayers and his vows alike partook of the vehemence of those contending passions by which he was moved and agitated. He wept upon the cross he pressed to his lips—but his tears were not all the holy dew of pious contrition; religion became debtor to the passions she opposed, and the ardour of his devotion borrowed its warmth and energy from the overflowing of those human feelings it sought to combat and to destroy. At last his emotions, worn out by their own force and activity, subsided into the torpor of extreme exhaustion. Throwing himself upon the earth, encompassed by those deep shades of darkness which precede the twilight dawn of day, he slept; but his slumber was broken and transient, and the dreams it brought to his disordered imagination were harassing to his spirits as the painful vigil which had preceded them; for the affliction which is deep rooted in the heart, which presses upon the vital spring of self-love, and disturbs the calm of conscientious principle, blasting hope, rousing remorse, and annihilating happiness, sets at defiance the soothing oblivion of sleep. Nature, thus opposed to herself, in vain presents the balmy antidote to the suffering she has inflicted—and the repose she offers, flies from the lids her unregulated feelings have sullied with a tear.

CHAPTER X.

The day arose brightly upon the valley of Cashmire. It came in all the splendid majesty of light, bathing in hues of gold the summits of the Indian Caucasus: it came in all the renovating influence of warmth, raising the blossom the night-breeze had laid low; it shed the dews of heaven upon the towering head of the mighty banyan, and steeped in liquid silver the flowers of the vesanti creeper; pervading, with a genial and delicious power, the most remote recess, the most minute production of nature, and pouring upon the face of the earth, the beneficent influence of that Being from whose word it proceeded. But the day brought no solace in its dawn, no joy in its course, to him, who, in the scale of creation, came nearest in his nature to the Creator;—it brightened not his thoughts; it revived not his hopes; and, for him, its beams shone, its dews fell, in vain.

The minister of the religion of peace arose from his harassing slumber with an heart heavy and troubled, with a frame chilled and unrefreshed. He arose, agitated by that vague consciousness of misery, which disturbs, without being understood, when the mind, suddenly awakened from the transient suspension of its powers, has not yet regained its full vigour of perception, nor the memory collected and arranged the freshly traced records of some stranger woe, and when the faculty of suffering, alone remains to us in all its original force and activity. Agitated by the tumults of passion, distracted by the suspicions of jealousy, torn by the anguish of remorse, and humbled by the consciousness of weakness, the Missionary now felt the full extent of his progressive and obstinate illusion, in the consequences it had already produced; he felt that the heart which once opens itself to the admission of a strong passion, is closed against every other impression, and that objects obtain or lose their influence, only in proportion as they are connected with, or remote from, its interest. Love was now to him what his religion had once been, and the strongest feeling that rules the human heart stood opposed to the most powerful opinion which governs the human mind:—the conflict was terrific, and proportioned in obstinacy and vigour to the strength of the character in which it was sustained. Knowing no solace in his misery but what arose from the belief that the secret of his weakness was known only to Heaven and to himself, he resolved not to trust its preservation to the issue of chance; but, ere the dreadful passions which shook his soul could realize their fatal influence in crime; ere the fluctuating emotions which degraded his mind could resolve themselves into iniquity; ere he debased the life which sin had not yet polluted, or broke the vows which were revered, even while they were endangered, he determined to fly the scenes of his temptation, and to cling to the cross for his redemption and support. Yet still, with an heart vibrating from the recent convulsion of its most powerful feelings, he remained irresolute even in his resolution. Convinced of the imperious necessity which urged him to leave, for ever, the object of a passion which opposed itself equally to his temporal and to his eternal welfare; to leave for ever, those scenes which had cherished and witnessed its progress; he still doubted whether he should again, and for the last time, behold her, whose falsehood it was his interest to believe, and his misery to suspect. Now governed by conscience and by jealousy; now by tenderness and passion—the alternate victim of feeling and religion, of love and of opinion; he continued (wretched in his indecision) to wander amidst the voluptuous shades of his perilous seclusion; hoping that chance might betray him into the presence of his dangerous and faithless disciple, and vowing premeditatedly to avoid her, or to behold her only to upbraid, to admonish, and to leave her for ever. The day, as it passed on, vainly told to his unheeding senses its rapid flight in all the sweet gradation of light and odour, in beams less ardent, and in gales more balmy; till the Missionary, unconsciously descending a path worn away through a gigantic mass of pine-covered rocks, found himself, at the setting of the sun, near the too well remembered stream of evening worship. He started and shuddered, and involuntarily recoiled; and that fatal moment when he had first seized the up-raised arm of the idolatrous Priestess, rushed to his recollection: the hour—the place—the stream which had since so often reflected in its course the pastor and the proselyte—the tree which had so often shaded their fervid brows when the glow which suffused them was not all the influence of season—the sun, whose descending beam had so often been the herald of their felicity—all looked, all was now, as it had been then, unaltered and unchanged. The Missionary gazed around him, and sighed profoundly: "All here," he said, "still breathes of peace, as when, myself at peace with all the world, I first beheld this scene of tranquil loveliness. All here remains the same. O man! it is then thy dreadful prerogative alone, to sustain that change of all thy powers which leaves thee a stranger to thyself, lost in the wild vicissitude of feelings, to which thy past experience can prove no guide, thy reason lend no light: one fixed immutable law of harmony and order, regulates and governs the whole system of unintelligent creatures; but thou, in thy fatal pre-eminence, makest no part in the splendid mechanism of nature: exclusive and distinct among the works of thy Creator, to thee alone is granted a self-existing principle of intellectual pain; a solitary privilege of moral suffering. Vicegerent of Heaven! thou rulest all that breathes, save only thyself: and boasting a ray of the divine intelligence, thou art the slave of instinct, thy principle of action a selfish impulse, and thy restraint an inscrutable necessity."—He paused for a moment, and raising his eyes to the sun, which was descending in all the magnificence of retiring light, still apostrophizing the species to which he belonged, and whose imperfections he felt he epitomized in himself, he continued: "That orb, which rises brightly on thy budding hopes, sets with a changeless lustre on their bloom's destruction; but, in the brief interval of time in which it performs its wonted course, in uninterrupted order, what are the sad transitions by which the mind of man is subject! what are the countless shades of hope and fear, of shame and triumph, of rapture and despair, by which he may be depressed or elevated, ennobled or debased!" He sighed profoundly, as he concluded a picture of which he was himself the unfortunate original; and, withdrawing his eyes from the receding sun, he threw them, with the looks of one who fears an intrusion upon his solitary misery, in that line where a gentle rustling in the leaves had called his attention. The branches, thick and interlaced, slowly unclasped their folds, and thrown lightly back on either side, by a small and delicate hand, the Priestess of Brahma issued from their dusky shade; her form lighted up by the crimson rays of that life-giving power, to which she was at this hour wont to offer her vesper homage. She had that day officiated in the Pagoda, where she served, and she was habited in sacerdotal vestments, but there was in her look more of the tender solicitude of an expecting heart, than the tranquil devotion of a soul which religion only occupied. Advancing with a rapid, yet doubtful step, she cast round her eyes with a look timid, tender, and apprehensive, as if she wished and feared, and hoped and dreaded the presence of some expected object—then pausing, she drew aside her veil, lest the almost impalpable web should intercept the fancied sound which expectation hung on. Thus, as she stood animated by suspenseful love, glowing with the hues of heaven, her up-held veil floating, like a sun-tinged vapour, round her; she looked like the tender vision which descends upon Passion's dream, like the splendid image, to whose creation Genius entrusts its own immortality.

O woman! Nature, which made you fair, made you fairest in the expression of this her best feeling; and the most perfect loveliness of a cold insensibility becomes revolting and deformed, compared to that intelligence of beauty which rushes upon the countenance from the heart that is filled with a pure and ardent affection: then thought breathes upon the lip, independent of sound; and the eye images in a glance, all that the soul could feel in an age!

Unseen, though haply not unexpected, the Missionary stood lost in gazing, and finely illustrated the doctrine which gave birth to his recent soliloquy; for in a moment, thought was changed into emotion, and musing into passion; resolves were shaken, vows were cancelled, sufferings were forgotten; on earth he saw only her, whom a moment before he had hoped never to behold again; and from the world of feelings which had torn his heart, one only now throbbed in its rapid pulse—it was the consciousness of being loved! He saw it in the look, intently fixed upon the path he was wont to take: he saw it on the cheek which lost or caught its colouring from sounds scarce audible: he saw it in the air, the attitude; he saw it in the very respiration, which gave a tremulous and unequal undulation to the consecrated vestment which shaded, with religious mystery, the vestal's hallowed bosom. Sight became to him the governing sense of his existence; and the image which fascinated his eye, absorbed and ruled every faculty of his mind. A moment would decide his destiny—the least movement, and he was discovered to Luxima: a look turned, or a smile directed towards him, and the virtues of his life would avail him nothing.— He trembled, he shuddered!—Love was not only opposed to religion, to reason—in his belief, it was at that moment opposed to his eternal salvation! Suddenly struck by the horrible conviction, he turned his eyes away, and implored the assistance of that Heaven he had abandoned. The voice of Luxima came between him and his God. His prayer died, unfinished, on his lips. He paused, he listened; but that voice, sweet and plaintive as it was, addressed not him—its murmuring sounds, broken and soft, seemed only intended for another; for one who had sprung from behind a clump of trees, and had fallen at her feet—It was the Prince Solyman Sheko!! The Missionary stood transfixed, as though a blast from Heaven had withered up his being!

Luxima, apparently agitated by amazement and terror, seemed to expostulate; but in a voice so tremulous and low, that it scarcely could have reached the ear it was intended for.

"Hear me," said the Prince, abruptly interrupting her, and holding the drapery of her robe, as if he feared she would escape him; "hear me! I who have lived only to command, now stoop to solicit; yet it is no ordinary suitor who pleads timidly at thy feet, desponding while he supplicates—it is one resolved to know the *best* or *worst*—to conquer thee, or to subdue himself. Amidst the dreams of glory, amidst the tumults of a warrior's life, the fame of thy unrivalled beauty reached my ear. I saw thee in the temple of thy gods, and offered to thee that homage thou dost reserve for them. From that moment my soul was thine. Thy loveliness hung upon me like a spell; and still I loitered 'midst the scenes thy presence consecrates, while duty and ambition, my fame and glory, vainly called me hence. Thy absence from the temple where thou dost preside, not more adoring than adored; thy holy seclusion, which all lament, and none dare violate, which even a Mussulman respects, blasted my hopes and crossed my dearest views: till yesterday a mandate from my father left to my heart no time for cool deliberation. With the shades of evening I sought the consecrated grove forbidden to the foot of man; and for the first time presented myself to eyes whose first glance fixed my destiny. Amazed and trembling, thou didst seem to hear me in pity and disdain; then thou didst supplicate my absence—yet still I lingered; but thou didst weep, and I obeyed the omnipotence of those sacred tears—yet, ere I reached the camp, I cursed my weakness, and, listening only to my imperious passion, returned to seek and sue, perhaps, to conquer and be blessed! But in thy stead, I saw, or fancied that I saw, some prying Brahmin, some jealous guardian of the vestal Priestess, placed in these shades to guard and to preserve her from the unhallowed homage of human adoration, as if none but the God she served was worthy to possess her. For thy sake, not for mine, I fled: but now, while all thy brethren are engaged, performing in their temples their solemn evening worship, I come to offer mine to thee. The sun has *their* vows—thou hast mine. They offer to its benignant influence, prayers of gratitude. Oh! let mine cease to be prayers of supplication; for I, like them, am zealous in my idolatry; and thus, like them, devote what yet remains of my existence to my idol's service." He ceased, and gazed, and sighed.

Luxima had heard him in silence, which was only interrupted by broken exclamations of impatience and apprehension; for her attitude imaged the very act of flight. The averted head, the advanced step, the strained eye, the timid disorder of her countenance, all intimated the agitation of a mind, which seemed labouring under the expectation of some approaching evil. A pause of a moment ensued; and the Prince, construing her silence and emotion as his wishes directed, would have taken her hand. The indignant glance of Luxima met his. There were, in his eyes, more terrors than his words conveyed. She would have fled. The arms of the unhallowed infidel were extended to inclose in their fold the sacred form of the vestal Priestess; but an arm, stronger than his, defeated the sacrilegious effort, and seizing him in its mighty grasp, flung him to a considerable distance. The Mussulman was stunned: amazement, consternation, and rage, mingled in his darkened countenance. He drew a dagger from his girdle, and flew at the intruder—who suddenly darted forward to ward off the death-blow which threatened him; and, seizing the up-raised arm of the infuriate Prince, he struggled with his strength, and wrenching the weapon from the hand that brandished it, flung it in the air. Then, with a look dignified and calm, he said, "Young stranger, thou wouldest have dishonoured thyself, and destroyed me. I have saved thee from the double crime; give Heaven thanks: return whence thou camest; and respect, in future, the sacred asylum of innocence, which thy presence and thy professions alike violate."

The Prince, struck, but not daunted, by a firmness so unexpected, replied, with indignation in his look, and rage storming on his brow, "And who are thou, insolent! who thus darest command? By thy garb and air, thou seemest some adventurer from the West, some wretched Christian, unconscious that, for the first time, thou art in the presence of a Prince."

The large dark eye of the Missionary rolled over the form of the youth in haughtiness and pity. His lips trembled with a rage scarcely stifled, his countenance blazed with the indignant feelings which agitated his mind. He struggled religiously against himself; but the saintly effort was unequal to combat the human impulse—he paused to recover his wonted equanimity of manner, and then returned:

"Who am I, thou wouldest know? I am, like thee, young Prince, a man, alive to the dignity of his nature as man, resolved, as able, to defend it; with sinews no less braced than thine, a heart as bold, an arm as strongly nerved; descended, like thyself, from royal race, and born, perhaps like thee, for toil and warfare, for danger and for conquest: but views of higher aim than those which kings are slaves to, replaced a worldly, with a heavenly object; and he, whom thou hast dared to call a wretch, tramples beneath his feet the idle baubles for which thy kindred steep their hands in brothers' blood; great in the independence of a soul which God informs, and none but God can move!" The Missionary paused—the grandeur of his imperious air fading gradually away, like the declining glories of an evening sky, as all their lustre melts in the solemn tints of twilight. His eyes fell to the earth, and a cast of meekness subdued the fire of their glance, and smoothed the lowering furrow of his close-knit brow.

"Prince," he added, "thou didst ask me, who I am.—I am a Christian Missionary, lowly and poor, who wandered from a distant land, to spread the truth my soul adores, to do what good I can, and still to live in peace and Christian love with thee and all mankind!" He ceased.

Wonder and amazement, shame and disappointment, mingled in the expressive countenance of the Mussulman: he remained silent, alternately directing his glance towards the Missionary, who stood awfully meek and grandly humble before him, and to Luxima, who, faint and almost lifeless, leaned against the trunk of a tree, beaming amidst its dark foliage like a spirit of air, whom the power of enchantment had spell-bound in the dusky shade. The young and ardent Solyman had nothing to oppose to the speech of the Missionary, and offered no reply; but rushing by him, he fell at the feet of the Priestess. "Fair creature," he said, "knowest thou this wondrous stranger, and has he any influence o'er thy mind? for though I hate him as an infidel, yet I would kneel to him, if he could but move thee in my favour."

"And what wouldst thou of a Brahmin's daughter, and a consecrated vestal?" interrupted the Missionary, trembling with agitation; while Luxima hid her blushing face in her veil.

"I would possess her affections!" returned the impassioned Solyman.

"She has none to bestow," said the Missionary, in a faltering voice; "her soul is wedded to Heaven."

"Perhaps thou lovest her thyself," said the Prince, rising from the feet of Luxima, and darting a searching glance at the Missionary; who replied, while a crimson glow suffused itself even to his brow, "I love her in Christian charity, as I am bound to love all mankind."

"And nothing more?" demanded the Prince, with a piercing look.

"Nothing more?" faintly demanded Luxima, turning on him eyes which melted with a tenderness and apprehension, as if her soul hung upon his reply.

"Nothing more!" said the Monk, faintly.

"Swear it then," returned Solyman, while his eyes ran over the anxious countenance of the drooping Neophyte, who stood pale and sad, chasing away with her long hair the tears which swelled to her eyes; "swear it, Christian, by the God you serve."

"And by what compulsion am I to obey thy orders," said the Missionary vehemently, and in unsubdued emotion, "and profane the name of the Most High, by taking it in vain, because a boy desires it?"

"Boy! boy!" reiterated the Prince, his lips quivering with rage; then, suddenly recovering himself, he waved his head, and smiled contemptuously; and turning his eyes on Luxima, whose loveliness became more attractive from the tender emotion of her varying countenance, he said, "Beautiful Hindu! it is now for thee to decide! Haply thou knowest this Christian; perhaps thou lovest him! as it is most certain that he loves thee. I also love thee: judge then between us. With me thou mayst one day reign upon the throne of India, and yet become the empress of thine own people; what he can proffer thee, besides his love, I know not."

"Besides his love!" faintly repeated Luxima; and a sigh, which came from her heart, lingered long and trembling on her lips, while she turned her full eyes upon the Missionary.

"Ah! thou lovest him then?" demanded the Prince, in strong and unsubdued emotion.

"It is my religion now to do so," replied the Indian, trembling and covered with blushes; and chasing away her timid tears, she added faintly, "Heaven has spoken through his lips to my soul."

A long pause ensued; the eyes of each seemed studiously turned from the other; and all were alike engrossed by their own secret emotions. Solyman was the first to terminate a silence almost awful.

"Unfortunate Indian!" exclaimed the Prince, with a look of mingled anger and compassion; "thou art then a Christian, and an apostate from thy religion, and must *forfeit cast.*"

[margin annotation: She is going to be excommunicated.]

At this denunciation, so dreadful, Luxima uttered a shriek, and fell at his feet, pale, trembling, and in disorder. "Mercy!" she exclaimed, "mercy! recall those dreadful words. Oh! I am not a Christian! not *all* a Christian! His God indeed is mine; but Brahma still receives my homage: I am still his Priestess, and bound by holy vows to serve him; then save me from my nation's dreadful curse. It is in thy power only to draw it on my head: for here, hidden from all human eyes, I listen to the precepts of this holy man, in innocence and truth."

The Prince gazed on her for a moment, lovely as she lay at his feet, in softness and in tears; then concealing his face in his robe, he seemed for some time to struggle with himself; at last he exclaimed, "Unhappy Indian, thou hast my pity! and if from others thou hast nought to hope, from me thou hast nought to fear." Again he paused and sighed profoundly; and then, in a low voice, added, "Farewell! Though I have but thrice beheld thy peerless beauty, I would have placed the universe at thy feet, had I been its master; but the son of the royal Daara cannot deign to struggle, in unequal rivalship, with an obscure and unknown Christian wanderer. Yet still remember, should the imprudence of thy Christian lover expose thee to the rage of Brahminical intolerance; or thy apostacy call down thy nation's wrath upon thy head; or should aught else endanger thee; seek me where thou mayest, I promise thee protection and defence." Then, without directing a glance at the Missionary, he moved with dignity away; and mounting a Tartar horse, whose bridle was thrown over the trunk of a distant tree, he was in a moment out of sight.

The Missionary, overwhelmed, as if for the first time his secret were revealed even to himself, stood transfixed in the attitude in which the Prince's last speech had left him; his arms were folded in the dark drapery of his robe; his eyes cast to the earth; and in his countenance were mingled expressions of shame and triumph, of passion and remorse, of joy and apprehension. Luxima too remained in the suppliant attitude in which she had thrown herself at the Prince's feet; not daring to raise those eyes in which a thousand opposite expressions blended their rays. Solyman had called the Missionary her *lover*; and this epithet, by a strange contrariety of feeling and of prejudice, at once human and divine, religious and tender, filled her ardent soul with joy and with remorse. The affectionate, the impassioned woman triumphed; but the pure, the consecrated vestal shuddered; and though she still believed her own feelings resembled the pious tenderness of *mystic love*, yet she trembled to expose them even to herself, and remained buried in confusion and in shame. A long and awful pause ensued, and the silent softness of the twilight no longer echoed the faintest sound; all around resembled the still repose of nature, ere the eternal breath had warmed it into life and animation; but all within the souls of the solitary tenants of shades so tranquil was tumult and agitation. At last, Luxima, creeping towards the Missionary, in a faint and tender voice, pronounced the dear and sacred epithet of "Father!" He started at the sound, and, turning away his head, sighed profoundly. "Look on me," said Luxima, timidly; "it is thy child, thy proselyte, who kneels at thy feet; the wrath of Heaven is about to fall heavily on her head; the gods she has abandoned are armed against her; and the Heaven, to which thou hast lured the apostate, opens not to receive and to protect her." She took the drapery of his robe as she spoke, and wept in its folds. She was struck to the soul by the cold resistance of his manner; and beholding not the passions which convulsed his countenance, she guessed not at those which agitated his mind. The instinctive tenderness and delicacy of a woman, whose secret has escaped her, ere an equal confidence has sanctioned the avowal of her love, was deeply wounded; and not knowing that man, who has so little power over the mere impulse of passion, could subdue, confine, and resist the expressions of his sentiments, she believed that the unguarded discovery of her own feelings had awakened the abhorrence of a soul so pure and so abstracted as the Christian's; and, after a pause, which sighs only interrupted, she added, "And have I also sinned against thee, for whose sake I have dared the wrath of the gods of my fathers; and, in declaring the existence of that divine love, enchanting and sublime, which thou hast taught me to feel, that mysterious pledge for the assurance of heavenly bliss, by which an object on earth, precious and united, yet distinct from our own soul, can—"

"Luxima! Luxima!" interrupted he, in wild and uncontrollable emotion, nor daring to meet the look which accompanied words so dangerous, "cease, as you value my eternal happiness. You know not what you do, nor what you say. You are confounding ideas which should be eternally distinct and separate: you deceive yourself, and you destroy me! The innocence of your nature, your years, your sex, the purity of your feelings, and your soul, must save you; but I! I!—Fatal creature! it must not be! Farewell, Luxima!—O Luxima! on earth at least we meet no more!" As he spoke, he disengaged his hand from the clasp of hers, and would have fled.

"Hear me," she said, in a faltering voice, and clinging to his robe; "hear me! and then let me die!"

The Missionary heard and shuddered: he knew that the idea of death was ever welcome to an Indian's mind; and, that the crime of suicide to which despair might urge its victim, was sanctioned by the religion of the country, by its customs and its laws.* He paused, he trembled, and turning slowly round, fearfully beheld almost lifeless at his feet, the young, the innocent, and lovely woman, who, for his sake, had refused a throne; who, for his sake, was ready to embrace death. "Let you die, Luxima?" he repeated, in a softened voice; and seating himself on a bank beside her, he chased away with her veil, the tears which hung trembling on her faded cheek—"Let you die?"

---

* To quit life, before it quits them, is among the Hindus no uncommon act of heroism; and this fatal custom arises from their doctrine of metempsychosis, in which the faith of all the various casts is equally implicit.

"And wherefore should I live?" she replied with a sigh. "Thou hast torn from me the solace of my own religion; and, when I lose thee, when I no longer look upon or hear thee, who can promise that the faith, to which thou hast won me from the altars of my ancient gods, will remain to soothe my suffering soul? and, O father! though it should, must I worship alone and secretly, amidst my kindred and my friends; or, must I, by a public profession of apostacy, lose my cast, and wander wretched and an alien in distant wilds, my nation's curse and shame? Oh! no; 't were best, ere that, I died! for now I shall become a link between thy soul and a better, purer state of things; spotless and unpolluted, I shall reach the realms of peace, and a part of thyself will have gone before thee to the bosom of that great Spirit, of which we are alike emanations. O father!" she added, with a mixture of despair and passion in her look and voice, "'t were best that *now* I died; and that I died for *thee*."

"For me, Luxima! for me!" repeated the Missionary, in a frenzied accent, and borne away by a variety of contending and powerful emotions—"die for me! and yet it is denied *me* even to *live* for thee!—And live I not for thee? O woman! alike fatal and terrific to my senses and my soul, thou hast offered thy life as a purchase of my secret—and it is thine! Now then, behold prostrate at thy feet, one who, till this dreadful moment, never bent his knee to aught but God alone; behold, thus grovelling on the earth, the destruction thou hast effected, the ruin thou hast made! behold the unfortunate, whose force has submitted to thy weakness; whom thou hast dragged from the proudest eminence of sanctity and virtue, to receive the law of his existence from thy look, the hope of his felicity from thy smile; for know, frail as thou mayest be, in all thy fatal fondness, he is frailer still; and that thou, who lovest with all a seraph's purity, art beloved with all the sinful tyranny of human passion, strengthened by restraint, and energized by being combatted. Now then, all consecrated as thou art to heaven; all pure and vestal by thy vows and life; save, if thou canst, the wretch whom thou hast made; for, lost alike to heaven and to himself, he looks alone *to thee* for his redemption!" As he spoke, he fell prostrate and almost lifeless on the earth: for two days no food had passed his lips; for two nights no sleep had closed his eyes; passion and honour, religion and love, opposed their conflicts in his mind; nature sunk beneath the struggle, and he lay lifeless at the feet of her who had for ever destroyed the tranquility of his conscience, and rendered valueless the sacrifices of his hitherto pure, sinless, and self-denying life.

Luxima, trembling and terrified, yet blessed in her sufferings, and energized by those strong affections which open an infinite resource to woman in the hour of her trial, gently raised his head from the earth and chafed his forehead with the drops which a neighbouring lotos-leaf had treasured from the dews of the morning. He loved her; he had told her so; and she again repeated in her felicity, as she had done in her despair, "It were best that I now died!" *"I've exposed myself, and now it's time for me to die" Luxima.*

CHAPTER XI.

Slowly restored to a perfect consciousness of his situation; to a recollection of the fatal avowal, by which he had irretrievably committed himself, and of the singular event which had produced it; the Missionary still lay motionless and silent; still lay supported by the Neophyte which love alone had given him. He dreaded a recovery from the partial suspension of all his higher faculties; he shrank from the obtrusive admonitions of reason and religion, and sought to perpetuate an apparent state of insensibility, which gave him up to the indulgence of a passive but gracious feeling, scarcely accompanied by any positive perception, and resembling, in its nature and influence, some confused but delightful dream, which, while it leaves its pleasurable impression on the senses, defies the accuracy of memory to recall or to arrange it. His heart now throbbed lightly, for it was disburdened of its fatal secret; his mind reposed from its conflicts, for it had passed the crisis of its weakness in betraying it: he felt the tears of love on his brow; he felt an affectionate hand returning the pressure of his; and a sense of a sacred communion, which identified the soul of another with his own, possessed itself of his whole being; and passion was purified by an intelligence which seemed to belong alone to mind. Alive to feelings more acute, to a sensibility more exquisite, than he had hitherto known; all external objects faded from his view for the moment; life was to him a series of ideas and feelings, of affections and emotions: he sought to retain no consciousness, but that of loving and being loved; and if he was absorbed in illusion, it was an illusion which, though reason condemned, innocence still ennobled and consecrated.

Luxima hung over him in silence, and her countenance was the reflection of all the various emotions which flitted over his. The repose which smoothed his brow, communicated to hers its mild and tranquil expression; her pulse quickened to the increasing throb of his temples; and the vital hues which revisited his cheek, rosed hers with the bright suffusion of love and hope. Fearing almost for his life, she bowed her head to catch the low-drawn respiration, and returned every breath of renovating existence with a sigh of increasing joy.

"Luxima!" said a voice, which, though low and tremulous, reached her inmost soul.

"I am here, father!" she replied in emotion, and bashfully withdrawing her arm from beneath a head which no longer needed support.

The Missionary took the hand thus withdrawn, and pressed it, for the first time, to his lips. The modest eyes of the vestal Priestess sank beneath the look which accompanied the tender act: it was the first look of love acknowledged and returned; it penetrated and mingled itself with the very existence of her to whom it was directed; it resembled, in its absorbing and delicious influence, the ecstacy of enthusiasm, which, in the days of her religious illusion, descended on her spirit to kindle and to entrance it; which had once formed the inspiration of the Prophetess, and animated beyond the charms of human beauty the loveliness of the woman. Turning away her glance in timid disorder, she sought for resource against herself in the objects which encompassed her: she threw up her eyes to that heaven, to whose exclusive love she had once devoted herself, and, from a sudden association of ideas, she turned them to the mouldering altar of the god whose service she had abandoned. The religion of her spirit and of her senses, of truth and error, alike returned with all their influence on her soul; and she shuddered as she looked on the shrine where she had once worshipped with a pure, pious, and undivided feeling: the moonlight fell in broken rays upon its shining fragments, and formed a strong relief to their lustre in the massive foliage of a dark tree which shaded it. The air was breathless, and the branches of this consecrated and gigantic tree alone were agitated; they waved with a slow but perceptible undulation; the fearful eyes of the apostate pursued their mysterious motion, which seemed influenced by no external cause: they bowed, they separated, and through their hitherto impervious darkness gleamed the vision of a human countenance! if human it might be called; which gave the perfect image of Brahma, as he is represented in the *Avatar* of "the Destroyer." It vanished—the moon sank in clouds—the vision lasted but a moment; but that moment for ever decided the fate of the Priestess of Cashmire! Luxima saw no more—with a loud and piercing shriek she fell prostrate on the earth.

The Missionary started in horror and amazement; the form which now lay pale and lifeless at his feet, had, an instant before, by its animated beauty rivetted his eyes, absorbed his thoughts, and engrossed his exclusive attention, as half-averted, half-reposing in his arms, it had mingled in its expression and its attitude the tender confidence of innocence and love, the dignified reserve of modesty and virtue; still seeing no object but herself, he remained ignorant of the cause of her emotion, and was overwhelmed by its effects. He trembled with a selfish fondness for a life on which his happiness, his very existence, now depended: he raised her in his arms; he murmured on her ear words of peace and love. He threw back her long dark tresses, that the air might play freely on her face; and he only withdrew his anxious looks from the beauty of her pale and motionless countenance, to try if he could discover, in the surrounding scene, any cause for a transition of feeling so extraordinary; but nothing appeared which could change happiness into horror, which could tend to still the pulse of love in the throbbing heart, or bleach its crimson hue upon the glowing cheek. The moon had again risen in cloudless majesty, rendering the minutest blossom visible: the stillness of the air was so profound, that the faintest sigh was heard in dying echoes. All was boundless solitude and soothing silence. The mystery, therefore, of Luxima's sudden distraction was unfathomable. She still lay motionless on the shoulder of the Missionary; but the convulsive starts, which at intervals shook her frame, the broken sighs which fluttered on her lips, betrayed the return of life and consciousness. "Luxima!" exclaimed the Missionary, pressing the cold hands he held; "Luxima, what means this heart-rending, this fearful emotion? Look at me! Speak to me! Let me again meet thine eye, and hang upon thy voice—fatal eye and fatal voice—my destruction and my felicity! still I woo and fear the return of their magic influence. Luxima, if Heaven forbids our communion in happiness, does it also deny us a sympathy in sorrow? Art thou to suffer alone? or rather, are my miseries to be doubled in my ignorance of thine? Oh! my beloved, if conscience speak in words of terror to thy soul, what has not mine to fear? It is I, I alone, who should be miserable in being weak. Created to feel, thou dost but fulfil thy destiny, and in thee nature contemns the false vow by which superstition bound thee to thy imaginary god. In thee it is no crime to love! in me, it is what I abhor no less than crime—it is sin, it is shame, it is weakness. It is I alone who should weep and tremble; it is I alone who have fallen, and whose misery and whose debasement demand pity and support. Speak to me then, my too well beloved disciple; solace me by words, for thy looks are terrific. O Luxima! give me back that soft sweet illusion, which thy voice of terror dissipated, or take from me its remembrance; give me up at once to reason and to remorse, or bid me, with one look of love, renounce both for ever at thy feet, and I will obey thee! I!—Redeemer of the World! hast thou then quite forsaken him whom thou didst die to save? Is the bearer of thy cross, is the minister of thy word, abandoned by his Saviour? Is he so steeped in misery and sin, that the spirit, which thy grace once enlightened, dares not lift itself to thee, and cry for mercy and salvation? Is the soul, which was tempted to error in its zeal for thy cause, to sink into the endless night prepared for the guilty? Woman! fiend! whatever thou art, who thus by the seeming ways of Heaven leadest me to perdition, leave me! fly me! loose thy fatal hold on my heart, while yet the guilty passions, which brood there, have made me criminal in thought alone."

Luxima shuddered; she raised her drooping head from the bosom which recoiled from supporting her, and she fixed on the agitated countenance of the Monk a look, tender, and reproachful, even through the expression of horror and remorse, which darkened its softness and its lustre. This look had all its full effect; but Luxima shrunk back from the arms which again involuntarily extended to receive and to support her; and, in a solemn and expressive voice, she said, "It is all over!—ere that orb shall have performed its nightly course we shall be *parted for ever*!"

The Missionary was silent, but horror and consternation were in his looks.

Luxima threw round her a wild and timid glance; then creeping toward him, she said, in a low whispering voice, "Sawest thou nothing, some few minutes back, which froze thy blood, and harrowed up thy soul?"

"Nothing," he replied, watching, in strong emotion, the sad wild expression of her countenance.

"That is strange," she returned, with a deep sigh, "most strange!" Then, after a pause, she demanded, with a vacant look, "Where are we, father?"

"Luxima! Luxima!" he exclaimed, gazing on her in fear and in amazement, "what means this sudden, this terrific change? Merciful Heaven! does thy mind wander; or hast thou quite forgotten thine own consecrated shades, the '*confluence of the streams*,' where first the Christian Missionary addressed the Priestess of Brahma? Hast thou forgotten the altar of thy once worshipped god?"

At these words, emphatically pronounced, to steady her wavering recollection, lightning from heaven seemed to fall upon the head of the apostate Priestess; her limbs were convulsed, her complexion grew livid, she threw her eyes wildly round her, and murmuring, in a low quick voice, a Brahminical invocation, she sprung forward with rapid bound, and fell prostrate before the shrine of her former idol. There the Christian dared not follow her: he arose, and advanced a few steps, and paused, and gazed; then, wringing his hands in agony, he said, "Happy in her illusion, she returns to her false gods for support and comfort, while I, debased and humbled, dare not raise my eyes and heart in supplications to the God of Truth." As he spoke, he cast a look on the cross, which hung from his rosary; but it was still humid with tears, which love had shed, it still breathed the odours of the tresses the wind had wafted on its consecrated surface. He shuddered, and let it fall, and groaned, and covered his eyes with his robe, as if he sought to shut out the light of the Heaven he had offended. When again he raised his head, he perceived that Luxima was moving slowly towards him, not, as she had left him, in delirium, and in tears; but in all the dazzling lustre of some newly-awakened enthusiasm; resembling in her motions and her look the brilliant, the blooming, the inspired Prophetess, who had first disturbed his imagination and agitated his mind, in the groves of Lahore; extending her right hand to forbid his approach, she paused and leaned on the branch of a blasted tree, with all the awful majesty of one who believed herself fresh from a communion with a celestial being, and irradiated with the reflection of his glory. "Christian!" she said, after a long pause, "the crisis of human weakness is past, and the powers of the immortal spirit assert themselves:—Heaven has interposed to save its faithless servant, and she is prepared to obey its mandate: a divine hand has extended itself to snatch her from perdition, and she refuses not its aid. Christian! the hour of sacrifice is arrived—Farewell. Go! while yet thou mayest go, in innocence; while yet the arm of eternal destruction has not reached thee. O Christian! dangerous and fatal! while yet I have breath and power to bid thee depart, leave me! The light of the great Spirit has revisited my soul. Even now

I am myself become a *part of the Divinity*." As she spoke, her eyes were thrown up, and the whites only were visible; a slight convulsive smile gleamed across her features; and she passed her right hand from her bosom to her forehead with a slow movement. This mysterious act seemed to bestow upon her a new sense of existence.* Her religious ecstacy slowly subsided—her eyes fell—the colour revisited her cheek—she sighed profoundly, and after a silent pause, she said,

"Christian, thou hast witnessed my re-union to the source of my spiritual being. Oppose not thyself to the Heaven, which opens to receive me: depart from me; leave me now—and for ever."

"Luxima," interrupted the Missionary, in the low wild accent of terror and amazement; and perceiving that some delirium of religious fanaticism had seized her imagination—"Luxima, what means this wondrous resolution, this sudden change? Are all our powers alike reversed? Has thou risen above humanity, or have I fallen below it? And art thou, the sole cause of all my weakness and my shame, to rise upon the ruin thou hast made, to triumph upon the destruction thou hast effected? Part with me now! abandon me in a moment such as this! O Luxima," he added, with tenderness and passion, and in a voice soft and imploring, "am I deceived, or do you love me?"

Luxima replied not, but her whole countenance and form changed their expression: she no longer looked like an inspired sibyl, borne away by the illusions of her own disordered imagination, but like a tender and devoted woman. She advanced; she fell at his feet, and kissed with humility and passion the hem of his robe; but when he would have raised her in his arms, she recoiled from his support, and seating herself on a bank, at a little distance from him, she wept. He approached, and stood near her: he saw in the rapid transitions of her manner, and her conduct, the violent struggles of feeling and opinion, the ceaseless conflicts of love and superstition; he saw imaged in her emotions the contending passions which shook him to dissolution. He sighed heavily, and mentally exclaimed,

"Alas! her virtue derives more strength even from error, than mine from truth: she obeys her ideas of right as a Brahmin; I, as a

---

* This mystery is called the *Matricha-machom*. The Brahmins believe that the soul is thus conducted to the brain, and that the spirit is re-united to the Supreme Being.

Christian, violate and forsake mine." He turned his eyes on Luxima, and percieved that she was now gazing with a look of exquisite fondness on him, tempered with something of melancholy and sadness.

"It is hard," said she, "to look on thee, and yet to part with thee! but who will dare to disobey the mandate of a *God*, who comes in his *own presence to save and to redeem us?*"

"What mean you, Luxima?" interrupted the Missionary, in emotion, and throwing himself beside her.

"Hear me," she returned; "*believe*, and *obey*.—From the moment I first beheld thee, first listened to thee, I have ceased to be myself; thy looks, thy words, encompassed me on every side; it seemed as if my soul had anticipated its future fate, and already fled to accomplish it in thee. I felt that, in ceasing to be near thee, I should cease to exist: therefore I concealed from thee the danger which hung upon our interviews, and all that might lead thee, for thine own sake or for mine, to withdraw from me the heaven of thy presence—but the dream is over! the God whom thou didst teach me to abandon, has this night appeared on earth to reclaim his apostate."

"Luxima! Luxima!"

"Hear me, father! If I live, this night the vision of Brahma, the God whom I forsook, appeared to me amidst the ruins of his own neglected altar!"

"Impossible! impossible!" exclaimed the Missionary vehemently.

"Then," she returned, in a voice which resembled the heart-piercing accent of melancholy madness, "then there lives some human testimony of our interview, and thou art lost! thou, my soul's own idol! Oh! then, fly—for ever fly: let me feel death and shame but once, and not a thousand, thousand times through thy destruction. But, no," she added in a calmer tone; "it was no human form I saw; I have oft before met that awful vision in my dream of inspiration! haply it came to warn me of thy danger, and to save *my* life through *thine*—then go, leave me while yet I have power to say—*leave me!*"

The Missionary heard her in uncontrolled emotion; but without any faith in a fancied event, which he deemed but the vision of her own disordered imagination, influenced by the agitation of her feelings, by the hour, the scene, and by the fanaticism and superstitious horrors which still governed her vacillating mind: but he saw that there was evidently, at that moment, an obstinacy in her illusion, a bigotry in her faith, it would be vain to attempt to dissipate or to vanquish, until a calmer mood of thought and feeling should succeed to their present tumultuous and unsettled state. Less surprised at the nature of her vision, than at the peculiar result of its influence, he could not comprehend the miracle by which she submitted to an eternal separation, at a moment when his mind, broken and enervated, sunk under the tyranny of a passion which had just reached its acmé. But he knew love only as a man, and could not comprehend its nature in the heart of a woman:— with him the existing moment was every thing, but her affection took eternity itself into its compass; and though she could have more easily parted with her life than with her lover, yet she did not hesitate to sacrifice her felicity to his safety, to his glory, and to the hope of that eternal reunion which might await two souls, which crime had not yet degraded; for her tolerant, but zealous, religion, shut not the gates of Heaven against all who sought it by a different path; and consecrating a human feeling, in ascribing to it an immortal duration, love itself enabled her to make the sacrifice religion demanded. The Missionary sought not to subdue the influence of that wild and fervid imagination, which now, he believed, held the ascendant; but he sought to combat the resolution it had given birth to—and gazing on a countenance, where the enthusiasm of religion still mingled with the expressions of tenderness and passion, he said,

"Wondrous and powerful being! equally fatal in thy weakness and thy force, in thy seducing softness, and resisting virtue; wilt thou now, thus suddenly, thus unprepared, abandon me?—now, that thou hast trampled on my religion and my vows; now, that thou hast conquered my habits of feeling, my principles of thinking, subdued every faculty of my being to thy influence, and bereft me of all, save that long latent power of loving passionately—that tyrannic and dreadful capability of an exclusive devotion to a creature frail and perishable as myself, by which thou hast effected my ruin, and changed the very constitution of my nature?"

"Oh, no!" returned Luxima, endeavouring to conceal her tenderness and her tears; "oh, no! Part we cannot. Go where thou mayest, my life must still hang upon thine! my thoughts will pursue thee. Indissolubly united, there is now but one soul between us. But, O father! to preserve that soul pure and untainted—the human intercourse, that dear and fatal symbol of our eternal union, ought, and can, no longer exist; the voice of God and the law of man, alike oppose it: let us not further provoke the wrath of both, let us remember our respective vows, and immolate ourselves to their performance." She arose as she spoke. The tears stood trembling in her inflamed eyes, and that deadly sickness of the soul which ushers in the moment of separation from all the heart holds dearest, spread its livid hues over her cheek, its agony of expression over her countenance.

"Woman! woman!" exclaimed the Missionary, wildly, and seizing her trembling hands, "give me back my peace, or remain to solace me for its loss; give me back to the Heaven from which you have torn me, or stay, stay, and teach me to forget the virtue by which I earned its protection. While yet a dreadful remembrance of my former self remains, you dare not leave me to horror and remorse! You dare not, cold, or cruel, or faithless, as you may be, you dare not say, 'This moment is our last.' O Luxima! Luxima!"— Overcome by a sense of his weakness, he drooped his head upon her hands, and wept. Had not the salvation of his life been the purchase of her firmness and her resistance, Luxima would have granted to the tears of love, what its ardour or its eloquence could now have obtained: but she knew the danger of remaining longer, or of again meeting him in a place, where they had either been discovered by the jealous guardians of her rigid order, or from which they had been warned by a divine intimation. Mingling her tears with his, after an affecting pause, she said, in a low voice, and scarcely articulate from contending emotions,

"To-morrow, then, we shall again meet, when the sun sets behind the mountains: but not here—not here! Oh, no! These shades have become fearful and full of danger to my imagination. But if thou wilt repair to the western arcades of the great banyan-tree, then—" The words died away upon her trembling lips, and she cast round a wild and timid look, as if some minister of Heaven's mercy was near to forbid an appointment, which might be, perhaps, pregnant with destruction to both.

"*And then*," repeated the Missionary, with vehemence and with firmness, "we meet to part *for ever*!—or—*to part no more!*"

Luxima, at these words, turned her eyes on him, with a look of love, passionate and despairing—then, folding her hands upon her bosom, she raised those eloquent eyes to Heaven, with a glance of sweet and holy resignation to its will. This seraph look of suffering and piety operated like a spell upon the frantic feelings of her lover. The arms, extended to detain her, fell back nerveless on his breast. He saw her move slowly away, resembling the pensive spirit of some innocent sufferer, whom sorrow had released from the bondage of painful existence. He saw her light and perfect form, faintly tinged with the moon-ray, slowly fading into distance, till it seemed to mingle with the fleecy vapours of the night: then he felt as if she had disappeared from his eyes for ever, and, turning to her image in his heart, he gave himself up to suffering and to thought, to the alternate influence of passion and remorse.

CHAPTER XII.

The habit of suffering brings not always with it the power of endurance; the nerves, too frequently acted on, become morbid and less capable of sustaining the pressure of a reiterated sensation; and the mind, no longer able to support or to resist a protracted conflict, sinks under its oppression, or by some natural impulse abandons the object of its painful cogitation, and finds relief in the effort of seeking change.

The Missionary had reached the crisis of passion, the feverish paroxysm of long-combatted emotions. He had reached the utmost limits of human temptation and human resistance, and shuddered at the risk he had run and the peril he had escaped. He resembled a wanderer in an unknown land, who reaches a towering and fearful eminence; who beholds at a single glance the dangers he has passed, and those he has still to encounter; and who endeavours to regulate his future course by the inferences of his past experience. That wild delirium of the senses which left him an unpractised victim to their tyranny, subsided in some degree with the absence of that tender and enchanting object who distanced all that his fancy had ever dared to picture of woman's loveliness or woman's love; and his mind, comparatively enabled to think and to decide, with something of its former tone and vigour, gave itself up to a meditation which had for its subject the consequences of that fatal avowal by which he had so irretrievably committed his character and his profession. The mysterious veil which the cold pure hand of religion had flung over his feelings, was now for ever withdrawn, and the frailties of a being once deemed infallible, the passions and weaknesses incidental to his nature as being human, were not only exposed to himself, but were betrayed to others; and to the followers of Brahma and Mahomet, the apostle of Christianity appeared alike frail, alike subdued by passion and open to temptation, as he on whom the light of revealed truth has never beamed. He felt that he had dishonoured the religion he professed, by making no application of its principles to his conduct in the only instance in which his virtue had been put to a severe test; and that the doctrine of opinion had failed practically in its influence upon the interests and feelings of self-love. He could no longer conceal from his awakened conscience, that the proselyte his zeal had sought for Heaven, had become the object of a human passion; of a passion, imprudent in the eye of reason, criminal in the eye of religion; and which, in its nature and consequences, was scarcely referable to any order, or to any state of society; for, by the doctrines of their respective religions, by the laws and customs of their respective countries, they could never be united by those venerated and holy ties, which regulate and cement the finest bonds of humanity, and which obtain from mankind, in all regions of the earth, respect and sanction, as being founded in one of the great moral laws of nature's own eternal code. No Brahmin priest could consecrate an union, sacrilegious according to his habits of thinking and believing. No Christian minister could bless an alliance formed upon the violation of vows solemnly pledged before the altar of the Christian's God. If, therefore, human opinion was of moment to one, whose secret ambition to obtain its favour had rendered even *religion* subservient to its purpose; if the habits, the principles, and the faith of a whole life, held any power over conduct and action in a particular instance; if self-estimation were necessary to the self-love of a proud and lofty character, between the Christian Priest and Heathen Priestess was placed an insuperable bar, which if once removed, risked their exposure to infamy and to shame in this world, and offered, according to their respective creeds, eternal suffering in the next. But the alternative was scarce less dreadful. In the first instance it was deemed impossible, for it was immediate and eternal separation! Reason dictated, religion commanded, even love itself, influenced by pity, admitted the terrific necessity. Yet still passion and nature struggled, and resisted, with an energy and an eloquence, to which the heart, the imagination, and the senses, devotedly listened. Oh! it is long, very long, before the strongest mind, in obedience to the dictates of prudence and of pride, can dismiss from its thoughts the object of an habitual meditation, before it can strike out some new line of existence, foreign to its most cherished sentiments and dearest views. It is long, very long, before we can look calmly into the deserted heart, and behold unmoved a dreary void, where late some image erected by our hopes, filled from the source of pleasure, every artery with the tide of gladness. It is difficult for human reason to argue away passion, by cold and abstract principles, and to substitute the torpor of indifference for the pang of disappointment; but it is still more difficult for human fortitude, though actuated by the highest human virtue, to tear asunder the ties of love, in all their force and vigour, ere habit may have softened their strength, or satiety relaxed their tension. To effect this sudden breaking up of the affections, ere they have been suffered gently to moulder away in the mild and sure decay of consuming time, the silent, certain progress of mortal oblivion, some power more than human is requisite.

On the luxurious shores of the confluence of the streams, with the light of heaven dying softly round them, the air breathing enjoyment, and the earth affording it, the stoicism of the man would not perhaps have continued proof against the charms of the woman. But in darkness, in solitude, and in silence, in a cavern cold and gloomy, religion borrowed a superadded influence from the impression of the senses; and at the foot of the cross, raised by his own hands in the land of the unbelieving, and faintly illuminated by the chill pure rays of an approaching dawn, that season of the day so solemn and so impressive, when passion slumbers, and visions of fear and gloom steal upon the soul, did the Christian Missionary vow to resign for ever, the object of the only human weakness which had disgraced his sinless life. The vow had passed his lips; it was registered in heaven; and nature almost sunk beneath the sacrifice which religion had exacted.

The great immolation resolved on, all that now remained to be effected, was to fly from a spot which he had found so fatal to his pious views, and to pursue the holy cause of the Mission in regions more favourable to its success; but the energy of zeal was subdued or blunted, and a complexional enthusiasm, once solely directed to the interest of Christianity, had now found another medium for its ardour and activity. Scarcely knowing whither to direct his steps, he mechanically inquired from a Goala, whom kindness that morning brought to his grotto with some fruit, the road, which at that season, the caravan passing through Cashmire from Thibet, usually took. The information he received tended to facilitate his departure from Cashmire, for the caravan had halted in the district of Sirinagar.

To behold Luxima for the last time was now all that remained! But the feelings of tenderness and despair, with which this trying interview was contemplated, plunged him in all the pangs of irresolution; vibrating between desire and fear, between the horror of leaving her, unprepared and unexpecting their eternal separation,

P. 72, 73

P. 225, 226, 241 – Presentation
classes
p. 97

p. 16, 19, 20

or of beholding her in love and in affliction, expressing in her beautiful and eloquent countenance, the agony of that tender and suffering heart which, but for him, had still been the asylum of peace and happiness.

At last, a day of conflict and of misery, alternately devoted to an heavenly and an earthly object, now passed in tenderness and grief, and now in supplication and in prayer, hastened to its conclusion! The sun had set—a few golden rays still lingered in the horizon, and found a bright reflection on the snows which covered the mountains of Thibet. It was the hour of *the appointed interview!* The Christian prostrated himself for the last time before the altar, and invoked the protection of Heaven to support him through the most trying effort of his life; to subdue the hidden "man of the heart,"[68] and, upon the ruins of a frail and earthly passion, to raise a sentiment of hope and faith, which should point alone to that eternal recompense reserved for those who suffer and who sustain, who are tempted and who resist. He arose, sublimed and tranquilized, from the foot of the altar. Religion encompassed him with her shield, and poured her spirit on his soul. He took from the altar the Scriptural volume, and placed it on his bosom; and grasping in his right hand the pastoral crosier, he paused for a moment, and gazed around him; then proceeding with a rapid step, he passed, for the last time, the rude threshold of a place which had afforded him so sweet and so fatal an asylum, which had so often re-echoed to his sighs of passion, and resounded to his groans of penitence. Yet once again he paused, and cast back his eyes upon this beloved grotto: but the faded wreath of the Indian Priestess, suspended from one of its projections, caught his glance. He shuddered. This simple object was fatal to his resolutions—it brought to his heart the recollection of love's delicious dawn; the various eras of its successive and blissful emotions. But he wished to meet *her*, on whose brow this frail memento had once exhausted its odours and its bloom, as he had first met her, with eyes so cold, and thoughts so pure and so free from human taint, that even Religion's self might say, "A communion such as this belongs to Heaven!" Yet he withdrew his eyes with a long and lingering look, and sighed profoundly as he retreated. He reached the arcade of the banyans, as the sunbeam reflected from the mountains threw its last light on a dark bower of branches, beneath whose shade he beheld the Indian Neophyte. She was kneeling on the earth, pale, and much changed in her appearance, and seemingly invoking the assistance of Heaven with fervid devotion. No consecrated flower bloomed amidst the dark redundancy of her neglected tresses. No transparent drapery shadowed, with folds of snow, the outlines of her perfect form: her hair, loose and dishevelled, hung in disorder round her; and she was habited in the dress of a Chancalas, or *outcast*—a habit coarse and rude, and calculated to resist the vicissitude of climate to which such unhappy wanderers are exposed. A linen veil partly shaded her head: her muntras were fastened round her arm with an idol figure of Camdeo: from the dsandam which encircled her neck, was suspended a small cross, given to her by the Missionary; and those symbols of faith and of idolatry expressed the undecided state of her mind and feelings, which *truth* taught by *love*, and *error* confirmed by *habit*, still divided—equally resembling in her look, her dress, and air, a Christian Magdalene, or a penitent Priestess of Brahma.[69]

In this object, so sad and so touching, nothing appeared to change the resolutions of the Missionary, but much to confirm them. It was a fine image of the conquest of virtue over passion—and the most tender of women seemed to set a bright example to the firmest of men. Yet, when Luxima beheld him, a faint colour suffused her cheek, her whole frame thrilled with obvious emotion. She arose, and extended her trembling hand—but he took it not; for her appearance awakened sensations of love and melancholy, which, when they mingle, are of all others the most profound; and casting down his eyes, he said,

"I am come, my daughter, in obedience to thy commands, to behold thee for the last time, and to give thee up exclusively to Him, whose grace may operate upon thy soul, without the wretched aid of one so frail and weak as I have proved. Thou wearest on thy breast, the badge of that pure truth which already dawns upon thy soul. Take also this book—it is all I have to bestow; but it is all-sufficient for thy eternal happiness." He paused, and the emotion of his countenance but ill accorded with the coldness of his words.

Luxima took the book in silence: something she would have said, but the words died away on her trembling lips; and she raised her eyes to his face, with a look so tender, and yet so despairing, that the Missionary felt how fatal to every resolution he had formed, another such look might prove.

Averting his eyes, therefore, and extending his hands over her head, he would have spoken—he would have blessed her—he would have said, "Farewell for ever!" but the power of articulation had deserted him. Again he tried to speak, and failed; his lips trembled, his eyes grew dim, his heart sickened, and the agonies of death seemed to convulse his frame. Luxima still clung to his arm. Had the lifeblood flowed from her bosom, beneath the sacrificial knife, her countenance could not have expressed more acute anguish. He sought, by a feeble effort, to release himself from her grasp: but he had not power to move; and the mutual glance which mingled their souls at the moment they were about to part for ever, operated with a force they had no longer power to resist. Faint and pale, Luxima sunk on his bosom. At that moment, sounds came confusedly on the winds, and growing louder on the ear, seemed to pierce the heart of the Indian. She started, she trembled, she listened wildly; and then with a shriek, exclaimed,

"So soon, so soon, does death overtake me. Now then, now, farewell for ever! Leave me to die, and save thyself!" As she spoke, she would have fallen to the earth, but that the Missionary caught her in his arms. All the powers of life seemed to rush upon him; a vague idea of some dreadful danger which threatened the object of his pity and his love, roused and energized his mind and nerved his frame. He no longer reasoned, he no longer resisted. Obedient only to the impulse of the immediate feeling, he bore away his lifeless charge in his arms, and plunging into the deepest shades of the banyan, endeavoured to reach a dark pile of towering rocks, whose sharp high points still caught a hue of light from the west, and among whose cavities he hoped to find refuge and concealment. The mists of evening had hid from his view a mighty excavation, which he now entered, and perceived that it was the vestibule of an ancient Pagoda: its roof, glittering with pendant stalactites, was supported by columns, forming a magnificent colonnade, disposed with all the grand irregularity which Nature displays in her greatest works, and reflecting the images of surrounding objects, tinged with the rich and purple shade of evening colouring. This splendid portico opened into a gloomy and terrific cavern, whose half-illuminated recess formed a striking contrast to the exterior lustre. Pillars of immense magnitude hewn out of the massive rocks, and forming an imperishable part of the whole mighty mass, sustained the ponderous and vaulted ceiling: receding in the perspective, they lost their magnitude in distance, till their lessening forms terminated in dim obscurity, and finely characterized the awful mystery of the impervious gloom. Idols of gigantic stature, colossal forms, hideous and grotesque images, and shrines emblazoned with offerings, and dimly glittering with a dusky lustre, were rudely scattered on every side. For the Missionary had borne the

Priestess of Brahma to the temple in which she herself presided: the most ancient and celebrated in India, after that of Elephanta. This sanctuary of the most awful superstition, worthy of the wildest rites of a dark idolatry, was now wrapt in a gloom, rendered more obvious by the faint blue light which issued from the earth, in a remote part of the cavern, and which seemed to proceed from a subterraneous fire,[*] which burst at intervals into flame, throwing a frightful glare upon objects in themselves terrific.

The Christian shuddered as he gazed around him: but every thought, every feeling of the lover and the man, was soon concentrated to the object still supported in his arms, and who he believed and hoped, in this sad and lonely retreat, had nothing to apprehend from immediate danger. Life again reanimated her frame, but she was weak and faint, and an expression of terror was still marked on her features. He placed her near a pillar, which supported her drooping form, and flew to procure some water from a spring, whose gushing fall echoed among the rocks; when the sound of solemn music, deep, sad, and sonorous, came upon the wind, which at intervals rushed through the long surrounding aisles of the cavern, disturbing with their hollow murmurs the death-like silence of the place. The Missionary listened: the sounds grew louder; they were no longer prolonged by the wind; they came distinctly on the ear; they were accompanied by the echo of many footsteps; and hues of light thrown on the darkness of the rocks, marked the shadows of an approaching multitude. The Missionary rushed back to his charge: she had raised her head from the earth, and listened with the air of a maniac to the increasing sounds.

"Unfortunate as innocent," he said, encircling her with his extended arms, "there is now, I fear, no refuge left thee but this. O Luxima! thy danger has re-united us, and I am alike prepared to die for or with thee." As he spoke, a blue phosphoric light glanced on the idols near the entrance of the Pagoda: it proceeded from a large silver censer, borne by a venerable Brahmin, who was followed by a procession of the same order, each Brahmin holding in his hand a branch of the gloomy and sacred ocynum, the symbol of the dreadful ceremony of *Brahminical excommunication*. The procession,

---

[*] The vapour of naphtha which issues through the crevices of the earth, is supposed to be the cause of the flame which is sometimes observed in India. At Chittagong is a fountain which bursts into flame, and which has its tutelar deities and presiding priests. When it is purposely extinguished, it rekindles spontaneously.

which passed near the pillar, by whose deep shadow the unfortunate victims who thus had rushed upon destruction, stood concealed, was closed by the venerable Guru of Cashmire; he was carried in a black palanquin, and his aged countenance was stamped with the impress of despair. The Brahmins circled round the subterraneous fire, each in his turn flinging on its flame the leaves of the sandal-tree and oils of precious odour. The kindling flames discovered on every side, thrones, columns, altars, and images; while the priests, dividing into two bands, stood on each side of the fire, and the Guru took his place in the centre of his disciples.

All now was the silence of death, and the subterraneous fire spread around its ghastly hues: the chief of the Brahmins, then prostrating himself before the shrine of Vishnu, drew from his breast the volume of the sacred laws of MENU, and read the following decree, in a deep and impressive voice: "Glory be to Vishnu! who thus speaks by the mouth of his Prophet Menu.* He who talks to the wife or the widow of a Brahmin, at a place of pilgrimage, in a consecrated grove, or at the confluence of rivers, incurs the punishment of guilt; the seduction of a guarded Priestess is to be repaid with life: but if she be not only guarded, but eminent for good qualities, he is to be burnt with the fires of divine wrath!"[71] At these words the solemn roll of the tublea, or drum of condemnation, resounded through the temple; and when the awful sound had died away in melancholy murmurs, two Brahmins coming forward, made their depositions of the guilt of the chief Priestess of the temple. They deposed, that, passing near the sacred grove which led to the pavilion of the Priestess, they observed issuing from its shades the Mogul Prince Solyman—that, induced by their zeal for the purity of their sacred order, they repaired at the same hour on the following evening to the place of her evening worship, where they had discovered the Brachmachira, not indeed as they had expected, with the worshipper of Mahomet, but with a Frangui or Impure, who has already endeavoured to seduce some of the children of Brahma to abandon the God of their fathers; that they found her supporting the infidel in her arms—a circumstance sufficient to confirm every suspicion of her guilt, and to call for her excommunication, or forfeiture of cast. The sanctity, the age and reputation of the Brahmins, gave to their testimony a weight which none dared dispute. It was now only reserved for the Guru

---

* See translation of the Laws of Menu, by Sir William Jones.[70]

to pronounce sentence on his grand-daughter. He was supported by two Yogis.[72] A ghastly and livid hue diffused itself over his countenance; and in his despairing look were mingled with the distracted feelings of the doting parent, the superstitious horrors of the zealous Priest. Thrice he essayed to pronounce that name, hitherto never uttered but with triumph; and to heap curses upon that beloved head, on which blessings and tears of joy had so often fallen together. At last, in a low, trembling, and hollow voice, he said,

"Luxima, the Brachmachira of Cashmire, Chief Priestess of the Pagoda of Sirinagar, and a consecrated vestal of Brahma, having justly forfeited cast, is doomed by the word of Brahma, and the law of Menu, to become Chancalas, a wanderer, and an outcast upon earth!—with none to pray with her, none to sacrifice with her, none to read with her, and none to speak to her; none to be allied by friendship or by marriage to her, none to eat, none to drink, and none to pray with her. Abject let her live, excluded from all social duties; let her wander over the earth, deserted by all, trusted by none, by none received with affection, by none treated with confidence—an apostate from her religion, and an alien to her country, branded with the stamp of infamy and of shame, the curse of Heaven and the hatred of all good men."*

The last words died on the lips of him who pronounced them; and the unfortunate grandsire fell lifeless in the arms of his attendants. The conch, or religious shell, was then blown with a blast so shrill and loud, that it resembled the sound of the last trump; the tublea rolled, and was echoed by endless reverberations; hideous shouts of superstitious frenzy mingling their discordant jar, ran along the mighty concave like pealing thunderbolts, until gradually these sounds of terror fainted away in sobbing echoes; and the awful procession departed from the temple to the same solemn strains, in the same order in which it had entered it. All was again silent, awful, and gloomy; like the night which preceded creation, or that which is to follow its destruction. The subterraneous fires still faintly emitted their flame above the surface of the earth, and threw their mystic light on the brow of the excommunicated Priestess. She lay lifeless on the earth, where she had fallen during the conclusion of the ceremony of her excommunication, with a shriek so loud and piercing, that the horrid crash of sounds, which

---

* Such is the form of the Indian excommunication.[73]

at that moment filled the Pagoda, could alone have drowned her shrill and plaintive voice, or prevented the discovery of her situation to the ministers of the temple. The Missionary knelt beside her, watching, in breathless agony, the slow departure and fading sounds of the procession. When all was still, he turned his eyes on the Outcast; he saw her lying without life or motion, cold and disfigured, and, save by him alone, abandoned and abhorred by all. Thus lost, thus fallen, he beheld her in a place where she had once received the homage of a deity: he saw her an innocent and unoffending victim, offered by himself, by his mistaken zeal and imprudent passion, on the altar of a rigid and cruel superstition: his brain maddened as he gazed upon her, for he almost believed her tender heart had broken its life-chords, under the pressure of feelings and sufferings beyond the power of human endurance; and, in this dreadful apprehension, all capability of thought or action alike deserted him. Alike bereaved of reflection or resource, alike destitute of effort or energy, he remained mute, agonized, and gazing on the object of his tenderness and his despair. At last a sigh, soft, yet convulsive, breathed from the lips of Luxima, and seemed to operate on his frame like electricity: it was a human sound, and it dispelled the dead-like silence of all around him; it was the accent of love and sorrow, and his heart vibrated to its respiration. He raised the sufferer in his arms; he addressed to her soothing murmurs of love and pity, of hope and consolation. At the sound of his voice, she raised her eyes, and gazed, with a look of fear and terror, round her, as if she expected to meet the forms, or to hear the voices, of the awful ministers of her malediction; but the moment which succeeded was cheaply purchased, even by its preceding horrors. She turned back her languid eyes in despair, believing herself abandoned alike by Heaven and earth, but she fixed them in transport on him who was now her universe; her whole being received a new impulse from the look which answered to her own.

"Thou art safe! thou art near me!" she exclaimed, in a sobbing accent; and, falling on his shoulder, she wept. Some moments of unbroken silence passed away, devoted to emotions too exquisite and too profound to be imaged by words. Where a true and perfect love exists, there is a melancholy bliss in the sacrifices made for its object; and the tender Indian was now soothed, under her affliction, by the consideration of him for whose sake she had incurred it: for to suffer, or to die, for him she loved, was more precious to her feelings, than even to have enjoyed security and life, independent of his idea, his influence, or his presence. But equal to sustain her own miseries, she was overpowered by the fate which remotely threatened him; and in a moment when her affection rose in proportion to the peril he risked for her sake, she resolved on the last and greatest sacrifice the heart of woman could make to effect his safety, by again urging his flight, and resigning him for ever. Gazing on him, therefore, with a melancholy smile, which love and agony disputed, she said, "My father and my friend! a creature avoided and abhorred by all, labouring under the curse of her nation and the wrath of Heaven, has no alternative but to submit to a fate, which she can neither avert nor avoid: but for thee, who hast incurred the penalty of a crime, of which thou art innocent, and which thy pure soul abhors, a life of safety and of glory is yet reserved. A law, which seems dictated by cruelty, is always reluctantly executed by the gentle and benevolent Hindus; and they shudder to take the life which they yet forbear not to render miserable. Provoke not then their wrath by thy presence, but fly, and live for those most happy and most blessed, who shall meet thy looks and hang upon thy words. For me, my days are numbered—sad and few, they will wear away in some trackless desert; where, lost to my cast, my country, and my fame, death, welcome and wished for, shall yet find my soul wedded to one deathless bliss, the bliss of knowing I was beloved by thee." As she spoke, her head drooped on the trembling hands which were clasped in hers; her tears bathed them. A long and an affecting pause ensued.

A thousand feelings, opposite in their nature and powerful in their influence, seemed to struggle in the bosom of the Missionary: a thousand ideas, each at variance with the other, seemed to rush on and to agitate his mind. At last, withdrawing the hand which trembled in hers, and with the look and voice of one whose soul, after a long tumultuous conflict, is wound up to unalterable resolution, he said, "Luxima, I am a Christian, and a priest, and I am bound by certain vows to Heaven, from the observance of which no human power can absolve me; but I am also a man; as such, led by feeling, impelled by humanity, and bound by duty, to aid the weak and to succour the unfortunate:—but when I am myself the cause of sorrow to the innocent! of affliction to the unoffending!—O Luxima!" he passionately added, "lost to thee for ever, as lover or as husband, thinkest thou that I can also abandon thee as pastor and as friend? Hast thou then, my daughter, the courage to leave for ever the temples of thy God, and the land of thy forefathers? Art thou so assured of thyself and of me, as to follow me through distant regions, to follow me as my *disciple only;* to take up the cross of Christianity, and to devote what remains of thy young and blooming life exclusively to Heaven? Luxima, wilt thou follow me to Goa?"

"Follow *thee?*" wildly and tenderly repeated the Indian. An hysteric laugh burst from her lips, a crimson blush rushed over her face, and again deserting it, left it colourless. "Follow thee! O Heaven! *through life to death!*"

The Missionary arose: he averted his eyes from the fatal eloquence of hers: he paced the temple with an unequal but rapid step; he seemed wrapt in thoughts wild and conflicting. At last, turning to Luxima, he fixed his eyes on her face, and said, with a voice firm, solemn, and impressive, "Daughter, it is well! from this moment I am thy guide on earth to heaven—no more!"

"No more!" faintly repeated Luxima, casting down her looks and sighing profoundly. Then, after a short pause, the Missionary extended his hand to raise her; but suddenly relinquishing the trembling form he supported, he moved away. Luxima, with a slow and feeble step, followed him to the entrance of the temple; but, as they reached together the extremity of the cavern, the blue light of the subterraneous fire flashed on an image of Camdeo, her tutelar deity. She started, involuntarily paused before the idol, and bowed her head to the earth.

The Missionary threw on her a glance of severe reproof, and, taking her hand, would have led her on; but this little image had touched on the chord of her most profound feelings, and awakened the most intimately associated ideas of her mind.

"Father," she said, in a timid supplication of look and voice, "forgive me; but here, in this spot, no less an idol than that at whose shrine I bow—my nation's pride and sex's glory—here did I devote myself to Heaven; and becoming the Priestess of mystic love, here did I renounce, by many a sacred vow, all human passion and all human ties."

"Luxima," he replied, still leading her on, "such as were thy vows, such *are* mine; let us alike keep them in our recollection, and renew them in our hearts. O my daughter! let us more than tacitly renew them in our hearts; let us together kneel, and—"

"*But not here, father!*" tremulously interrupted Luxima, looking fearfully round her—"not here!"

"No," he replied, and shuddered as he spoke, "not here!"

In silence, and with rapid steps, they passed beneath the frowning and gigantic arch, which hung its ponderous vault above the threshold of the Pagan temple; to its impervious gloom, its mysterious obscurity, succeeded the sudden brightness of the moonlight glen, in whose lovely solitudes the awful pile reared its massive heights, to intercept the rising, or catch the parting beam of day. Here the proscribed wanderers paused; they listened breathlessly, and gazed on every side; for danger, perhaps death, surrounded them: but not a sound disturbed the mystic silence, save the low murmurs of a gushing spring, which fell with more than mortal music from a mossy cliff, sparkling among the matted roots of overhanging trees, and gliding, like liquid silver, beneath the network of the parasite plants. The flowers of the Mangoosten gave to the fresh air a balmy fragrance. The mighty rocks of the Pagoda, which rose behind in endless perspective, scaling the heavens, which seemed to repose upon their summits, lent the strong relief of their deep shadows to the softened twilight of the foreground.

"All is still," said the Missionary, pausing near the edge of the falling stream, and relinquishing the hand he had till now clasped; "all is still, and spirits of peace seem to walk abroad, to calm the tumult of human cares, to whisper hope, and to inspire confidence. My daughter, eternity is in these moments. The brief and frail authority of man, reduced to its own insignificance, holds no jurisdiction now, and the spirit ascends free and fearless to the throne of its Creator." The Missionary stood gazing on the firmament as he spoke, his soul mingling with the magnificent and sublime objects he contemplated; then, turning his eyes on Luxima, he was struck with the peculiar character of her air and person. She looked, as she stood at a little distance, half hid in the mists of shade, like some impalpable form, which imaged on the air the spirit of suffering innocence, in the first moment of its ascent to heaven. Her head was thrown back, and a broken moonbeam, falling through the trees, encompassed it with a faint glory: the tears of human suffering had not yet dried upon her cheek of snow; but it was the only trace of human feeling visible: her soul seemed to commune with him of whom it was an emanation.

"Luxima," said the Missionary, approaching her, "the moment of thy perfect conversion is surely arrived: in spirit thou belongest to Him who died to save thee; be then his also by those rites, which, in a place like this, he thought it not beneath him to receive, from the hands of one by whom he was preceded, as the star of the morning ushers in the radiance of the rising sun. O my daughter!

ere together we commence our perilous and trying pilgrimage, we have need of all the favour which Heaven's mercy can afford us, for we have much to dread, from others and ourselves; let then no tie be wanting which can bind us faster to virtue and religion. Luxima, innocent and afflicted as thou now art, pure and sublime as thou now lookest, feelest thou thyself not worthy to become a Christian in form as in faith?"

"If *thou* thinkest me not unworthy," she replied, in a low voice, "that which thou art, I am willing to be."

The Missionary led her forward, in silence, to the edge of the spring, and blessing the living waters as they flowed, he raised his consecrated hands, and shed the dew of salvation upon the head of the proselyte, pronouncing, in a voice of inspiration, the *solemn sacrament of baptism.*[74] All around harmonized with the holy act; Nature stood sole sponsor; the incense which filled the air, arose from the bosom of the earth; and the light which illuminated the ceremony, was light from heaven.

A long and solemn pause ensued; then the Missionary, clasping and holding up the hands of Luxima in his, said, "Father, receive into thy service this spotless being; for to thy service do I consecrate her."

A beam of religious triumph shone in the up-turned eyes of the Missionary. The conversion of the Priestess of Brahma was perfected, and human passion was subdued. "Daughter of heaven!" he said, "thou hast now nothing to fear; and I, on this side eternity, have nothing to hope." As he spoke the last words, an involuntary sigh burst from his lips, and he turned his eyes on the Christian vestal; but hers were fixed upon the Pagoda, the temple of her ancient devotion. Her look was sad and wild; she seemed absorbed and overwhelmed by the rapidity of emotions which had lately assailed her. "Let us proceed," he said, in a softened voice, "if thou be able; let us leave for ever the monument of the dark idolatry which thou hast abjured." As he spoke, he took her arm to lead her on; but he started, and suddenly let it fall, for he found it was encircled with the muntra, or Brahminical rosary, from which the image of Camdeo was suspended. "Luxima," he said, "these are not the ornaments of a Christian vestal."

Luxima clasped her hands in agony; the tears dropped fast upon her bosom; and she fell at his feet, exclaiming, in a voice of tenderness and despair, "Oh! thou wilt not deprive me of these also? I have nothing left now *but these*! nothing to remind me, in the land of strangers, of my country and my people, save only these: it makes a part of the religion I have abandoned, to respect the sacred ties of nature; does my new faith command me to break them? This rosary was fastened on my arm by a parent's tender hand, and bathed in Nature's holiest dew—a parent's tender tears; hold not the Christians relics, such as these, precious and sacred? Thou hast called thy religion the religion of the heart; will it not then respect the heart's best feelings?" A deep convulsive sob interrupted her words; all the ties she had broken pressed upon her bosom, and the affections of habit, those close-knit and imperishable affections, interwoven, by time and circumstance, with the very life-nerves of the heart, bore down for the moment, every other passion. The Outcast, with her eyes fixed upon the religious ornaments of her youth, wept, as she gazed, her country, parents, friends—"and would not be comforted."[75]

The Missionary sighed and was silent: he sighed to observe the strong influence of a religion, which so intimately connected itself with all the most powerful emotions of nature and earliest habits of life; and which, taking root in the heart, with its first feelings, could only be perfectly eradicated by the slow operation of expanding reason, by the strengthening efforts of moral perception, or by the miraculous effects of divine grace, and he was silent; because, the appeal which the tender and eloquent Indian made to his feelings, found an advocate in his breast it was impossible to resist. Instead, therefore, of reproving her emotion, he suffered himself to be infected by its softness, and mingled his tears with hers.

The grief of Luxima subsided in the blessed consciousness of a sympathy so precious, so unexpected; and love's warm glow dried up the tear, which the grief of natural affection shed on the cheek of the Outcast. "Thou weepest for me," she said, chasing away the trembling drops which hung in her up-turned eyes; "and in the indulgence of a selfish feeling, I hazard thy safety and thy life! That cruel, that accusing Brahmin, who has watched my steps to my destruction, whom I mistook last night for the vision of that God he too zealously serves—may he not even now lurk in these shades; or may he not, when we are vainly sought for in our respective asylums, seek us here?—O my father! forgive these tears. But it was the tenderness of him who lately cursed me; it was my aged grandsire, whom I have dragged to death and covered with shame (for something of my infamy must light on all my kindred); it was he who, with the morning's dawn, sent me the tidings of my approaching fate, and bade me fly and shun it: he would not see, he would not hear me; nor dare he breathe my name, but to heap curses on my head. But for this timely tender warning I should have else been hunted, like some noxious reptile, to wilds and wastes, there to die and be forgotten. All day I lay concealed amidst the shades of the impervious banyan, to wait thy coming with the evening sun, to bid thee a last farewell, and urge thee to save thyself by an immediate flight; but by a miracle, wrought doubtlessly by thy God for thee, that which seemed to lead us to destruction, became the wondrous mean of preservation; and we found safety where we could only hope for death."

"Luxima," said the Missionary, "let us believe that He, who alone could save us, still extends around us the shelter of his wing. Let us, while yet thou hast strength, fly these fatal shades. Behind those pine-covered rocks, which the moon now silvers, there lies, I know, a deep and entangled glen, which, I have heard, is held in superstitious horror, and never approached by pious Hindus. This glen leads to Bimbhar, by many a solitary path, made to facilitate the march of the caravan from Thibet to Tatta, at this season of the year.* It was but yesterday, some straggling troops, belonging to the caravan, passed through the valley, and halted at no great distance hence, to traffic with the Cashmirian merchants: these, as they often halt, we may overtake in some lone way, out of the view of thy intolerant countrymen." While he spoke, they had proceeded on, and reached the entrance to a ravine in the rocks, which, dark and tremendous, seemed like a closing chasm above their heads, threatening destruction; but, when they had reached its extremity, they found themselves in a delicious glen, through whose trees were discernible the crescent banners of the Mogul camp; and the sky-lamps, which marked the outposts of the midnight guards. At this sight, the prophetic warning and generous offers of the gallant Solyman rushed with equal force to the minds of the wanderers; but both remained silent—Luxima, from an instinctive delicacy, which mocked the refinement of acquired sentiment; the Missionary, from a feeling less laudable and less disinterested. Both involuntarily turned their eyes on each other, and suddenly withdrawing them, changed colour; for, in spite of the awful vows since made, and the virtuous resolution since formed, the hearts of each throbbed responsively to the dangerous recollection of that fatal

---

* "Selon les témoignages de tous les Katchmeriens, on voyoit partir chaque année de leur pays plusiers caravans."—*Voyages de* BERNIER.[76]

scene, to which the unexpected presence of the Mogul Prince had given birth.

Ere the mild and balmy night had passed its noon, the weary proselyte, exhausted equally from fatigue of mind and body, felt that she would be unable to proceed, if she snatched not the invigorating refreshment of a short repose. The Missionary, with tender watchfulness, was the first to observe her faltering steps, and sought out for her a mossy bank, cradled by the luxuriant branches of a mango-tree; and, withdrawing to a little distance, he at once guarded her slumber and gave himself up to meditate on some precise plan for their future pilgrimage; which, if they could overtake the caravan, whose track they had already discovered, would be attended with but few difficulties. Yet he dared no longer seek "the highways and public places,"[77] to promulgate his doctrines, and to evince his zeal. Withheld less by a principle of self-preservation than by his fears for the safety and even life of his innocent proselyte; he also felt his enthusiasm in the cause weakened, by the apparent impossibility of its success; for he perceived that the religious prejudices of Hindostan were too intimately connected with the temporal prosperity of its inhabitants, with the established opinions, with the laws, and even with the climate of the country, to be universally subverted, but by a train of moral and political events, which should equally emancipate their minds from antiquated error, in which they were absorbed, and which should destroy the fundamental principles of their loose and ill-digested government. He almost looked upon the Mission, in which he had engaged, as hopeless; and he felt that the miracle of that conversion, by which he expected to evince the sacred truth of the cause in which he had embarked, could produce no other effect than a general abhorrence of him who laboured to effect it, and of her who had already paid the forfeit of all most precious to the human breast, for that partial proselytism, to which her affections, rather than her reason, had induced her. Yet, when he reflected that he should return to Goa, the scenes of his former triumphs, followed only by one solitary disciple, and that disciple a young and lovely woman, his mind became confused, and he trembled to dwell on an idea fraught with a thousand mortifying and cruel recollections. The dawn had already beamed upon his harassing vigils, when Luxima stood before him, resembling the star of the morning, bright in her softness, the mists of a tender sadness hanging on the lustre of her looks. The Missionary was revived by her presence; but the sweet and subtle transport, which circulated through his veins, as he gazed on the being who now considered him as her sole providence, he endeavoured to conceal beneath a tranquil coldness of manner, which the secret ardour of his feelings, the delicacy of his situation, and the pure and virtuous resolutions of his mind, alike rendered necessary and laudable.

As they proceeded, he spoke to her of the plans he had devised, and of his intention of placing her in a religious house when they arrived at Goa. He spoke to her of the false religion that she had abandoned, and of the pure faith she had embraced.

Luxima answered only by gentle sighs, and by looks, which seemed to say, "Whatever may be my future destiny, I am at least *now* near you."

The Missionary sought to avoid these looks, which, when they met his eye, sunk to his heart, and disturbed his best resolutions; for never had his Neophyte looked more lovely. Supported by a white wand, which he had formed for her, of a bamboo, she moved lightly and timidly by his side, like the genius of the sweet and solitary shades, in which they wandered. The course of the rivers, the variation of the soil, and the beacons held out to them by the surrounding mountains, with whose forms they were well acquainted, were their guides; while the milk of the young and luscious cocoa-nut, the cheering nectar extracted from the pulp of the bilva-fruit, and the rice, and delicious fruits, which on every side presented themselves, afforded at once nutrition and refreshment.*
Sometimes catching, sometimes losing, the faint track of the caravan, the conviction of increasing safety, and the certainty of overtaking it at Bimbhar, left them scarcely a fear, and scarcely a hope, on the subject. For to wander through the lovely and magnificent valley of Cashmire, was but to loiter amidst the enjoyments of Eden; and to proceed by each other's side—to catch the half-averted eyebeam, which penetrated the soul—to observe the sudden glow which mantled on the cheek—to participate in the same blissful feelings, and yet to heighten, by submitting it to the same pure sense of virtue, was a state of being too exquisite not to obliterate, in its transient enjoyment, the memory of the past and the apprehension of the future. Restrained and reserved even in the intimacy of their intercourse, they sought to forget the existence

---

* "Il faut surtout considérer que l'abstinence de la chair des animaux est une suite de la nature du climat."—*Essai sur les Mœurs des Nations, &c. &c. &c.*[78]

of a passion it was now so dangerous to cherish. The Missionary was regulated by religion and by honour; the Indian, by sentiment and by instinctive delicacy. Solicitude tempered by reserve, tenderness blended with respect, distinguished the manner of the Priest. Modesty, which shrunk from the appearance of intrusion; and bashfulness, trembling to betray the feelings it guarded, marked the conduct of the Neophyte. Silent, except on subjects of religious sublimity, a look, suddenly caught and as suddenly withdrawn, alone betrayed their dangerous secret. They were frequently parted during the ardours of the day, which prevented their continuing their journey; and sometimes, when the night-dews fell heavily, the guardian Priest sought out for his weary charge a grassy couch, where the madhucca had spread its downy leaves; or where a luxurious and perfumed shade was afforded by the sephalica, whose flowers unfold only their bloom and odour to the sighs of night, and droop and wither beneath the first ray the sun darts o'er their fragile loveliness: while *he*, not daring, even by a look, to violate the pure and seraph slumber of confiding innocence, waked only to guard her repose; or slept, to woo to his fancy the dream, which too often, in illusive visions, gave to his heart her whom waking he trembled to approach. When they arose, the twilight of the dawn conducted them to the respective bath, which innumerable springs afforded; and, when again they met, they offered together the incense of the heart to Heaven, and proceeded on their pilgrimage. The path they had taken was so sequestered, that they seldom risked discovery; but when, amidst the haze of distance, they observed a human form, or caught a human sound, they plunged into the umbrage of the surrounding shades, until the absence of the intruder again gave them up to solitude and silence. It was in moments such as these only, that the high mind of the Missionary felt that it had forfeited its claim to the independence which belongs to unblemished rectitude, and that the Indian remembered she was an alien and Outcast.

THE END OF VOL. II.

VOLUME III

CHAPTER XIII.

On the second day of their wandering, the deep shade of the forest scenery, in which they had hitherto been involved, softened into a less impervious gloom, the heights of the black rock of Bembhar rose on their view, and the lovely and enchanting glen which reposes at its northern base, and which is called the Valley of Floating Islands, burst upon their glance. These phenomena, which appear on the bosom of the Behat, are formed by the masses of rock, by the trees and shrubs which the whirlwind tears from the summits of the surrounding mountains, and which are thus borne away by the fury of the torrents, and plunged into the tranquil waters beneath; these rude fragments collected by time and chance, cemented by the river Slime, and intermixed by creeping plants, and parasite grasses, become small but lovely islets, covered with flowers, sowed by the vagrant winds, and skirted by the leaves and blossoms of the crimson lotos, the water-loving flower of Indian groves. This scene, so luxuriant and yet so animating, where all was light, and harmony, and odour, gave a new sensation to the nerves, and a new tone to the feelings of the wanderers, and their spirits were fed with the balmier airs, and their eyes greeted with lovelier objects, than hope or fancy had ever imaged to their minds.—Sometimes they stood together on the edge of the silvery flood, watching the motion of the arbours which floated on its bosom, or pursuing the twinings of the harmless green serpent, which, shining amidst masses of kindred hues, raised gracefully his brilliant crest above the edges of the river bank. Sometimes from beneath the shade of umbrageous trees, they beheld the sacred animal of India breaking the stubborn flood with his broad white breast, and gaining the fragrant islet, where he reposed his heated limbs; his mild countenance shaded by his crooked horns, crowned by the foliage in which he had entangled them; thus reposing in tranquil majesty, he looked like some river-deity of ancient fable.

Flights of many-coloured perroquets, of lorys, and of peacocks, reflected on the bosom of the river the bright and various tints of their splendid plumage; while the cozel, the nightingale of Hindoo bards, poured its song of love from the summit of the loftiest *mergosa*, the eastern lilac. It was here they found the *Jama*, or rose apple-tree, bearing ambrosial fruit—it was here that the sweet sumbal, the spikenard of the ancients, spread its tresses of dusky gold over the clumps of granite, which sparkled like coloured gems amidst the sapphire of the mossy soil—it was here that, at the decline of a lovely day, the wanderers reached the shade of a natural arbour, formed by the union of a tamarind-tree with the branches of a *covidara*, whose purple and rose-coloured blossoms mingled with the golden fruit which, to the Indian palate, affords so delicious a refreshment.

It was Luxima who discovered this retreat so luxurious, and yet so simple. The purity of the atmosphere, the brilliancy of the scene, had given to her spirits a higher tone than usually distinguished their languid character. Looking pure and light as the air she breathed, she had bounded on before her companion, who, buried in profound reverie, seemed at once more thoughtful and more tender than he had yet appeared in look or manner. When he reached the arbour, he found Luxima seated beneath its shade—her brow crowned with Indian feathers, and her delicate fingers engaged in forming a wreath of odoriferous berries; looking like the emblem of that lovely region, whose mild and delicious climate had contributed to form the beauty of her person, the softness of her character, and the ardour of her imagination. No thought of future care contracted her brow, and the smile of peace and innocence sat on her lips. Not so the Missionary: the morbid habit of watching his own sensations had produced in him an hypochondriasm of conscience, which embittered the most blameless moments of his life; his diseased mind discovered a lurking crime in the most innocent enjoyments; and the fear of offending Heaven, fastened his attention to objects which were only dangerous, by not being immediately dismissed from his thoughts. The moral economy of his nature suffered from the very means he took to preserve it; and his danger arose less from his temptation, than from the sensibility with which he watched its progress, and the efforts he made to combat and to resist its influence. He now beheld Luxima more lovely than he had ever seen her; she was gracefully occupied, and there was something picturesque, something almost *fantastic*, in her appearance, which gave the poignant charm of novelty to her air and person. She was murmuring an Indian song, as he approached her. The Missionary stood gazing on her for some moments in silence, then suddenly averting his eyes, and seating himself near her, he said—"And to what purpose, my dearest daughter, dost thou so industriously weave those fragrant wreaths?"

"To hang upon the bower of thy repose," she replied, "as a spell against evil;—for dost thou not, on every side, perceive the *bacula* plant, so injurious to the nerves, and whose baneful influence the odour of these berries can alone dispel?"*

"Alas!" he exclaimed, "in scenes so lovely and remote as those in which we now wander, who could suspect that latent evil lurked? But the evil which always exists, and that against which it is most difficult to guard, exists within ourselves, Luxima."

"Thou sayest it," returned Luxima, "and therefore must it be true; and yet, methinks, in us at least no evil can exist—look around thee, Father; behold those hills which encompass us on every side, and which, seeming to shut out the universe, exclude all the evil passions by which it is agitated and disordered; and since absent from all human intercourse, our feelings relate only to each other, surely in us at least no evil *can* exist."

"Let us hope, let us trust there does not, Luxima," said the Missionary, in strong emotion; "and oh! my daughter, let us watch and pray that there *may not.*"

"And here," said Luxima with simplicity, and suspending her work, "where all breathes of peace and innocence, against what are we to pray?"

"Even against *those thoughts* which involuntarily start into the mind, and which, though confined, and perhaps referring exclusively to each other, may yet become fatal and seductive, may yet plunge us into error beyond the mercy of Heaven to forgive!"

"But if one *sole* thought occupies the existence!" said Luxima, tenderly and with energy, "and if it is sanctified by the perfection of its object!"

"But to what earthly object does perfection belong, Luxima?"

"To thee;" replied the Neophyte, blushing.

"It is the ardour of thy gratitude only," said the Missionary with vehemence, "which bestows on me, an epithet belonging alone to Heaven. And lovely as is this purest of human sentiments, yet, *being human*, it is liable to corruption, and may be carried to an excess fatal to us both; for, oh! Luxima, were I to avail myself of this excess of gratitude, this pure but unguarded tenderness, and in wilds solitary and luxuriant as these, where happiness and security might mingle, where, forgetting the world, and its opinions, abandoning alike *heaven* and its *cause!*"—he paused abruptly—he trembled, and a deep groan burst from a heart, agitated by all the conflicting emotions of a sensitive conscience, and an imperious passion.

---

* The odour of this flower produces violent head-aches.

Luxima, moved by his agitation—tender, timid, yet always happy and tranquilly blessed in the presence of him, the idol of her secret thoughts, and fearing only those incidents which might impede the innocent felicity of being near him—endeavoured to soothe his perturbation, and, taking his hand in hers, and bending her head towards him, she looked on his eyes with innocent fondness, and her sighs, sweet as the incense of the evening, breathed on his burning cheek! Then the sacred fillet of religion fell from his eyes; he threw himself at her feet, and pressing her hands to his heart, he said passionately—"Luxima, tell me, dost thou not belong exclusively to Heaven? Recall to my wandering mind that sacred vow, by which I solemnly devoted thee to its service, at the baptismal font! Oh! my daughter, thou wouldst not destroy me? thou wouldst not arm Heaven against me, Luxima?"

"I!" returned Luxima tenderly, "I destroy thee, who art dear to me as heaven itself!"

"Oh! Luxima," he exclaimed in emotion, "look not thus on me! tell me not that I am dear to thee, or...." At that moment his rosary fell to the earth, and lay at the feet of the Indian.

An incident so natural and so simple struck on the conscience of the Missionary, as though the Minister of Divine wrath had blasted his gaze with his accusing presence;—he grew pale and shuddered, his arms fell back upon his breast;—overpowered by shame, and by self-abhorrence, rushing from the bower, he plunged into the thickest shade of the grove; there he threw himself on the earth; and that mind, once so high and lofty in its own conscious triumph, was now again sunk and agonized by the conviction of its own debasement. From this state of unsupportable humiliation, he was awakened by the sound of horses' feet; he raised his eyes, and beheld approaching an Indian, who led a small Arabian horse, laden with empty panniers: the Missionary hastily arose—and the stranger, moved by the dignity of his form, and the disorder of his pale and haggard countenance, gave him the *Salaam;* and invited him, with the hospitable courtesy of his country, to repair to his cottage, which lay at a little distance,—"Or perhaps," he said, "you wish to overtake the caravan, and—"

"To *overtake* it!" interrupted the Missionary; "has it then long passed?"

"It halts now," returned the peasant; "on the other side of *Bem-*

bhar, I have been disposing of some *touz** to a merchant of Tatta; if you have no other mode of proceeding, you will scarcely overtake it on foot."

A new cause of suffering now occupied his mind.—Luxima, hitherto cheered and supported by the lovely and enlivening scenes through which she passed, by the smoothness of her path and the temperature of her native climes, was yet wearied and exhausted by a journey performed in a manner to which the delicacy of her frame was little adequate—but it was now impossible she could proceed as she had hitherto done; in a few hours the Eden which had cheated fatigue of its influence, would disappear from their eyes; and, should the caravan have proceeded much in advance, it was impossible that the delicate Indian could encounter the horrors of the desert which lay on the southern side of Bembhar.

It was then that, believing Providence had sent the Indian in his path, a new hope revived in his heart, a new resource was opened in his mind:—he offered a part of what remained of the purse of rupees he had brought with him from Lahore, for the Arabian horse. It was more than its value, and the Indian gladly accepted his proposal, and, pointing out to him the shortest way to *Bembhar*, and offering his good wishes for the safety of his journey, he pursued his way to his cottage. As soon as he had disappeared, Hilarion led the animal to the bower, where Luxima still remained, involved in reveries so soft, and yet so profound, that she observed not the approach of him who was their sole and exclusive object.

"Luxima!" he said in a low and tremulous voice—Luxima started, and, covered with blushes, she raised her languid eyes to his, and faintly answered—"*Father!*"

"My daughter," he said, "that Heaven, of whose favour I at least am so unworthy, has mercifully extended its providential care to us. A stranger, whom I met in the forest, has informed me, that the caravan has passed the rock of Bembhar; but I have purchased from him this animal, by which thou wilt be able to proceed!"

Luxima arose, and, drawing her veil over a face in which the lovely confusion of a sensitive modesty and ardent tenderness still

---

* Une laine, ou plutôt un poil, qu'on nomme *touz*, se prend sur les poitrines des chèvres sauvages des montagnes de Cashmire.—*Bernier.*
It is of this wool the Cashmirian shawls are formed.[79]

lingered, she suffered the Missionary to place her on the gentle Arabian—and he moving with long and rapid steps by her side, they again renewed their pilgrimage.

Already the bloom and verdure of Cashmire appeared fading into the approaching heights of the sterile Bembhar, and the travellers, silent and thoughtful, ascended those acclivities, which seemed but to reflect the smiling lustre of the scenes they left; no sound, even of nature, disturbed the profound silence of scenes—so still and solemn, that they resembled the primæval world, ere human existence had given animation to its pathless wilds, or human passions had disturbed the calm of its mild tranquillity! No sound was heard, save the jackal's dismal yell, which so often disturbs the impressive and serene beauty of Indian scenery.

But this death-like calm failed to communicate a correspondent influence to the bosom of the solitary wanderers:—again together, in a boundless solitude, they were yet silent, as though they feared a human accent would destroy the impassioned mystery which existed between them; while religion and penitence, and delicacy and self-distrust, enforced the necessity of a reserve, to which both alike submitted with difficulty but with fortitude. Solitude, with the object of a suppressed tenderness, is always too dangerous! and that great passion which seeks a desert, finds the proper region of its own empire. Thus, those helpless and tender friends, in whom love and grace struggled with equal sway, now eagerly looked forward to their restoration to society, which would afford them that protection against themselves, which nature, in her loveliest regions, had hitherto seemed to refuse them.

The travellers at last reached the summit of the *rock of Bembhar;* and, ere they descended the wild and burning plains of Upper Lahore, the Indian turned round to take a last view of her native Eden. The sun was setting in all his majesty of light upon the valley; and villages, and pagodas, and groves, and rivers, were brilliantly tinted with his crimson rays. Luxima cast one look in that direction where lay the district of Sirinagar—another towards Heaven—and then fixed her tearful eyes on the Missionary, with an expression so eloquent and so ardent, that they seemed to say, "Heaven and earth have I resigned for thee!"—The Missionary met and returned her look, but dared not trust his lips to speak; and, in the sympathy and intelligence of that silent glance, the Indian found country, kindred, friends; or ceased for a moment to remember she had lost them all.

Sad, silent, and gloomy, resembling the first pair, when they had reached the boundary of their native paradise, they now descended the southern declivities of Bembhar: the dews of Cashmire no longer embalmed the evening air, and the heated vapours which arose from the plains below, rendered the atmosphere insupportably intense.

As they reached the plains of Upper Lahore, a few dark shrubs and blasted trees alone presented themselves in the hot and sandy soil; and when a stalk of rosemary and lavender, or the scarlet tulip of the desert, tempted the hand of the Missionary, for her to whom flowers were always precious, they mouldered into dust at his touch!

Luxima endeavoured to stifle a sigh, as she beheld nature in this her most awful and destructive aspect—and the Missionary, with a sad smile, sought to cheer her drooping spirit, by pointing out to her the track of the caravan, or the snowy summit of *Mount Alideck*, which arose like a land-mark before them. Having paused for a short time, while the Missionary ascended a rock, to perceive if the caravan was in view—which if it had been, the light of a brilliant moon would have discovered,—they proceeded during the night, in sadness and in gloom, while the intense thirst produced by the ardour of the air had already exhausted the juicy fruits with which the Missionary had supplied himself for Luxima's refreshment; at last the faint glimmering of the stars was lost in the brighter lustre of the morning-planet; the resplendent herald of day, riding in serene lustre through the heavens, ushered in the vigorous sun, whose potent rays rapidly pervaded the whole horizon.—The fugitives found themselves near a large and solitary edifice; it was a *Choultry*, built for the shelter of travellers, and, as an inscription indicated, "built by *Luxima*, the *Prophetess and Brachmachira of Cashmire!*"—At the sight of this object, the Indian turned pale—all the glory and happiness of her past life rushed on the recollection of the excommunicated Chancalas; and her guide, feeling in all their force the sacrifices which she had made for him, silently and tenderly chased away her tears, with her veil. As it was impossible to proceed during the meridional ardours of the day, the wearied and exhausted Indian sought shelter and repose beneath that roof which her own charity had raised; and a cocoatree, planted on the edge of a tank which she had excavated, afforded to her that refreshment, which she had benevolently provided for others. Here, it was evident, the caravan had lately halted; for the remains of some provisions, usually left by Indian travellers for those who may succeed them, were visible, and the track of wheels, of horses, and of camels' feet, was every where apparent. Revived and invigorated by an hour's undisturbed repose, they again re-commenced their route; still pursuing the track of the caravan, while, in forms rendered indistinct by distance, they still fancied they beheld the object of their pursuit. Scenes more varied than those through which they had already journeyed, now presented themselves to their view. Sometimes they passed through a ruined village, which the flame of war had desolated; sometimes beneath the remains of a Mogul fortress, whose mouldering arches presented the most picturesque specimens of eastern military architecture; while from the marshy fosse, which surrounded the majestic ruins, arose a bright blue flame, and moving with velocity amidst its mouldering bastions, floating like waves, or falling like sparks of fire, became suddenly extinct—Luxima gazed upon this spectacle with fear and amazement, and, governed by the superstition of her early education, saw, in a natural phenomenon, the effects of a supernatural agency; trembling, she clung to her pastor and her guide, and said, "It is the spirit of one who fell in the battle, or who died in the defence of these ruins, and who, for some crime unredeemed, is thus destined to wander till the time of expiation is accomplished, and he return into some form on earth."

The Missionary sought to release her mind from the bondage of imaginary terrors, and at once to amuse her fancy, to enlighten her ideas, and to elevate her soul; he explained to her, with ingenious simplicity, the various and wonderful modes by which the Divine Spirit disposes of the different powers of nature, still teaching her to feel "God in all, and all in God."[80]

Luxima gazed on him with wonder while he spoke, and hung in silent admiration on words she deemed inspired; yet when, as it sometimes occurred, she beheld the rude altars raised, even in the most unfrequented places to *Boom-Daivee*, the goddess of the earth;* or to the Daivadergoel, the tutelar guardians of wilds and forests, her senses acknowledged these images of her ancient superstition, in spite of her reason, and she involuntarily bowed before the objects of her habitual devotion. Then the Missionary reproved her severely for the perpetual vacillation of her undecided faith; but, disarming his severity by looks and words of tenderness, she would fondly reply—"Oh! my Father! it is not all devotion which

---

* See Kindersley's History of the Hindu Mythology.[81]

bows my head and bends my knee before these well remembered shrines of my ancient faith! Alas! it is not all a pious impulse, but a natural sympathy: for the genii to whom these altars are raised, were once, as I was, happy and glorified; but they incurred the wrath of *Shiven*,* by abandoning his laws; and, banished from their native heaven, were doomed to wander in solitary wastes to expiate their error:—but here, that sympathy ceases; for *they* found not, like me, a compensation for the paradise they forfeited; they found not on earth, something which partook of heaven, and they knew not that perfect communion, which images to the soul, in its transient probation through time, the bliss which awaits it in eternity."

It was by words like these, timidly and tenderly pronounced, that the feelings of the spiritual guide were put to the most severe test; it was words like these, which chilled his which increased the hidden sentiment, manner, while they warmed his heart;[83] and restrained the external emotion, and which cherished and fed his passion, while they awakened his self-distrust: but Luxima, at once his peril and his salvation, counteracted by her innocence the effects of her tenderness, and alternately awakened, excited or subdued, by that feminine display of feeling and sentiment, which blended purity with ardour, and elevation of soul with tenderness of heart. More sensitive than reflecting, she was guided rather by an instinctive delicacy, than a prudent reserve; in *her*, sentiment supplied the place of reason, and she was the most virtuous, because she was the most affectionate of women.

The evening again arose upon their wanderings, and they paused ere they proceeded to encounter the pathless way through the gloom of night; they paused near the edge of a spring, which afforded a delicious refreshment; and, under the shadow of a lofty tamarind-tree, which, blooming in solitary beauty, supplied at once both fruit and shade, and seemed dropt in the midst of a lonesome waste, as a beacon to hope, as an assurance of the providential care of *him*, who reared its head in the desert for the relief of his creatures. Here the Missionary left Luxima to take repose; and, having fastened the *Arabian* to a neighbouring rock, embossed with patches of vegetation, he proceeded across some stony acclivities which were covered by the caprice of nature with massy clumps of the *bamboo tree*. When he had reached the opposite side, he looked

---

* "C'est dans le *Shasta* que l'ou trouve l'histoire de la Chûte des Anges."— *Essai sur les Mœurs des Nations*. P. 2, T. 2.[82]

back to catch, as he was wont, a glimpse of Luxima; but, for the first time since the commencement of their pilgrimage, she was hidden from his view by the intervening foliage of the plantation, trembling at the fancied dangers which might assail her in his absence: he proceeded with a rapid step towards an eminence, in the hope of ascertaining, from its summit, the path of the caravan, or of discovering some human habitation, though but the hut of a *pariah*, whose owner might guide their now uncertain steps. Turning his eyes towards the still glowing West, he perceived a forest whose immense trees marked their waving outline on saffron clouds, which hung radiantly upon their gloom, tinging their dark branches with the yellow lustre of declining light; he perceived also, that this awful and magnificent forest was skirted by an illimitable jungle, through whose long-entangled grass a broad path-way seemed to have been recently formed, and, vision growing strong by exercise, the first confusion of objects which had distracted his gaze, gradually subsiding into distinct images, he perceived the blue smoke curling from a distant hut, which he knew, from its desolate situation, to be the miserable residence of some *Indian outcast;* he soon more distinctly observed some great body in motion: at first it appeared compact and massive; by degrees broken and irregular; and at last the form and usual pace of a troop of camels were obvious to his far-stretched sight, by a deep red light which suddenly illumined the whole firmament, and, throwing its extended beams into the distant fore-ground, fell, with bright tints, upon every object, and confirmed the Missionary in hopes, he almost trembled to encourage, that the caravan at that moment moved before his eyes! But the joy was yet imperfect; unshared by *her*, who was now identified with all his hopes and all his fears; and descending the hill with the rapidity of lightning, he suddenly perceived his steps impeded by a phenomenon which at first seemed some sudden vision of the fancy, to which the senses unresistingly submitted; for a brilliant circle of fire gradually extending, forbid his advance, and had illuminated, by its kindling light, the surrounding atmosphere! Recovering from the first emotion of horror and consternation, his knowledge of the natural history of the country soon informed him of the cause of the apparent miracle,[*] without reconciling him

---

[*] This singular spectacle frequently presents itself to the eye of the traveller in the hilly parts of the Carnatic, as well as in Upper India, particularly about the *Ghauts*, which are covered with the bamboo tree.[84]

to its effects; he perceived that the *bamboos*, violently agitated by a strong and sultry wind, which suddenly arose from the South, and crept among their branches, had produced a violent friction in their dry stalks, which emitted sparks of fire, and which, when communicated to their leaves, produced on their summits one extended blaze, which was now gradually descending to their trunks.[85] Though this extraordinary spectacle fulfilled, rather than violated, a law of nature, the Missionary's heart, struck by the obstacle it opposed to his wishes and his views, and the terrors it held out to his imagination, felt as if, by some interposition of Divine wrath, he had been separated, for ever, from her who had thus armed Heaven against him. Given up to a distraction which knew no bounds from reason or religion, he accused the Eternal Judge, who, in making the object of his error the cause of his retribution, had not proportioned his punishment to his crime, and who had implicated in the vengeance which bowed *him* to the earth, a creature free and innocent of voluntary error.—Yet, considering less his own sufferings, than the probable and impending destruction of Luxima, thus exposed, alone, in solitary deserts, to want! to the inclemency of treacherous elements! to the fury of savage beasts! perhaps to men, scarce less savage! who might refuse her that protection, their very presence rendered necessary—his mind and feelings were roused, even to frenzy, by the frightful images conjured up by a heart distracted for the safety of its sole object; and the instinct of self-preservation, that strong and almost indestructible instinct, submitted to the paramount influence of a *sentiment;* but that sentiment before which nature stood checked, blended the united passions of *love* and *pity*, the best and dearest which fill the human breast—and, resolved to risk his life for the salvation of hers, dearer to him still than life,—he threw around him a rapid glance, in the faint hope of discerning some object which might assist him in the perilous enterprise he meditated, and enable him to encounter the rage of those flames which opposed his return to the goal of his solicitude and anxiety. It was then he perceived that the surrounding rocks were covered with the entangled web of the *mountain flax*, the inconsumable *amianthus* of India.[*]

---

[*] One of the varieties of the *asbestos*, which when long exposed to air, dissolves into a downy matter, unassailable by common fire.

At this sight, the providential care of the Divinity, who every where presents an *antidote* to that evil which may eventually become the bane of human preservation, smote his heart—and, raising his soul and eyes in thankfulness to Heaven, he wrapped round his uncovered head, the fibres of this singular and indestructible fossil, and, folding his robe closely round his body, he plunged daringly forward, throwing aside the branches of the burning trees, which flamed above his head, with the iron point of his crosier, as he flew over the arid path, and looking as he moved like the mighty *spirit* of that *element* to which the popular superstition of the region he inhabited would have offered its homage.* The fire had nearly exhausted itself in the direction in which he moved, and soon left nothing but its smoking embers to impede his course. Scorched, spent, and almost deprived of respiration, he reached the opposite side of the plantation, and, with the recovery of breath and strength, he flew towards the spot where he had left his charge, whom every new peril, by adding anxiety to love, bound more closely to his heart. He found her wrapt in profound slumber; the moonlight, checquered by the branches of the tree through which it fell, played on her face and bosom; but her figure was in deep shade, from its position; and a disciple of her own faith would have worshipped her, had he passed, and said, " 'Tis the messenger of Heaven,† who bears to earth the mandate of *Vishnoo*;" for it is thus the Indian *Iris* is sometimes mystically represented—nothing visible of its beauty, but the countenance of a youthful seraph. Close to the brow of the innocent slumberer lay, in many a mazy fold, a serpent of immense size: his head, crested and high, rose erect; his scales of verdant gold glittered to the moon-light, and his eyes bright and fierce were fixed on the victim, whose first motion might prove the signal of her death. These two objects, so singular in their association, were alone conspicuous in the scene, which was elsewhere hid in the massive shadows of the projecting branches. At the sight of this image, so beautiful and so terrific, so awfully fine, so grandly dreadful, where loveliness and death, and peace and destruction, were so closely blended, the distracted and solitary spectator stood aghast!—A chill of horror running through his

---

* *Augne-Baugauvin*, the God of Fire, and one of the eight keepers of the world.
† Saindovoer.

veins, his joints relaxed; his limbs, transfixed and faint, cold and powerless, fearing lest his very respiration might accelerate the dreadful fate which thus hung over the sole object and tie of his existence,—breathless, motionless,—he wore the perfect semblance of that horrible suspense, which fills the awful interval between impending death, and lingering life! Twice he raised his crosier to hurl it at the serpent's head; and twice his arm fell nerveless back, while his shuddering heart doubted the certain aim of his trembling hand,—and whether, in attempting to strike at the vigilant reptile, he might not reach the bosom of his destined victim, and urge him to her immediate destruction!—But, feelings so acute were not long to be endured: cold drops fell from his brow, his inflamed eye had gazed itself into dimness, increasing agony became madness,—and, unable to resist the frenzy of his thronging emotions, he raised the pastoral spear, and had nearly hurled it at the destroyer, when his arm was checked by a sound which seemed to come from Heaven, breathing hope and life upon his soul; for it operated with an immediate and magic influence on the organs of the reptile, who suddenly drooped his crested head, and, extending wide his circling folds, wound his mazy course, in many an indented wave, towards that point, where some seeming impulse of the "vocal aid"[86] lured his nature from its prey.

Luxima slowly awakening from her sweet repose, to sounds too well remembered, for it was the vesper hymn of the Indian huntsmen, raised her head upon her arm, and threw wildly round her the look of one wrapt in visionary trance—now resting her eye upon the Missionary, who stood before her motionless, suspended between joy and horror, between fear and transport—now upon the flaming circles which hung upon the burning *bamboos*—and now on the receding serpent, whose tortuous train, veering as he moved, still glistened brightly on the earth, till slowly following the fainting sounds, his voluble and lengthening folds were lost in the deep shade of a sombre thicket;—then the Indian raised her hands and eyes to heaven in thankfulness to that Power who had mercifully saved her from a dreadful death. The music ceased; nature had reached the crisis of emotion in the breast of the Missionary: without power to articulate or to move, he bent one knee to the earth; he raised his folded hands to Heaven; but his eyes were turned on the object of its protection: he sighed out her name, and Luxima was in a moment at his side.

CHAPTER XIV.

The left arm of the Missionary had suffered from the flames; Luxima was the first to perceive it: she applied to it the only remedy which nature afforded them in a spot so desolate; and the ingenuity of love, and of necessity, supplied the place of skill. She gathered from the neighbouring spring, the oily *naptha*, whose volatile and subtil fluid so frequently floats on the surface of Indian wells, and, steeping in it the fragment of her veil, she bound it round the arm of her patient. Thus engaged, the thoughts of the wanderers, by a natural association, mutually reverted to their first interview in the grotto of Congelations; when the rigid distinctions of prejudice first gave way to an impulse of humanity, and the Priestess of Brahma, no less in fear than pity, bound up the wound of him whom she then deemed it a sacrilege to approach! The sympathy of the recollection was visible in the disorder of their looks, which were studiously averted from each other; and the Neophyte, endeavouring to turn the thoughts of her spiritual guide from a subject she trembled to revert to, spoke of the danger which he had recently incurred for her sake, and spoke of it with all the fervour which characterized her eloquence.

The Missionary replied with the circumspect reserve of one who feared to trust his feelings: he said, "That which I have done *for thee*, I would have done for another, for it is the spirit of the religion I profess, to sacrifice the selfish instinct of our nature to the preservation of a fellow-creature whose danger claims our interference, or whose happiness needs our protection."

"Oh! Father," she returned in emotion, "refer not to thy faith alone, a sentiment inherent in thyself; let us be more just *to him* who made us, and believe, that there is in nature, a feeling of benevolence which betrays the original intention of the Deity, to promote the happiness of his creatures. If thou art prone to pity the wretched, and aid the weak, it is because thou wast thyself created of those particles which, at an infinite distance, constitute the Divine essence."

The Missionary interrupted her by a look of reprehension; he knew such was the doctrine, and such the phrase of the Brahmins, with respect to those of their holy men who led a religious and sinless life: but he felt, at the moment, how little claim he had to make any application of it to himself.

"Thy religion, at least," continued Luxima, with softness and timidity, "forbids not the expression of *gratitude*. It is said in the

Shaster, that the first thought of Brahma, when created by the great Spirit, was a sentiment of gratitude; he offered up thanks to the Author of his existence, for the gift of life, and a reasonable soul: is then the Christian doctrine less amiable than that I have abandoned? and, if through thee, my life has been preserved, and my soul enlightened, must I stifle in my heart, the gratitude thou hast awakened there?"

"Luxima," exclaimed the Missionary, with vehemence, "*all* sentiments merely of the heart are dangerous, and to be distrusted; whatever soothes the passions, tends to cherish them,—whatever affords pleasure, endangers virtue,—and even the love we bear to Heaven, we should try, were it possible, to separate from the happiness which that love confers. Oh! Luxima, it is a dangerous habit,—the habit of enjoying any earthly good, and until now—" he broke off suddenly, and sighed, then added, "Thou talkest much of gratitude, Luxima; but wherefore? It was for Heaven I sought thee—it is for Heaven I saved thee! It was not for *thy* sake, nor for mine, that I lured thee from the land of the unbelieving, or that I would risk a thousand lives to save thine,—it is for *his* sake, whose servant I am. But, if *thou* talkest of gratitude, to whom is it due? *Art thou not here?* in dreary deserts, encompassed round by danger and by death: to follow me, thou art here,— thou, the native of an earthly paradise,—the idol of a nation's homage. Oh! I should have left thy pure soul, all innocent as it was of voluntary error, to return to its Creator, untried by the dangers, unassailed by the tempting evils of passion and of life, virtuous in thy illusions, pure from the errors and misfortunes of humanity, an inmate fit for the Heaven which awaited thee."

"Be that Heaven my witness," returned Luxima, with devotion and solemnity, "that I would not for the happiness I have abandoned, and the glory I have lost, resign that desert, whose perilous solitudes I share with thee. Oh! my father, and my friend, thou alone hast taught me to know, that the paradise of woman is the creation of her heart; that it is not the light or air of Heaven, though beaming brightness, and breathing fragrance, nor all that is loveliest in nature's scenes, which form the *sphere* of *her* existence and enjoyment!—it is alone the presence of *him she loves*: it is that mysterious sentiment of the heart, which diffuses a finer sense of life through the whole being; and which resembles, in its singleness and simplicity, the *primordial idea*, which, in the religion of my fathers, is supposed to have preceded *time* and *worlds*, and from which all created good has emanated."

The Missionary arose, in disorder; he turned, for a moment, his eyes on Luxima: the glow which mantled to her brow, the bashful confusion of her look, the modesty with which she drew her veil over her downcast eyes, spoke the involuntary error of one, whose ardent feelings had for a moment over-ruled the circumspect reserve of a rigid virtue. He sighed profoundly, and withdrew his glance. Luxima now also arose; and they were both proceeding on in silence, when a rustling in the thicket was distinctly heard, and the next moment a large but meagre dog sprang forward, followed by an Indian, on whose dark and melancholy countenance the light of the moon fell brightly; a scanty garment, woven of the fibres of trees, partially concealed his slender and worn form; an Indian pipe was suspended from his girdle; and he leaned, as he paused, to gaze on the wanderers, upon a huntsman's *spear*. But, scarcely had he fixed his haggard eyes on the brow of Luxima, which still bore the consecrated *mark of the tellertum*,* than he fell prostrate on the earth, in token of reverential homage. Luxima shrieked, and hiding her head in the bosom of the Missionary, exclaimed, "Let us fly, or we are lost! it is a *pariah*!"

The *unfortunate*, rising from the earth, and withdrawing a few paces, said, in a timid and respectful accent:—"I am indeed of that wretched cast, who live under the curse of Heaven—an outcast! an alien! I claim no country. I *own no kindred*, but still I am human, and can pity in others the suffering I myself endure: I ask not the daughter of Heaven, who sprang from the head of Brahma, to repose beneath the roof of a pariah; but I will conduct her to a spot less perilous than this, and I will lay at her feet the pulp of the young cocoa-nut, which grows by the side of my hut; and when the morning star dawns above yonder forest, I will guide her steps to a path of safety, and teach her how to shun the abode of the wild beast, and to avoid the nest of the serpent."

To these humane offers, Luxima replied only by tears: an *outcast* herself, the unconquerable prejudice and religious pride of the cast she had forfeited, still operated with unabated influence on her mind, and she shuddered when she beheld the Missionary stretch out his hands and press in their grateful clasp those of the unfortunate and benevolent *pariah*: he had been the saviour of the life of her he loved; for it was the music of his sylvan reed, which he

---

* The *tellertum* is a mark which is at once an ornament and an indication of cast and religious profession.

seduced the serpent from his prey, and the point of his spear was still red with the blood of the reptile he had destroyed.*

But for the first time, neither the example nor the persuasions of the Missionary had any effect upon the mind of his neophyte. Suddenly awakened to all the tyranny of habitual prejudice and superstitious fear, she rejected the repose and safety to be found beneath the shadow of a pariah's *hut*, she rejected the fruit planted by a pariah's hand; and the pride of a Brahmin's daughter, and the bigotry of a Brahmin priestess, still governed the conduct of the excommunicated *chancalas*, still over-ruled the reason of the Christian neophyte: accepting, therefore, only the advice of the unhappy pariah, who directed them to a woody path, by which they might soonest gain the caravan road, and who taught them how to avoid whatever was most dangerous in these unfrequented wilds, they again re-commenced their wanderings. The Missionary, with difficulty guiding the Arabian through the intricacies of the forest-path, remained silent and thoughtful; while Luxima, fearing that she had displeased him by an unconquerable obstinacy, which had its foundation in the earliest habits and feelings of her life, sought to cheer his mind and amuse his attention by the repetition of some of those mythological romances, which had formed a part of her professional acquirements. But the Missionary, alive to dangers which in his society *she* felt not, and borne down by the recent disappointment of his flattering hopes, of which *she* was ignorant, gave not to her brilliant and eloquent details, the wonted look of half-repressed transport, the wonted reserved smile of tenderness and admiration; his whole thoughts rested in a faint expectation of overtaking the caravan, which moved slowly, and which had taken a more circuitous road than that to which the pariah had directed him.

In the unfrequented wilds through which they now passed, no trace of human life appeared, save that once, and at an immense distance, they beheld the arms of some Indian troops glittering brightly to the moon-beams; but the welcome spectacle passed away like a midnight phantom; and, that again they observed a circle of glimmering fires, before which the remote shadows of an

---

* According to the *Abbé* Guyon, there is in India a species of serpent, which even in the pursuit of its prey is to be lulled into a profound slumber by the sounds of *musical instruments*. The Indian serpent-hunters frequently make use of this artifice, that they may destroy them with greater facility.

elephant's form seemed to pass. Luxima, acquainted with the customs of her country, believed this spectacle to belong to a hunting match of elephants; a diversion in India truly royal. At last, having recovered the traces of the caravan, which were deeply impressed on the soil, they found themselves on a wild and marshy waste, skirted by the impenetrable forest, from whose gloom they now emerged;—the earth trembled beneath their sinking feet, and particles of light arising from putrescent substances, rose like meteors before them; while frequently the high jungle grass, almost surmounting the lofty figure of the Missionary, stubbornly resisted the efforts which he made with his extended arms to clear a passage for the animal on which Luxima was mounted;—the moon, suddenly absorbed in clouds, left them with "*danger and with darkness compassed round;*"[87]—while the low and sullen murmurs of the elements foretold a rising storm. Exhausted by heat and by fatigue, no longer able to perceive the track of the caravan, the unfortunate wanderers sought only to avoid the dreadful inclemency of the moment: sounds of horror mingled in the wild expanse; the hiss of serpents, and the yell of ferocious animals which instinctively sought shelter amidst the profound depths of the forest, (whose mighty trees, bending their summits to the sweeping blast, rolled like billows in deep and dying murmurs) all around bowed as in awful reverence to the omnipotent voice of nature, thus pouring her accents of terror in the deep roll of endless thunder; the crush of shattered rocks, the groans of torn-up trees, and all those images of terror which mark the *land-tempests* in those mighty regions, where even destruction wears an aspect of magnificence and sublimity, all struck upon the soul of the fainting Indian, and left there an impression never to be effaced. It was then that the religion which she had abandoned, less from *conviction* than from *love*, and the superstitious errors which were still latent in her mind, resumed at this moment (to her, of dreadful retribution) all their former influence; and she felt the wrath of Heaven in every flash of lightning which darted round her head: for the mind long devoted to an illusion interwoven with all its ideas, however it may abandon its influence in the repose of safety, or the blessings of enjoyment, still clings to it, as to a resource, in suffering and in danger; and, contrite for the transient apostacy, adds the energy of repentance to the zeal of returning faith.

The Missionary, who beheld remorse in the bosom of his proselyte strengthening under the dangers which had awakened it, in vain endeavoured to soothe and to support her; she shrank from his arms, and, prostrate on the earth, invoked those deities whom she still believed to have been the tutelar guardians of the days of her innocence and her felicity; while he, still feeling only through her, stood near to shield and to protect her: awed, but not subdued, he presented a fine image of the majesty of man;—his brow fearlessly raised to meet the lightning's flash, a blasted tree in ruins at his feet, and while all lay desolate and in destruction round him, looking like one whose spirit, unsubdued by the mighty wreck of matter, defied that threatened annihilation, which could not reach the immortality it was created to inherit!

The storm ceased in a tremendous crash of the elements, with all the abrupt grandeur with which it had arisen; and a breathless calm, scarcely less awful, succeeded to its violence; the clouds dispersed from the face of the Heavens, and the moon, full and cloudless, rose in the firmament: every thing urged the departure of the wanderers, for danger, in various forms, surrounded them.—Luxima, alive to every existing impression, was cheered even by the solemn calm, but nearly exhausted and overcome by suffering and fatigue, the Missionary was obliged to support her on the horse; and though she tried to smile, yet her silent tears, and uncomplaining sufferings, relaxed the firmness of his mind; he felt, that, were even her conversion perfected, which he hourly discovered it was far from being, she would have purchased the sacred truths of Christianity at the dearest price, and that Heaven alone could compensate the unhappy and apostate Indian, who thus sought it at the expence of every earthly good and human happiness.

At length the trees of the forest, on whose remotest skirts they wandered, gradually disappeared; and, still following the track of the caravan, which in the course of the night they had again recovered as well as the moon's declining light would permit, they crossed a hill, where it seemed by its impressions on the soil recently to have passed: they then descended into a boundless plain, dismal, wild, and waste. Ere the sun had risen in all its fiercest glories above the horizon, they found themselves surrounded by a desert: the guiding track indeed still remained; but, in the illimitable waste, far as the eye could stretch its view, no object which could cheer their hearts, or dispel their fears, presented itself:—sky and earth alone appeared, alike awful, and alike unvaried; the heavens, shrouded with a deep red gloom, spread a boundless canopy to the view, like the concave roof of some earth-embosomed mine, whose golden veins shine duskily in gloomy splendour; and the sandy and burning soil, unvaried by a single tree or shrub, reflected back the scorching ardour of the skies, and mingled its brilliant surface with the distant horizon; both alike were terrific to the fancy, and boundless to the eye; both alike struck horror on the mind, and chased hope from the heart; alike denying all resource, withholding all relief; while the disconsolate wanderers, as they trod the burning waste, now turned their looks on the bleak perspective, now tenderly and despairingly on each other. Convinced that to return or to advance threatened alike destruction, thus they continued to wander in the lonesome and desolate wild, enduring the intense heat of the ardent day, the noxious blast of the chilly night, with no shelter from the horrors of the clime but what a clump of naked rocks at intervals afforded them; and when this rude asylum presented itself, the Missionary spread his robe on the earth for Luxima—endeavouring to soothe her to repose, only leaving her to seek some spring, always vainly sought, or to look for those hardy shrubs which even the desert sometimes produces, and which frequently treasure in their flowers the lingering dews of moister seasons; if he found them, it was mouldering amidst the dry red sand of the soil. At last the delicate animal, which had hitherto afforded them so much relief and aid, sunk beneath the intemperature of the clime, and expired at their feet. Luxima was now borne hopelessly along by the associate and the cause of her sufferings; and they proceeded slowly and despairingly, their parched and burning lips, their wearied and exhausted frames, scarcely permitting them to speak without effort, or to move without pain. But it was for Luxima only the Missionary suffered—he saw her whom he had found in the possession of every enjoyment, now almost expiring beneath his eyes; her lips of roses, scorched by the noxious blasts, and gust after gust of burning vapour, drying up the vital springs of life; while she, confounding in her mind her afflictions, and what she believed to be their cause, offered up faint invocations to appease those powers, whom love had induced her thus to provoke and to abandon.

It was in moments such as these, that the unfortunate Hilarion beheld that hope frustrated, which had hitherto solaced him in all the sufferings he had caused, and those he sustained; it was then that he felt it was the heart of the woman he had seduced, and not the mind of the heathen he had converted. At last, wholly overcome by the intense heat and immoderate fatigue, by insupportable thirst and a long privation of sustenance and sleep, Luxima was unable to proceed. The Missionary bore her in his feeble clasp to the base of a rock, which afforded them some shelter from the rays of the sun. He would have spoken to her of the Heaven to which her soul seemed already taking its flight; he would have assured her that his spirit would soon mingle with hers, and that an eternal union awaited them: but, in a moment, when love was strengthened by mutual suffering, and despair gave force to passion, and when each at once only lived and died for the other, words were poor vehicles to feelings so acute; and sighs, long and deep drawn, were the only sounds which emotions so profound, so tender, and so agonizing, would admit of: all was the silence of love unspeakable, and the awful stillness of dissolution. But when over the beautiful countenance which lay on his bosom, the Missionary beheld the sudden convulsion of pain throw its dread distortion,—madness seized the brain of the frantic lover, and he threw round a look wild and inquiring, but looked in vain; all was still, hopeless, and desolate. At last, something like a vapour appeared moving at a distance. He sprung forward, and, ascending the point of a rock, discovered at a distance a form which resembled that of a camel: faint as was the hope now awakened, it spread new life through his whole being; he snatched the dying Indian to his bosom; strength and velocity seemed a supernatural gift communicated to his frame; he flew over the burning sand, he approached the object of his wishes; hope with every step realizes the blessed vision; human forms grew distinct on his eye, human sounds vibrate on his ear—"She lives, she is saved!" he exclaims with a frantic shriek, and falls lifeless beneath his precious burthen in the midst of the multitude which forms the rear of the caravan. The caravan had stopped in this place near a spring, accidentally discovered, and the motley crowd which composed it, were all verging towards one point, eagerly contending for a draught of muddy water; but the sudden and extraordinary appearance of the now almost lifeless strangers, excited an emotion in all who beheld them. The few Hindus who belonged to the caravan shrank in horror from the unfortunate *Chancalas*, thus so closely associated with a *frangui*, or impure; but those in whom religious bigotry had not deadened the feelings of nature, beheld them with equal pity and admiration. Every assistance which humanity could devise was administered; and cordials, diluted with water, moistened lips parched with a long consuming thirst, and recalled to frames nearly exhausted, the fading powers of life. The Missionary, more overcome by his anxiety for Luxima, and the sudden transition of his feelings from despair to hope, than even by weakness, or personal suffering, was the first to recover consciousness and strength, and love instinctively claimed the first thought of reviving existence. In the transport of the moment he forgot the crowd that was its witness; he flew to Luxima, and shed tears of love and joy on the hands extended to him. He beheld the vital hues revisiting that cheek which he had lately pressed in hopeless agony, and saw the light of life beaming in those eyes whose lustre he had so lately seen darkened by the shades of death. Again, too, the voice of Luxima addresses him by the endearing epithet of "Father:" and though the venerated title found no sanction in their looks or years, yet many who beheld the scene of their re-union were touched by its affecting tenderness; and a general interest was excited for persons so noble, and so distinguished in their appearance, so interesting by their sufferings and misfortunes, which were registered in their looks, and attested by the singularity of their situations.

CHAPTER XV.

Luxima, restored to life, was still feeble and exhausted: but though faded, she was still lovely; and, being immediately recognized as a *Hindu*, that peculiar circumstance awakened curiosity and surmise. Those of her own nation and religion still shrank from her in horror, and declared her to be a *Chancalas*, or outcast; the Moslems who beheld her, sought not to conceal their rude admiration, and recognized her at once for a *Cashmirian* by her complexion and her beauty; but the persons who seemed to observe her with the most scrutiny, were *two Europeans*, whose features were concealed by hoods, worn apparently to shade off the ardour of the sun. Luxima was permitted to share the *mohaffah* or litter of a female seik who was going with her husband, a dealer in gems, to Tatta.[88] The Missionary was suffered to ascend the back of a camel, whose proprietor had expired the day before in the desert. Having declared himself a Portuguese of distinction, a Christian missionary, and shewed the briefs which testified his rank, he found no difficulty in procuring such necessaries as were requisite for the rest of their journey, until his arrival at Tatta should enable him to defray the debt of obligation which he of necessity incurred.

But though he had declared the nature of the relation in which he stood to his Neophyte to those immediately about him, yet he fancied, that the fact was, received by some with suspicion, and by others with incredulity. He was evidently considered the seducer of the fugitive Indian; and neither his innocence nor his dignity could save him from a profound mortification, new and insupportable to his proud and lofty nature: yet, trembling to observe the admiration which Luxima inspired, he still hovered near her in ceaseless disquietude and anxiety. The caravan was composed of five hundred persons of various nations and religions;—Mogul pilgrims, going from India to visit the tomb of their prophet at Mecca; merchants from Thibet and China, carrying the produce of their native climes, the Western coasts of Hindostan; Seiks, the Swiss of the East, going to join the forces of rebelling Rajahs; and faquirs and dervises, who rendered religion profitable by carrying for sale in their girdles, spices, gold-dust, and musk. Luxima, obviously abhorred by those of her own religion, closely observed by some, and suspected by all, felt her situation equally through her sex and her prejudices, and shrunk from the notice she unavoidably attracted in shame and in confusion: it was now that her forfeiture of cast for the first time appeared to the Missionary in all its horrors, and he no longer wondered that so long as the prejudice existed, with which it is connected, it should hold so tyrannic an influence over the Indian mind. His tenderness increasing with his pity, and his jealousy of those who attempted to approach, or to address her, giving a new force and character to his passion, he seldom left the side of her *litter:* yet he endeavoured to moderate the warmth of feelings it was now more than ever necessary to conceal. That passion, dangerous in every situation, was now no longer solitary as the wilds in which it sprang, but connected with society, and exposed to its observation; and the reserve with which he sought to temper its ardour, restored to it all that mysterious delicacy, which constitutes, perhaps, its first, and perhaps its best charm.

The caravan proceeded on its route, and, having passed the Desert, crossed the *Setlege*, and entered the *Moultan*, it halted at one of its usual stations, and the tents of the travellers were pitched on the shores of the Indus: the perils of the past were no longer remembered, and the safety of the present was ardently enjoyed, while the views and interests of the motley multitude, no longer subdued by personal danger, or impeded by personal suffering, again operated with their original force and activity. The merchants bartered with the traders, who came from the surrounding towns for the purpose; and the professors of the various religions and sects preached their respective doctrines to those whom they wished to convert, or to those who already believed, all but the Christian Missionary! Occupied by feelings of a doubtful and conflicting nature, sometimes hovering round the tent which Luxima shared with the family of the Seik, sometimes buried in profound thought, and wandering amidst the depths of a neighbouring forest, where he sought to avoid the idle bustle of those among whom he was adventitiously thrown; anxious, unquiet, and distrustful even of himself, he was now lost to that evangelic peace of mind, to that sober tranquility of feeling, so indispensable to the exercise of his mission. Though buried in a reserve which awed, while it distanced, there was a majesty in his air, and a dignified softness in his manner, which daily increased that popular interest in his favour, which his first appearance had awakened: to this he was not insensible; for, still ambitious of distinction as saint or as man, he beheld his influence with a triumph natural to one, who, emulous of unrivalled superiority, feels that he owes it not to extraneous circumstance, but to that proud and indefeasible right of supreme eminence, with which nature had endowed him. But he could not but particularly observe, that he was an object of singular attention to the two European travellers, who, wrapped in mystery, seemed to shun all intercourse, and avoid all observation; and, though they crossed him in his solitary walks, pursued him to the entrance of Luxima's tent, and hung upon his every word and action, yet so subtilely had they eluded his notice, that he had not yet obtained an opportunity of either distinctly seeing their features, or of addressing them; all he could learn was, that they had joined the caravan from *Lahore*, with two other persons of the same dress and description as themselves, who had proceeded with the advanced troop of the caravan, and that they were known to be Europeans and Christians. It was not till the caravan had entered the province of *Sindy*, that one of them, who rode near the camel of the Missionary, seemed inclined to address him; after some observations he said, "It is understood that you are a Christian Missionary! but, while in this mighty multitude the professor of each false religion appears anxious to advance his doctrine, and to promulgate his creed, how is it that the *apostle of Christianity* is alone silent and indifferent on the subject of that pure faith, to the promulgation of which he has devoted himself?"—

The Missionary threw a haughty look over the figure of the person who thus interrogated him; but, with a sudden recollection, he endeavoured to recall the humility of his religious character, and replied: "The question is natural—and the silence to which you allude is not the effect of weakened zeal, nor the result of abated

enthusiasm, in the sacred cause to which I have devoted myself—
it is a silence which arises from a consciousness that though I spoke
with the tongues of angels, it *would be here but as the sound of tinkling brass*;[89] for *truth*, which always prevails over unbiassed ignorance, has ever failed in its effect upon bigoted error—and the
dogma most difficult to vanquish, is that which is guarded by self-
interest."

"You allude to the obstinate paganism of the Brahmins?"

"I allude to the power of the most powerful of all human superstitions; a superstition which equally presides over the heavenly
hope, and directs the temporal concern; and which so intimately
blends itself with all the relations of human life, as equally to dic-
tate a doctrinal tenet, or a sumptuary law, to regulate alike the salvation of the soul, and fix the habits of existence."

"It is the peculiar character of the zeal of Christianity to rise in
proportion to the obstacles it encounters!"

"The zeal of Christianity should never forsake the mild spirit of
its fundamental principles; in the excess of its warmest enthusiasm,
it should be tempered by charity, guided by reason, and regulated
by possibility; forsaken by these, it ceases to be the zeal of religion,
and becomes the spirit of fanaticism, tending only to sever man
from man, and to multiply the artificial sources of aversion by
which human society is divided, and human happiness destroyed!"

"This temperance in doctrine, argues a freedom in opinion, and
a languor in zeal, which rather belongs to the character of the heathen philosophy, than to the enthusiasm of Christian faith; had its
disciples been always thus moderate, thus languid, thus philosoph-
ically tolerant, never would the cross have been raised upon the
remotest shores of the Eastern and Western oceans!"

"Too often has it been raised under the influence of a sentiment
diametrically opposite to the spirit of the doctrine of him who *suffered on it*, and who came not to *destroy*, but to *save* mankind. Too
often has it been raised by those whose minds were guided by an
evil and interested policy, fatal to the effects which it sought to
accomplish, and who lifted to Heaven, hands stained with the blood
of those, to whom they had been sent to preach the religion of
peace, of love, and of salvation; for even the zeal of religion, when
animated by human passions, may become fatal in its excess, and that
daring fanaticism, which gives force and activity to the courage of
the man, may render merciless and atrocious, the zeal of the bigot."

"You disapprove then of that energy of conversion which either
by art or force secures or redeems the soul from the sin of idolatry?"

"*Force* and *art* may indeed effect profession, but cannot induce the conviction of faith; for the individual perception of truth is not to be effected by the belief of others, and an act of faith must be either an act of private judgement, or of free will, which no human artifice, no human authority can alter or controul."

"You disapprove then of the zealous exertions of the Jesuits in the cause of Christianity, and despair of their success?"

"I disapprove not of the zeal, but of the mediums by which it manifests itself: I believe that the coercion and the artifice to which they resort, frequently impel the Hindus to a resistance, which they perhaps too often expiate by the loss of life and property, but seldom urge them to the abjuration of a religion, the loss of whose privileges deprives the wretched apostate of every human good! It is by a previous cultivation of their moral powers, we may hope to influence their religious belief; it is by teaching them to love us, that we can lead them to listen to us; it is by inspiring them with respect for our virtues, that we can give them a confidence in our doctrine: but this has not always been the system adopted by European reformers, and the religion we proffer them is seldom illustrated by its influence on our own lives. We bring them a spiritual creed, which commands them to forget the world, and we take from them temporal possessions, which prove how much *we live for it.*"

"With such mildness in opinion, and such tolerance towards the prejudices of others, you have doubtless succeeded in your mission, where a zeal not more pure, but more ardent, would have failed?"

The Missionary changed colour at the observation, and replied—"The zeal of the members of the congregation of the Mission can never be doubted, since they voluntarily devote themselves to the cause of Christianity; yet to effect a change in the religion of sixty millions of people, whose* doctrines claim their authority from the records of the most ancient nations,—whose faith is guarded by the pride of rank, the interest of priesthood, by its own abstract nature, by local habits, and confirmed prejudices; a faith which resisted the sword of Mahmoud and arms of Timur,[91]—requires a power seldom vested in man, and which

---

* "Notwithstanding the labours of the Missionaries for upwards of two hundred years, out of perhaps one hundred millions of *Hindus*, there are not twelve thousand *Christians*, and those are almost all entirely *chancalas*, or *outcasts*."—*Sketches of the History of the Religion, Learning, and Manners of the Hindus*, p. 48.[90]

time, a new order of things in India, and the Divine will, can alone, I believe, accomplish."

"You return to the centre of your mission without any converts to your exertion and your eloquence?"

"No fruit has been indeed gathered equal to the labour or the hope; for I have made but one proselyte, who purchases the truths of Christianity by the forfeiture of every earthly good!"

"A *Brahmin* perhaps?"

"A Brahmin's daughter! the chief priestess of the pagoda of Sirinagar, in Cashmire, a prophetess, and *Brachmachira;* whose conversion may indeed be deemed a miracle!"

"Your neophyte is then that young and beautiful person we first beheld lifeless *in your arms*, in the desert?"

"The same," said the Missionary, again changing colour: "She has already received the rites of baptism, and I am conveying her to *Goa*, there her profession of some holy order may produce, by its example, a salutary effect, which her conversion never could have done in Cashmire; a place where the Brahminical bigotry has reached its zenith, and where her forfeiture of cast would have rendered her an object of opprobrium and aversion!"—As the Missionary spoke, he raised his eyes to the face of the person he addressed; but it was still shaded by the hood of his cloak, yet he met an eye so keen, so malignant in its glance, that, could he have shrunk from any mortal look, he would have shrunk from this. Struck by its singular expression, and by the certainty of having before met it, he remained for many minutes endeavouring to collect his thoughts, and, believing himself justified by the freedom of the stranger's inquiries, to question him as to his country and profession, he turned round to address him: but the strangers had now both moved away, and the Missionary then first observed, that he who had been silent during this short dialogue, and whom he still held in view, was employed in writing on a tablet, as though he noted down the heads of the conversation. This circumstance appeared too strange not to excite some curiosity, and much amazement. The person who addressed him spoke in the Hindu dialect, as it was spoken at *Lahore*; but he believed it possible, that he might have been some emissary from the Jesuits' convent there, on his way to the Inquisitorial college at Goa: this for a moment disquieted him; for his mind, long divided by conflicting passions, had lost its wonted self possession and lofty independence: he had been recently accustomed to suspect himself; and he now feared that his zeal, relaxed by passion, had weakened that severity of principle which once admitted of no innovation, and thought it not impossible that he might have expressed his sentiments with a freedom which bigotry could easily torture into an evidence of heresy itself. He again sought the two strangers, but in vain; for they had joined the advanced troop of the caravan; while a feeling, stronger than any they had excited, still fixed him in the rear, near the mohaffah of Luxima.

The caravan now pursued its toilsome route through the rich and varying district of *Scindi*;[92] and the fresh and scented gales, which blew from the Indian sea, revived the languid spirits of the drooping Neophyte; and gave to her eye and cheek, the beam and glow of health and loveliness. Not so the Missionary:—as he advanced towards the haunts of civilized society, the ties by which he was bound to it, and its influence and power over his opinions and conduct, which a fatal passion, cherished in wilds and deserts, had banished from his mind, now rushed to his recollection with an overwhelming force—he gloomily anticipated the disappointment which awaited his return to Goa; the triumph of his enemies, and the discomfiture of his friends; the inferences which might be drawn from the sex and beauty of his solitary Neophyte; and, above all, the eternal separation from the sole object, that alone had taught him the supreme bliss, which the most profound and precious feeling of nature can bestow,—a separation, imperiously demanded by religion, by honour, and by the respect still due to his character and holy profession. It was his intention to place her in a house of Franciscan Sisters, an order whose purity and mildness was suited to her gentle nature. But, when he remembered the youth and loveliness he was about to entomb, the feelings and affections he was about to sacrifice—the warm, the tender, the impassioned heart he should devote to a cold and gloomy association, with rigid and uncongenial spirits—when he beheld her in fancy ascending the altar steps, resigning, by vows she scarcely understood, the brilliant illusions of her own imposing and fanciful faith, and embracing doctrines to which her mind was not yet familiarized, and against which her strong rooted prejudices and ardent feelings still revolted,—when he beheld her despoiled of those lovely and luxuriant tresses which had so often received the homage of his silent admiration, and almost felt his own hands tremble, as he placed on her brow the veil which concealed her from him for ever,—when he caught the parting sigh,—when his glance died under the expression of those dove-like eyes, which, withdrawing their looks from the cross, would still throw their lingering and languid light upon his receding form!—then, worked up to a frenzy of love and of affection, by the image which his fancy and his feelings had pictured to his heart, he eagerly sought her presence as though the moment was already arrived, when he should lose her love for ever; and he hung, in such despairing fondness round her, that Luxima, touched by the expression of his countenance, sought to know the cause of his agitation, and to soothe his spirits. The Missionary leaned over the vehicle, in which she reposed, to catch the murmurings of her low and tender voice.

"Thou art sad," she said, "and melancholy hangs upon thy brow, now that danger is over, and suffering almost forgotten. Is it only in the midst of perils, which strike death upon weaker souls, that *thine* rejoices? for amidst the conflicts of varying elements, thou wast firm; in the burning desert, thou wast unsubdued—Oh! how often has my fancy likened thee to the great *vesanti* plant, which, when it meets not the mighty stem round which it is its nature to twine and flourish, droops not, though forsaken, but assuming the form and structure of a towering tree, betrays its aspiring origin, and points its lofty branches towards the heavens, whose storms it dares—and thus doth thou seem greatest, when most exposed— and firmest, when least supported. Oh! father," she added, with an ardour she had long suppressed, "didst thou feel as I feel, one look of love would chase all sorrow from thy heart, and sadness from thy brow."

"But Luxima," returned the Missionary, infected by her impassioned tenderness, as if that were almost love's last look, "if, when every tie was drawn so closely round the heart, that both must break together—if the fatal consciousness of being loved, have become so necessary to existence, that life seems without it, a cold and dreary waste—if under the influence of feelings such as these, the moment of an eternal separation dawns in all its hopeless and insupportable misery on the soul, then every look which love bestows, mingles sadness with affection, and despair with bliss." Luxima turned pale; and she raised her tearful eyes to his face, not daring to inquire, but by look, how far that dreadful moment was yet distant. The Missionary pointed out to her a distant view of Tatta, whence they were to sail for Goa; and, stifling the emotions of the lover, and the feelings of the man, he endeavoured to rally back his fading zeal; he spoke to her only in the language of the Missionary and the Priest; he spoke of resigning her to *God alone;* of that perfect conversion which his absence even *more* that his presence would effect!—he described to her the nature and object of the life she was about to embrace,—its peace—its sanctity—its exemptions from human trials, and human passions—and above all, the eternal beatitude to which it led;—he spoke to her of their separation, as inevitable,—and, concealing the struggles which existed in his own mind, he sought only to soothe, to strengthen, and to tranquillize hers. Luxima heard him in silence: she made neither objections nor reply. He was struck by the sudden change which took place in her countenance, when she learned how soon they were to part, and how inevitable was their separation; it was a look resolute and despairing,—as if she defied the destiny, cruel as it was, which seemed to threaten her. At some distance from Tatta, the ardours of a vertical sun obliged the caravan to halt, and seek a temporary shade amidst the umbrageous foliage of a luxuriant grove, refreshed by innumerable streams, flowing into the Indus.

Luxima left her mohaffah, and, supported by the Missionary, sought those shades, which so strongly recalled to her remembrance, the lovely groves of Cashmire,—and the recollections so sad, and yet so precious, which rushed on her mind, were opposed by those feelings which swelled in her bosom, when a distant view of Tatta recalled to her memory the approach of that hour which was so soon to lead her to Goa, to the destined altar of her immolation!—She reflected on the past—she anticipated the future;—and, for the first time, the powerful emotions of which she was capable, betrayed themselves with a violence almost irreconcilable with her gentle and tender nature.—Convulsed with long-stifled feelings, to which she now gave vent, she bathed the earth whereon she had thrown herself, with tears; and, with an eloquence dictated by love and by despair, she denied the existence of an affection which could voluntarily resign its object;—she upbraided equally her lover and herself; and, amidst expressions of reproach and remorse, was still less penitent than tender,—still less lamented her errors, than the approaching loss of him, for whom she had committed them.

"Thou sayest that I am dear to thee," she said; "and yet I am sacrificed; and by him for whom I have abandoned all, I am now myself abandoned.—Oh! give me back to my country, my peace, my fame; or suffer me still to remain near thee, and I will rejoice in the loss of all.—Thou sayest it is the law of thy religion that thou obeyest, when thou shalt send me from thee:—but, if it is a virtue in thy religion to stifle the best and purest feelings of the heart, that nature implants, how shall I believe in, or adopt, its tenets?—I, whose nature, whose faith itself, was love—how from thee shall I learn to subdue my feelings, who first taught me to substitute a human, for a heavenly passion?—Alas! I have but changed the object, the *devotion* is still the same; and thou art loved by the *outcast*, as the Priestess once loved Heaven only."

"Luxima," returned the Missionary, distracted equally by his own feelings and by hers, "let us from the sufferings we now endure, learn the extent of the weakness and the errors which we thus, be it hoped, so painfully expiate; for, it is by despair, such as now distracts us, that Heaven punishes the unfortunate, who suffers a passionate and exclusive sentiment to take possession of the heart, for a creature frail and dependant as ourselves. Oh! my daughter, had we but listened to the voice of religion, or of reason, as we have hearkened to our own passions, the most insupportable of human afflictions could not now have befallen us; and that pang by which we are agonized, at the brink of eternal separation, would have been spared to those souls, which a divine and imperishable object would then have solely occupied and involved."

"I, at least," said Luxima, firmly, yet with wildness, "I shall not long endure that pang:—Thinkest thou that I shall long survive *his* loss for whom I have sacrificed all? Oh! no; it was *thou* I followed, and not thy doctrines; for, pure and sublime as they may be, they yet came darkly and confusedly to my soul: but the sentiments thy presence awakened in my heart, were not opposed by any previous thought or feelings of my life; they were true to all its natural impulses, and, if not understood, they were *felt* and *answered;* they mingled with my whole being, and now, even now, form an imperishable part of my existence.—Shudder not thus, but pity, and forgive me! nor think that, weak as I am, I will deprive thee of thy triumph:—yes, thou shalt lead to the Christian Temple, the descendant of Brahma! thou shalt offer up, a sacrifice on the Christian altar, the first apostate, drawn from the most illustrious of the Indian casts,—a Prophetess! who for thee abandoned the homage of a Divinity,—a woman, who for thee resisted the splendours of an empire.—And this I will tell to the Christians in the midst of their temple, and their congregation—that they may know the single solitary convert thy powers have made, is more than all the proselytes thy brethren e'er brought to kiss the Cross:—this I shall do *less in faith* than *love;* not for *my* sake, but for *thine.*—Yet, oh! be thou near me at the altar of sacrifice; let me cling to thee to the last—for, stern and awful as thy religion is, its severity will not refuse me that: yet, if it punish thee, even for pitying—"

"And thinkest thou," interrupted the Missionary wildly, "that it is *punishment* I fear, or that if the enjoyment of thy love, fatal and dear as thou art, could be purchased by suffering, that I would shrink from its endurance? No! it is not torture the most acute I shun—it is *crime that I abhor*—and, equal to sustain all sufferings but those of conscience, I now live only in dread of myself! For oh! Luxima, even yet I might spare myself and thee a life so cold, so sad and dreary, that conscious virtue and true religion only can support us through it,—even yet, escaping from every eye, save Heaven's, we might together fly to the pathless wilds of these delicious regions, and live in sinful bliss, the commoners of nature:—But, Luxima, the soul of him who loves, and who resists thee, is formed of such a temper, that it can taste no perfect joy in weakness or in crime. Pity then, and yet respect, him who, loving thee and virtue equally, can ne'er know happiness without nor with thee,—who, thus condemned to suffer, without ceasing, submits not to his fate, but is overpowered by its tyranny, and who, alike helpless and unresigned, opposes while he suffers, and repines while he endures; knowing only the remorse of guilt without its enjoyments, and expecting its retribution, without daring to deprecate its weight."—Exhausted and overpowered, he fell prostrate on the earth; cold damps hung on his brow, and burning tears fell from his inflamed eyes.—Luxima, terrified by his emotion, faint and trembling, crept timidly and tenderly towards him; and, pressing his hands, she murmured soothingly, yet with firmness, "Since then we can both only live to suffer or to err, to be miserable or to be guilty, wherefore should we not die?"

The Missionary raised his eyes to her face, and its expression of loveliness and love, though darkened by despair, rendered her more enchanting in his eyes, than she had ever yet appeared: he felt her tears on his hands, which she pressed alternately to her eyes and to her lips; and this eloquent though silent expression of an affection so pure, which he believed was to be the last proof of love he might ever receive, overwhelmed him.

Silent and motionless, he withdrew not his hands from the clasp of hers; he gazed on her with unrestrained feelings of love and pity, his whole soul seeming to diffuse itself through his eyes, over her countenance and figure. It was in this transient moment of high-wrought emotions, that they were suddenly surrounded by a group of persons who sprang from behind a rock. Luxima was torn from the arms, which but now protectingly encircled her; and the Missionary was seized with a violence, that, in the first moment of amazement and horror, deprived him of all presence of mind. But the feeble plaints of Luxima, who was borne away in the arms of one of the assailants, recalled to his bewildered mind a consciousness of their mutual sufferings, and situations:—he struggled with all the strength of frenzy, in the strong grasp of the two persons who held him;—he shook them from him as creatures of inferior force and nature; and looked so powerful, in his uncurbed rage, that a third, who stood armed before him, attempted not to arrest his flight, as he sprang forward to the rescue of Luxima, who lay lifeless in the arms of the person who was carrying her away; but in the next moment his own encircled her: the person from whom he had torn her, seemed no less bold, no less resolved than he; drawing a pistol from beneath his robe, he pointed it to the Missionary's breast; and exclaimed, "To resist, is but to increase your crimes, and to endanger your life." The Missionary gently disengaged himself from Luxima, who sunk to the earth, and, springing like a lion on his opponent, he seized his arm;—closely entwined in bonds of mutual destruction, they wrestled for life and death, with a strength almost supernatural,— at last, Hilarion wresting the pistol from the hand of his adversary, flung him against a rock, at whose base he lay apparently without life.—His three associates now came to the scene of action— armed, and with looks that threatened to avenge the fate of their companion; but the Missionary stood firm and unappalled, his eye lowring defiance, and raising Luxima in one arm, while with the other he pointed the pistol towards them, he said boldly, "Whoe'er you be, and whatever may have tempted you to this desperate outrage, I shall not spare the life of him who dares approach one single step."

The persons looked in consternation on each other; but one of them, whose face was till now concealed, threw back his hood and robe, and discovered on his breast, the Badge which distinguishes *the officers of the Inquisition!** It was then, that the Missionary recognized in the European traveller the Coadjutor whom he had

---

* "They all wear (the Familiares de Santo Officio), as a mark of creditable distinction, a gold medal, upon which are engraven the Arms of the Inquisition." *Stockdale's History of the Inquisitions.*

disgraced and dismissed from his appointment, during their voyage to India. Amazed, confounded, but not subdued, he met, with an undaunted look, the keen, malignant, and avengeful glance, which was now directed at him: "Knowest thou me?" demanded the Inquisitor scoffingly, "who, now high in power in the highest of all human tribunals, was once covered with shame and opprobrium, by thy superior excellence! Where now are all the mighty virtues of the *man without a fault*? where now are the wonders which his zeal and genius promised? what are the fruits of his unrivalled Mission? Behold him! supporting on his bosom, the victim of his seductive arts!—his sacrilegious hand, pointing an instrument of death at those who are engaged in the duties of that holy office, whose censure he has incurred by dreadful heresies, by breach of solemn vows, and by his heretical defamation of a sacred Order!"— While the Inquisitor yet spoke, several persons from the Caravan had arrived on the spot, to witness a scene so singular and so unexpected: Luxima too, who had recovered her senses, still trembling and horror-struck, clung to the bosom, which now so wildly heaved to the emotions of rage and indignation.

Silent for many minutes, the Missionary stood gazing with a look of proud defiance and ineffable contempt upon his avengeful enemy: "And know *you* not me?" he at last exclaimed, with a lofty scorn— "you knew me once, supreme, where *you* dared not *soar*!—Such as *I then was*, such *I now am;* in every thing unchanged—and still, in every thing, *your* superior!—Grovelling and miserable *as you are* even in your unmerited elevation—this you *still* feel;—speak, then; what are your orders!—tremble not, but declare them!—It is the Count of Acugna, it is the Apostolic *Nuncio* of *India*, who commands you!"— Pale with stifled rage, the Inquisitor drew from his bosom the brief, by which he was empowered to call those before the Inquisitorial Court, whose conduct and whose opinions should fall under the suspicions of those emissaries, which it had deputed to visit the Christian establishments in the interior of India.—The Missionary glanced his eye over the awful instrument, and bowed low to the Red Cross imprinted at its head: the Inquisitor then said, "Hilarion, of the Order of St. Francis, and member of the Congregation of the Mission;—I arrest you in the name of the Holy Office, and in the presence of these its ministers, that you may answer to such charges as I shall bring against you, before *the tribunal* of the Inquisition." At these words, the Missionary turned pale!—nature stood checked by religion!—passion submitted to opinion, and prejudice governed those *feelings*, over which *reason* had lost all sway. He let fall the instrument of death, which he had held in his hand till now; the voice of the Church had addressed him, and all the powerful force of his religious habits returned upon his soul: he, who till now had felt only as a *man*, remembered he was a *religious*; he who had long, who had so recently, acknowledged the precious influence of human feeling, now recalled to mind that he had vowed the sacrifice of *all* human feeling to Heaven!—and he who had resisted oppression, and avenged insult, now recollected, that by the religion he professed, he was bound when one *cheek was smitten, to turn the other.*[93]

The rage which had blazed in the eyes of the indignant, the blood which had boiled in the veins of the brave, no longer flashed in the glance, or crimsoned the cheek of the Christian Missionary; yet still it was—

> "Awe from above, that quelled his heart,
> nought else dismayed."[94]

The officers of the Inquisition now approached, to bind his arms, and to lead him away; but Luxima, with a shriek of horror, threw herself between them, ignorant of the nature of the danger which assailed her lover and her friend, and believing it nothing less than death itself: her wild and frenzied supplications, her beauty and affection, touched the hearts of those who surrounded them. The Missionary had already excited a powerful interest in his favour: the popular feeling is always on the side of resistance against oppression—for men, however vicious individually, are generally virtuous in the mass: his fellow-travellers, therefore, boldly advanced, to rescue one, whose air and manner had captivated their imaginations. The passions of a multitude know no precise limit; the partisans of the Missionary only waited for the orders of him whom they were about to avenge: they said, "Shall we throw those men under the camels' feet? or shall we bind them to those rocks, and leave them to their fate?"

The Europeans shuddered, and turned pale!

The Missionary cast on them a glance of contempt and pity, and, looking round him with an air at once dignified and grateful, he said, "My friends, my heart is deeply touched by your generous sympathy; good and brave men ever unite, of whatever region, or whatever faith they may be: but I belong to a religion whose spirit it is to save, and not to destroy; suffer then, these men to live; they are but the agents of a higher power, whose scrutiny they challenge me to meet.—I go to appear before that tribunal of that church, whose voice is my law, and from which a Christian minister can make no appeal,—I trust I go to contend *best* with the *best;* prepared rather to suffer death myself, than to cause the death of others."

Then turning to the Inquisitor he said, pointing to Luxima, whom he again supported in his arms, "Remember, that by a word I could have had you mingled with the dust I tread on; but, as you prize that life I have preserved, guard and protect this sacred, this consecrated vestal!—*look at her!*—otherwise than pure and innocent, you dare not believe her: know then, also, she is a Christian Neophyte, who has received the Baptismal rites, and who is destined to set a bright example to her idolatrous nation, and to become the future spouse of God."

Subdued and mortified, the officers of the Inquisition made no reply. He whom the Missionary had wounded, now crawled towards the others—they surrounded their unresisting prisoner, who bore along the feeble form of the Indian: silent, and weeping, she was consigned to the mohaffah she had before occupied; and, the Missionary having ascended the back of his camel, the caravan was again in motion—two of the Inquisitors remained with their prisoner—the other two had rode on before the caravan to *Tatta.*

CHAPTER XVI.

It was night when the travellers reached the suburbs of the ancient city of Tatta; the caravan had been lessened of its numbers during its progress; those who remained, now dispersed in various directions: the Inquisitors, instead of proceeding with their charge to a *Caravansera,* carried him and the Neophyte to a small fortress which belonged to a Spanish garrison; a guard of soldiers, headed by the two Inquisitors, who had preceded the caravan, received them at its portals.

The Missionary guessed his fate—dreadful as it was, he met it not unprepared: he saw himself surrounded by an armed force; he knew that, were he inclined to offer it, all resistance would be vain; and he submitted, with all the grandeur of human dignity, with all the firmness of religious fortitude, to a destiny now inevitable.

But Luxima still clung to him: the gloomy air of all around her, the fierce looks of the soldiers, their arms glittering to the dusky light of a solitary lamp, which hung suspended in the centre of a vast and desolate guardroom; the black cowls and scowling countenances of the Inquisitors, all struck terror on the timid soul of the Indian. She cast round a fearful and terrified glance, and would then have sunk upon the bosom of her sole protector and friend on earth, but, exposed as they were to the observation of their persecutors, the Missionary, for her sake even more than for his own, rejected the impulse of his feelings, and, turning away his head to conceal the agony of his countenance, he held her from him.—It was then that the heart of Luxima, sinking within her bosom, seemed to have received its death wound;—she fixed her closing eyes on him, who thus almost seemed to resign her to misery and to suffering, unsupported and unpitied—but she wept not, and one of the Inquisitors bore her away, unresisting, and almost lifeless, in his arms. An exclamation of horror burst from the lips of the Missionary; and, with an involuntary motion, he advanced a few steps to follow her; betraying, in his wild and haggard looks, the feelings by which his soul was torn. But the guards interposed—he could not even himself desire, that she might remain with him; and the Inquisitor, fixing his eyes on his agitated countenance, with a look of scoffing malignancy, said: "Fear not for your concubine, she shall be taken care of."—At these words, a deep scarlet suffused the cheek of the Missionary; fire flashed from his dark rolling eye, and he cast a look on his insulting oppressor, so blasting in its glance, that he seemed to wither beneath its terrific influence.—"Observe!" he said, with a voice of thunder, "I repeat it to you, it is a Christian Neophyte, pure, spotless, and unsullied, which you have now taken under your protection; look therefore that you consider her as such, as you shall answer it to that God, to whom she is about to consecrate her sinless life; as you shall answer it to that Church, whose ministers you are.—Be this remembered by you as priests; as *men*, forget not *she is a woman!*" Then, turning to his guards, he said with haughtiness, "Lead on;"—as though he still commanded, even in obeying; and he was immediately led to a tower in a remote part of the fortress.

The members of the Inquisitorial Court, into whose power a singular coincidence of circumstances had thrown the Missionary, were returning from visiting the Christian institution at Lahore, of whose abuses and disorders the grand Inquisitor had received secret intelligence, when the chief of the party, who had been raised to his present dignity by the low arts of cunning and duplicity, discovered in the supposed lover of a fugitive Indian, that once infallible man, of whose rigid virtue, and severe unbending justice, he had been the victim; conscious, that in detecting and exposing the frailty of one who had "bought golden opinions, from all sorts of persons," he should, while he gratified his own private vengeance, present a grateful victim to the Jesuits and Dominicans, who equally hated the Franciscan, for his order, his popularity, and his unrivalled genius,—he soon sought and found sufficient grounds of accusation, to lay the basis of his future ruin.[95] With an artifice truly jesuitical, he drew the Missionary into a conversation, which he obliged one of his brethren to listen to, and note down; and, from the freedom of those religious opinions he had induced the Missionary to discuss, and from the tender nature of the ties which seemed to exist between him and his lovely associate,— Heresy, and the seduction of a Neophyte, were the crimes to be alleged against a man, whose disgrace was destined to be commensurate to the splendour of his triumphs.

On the day following their arrival at Tatta, the Missionary was conveyed on board a Spanish vessel, which lay in the Indus, and was bound for Goa. On his way he passed the *litter* which Luxima, he believed, occupied; but it was closely covered. He shuddered, and for a moment the heroism of virtue deserted him—he doubted not that she would be conveyed in the same vessel with him to Goa; and, as he knew that supplication would be fruitless, and that in humbling himself to intreaty he would not effect the purpose for which he stooped, he made no effort to obtain an interview with her: he believed too that the insatiable desire of the Jesuits for conversion would render her safety and preservation an object to them; and that she would owe to the bigotry of their zeal, that mercy which she could not expect from the suggestions of their humanity—but that he should never again behold her, the object of his only love, the companion of his wandering, and the partner of his sufferings, was an idea dictated by despair, from which religion withdrew her light, and hope her solace. Placed in a close and unwholesome confinement, it was in vain he sought to catch the sound of Luxima's voice; it was in vain he hazarded an inquiry relative to her situation: silence and mystery still surrounded him; no beam shone upon the darkness of his days; no answer was returned to his inquiries; no pity was given to his sufferings; all was dreary hopeless gloom! all was the loss of fame, the loss of love! of all that the high ambition of piety had promised! of all that the exquisite feelings of nature had bestowed!—Still pursued "by thoughts of lost happiness and lasting shame," and joined only in *equal ruin* with her for whom he had encountered misery and affliction,[96] and on whose innocent head he had heaped it,—he now saw that the sufferings of man resulted less from the constitution of his nature, than from the obstinacy with which he abandons the dictates of Providence, and devotes himself to those illusions which the law of human reason, and the impulse of human affection, equally oppose. He remembered the feelings with which the Brahmin Priestess and the Christian Missionary had first mutually met; he contrasted their first interview with their present situations, alike as they now were *the victims of mistaken zeal*; and he accused that misconstruction of the laws of Providence, those false distinctions, which superstition has erected between the species, as the source of the severest sufferings to which mankind was condemned. For himself, he had no hope: he knew the character of his judges, the sentiments they bore in general to his order, and in particular to him; he knew the influence of the tribunal at which they presided, he knew that those whom they intended to destroy, no human power could preserve. But while he accused himself of relaxation in his zeal, of negligence in his mission, of suffering a guilty passion to subdue the force of his mind, and the influence of his religion, he believed his enemies to be but the blind agents of that Heaven, whose wrath he had justly provoked; for, still bringing his new-born feelings to the test of his ancient opinions, he continued to oppose religion to nature, and deemed himself sunk in guilt, because he had not risen above humanity.

It was on a day bright and sunny as that on which the Apostolic Nuncio left *Goa* in all the triumph of superior and unrivalled excellence, that he returned to it a *prisoner* and in *chains*. His enemies had determined that his disgrace should be as striking and as public as his triumph; that the idol of the people should be dashed before their eyes from the shrine erected to his glory; and that envy and bigotry, under the guise of religion and justice, should gratify the insatiate spirit of persecution and vengeance. Before the illustrious criminal was permitted to land, the intelligence of his return under circumstances so different from those his departure had promised, and dark innuendos of the nature and extent of his fault, were artfully circulated through *Goa*, till the public mind, soured by the disappointments of its hopes and its confidence, was prepared to receive the Nuncio with a contempt equal to the admiration it formerly bestowed on him. At last a guard of Spanish soldiers, accompanied by the officers of the Holy Office, were sent to conduct him to the prison of the Inquisition. A multitude of persons had assembled to see him pass; but they no longer beheld the same creature whom they had last so loudly greeted with acclamations of reverential homage, and on whose mild and majestic brow passion had impressed no trace, whose commanding eye was brightened by holy joy, and whose life of sinless purity was marked in the seraphic character of his inspired countenance! His person was now almost as changed as his fate: it was worn away by suffering, by fatigue, by internal conflicts, and faded by its exposure to the varying clime; the experience of human frailty in himself, and of human turpitude in others, marked his brow with traces of distrust and disappointment;—his enthusiasm was fled! his zeal subdued by the fatal consequences of its unsuccessful efforts! and love, and affliction, and shame, and indignation, the opprobrium he endured, and the innocence he could not establish; the injustice under which he laboured, and the malignity he despised—all mingled their conflicts in his soul, all shed over his air and look the sullen grandeur of a proud despair, superior to complaint, and inaccessible to hope; yet "not all *lost* in *loss* itself," gleams of his mind's untarnished glory still brightened at intervals his look of gloom—and, still appearing little less than "archangel ruined," he proceeded, manacled, but lofty and tower-ing above the guards who surrounded him.[97] An awful silence reigned on every side; and even those who deemed him culpable, saw him so mighty in *his fall*, that while they accused him of guilt, they believed him superior to weakness; respecting while they condemned, and admiring while they pitied him. As a member of the noble house of *Acugna*, whatever were the charges brought against him, he could not fail to excite interest in Goa, where the Portuguese were coalesced by a common feeling of suffering under the oppression of the Spanish government: but the terrors which surrounded the most dreadful of all human tribunals; a tri-bunal which was seconded, in the hierarchy of Goa, by all the influence of civil authority; its being invested with the power of life and death, and superstitiously believed even with that of sal-vation itself, awed the boldest heart, and alike silenced the feelings of patriotism, and stilled the impulse of humanity! Not even a murmur of resistance was heard; the accused and his guards passed silently on to the prison of the Holy Office; they reached its gloomy court; the portals closed upon the victim, and the light of hope was shut out for ever!

No breath transpired of the dark mysterious deeds which passed within the mansion of horror and superstition; and its awful investigations were conducted with a secresy which baffled all inquiry:* the impenetrable cloud which hung over the fate of the Missionary, could only be cleared up when that dreaded day arrived, upon which the dungeons of the Inquisition were to yield up their tenants to punishment, to liberty, or—to death!

At this period a sullen gloom hung over the city of Goa, resembling the brooding of a distant storm:—it was rumoured, that the power of the Spanish government in Portugal and its colonies was on the point of extinction, and it was known by many fatal symptoms, that the Indians were ripe for insurrection. The arts used by the Dominicans and the Jesuits for the conversion of the followers of Brahma, the evil consequences which had arisen by forfeiture of cast, (for many families had shared the ignominy heaped on the devoted head of the individual apostate) with the coercive tyranny of the Spanish government, had excited in the breasts of the mild, patient, and long-enduring Hindus, a principle of resistance, which waited only for some strong and sudden impulse to call it into action;† and it was observed that this disposition had particularly betrayed itself on a recent and singular occasion.

A woman who bore on her forehead the mark of a descendant of Brahma (the sacred *tellertum*), and round her neck the sacrificial threads or *dsandam* of their tutelar god, was seen to enter a convent of Dominican nuns, led by an officer of the Inquisition, and surrounded by Dominican and *Jesuit priests!* The faded beauty of her perfect form, her noble and distinguished air, the agony of her countenance, and the silent tears which fell from her eyes when she turned them on those of her own cast and country, who stood near the litter from which she alighted, awakened a strong and

---

* The people also dare not speak of this Inquisition, but with the utmost respect and reverence; and if by accident the slightest word should escape one, which concerned it ever so little, it would be necessary immediately to accuse and inform against one's self. People are frequently confined to the prison for one, two, or three years, without knowing the reason, and are visited only by officers of the Inquisition, and never suffered to behold any other person.—*History of the Inquisition by Stockdale*, p. 213.

† An insurrection of a fatal consequence took place in *Vellore* so late as 1806, and a mutiny at Nundydrag and Benglore, occurred about the same period: both were supposed to have originated in the religious bigotry of the natives, suddenly kindled by the supposed threatened violation of their faith from the Christian settlers.[98]

powerful emotion in their feelings; and it was not decreased, when a Cashmirian, who was present, declared that the said apostate was Luxima, the Brachmachira and prophetess of Cashmire. The person who industriously circulated this intelligence, was the *pundit* of Lahore, the preceptor of the Missionary. His restless and unsettled spirit had led him to Goa: some imprudent and severe observations which he had let fall against the Inquisitorial power, had nearly proved his destruction, but his talents had extricated him; he had engaged as secretary and interpreter to the Spanish Viceroy, and obtained his favour and protection by those arts of conciliation, of which he was so perfectly the master. His hatred of the Inquisition, and his love of intrigue and of commotion, which gave play to the finesse of his genius, and the activity of his mind, led him to seize every opportunity of exciting his compatriots to resist the European power in Goa; and it was about this period that the arrival of Luxima furnished him with an event favourable to his views. He had in vain sought to attract her attention on her way to the Convent of the Dominicans; nor until her arrival at its portal had he succeeded in catching her eye; he then effected it by dropping his muntras at her feet. Absorbed as she appeared to be, this little incident did not escape her attention: she raised her tear-swollen eyes to his, with a look of sudden recognition, for she had known him in the day of her glory; but the Cashmirian, with an almost imperceptible motion of his finger across his lips, implying silence, carelessly picked up his beads and passed on, as the doors of the Christian sanctuary shut out from the eyes of the multitude the priestess of Brahma.

It was on the eve of St. Jago de Compostello,[99] that the usually tranquil abode of the Dominican sisters exhibited a scene of general consternation: the *Indian Catechuman*, committed to their pious care, had mysteriously disappeared a few days after her reception into their Order. Her conduct had not prepared them for an event so extraordinary from her: either unable or unwilling to speak their language, they had not once heard the sound of her voice, save that at sun-set she sung a few low wild notes, through the bars of the casement of her cell, which the younger nuns delighted to catch in the garden beneath, believing that the day was not distant, when a voice so angelic would blend its melody with the holy strains of the Christian choir; but she appeared in every other respect docile, unresisting, and timid almost to wildness. She had suffered them to exchange her Indian dress for the habit of a novice of St. Dominick; she had unreluctantly accompanied them to their church, and assisted at their devotions: her looks were indeed wandering and wild, and seemingly always sent in search of some particular object; but she made no inquiry, she uttered no complaint, and the secret disorder of her mind was only visible in her countenance; which wore the general expression of confirmed melancholy, the sadness of unutterable affliction. A meekness so saintly, a gentleness so seraphic, excited hopes in the breast of the abbess and the sisterhood, which were suddenly destroyed by the miraculous disappearance of the Catechuman. The convent grounds, the gardens of the Viceroy, which were only divided from them by a low wall, were vainly searched; and no circumstance attending her flight could be ascertained, but that she had escaped by the casement of her cell; one of the bars of which had been removed from the brick-work. The *Provincial* of the Order having been made acquainted with the event, which was placed to the account of *pagan sorcery*, an order was issued from the Holy Office, offering a reward to whoever should give up the *relapsed infidel*, and threatening death to those who should conceal her; but week after week elapsed, and no one came forward to claim the recompense, or to avert the punishment. The pagan sorceress was no where to be heard of.[*]

CHAPTER XVII.

However a propensity to evil may be inherent in human nature, it is impossible to conceive an idea of abstract wickedness, uninfluenced by some powerful passion, and existing without any decided reference to some object we wish to attain, or some obstacle we desire to vanquish.

The Pundit of Lahore had seen the Christian Missionary dragged in chains to the dungeon of the Inquisition, and the Priestess of Cashmire delivered up to the tyranny of a fanaticism no less dreadful in the exercise of its power than that from which she had escaped. He considered himself as the remote cause of their mutual sufferings: equally incredulous as to the truth or influ-

---

[*] The Pagans and Moors of Goa are not subject to the Inquisition till they have been baptized. A disgusting and absurd cruelty is displayed in its treatment of those unfortunate Indians who are accused of magic and sorcery, and, as guilty of such offences, are committed to the flames.—*See Hist. of the Inquisition*, p. 243.

ence of their respective doctrines, when opposed to the feelings of nature, he had felt a kind of triumph in putting their boasted infallibility to the test, which deserted him the moment he discovered the fatal consequences which arose from the success of his design. Unprincipled and corrupt to a certain degree, when a dereliction from right favoured the views of his interests, or established the justness of his opinions, (for the human mind, whether it credulously bends to imposition, or boldly resists in scepticism, can never wholly relinquish the intolerance of self-love), he was yet naturally humane and benevolent; and the moment he discovered the fate which awaited the Missionary and his proselyte, he determined to use every exertion to avert it.

Free at all times of admittance to the Viceroy's gardens, he continued to wander incessantly beneath the wall which divided them from the grounds of the convent. He had caught a few notes of Luxima's vesper song, and recognized the air of an Indian hymn, sung upon certain festivals by the priestesses of *Brahma*; he ventured therefore to scale the wall, veiled by the obscurity of a dark night; and by means of a ladder of ropes, he finally effected the escape of the Neophyte: he conveyed her to his own lodging in a retired part of the city, and gave her up to the care of a Jewess, who lived with him, and who, though outwardly professing Christianity from fear and policy, hated equally the Christians and the Pagans; love, however, secured her fealty to her protector, to whom she was ardently devoted; and pity secured her fidelity to the trust he had committed to her care; for the unfortunate Indian was now alike condemned by the religion of truth and the superstition of error— driven with shame and obloquy from the altar of Brahma, her life had become forfeit by the laws of the Inquisition as a relapsed Christian.[*] It was from the order issued from the Holy Office that the Pundit learned the latter circumstances. It was from the lips of the apostate that he learned she had forfeited cast, according to all the awful rites of Brahminical excommunication. It was therefore impossible to restore her to her own cast, and difficult to preserve her from the power of her new religion; and he found with regret and dismay, that the efforts he had made to save her, might but ultimately tend to her destruction;—he now considered that his life was involved in hers, and that his own preservation depended

---

[*] The Inquisition, which punishes with death relapsed Christians, never inflicts any capital punishment on those who have not received the rites of baptism.—*History of the Inquisition,* p. 244.

upon her concealment. His first thought was to remove her from Goa: but the disorder of her mind had fallen upon her constitution, and she was seized with the *mordechi**—that disease so melancholy, and so dangerous, in those burning climes, where exercise, the sole preventative, is impossible. The ill success of his endeavours hitherto, the impossibility of gaining admittance into the interior of the Santa Casa, destroyed the hopes and checked the intentions of the Pundit, which pointed to the liberation of the Missionary; and the mystery which hung over the fate of a man for whom all Goa was interested, no human power could fathom. But the festival upon which the next *auto da fè* was to be celebrated was fast approaching: and the result of those trials, the accused had sustained at the *messa di santo officio*, could at that period only be ascertained.

The day had already passed, upon which the ministers of the Inquisition, preceded by their banners, marched from the palace of the Holy Office to the *Campo Santo*, or place of execution, and there by sound of trumpet proclaimed the day and hour on which the *solemn act* of faith was to be celebrated.

That awful day at length arrived—its dawn, that beamed so fearfully to many, was ushered in by the deep toll of the great bell of the Cathedral; a multitude of persons, of every age and sex, Christians, Pagans, Jews, and Mussulmen, filled the streets, and occupied the roofs, the balconies and windows of the houses, to see the procession pass through the principal parts of the city. The awful ceremony at length commenced—the procession was led by the Dominicans, bearing before them a white cross; the scarlet standard of the Inquisition, on which the image of the founder was represented armed with a sword, preceded a band of the *familiars of the Holy Office*, dressed in black robes, the last of whom bore a green cross, covered with black crape; six penitents of the *San Benito* who had escaped death, and were to be sent to the galleys, each conducted by a familiar, bearing the standard of St. Andrew, succeeded, and were followed by the penitents of the *Fuego Revolto*, habited in grey scapulars, painted with reversed flames; then followed some persons bearing the effigies of those who had died in prison, and whose bones were also borne in coffins; the victims condemned to death appeared the last of the awful train; they were preceded by the *Alcaid* of the Inquisition, each accompanied on

---

* A species of delirious fever.[100]

either side by two officers of the Holy Office, and followed by an officiating priest: a corps of *Halberdeens*, or guards of the Inquisition, closed the procession. In this order it reached the church of St. Dominick, destined for the celebration of *the act of faith*. On either side of the great altar, which was covered with black cloth, were erected two thrones; that on the right was occupied by the Grand Inquisitor; that on the left by the Viceroy and his court: each person having assumed the place destined for him, two Dominicans ascended a pulpit, and read aloud, alternately, the sentences of the guilty, the nature of their crimes, and the species of punishment to which they were condemned. While this awful ceremony took place, each unfortunate, as his sentence was pronounced, was led to the foot of the altar by the Alcaid, where he knelt to receive it. Last of this melancholy band, appeared the *Apostolic Nuncio of India*. Hitherto no torture had forced from him a confession of crimes of which he was guiltless; but the power of his enemies had prevailed, and his innocence was not proof against the testimony of his interested accusers. Summoned to approach the altar, he advanced with the dignity of a self-devoted martyr to receive his sentence; firm alike in look and motion, as though created thing "nought value he or shunned,"[101] he knew his doom to be irrevocable, and met it unappalled.

Man was now to him an atom, and earth a speck! the collective force of his mind was directed to *one sole* object, but that object was—*eternity!* The struggle between the mortal and immortal being was over; passion no longer gave to his imagination the vision of its disappointed desires, nor love the seductive images of its frail enjoyment: the ambition of religious zeal, and the blandishments of tender emotion, no longer influenced a soul which was, in so short a space of time, to be summoned before the tribunal of its God.

Less awed than awful, he stood at the foot of the judgement seat of his earthly umpire, and heard unshrinking and unmoved his accusation publicly pronounced; but when to the sin of heresy, and breach of monastic vow, was added the *seduction of a Neophyte*, then *nature* for a moment asserted her rights, and claimed the revival of her almost extinguished power—his spirit again descended to earth, his heart with a resistless impulsion opened to the influence of human feeling! to the recollection of human ties! and Luxima, even at the altar's feet, rushed to his memory in all her loveliness, and all her affliction; innocent and persecuted, abandoned and despairing: then, the firmness of his look and mind alike deserted him—his countenance became convulsed—his frame shook—an agonizing solicitude for the hapless cause of his death disputed with Heaven the last thoughts of his life—and his head dropped upon the missal on which his hand was spread according to the form of the ceremony:—but when closely following the enumeration of his crimes, he heard pronounced the awful sentence of a dreadful and *an immediate death*, then the inspired fortitude of the martyr re-called the wandering feelings of the man, steadied the vibration of nerves, which love, for the last time, had taught to thrill, strengthened the weakness of the fainting heart, and restored to the troubled spirit the soothing peace of holy resignation and religious hope.

The fate of those condemned to the flames was at last announced—the officers of the secular tribunal came forward to seize the victims of a cruel and inexorable bigotry; and the procession increased by the Vice-roy, and the Grand Inquisitor, with their respective courts, proceeded to the place of execution.—It was a square, one side of which opened to the sea; the three others were composed of the houses of the Spanish grandees, before which a covered platform was erected, for the *Grand Inquisitor* and the Viceroy; in the centre of the square, three piles of faggots were erected, at a certain distance from each other, one of which was already slowly kindling; the air was still, and breathed the balmy softness of an eastern evening; the sun, something shorn of his beams, was setting in mild glory, and threw a saffron hue on the luxuriant woods which skirt the beautiful bay of Goa—not a ripple disturbed the bosom of the deep; every thing in the natural scene declared the beneficent intentions of the Deity, every thing in the human spectacle declared the perversion of man from the decrees of his Creator. It was on such an evening as this, that the Indian Priestess witnessed the dreadful act of her excommunication; the heavens smiled then, as now; and man, the minister of error, was then, as now, cruel and unjust,—substituting malevolence for mercy, and the horrors of a fanatical superstition for the blessed peace and loving kindness of true religion.

The secular judges had already taken their seats on the platform; the Grand Inquisitor and the Viceroy had placed themselves beneath their respective canopies; the persons who composed the procession were ranged according to their offices and orders,—all but the three unhappy persons condemned to death; they alone were led into the centre of the square, each accompanied by a familiar of the Inquisition, and a confessor. The condemned consisted of two relapsed Indians, and *the Apostolic Nuncio of India.* The pile designed for him, was distinguished by a *standard** on which, as was the custom in such cases, an inscription was written, intimating, "that he was to be burnt as a *convicted Heretic who refused to confess his crime!*"

The timid Indians, who, in the zeal and enthusiasm of their own religion, might have joyously and voluntarily sought the death, they now met with horror, hung back, shuddering and weeping in agony and despair, endeavouring to defer their inevitable sufferings by uttering incoherent prayers and useless supplications to the priests who attended them. The Christian Missionary, who it was intended should suffer first, alone walked firmly up to the pile, and while the martyr light flashed on his countenance, he read unmoved the inscription imprinted on the standard of death; which was so soon to wave over his ashes—then, withdrawing a little on one side, he knelt at the feet of his confessor; the last appeal from earth to heaven was now made; he arose with a serene look; the officers of the bow-string advanced to lead him towards the pile: the silence which belongs to death, reigned on every side; thousands of persons were present; yet the melancholy breeze that swept, at intervals, over the ocean, and died away in sighs, was distinctly heard. Nature was touched on the master-spring of emotion, and betrayed in the looks of the multitude, feelings of horror, of pity, and of admiration, which the bigoted vigilance of an inhuman zeal would in vain have sought to suppress.

In this awful interval, while the presiding officers of death were preparing to bind their victim to the stake, a form scarcely human, darting with the velocity of lightning through the multitude, reached the foot of the pile, and stood before it, in a grand and aspiring attitude; the deep red flame of the slowly kindling fire shone through a transparent drapery which flowed in loose folds from the bosom of the seeming vision, and tinged with golden hues, those long dishevelled tresses, which streamed like the rays of a meteor on the air;—thus bright and aerial as it stood, it looked like a spirit sent from Heaven in the awful moment of dissolution to cheer and to convey to the regions of the blessed, the soul which would soon arise, pure from the ordeal of earthly suffering.

The sudden appearance of the singular phantom struck the imagination of the credulous and awed multitude with supersti-

---

* "Morreo queimado por hereje convitto negativo."

tious wonder.—Even the ministers of death stood for a moment, suspended in the execution of their dreadful office. The Christians fixed their eyes upon the *cross*, which glittered on a bosom whose beauty scarcely seemed of mortal mould, and deemed themselves the witnesses of a miracle, wrought for the salvation of a persecuted martyr, whose innocence was asserted by the firmness and fortitude with which he met a dreadful death.

The Hindoos gazed upon the sacred impress of *Brahma*, marked on the brow of his consecrated offspring; and beheld the fancied *herald* of the tenth *Avatar*, announcing vengeance to the enemies of their religion. The condemned victim, still confined in the grasp of the officers of the bow-string, with eyes starting from their sockets, saw only the *unfortunate* he had made—the creature he adored—his disciple!—his mistress!—the Pagan priestess—the Christian Neophyte—his still lovely, though much changed Luxima. A cry of despair escaped from his bursting heart; and in the madness of the moment, he uttered aloud her name. Luxima, whose eyes and hands had been hitherto raised to Heaven, while she murmured the *Gayatra*, pronounced by the Indian women before their voluntary immolation, now looked wildly round her, and, catching a glimpse of the Missionary's figure, through the waving of the flames, behind which he struggled in the hands of his guards, she shrieked, and in a voice scarcely human, exclaimed, "My beloved, I come!—*Brahma* receive and eternally unite our spirits!"—She sprang upon the pile: the fire, which had only kindled in that point where she stood, caught the light drapery of her robe—a dreadful death assailed her—the multitude shouted in horrid frenzy—the Missionary rushed forward—no force opposed to it, could resist the energy of madness, which nerved his powerful arm—he snatched the victim from a fate he sought not himself to avoid—he held her to his heart—the flames of her robe were extinguished in his close embrace;—he looked round him with a dignified and triumphant air—the officers of the Inquisition, called on by their superiors, who now descended from the platforms, sprang forward to seize him:—for a moment, the timid multitude were *still* as the pause of a brooding storm.—Luxima clung round the neck of her deliverer—the Missionary, with a supernatural strength, warded off the efforts of those who would have torn her from him—the hand of fanaticism, impatient for its victim, aimed a dagger at his heart; its point was received in the bosom of the Indian;—she shrieked,—and called upon "Brahma!"—Brahma! Brahma! was re-echoed on every side. A sudden impulse was given to feelings long suppressed:—the timid spirits of the Hindoos rallied to an event which touched their hearts, and roused them from their lethargy of despair;—the sufferings, the oppression they had so long endured, seemed now epitomized before their eyes, in the person of their celebrated and distinguished Prophetess—they believed it was their god who addressed them from her lips—they rushed forward with a hideous cry, to rescue his priestess—and to avenge the long slighted cause of their religion, and their freedom;—they fell with fury on the Christians, they rushed upon the cowardly guards of the Inquisition, who let fall their arms, and fled in dismay.

Their religious enthusiasm kindling their human passions, their rage became at once inflamed and sanctified by their superstitious zeal. Some seized the prostrate arms of the fugitives, others dealt round a rapid destruction by fire; they scattered the blazing faggots, and, snatching the burning brands from the pile, they set on fire the light materials of which the balconies, the verandahs, and platforms were composed, till all appeared one horrid and entire conflagration. The Spanish soldiers now came rushing down from the garrison upon the insurgents,—the native troops, almost in the same moment, joined their compatriots—the engagement became fierce and general—a promiscuous carnage ensued—the Spaniards fought as mercenaries, with skill and coolness; the Indians as enthusiasts, for their religion and their liberty, with an uncurbed impetuosity; the conflict was long and unequal; the Hindoos were defeated; but the Christians purchased the victory of the day by losses which almost rendered their conquest a defeat.

CONCLUSION.

In the multitude who witnessed the awful ceremony of the *auto da fe*, in the church of St. Dominick, stood the Pundit of Lahore; and he heard with horror the sentence of death pronounced against the Christian Missionary. Considering himself as the remote cause of his destruction, he was overwhelmed by compassion and remorse—aware of the ripeness of the Indians to a revolt, he determined on exciting them to a rescue of their compatriots at the place of execution; he knew them prompt to receive every impression which came through the medium of their senses, and connected with the popular prejudices of their religion; when he beheld them following, with sullen looks, the slow march of the procession, to witness the execution of their countrymen, whom they conceived by their obstinate abjuration of the Christian religion to have been seduced from their ancient faith, his hopes strengthened, he moved rapidly among them, exciting the pity of some, the horror of others, and a principle of resistance in all: but it was to an unforeseen accident that he owed the success of his hazardous efforts.

Of the disorder by which Luxima had been attacked, a slight delirium only remained; her health was restored, but her mind was wandering and unsettled; the most affecting species of mental derangement had seized her imagination—the melancholy insanity of sorrow: she wept no tears, she heaved no sighs—she sat still and motionless, sometimes murmuring a Brahminical hymn, sometimes a Christian prayer—sometimes talking of her grandsire, sometimes of her lover—alternately gazing on the muntras she had received from one, and the cross that had been given to her by the other.

On the day of the *auto da fè*, she sat, as was her custom since her recovery, behind the gauze blind of the casement of the little apartment in which she was confined; she beheld the procession moving beneath it with a fixed and vacant eye, until a form presented itself before her, which struck like light from heaven on her darkened mind; she beheld the friend of her soul; love and reason returned together; intelligence revived to the influence of affection—she felt, and thought, and acted—whatever were his fate, she resolved to share it:—she was alone, her door was not fastened, she passed it unobserved, she darted through the little vestibule which opened to the street; the procession had turned into another, but the street was still crowded—so much so, that even her singular appearance was unobserved; terrified and bewildered, she flew down an avenue that led to the sea, either because it was empty and silent, or that her reason was again lost, and she was unconscious whither she went, till chance brought her into the "square of execution!"—she saw the smoke of the piles rising above the heads of the multitude—in every thing she beheld, she saw a spectacle similar to that which the self-immolation of the Brahmin women presents:—the images thus presented to her disordered mind, produced a natural illusion—she believed the hour of her sacrifice and her triumph was arrived, that she was on the point of being united in heaven to him whom she had alone loved on earth; and when she heard her name pronounced by his well-known voice, she rushed to the pile in all the enthusiasm of love and of devotion. The effect produced by this singular event was such as, under the existing feelings of the multitude, might have been expected. During the whole of the tumult, the Pundit did not for a moment lose sight of the Missionary, who, still clasping Luxima in his arms, was struggling with her through the ranks of destruction; the Pundit approaching him, seized his arm, and, while all was uproar and confusion, dragged him towards the shore, near to which a boat, driven in by the tide, lay undulating; assisting him to enter, and to place Luxima within it, he put the only oar it contained into his hands; driving it from the shore, he himself returned to the scene of action.

The Missionary, wounded in his right arm, with difficulty managed the little bark; yet he instinctively plied the oar, and put out from the land, without any particular object in the effort—his thoughts were wild, his feelings were tumultuous—he was stunned, he was bewildered by the nature and rapidity of the events which had occurred. He saw the receding shore covered with smoke; he saw the flames ascending to Heaven, which were to have consumed him; he heard the discharge of fire-arms, and the shouts of horror and destruction: but the ocean was calm; the horizon was bathed in hues of living light, and the horrors he had escaped, gradually faded into distance, and sunk into silence. He steered the boat towards the rocky peninsula which is crowned by the fortress of Alguarda; he saw the crimson flag of the Inquisition hoisted from its ramparts—he saw a party of soldiers descending the rocks to gain a watchtower, placed at the extremity of the peninsula, which guards the mouth of the bay:—here, remote as was the place, there was for him no asylum, no safety; he changed his course, and put out again to sea—twilight was deepening the shadows of evening; his little bark was no longer discernible from the land; he threw down the oar, he raised Luxima in his arms—her eye met his—she smiled languidly on him—he held her to his heart, and life and death were alike forgotten—but Luxima returned not the pressure of his embrace, she had swooned; and as he threw back her tresses, to permit the air to visit her face more freely, he perceived that they were *steeped in blood!* He now first discovered that the poignard he had escaped, had been received in the bosom of the Indian: distracted, he endeavoured to bind the wound with the scapular which had made a part of his death dress; but though he thus stopped for the time the effusion of blood, he could not recall her senses. He looked round him wildly, but there was no prospect of relief; he seized her in his arms, and turned his eyes on the deep, resolved to seek with her eternal repose in its bosom—he approached the edge of the boat—"To what purpose," he said, "do I struggle to protract, for a few hours, a miserable existence? Death we cannot escape, whatever way we turn—its horrors we may—O God! am I then obliged to add to the sum of my frailties and my sins the crimes of suicide and murder?" He gazed passionately on Luxima, and added, "Destroy thee, my beloved! while yet I feel the vital throb of that heart which has so long beaten only for me—oh no! The Providence which has hitherto miraculously preserved us, may still make us the object of its care."—He laid Luxima gently down in the boat, and, looking round him, perceived that the moon, which was now rising, threw its light on a peninsula of rocks, which projected from the main land to a considerable distance into the sea— it was the light of heaven that guided him—he seized the oar, and plying it with all the strength he could yet collect, he soon reached the rocks, and perceived a cavern that seemed to open to receive and shelter them.

★ ★ ★

The Pundit of Lahore was among the few who escaped from the destruction he had himself excited. Pursued by a Spanish soldier, he had fled towards the shore, and, acquainted with all the windings of the rocks, their deep recesses and defiles, he had eluded the vigilance of the Spaniard, and reached a cavern, which held out a prospect of temporary safety, till his strength should be sufficiently recruited to permit him to continue his flight towards a port, where some Bengal vessels were stationed, which might afford him concealment, and convey him to a distant part of India: as he approached the cavern, he looked round it cautiously, and by the light of the moon, with which it was illuminated, he perceived that it was already occupied—for kneeling on the earth, the *Apostolic Nuncio* of India, supported on his bosom the dying *Priestess of Cashmire*. The Pundit rushed forward; "Fear not," he said, "be cheered, be comforted, all may yet go well: here we are safe for the present, and when we are able to proceed, some Bengalese merchantmen who lie at a little port at a short distance from hence, will give us conveyance to a settlement, where the power of Spain or of the Inquisition cannot reach us."

The presence, the words of the Pundit were balm to the harassed spirits of the Missionary; a faint hope beamed on his sinking heart, and he urged him to procure some fresh water among the rocks, the only refreshment for the suffering Indian, which the desolate and savage place afforded. The Pundit, having sought for a large shell to contain water, flew in search of it; and the Missionary remained gazing upon Luxima, who lay motionless in his arms. The presence of the Pundit suddenly recalled to his memory the first scene of his mission; and he again beheld in fancy the youthful priestess of mystic love, borne triumphantly along amidst an idolizing multitude; he cast his eyes upon the object that lay faint and speechless in his arms; and the brilliant vision of his memory faded away, nor left upon his imagination one trace of its former lustre or its beauty; for the image which succeeded, was such as the *genius* of Despair could only portray in its darkest mood of gloomy creation.

In a rude and lonesome cavern, faintly lighted up by the rays of the moon, and echoing to the moaning murmurs of the ocean's tide, lay *that Luxima*, who once, like the delicious shade of her native region, seemed created only for bliss, and formed only for delight; those eyes, in whose glance the spirit of devotion, and the enthusiasm of tenderness, mingled their brilliancy and their softness, were now dim and beamless; and that bosom, where love lay enthroned beneath the vestal's veil, was stained with the life-blood which issued from its almost exhausted veins. Motionless, and breathing with difficulty, and with pain, she lay in his arms, with no faculty but that of suffering, with no sensibility but that of pain:— he had found her like a remote and brilliant planet, shining in lone and distant glory, illuminating, by her rays, a sphere of harmony and peace; but she had for him deserted her *orbit*, and her light was now nearly extinguished for ever.

When the Pundit returned, he moistened her lips with water, and chafed her temples and her hands with the pungent herbs the surrounding rocks supplied; and when the vital hues of life again faintly revisited her cheek, the Missionary, as he gazed on the symptoms of returning existence, gave himself up to feelings of suspense and anxiety, to which despondency was almost preferable, and pressing those lips in death, which in life he would have deemed it the risk of salvation to touch, his soul almost mingled with that pure spirit, which seemed ready to escape with every low-drawn sigh; and his heart offered up its silent prayer to Heaven, that thus they might unite, and thus seek together mercy and forgiveness at its throne. *Luxima* revived, raised her eyes to those which were bent in agony and fondness over her, and on her look of suffering, and smile of sadness, beamed the ardour of a soul whose warm, tender, and imperishable feelings were still triumphant over even pain and death.

"Luxima!" exclaimed the Missionary, in a melancholy transport, and pressing her to a heart which a feeble hope cheered and re-animated, "*Luxima*, my beloved! wilt thou not struggle with death? wilt thou not save me from the horror of knowing, that it is *for me thou* diest? and that what remains of my wretched existence, has been purchased at the expense of thine? Oh! if *love*, which has led thee to death, can recall or attach thee to life, still live, even though thou livest *for my destruction*." A faint glow flushed the face of the Indian, her smile brightened, and she clung still closer to the bosom, whose throb now replied to the palpitation of her own.

"Yes," exclaimed the Missionary, answering the eloquence of her languid and tender looks, "yes, dearest, and most unfortunate, our destinies are now inseparably united! Together we have loved, together we have resisted, together we have erred, and together we have suffered; lost alike to the glory and the fame, which our virtues, and the conquest of our passions, once obtained for us; alike condemned by our religions and our countries, there now remains nothing on *earth* for us, but each other!—Already have we met the horrors of death, without its repose; and the life for which thou hast offered the precious purchase of thine own, must *now belong alone to thee.*"

Luxima raised herself in his arms, and grasping his hands, and fixing on him her languid eyes, she articulated in a deep and tremulous voice, "*Father!*" but, faint from bodily exhaustion and mental emotion, she again sunk in silence on his bosom! At the plaintive sound of this touching and well-remembered epithet, the Missionary shuddered, and the blood froze round his sinking heart; again he heard the voice of the proselyte, as in the shades of Cashmire he had once heard it, when pure, and free from the taint of human frailty, he had addressed her only in the spiritual language of an holy mission, and she had heard him with a soul ignorant of human passion, and opening to receive that sacred truth, to whose cause he had proved so faithless: the religion he had offended, the zeal he had abandoned, the principles, the habits of feeling, and of thinking, he had relinquished, all rushed in this awful moment on his mind, and tore his conscience with penitence, and with remorse; he saw before his eyes the retribution of his error in the sufferings of its innocent cause; he sought to redeem what was yet redeemable of his fault, to recall to his wandering soul the duties of the minister of Heaven, and to put from his guilty thoughts the feelings of the impassioned man! He sought to withdraw his attention from the perishable woman, and to direct his efforts to the salvation of the immortal spirit; but when again he turned his eyes on the Indian, he perceived that hers were ardently fixed on the rosary of her idolatrous creed, to which she pressed with devotion her cold and quivering lips, while the crucifix which lay on her bosom was steeped in the blood she had shed to preserve him.

This affecting combination of images so opposite and so eloquent in their singular but natural association, struck on his heart with a force which his reason and his zeal had no power to resist:— and the words which religion, awakened to its duty, sent to his lips, died away in sounds inarticulate, from the mingled emotions of horror and compassion, of gratitude and love—and, wringing his hands, while cold drops hung upon his brow, he exclaimed in a tone of deep and passionate affliction, "Luxima, Luxima! are we then to be *eternally disunited?*"

Luxima replied only by a look of love, whose fond expression was the next moment lost in the convulsive distortions of pain. Much enfeebled by the sudden pang, a faintness, which resembled the sad torpor of death, hung upon her frame and features; yet her eyes were still fixed with a gaze so motionless and ardent, on the sole object of her dying thought, that her look seemed the last look of life and love, when both inseparably united dissolve and expire together. "Luxima," exclaimed the Missionary wildly, "Luxima, thou wilt not die! thou wilt not leave me alone on earth to bear thy innocent blood upon my head, and thy insupportable loss for ever in my heart!—to wear out life in shame and desolation—my hope entombed with thee—my sorrows lonely and unparticipated—my misery keen and eternal!—Oh! no, fatal creature! sole cause of all I have ever known of bliss or suffering, of happiness or of despair, thou hast bound me to thee by dreadful ties; by bonds, sealed with thy blood, indissoluble and everlasting! And if thy hour is come, mine also is arrived, for triumphing over the fate which would divide us: we shall *die*, as we dared not *live*—together!"

Exhausted by the force and vehemence of an emotion which had now reached its crisis—enervated by tenderness, subdued by grief, and equally vanquished by bodily anguish, and by the still surviving conflicts of feeling and opinion—he sunk overpowered on the earth; and Luxima, held up by the sympathizing Pundit, seemed to acquire force from the weakness of her unfortunate friend, and to return from the grasp of death, that she might restore him to life. Endeavouring to support his head in her feeble arms, and pressing her cold cheek to his, she sought to raise and cheer his subdued spirit, by words of hope and consolation. At the sound of her plaintive voice, at the pressure of her soft cheek, the creeping blood quickened its circulation in his veins, and a faint sensation of pleasure thrilled on his exhausted nerves; he raised his head, and fixed his eyes on her face with one of those looks of passionate fondness, tempered by fear, and darkened by remorse, with which he had so frequently, in happier days, contemplated that exquisite loveliness which had first stolen between him and Heaven. Luxima still too well understood that look, which had so often given birth to emotions, which even approaching death had not quite annihilated; and with renovated strength (the illusory herald of dissolution) she exclaimed—"Soul of my life! the God whom thou adorest, did doubtless save thee from a dreadful death, that thou mightest live for others, and still he commands thee to bear the painful burthen of existence: yet, oh! if for others thou *wilt not live,* live at least for *Luxima!* and be thy beneficence to her nation, the redemption of those faults of which for thy sake she has been guilty!—Thy brethren will not dare to take a life, which God himself has miraculously preserved—and when *I* am no more, thou shalt preach, not to the Brahmins only, but to the Christians, that the sword of destruction, which has been this day raised between the followers of thy faith and of mine, may be for ever sheathed! Thou wilt appear among them as a spirit of peace, teaching mercy, and inspiring love; thou wilt soothe away, by acts of tenderness, and words of kindness, the stubborn prejudice which separates the mild and patient Hindu from his species; and thou wilt check the Christian's zeal, and bid him follow the sacred lesson of the God he serves, who, for years beyond the Christian era, has extended his merciful indulgence to the errors of the Hindu's mind, and bounteously lavished on his native soil those wondrous blessings which first tempted the Christians to seek our happier regions. But should thy eloquence and thy example fail, tell them my story! tell them how I have suffered, and how even thou hast failed:—thou, for whom I forfeited my cast, my country, and my life; for 'tis too true, that still *more loving* than enlightened, my ancient habits of belief clung to my mind, thou to my *heart:* still I lived thy seeming proselyte, that I might *still live thine;* and now *I die* as Brahmin women *die,* a *Hindu* in my feelings and my faith—dying for him I loved, and believing as my fathers have believed."

Exhausted and faint, she drooped her head on her bosom—and the Missionary, stiffened with horror, his human and religious feelings alike torn and wounded, hung over her, motionless and silent. The Pundit, dropping tears of compassion on the chilling hands he chafed, now administered some water to the parched lips of the dying Indian, on whose brow, the light of the moon shone resplendently. Somewhat revived by the refreshment, she turned on him her languid but grateful eyes, and slowly recognizing his person, a faint blush, like the first doubtful colouring of the dawn, suffused the paleness of her cheek; she continued to gaze earnestly on him for some moments, and a few tears, the last she ever shed, fell from her closing eyes,—and though the springs of life were nearly exhausted, yet her fading spirits rallied to the recollection of *home*! of *friends*! of *kindred*! and of *country*! which the presence of a sympathizing compatriot thus painfully and tenderly awakened—then, after a convulsive struggle between life and death, whose shadows were gathering on her countenance, she said in a voice scarcely audible, and in great emotion—"I owe thee much, let me owe thee more—thou seest before thee Luxima! the Prophetess and Brachmachira of Cashmire!—and thou wast haply sent by the interposition of Providence to receive her last words, and to be the testimony to her people of her innocence; and when thou shalt return to the blessed paradise of her nativity, thou wilt say—'that having gathered *a dark spotted flower in the garden of love*,[102] she expiates her error by the loss of her life; that her disobedience to the forms of her religion and the laws of her country, was punished by days of suffering, and by an untimely death; yet that her *soul* was pure from sin, as, when clothed in transcendent brightness, she outshone, in faith, in *virtue*, all women of her nation!'"

This remembrance of her former glory, deepened the hues of her complexion, and illumined a transient ray of triumph in her almost beamless eyes: then pausing for a moment, she fixed her glance on the image of her tutelar god, which she still held in her hand—the idol, wearing the form of infant beauty, was symbolic of that religious mystic love, to which she had *once* devoted herself! she held it for a moment to her lips, and to her heart—then, presenting it to the Cashmirian, she added, "Take it, and bear it back to him, from whom I received it, on the day of my consecration, in the *temple* of *Sirinagar*! to him! the aged grandsire whom I abandoned!—dear and venerable!—should he still survive the loss and shame of her, his child and his disciple! should he still deign to acknowledge as *his* offspring the outcast whom he cursed—the Chancalas whom—" the words died away upon her quivering lips, "Brahma!" she faintly exclaimed,

"Brahma!" and, grasping the hands of the Missionary, alternately directed her looks to him and to Heaven; but he replied not to the last glance of life and love. He had sunk beneath the acuteness of his feelings; and the Indian, believing that his spirit had fled before her own to the realms of eternal peace, and there awaited to receive her, bowed her head, and expired in the blissful illusion, with a smile of love and a ray of religious joy shedding their mingled lustre on her slowly closing eyes.

* * *

The guards, who by order of the Inquisition were sent in pursuit of the fugitives, reached the cavern of their retreat three days after that of the insurrection; but here they found only a pile partly consumed, and the ashes of such aromatic plants as the interstices of the surrounding rocks afforded, which the Hindus usually burn with the bodies of their deceased friends, at the funeral pyre; they continued therefore their search farther along the shore; it was long, persevering and fruitless. The Apostolic Nuncio of India was *never heard of more*.

Time rolled on, and the majestic order of nature, uninterrupted in its harmonious course, finely contrasted the rapid vicissitudes of human events, and the countless changes in human institutions! In the short space of *twenty* years, the mighty had fallen, and the lowly were elevated; the lash of oppression had passed alternately from the grasp of the persecutor to the hand of the persecuted; the slave had seized the sceptre, and the tyrant had submitted to the chain. Portugal, resuming her independence, carried the standard of her triumph even to the remote shores of the Indian ocean, and, knowing no ally but that of *compatriot unanimity*, resisted by her single and unassisted force, the combined powers of a mighty state, the intrigues of a wily cabinet, and the arms of a successful potentate.*
While *Freedom* thus unfurled her spotless banner in a remote corner of the West, she lay mangled and in chains, at the foot of victorious tyranny in the East. *Aurengzebe* had waded through carnage and destruction to the throne of India—he has seized a sceptre stained with a brother's blood, and wore the diadem, torn from a parent's brow! worthy to represent the most powerful and despotic dynasty of the earth, his genius and his fortunes resembled the

---

* Revolution of Portugal.

regions he governed, mingling sublimity with destruction; splendour with peril;—and combining, in their mighty scale, the great extremes of good and evil. Led by a love of pleasure, or allured by a natural curiosity, he resolved on visiting the most remote and most delicious province of his empire, where his ancestors had so often sought repose from the toils of war, and fatigue of government; and where, *twenty years* before, his own heroic and unfortunate nephew, Solyman Sheko, had sought asylum and resource against his growing power and fatal influence. He left *Delhi* for Cashmire, during an interval of general prosperity and peace, and performed his expedition with all the pomp of eastern magnificence.*

In the immense and motley multitude which composed his suite, there was an European *Philosopher*,[104] who, highly distinguished by the countenance and protection of the emperor, had been led, by philosophical curiosity and tasteful research, to visit a country, which, more celebrated than known, had not yet attracted the observation of genius, or the inquiry of science. He found the natural beauty of the vale of *Cashmire*, far exceeding the description of its scenes which lived in the songs of the Indian bards, and its mineral and botanic productions curious, and worthy of the admiration and notice of the naturalist; and in a spot which might be deemed the region of natural phenomena, he discovered more than *one* object to which a moral interest was attached. Yet to *one object only* did the *interest of sentiment* peculiarly belong; it was a sparry cavern, among the hills of Sirinagar, called, by the *natives* of the valley, the "*Grotto of congelations!*"† They pointed it out to strangers as a place constructed by magic, which for many years had been the residence of a recluse! a stranger, who had appeared suddenly among them, who had been rarely seen, and more rarely addressed, who led a lonely and an innocent life, equally avoided and avoiding, who lived unmolested, awakening no interest, and exciting no persecution—"he was," they said, "a wild and melancholy man! whose religion was unknown, but who prayed at the confluence of rivers, at the rising and the setting of the sun; living on the produce of the soil, he needed no assistance, nor sought any intercourse; and his life, thus slowly wearing away, gradually faded into death.

---

* Historical.[103]

† Monsieur de Bernier laments, in his interesting account of his journey to Cashmire which he performed in the suite of Aurengzebe, that circumstances prevented him visiting the grotto of congelations, of which so many strange tales were related by the natives of the valley.

A *goala*, or Indian shepherd, who missed him for several mornings at his wonted place of matinal devotion, was led by curiosity or by compassion to visit his grotto. He found him dead, at the foot of an altar which he had himself raised to the deity of his secret worship, and fixed in the attitude of one who died in the act of prayer. Beside him lay a small urn, formed of the sparry congelations of the grotto—on opening it, it was only found to contain some ashes, a cross stained with blood, and the dsandum of an Indian Brahmin. On the lucid surface of the *urn* were carved some characters which formed the name of "*Luxima!*"—It was the name of an *outcast*, and had long been condemned to oblivion by the crime of its owner. The Indians shuddered when they pronounced it! and it was believed that the *Recluse* who lived so long and so unknown among them, was the same, who once, and in days long passed, had seduced, from the altar of the god she served, the most celebrated of their religious women, when he had visited their remote and lovely valley in the character of

A Christian Missionary.

THE END

Explanatory Notes

Readers should keep in mind that orientalist materials of Owenson's day are often contradictory, and tend to fall rather short of the standards of twentieth-century scholarship (in some measure because of the newness of the field and language difficulties as well as Eurocentric cultural assumptions). Owenson, moreover, often tailors such material to fit her literary purposes. It is consequently best to approach orientalist references in *The Missionary* on the cursory terms that Owenson provides, and to consider them as alluding to, and yet finally distinct from, Romantic-era orientalist scholarship—and, most certainly, seventeenth-century India. Owenson seems less inclined to alter details drawn from European history and literature, perhaps because they would be more familiar to her expected audience.

For complete bibliographical information on sources cited here, as well as those cited in Owenson's footnotes, see the Select Bibliography. All translations below are mine.

1 *"Olivarez, the gloomy minister of Philip the Fourth"*: Owenson here introduces the conflicts between Spain and Portugal, neighbours in the Iberian peninsula of southwestern Europe. In 1580, after a dispute over the succession, Philip II (1527-98), king of Spain, 1556-98, took control of Portugal. Philip IV (1605-65), king of Spain, Naples, and Sicily, 1621-65, ruled Portugal for the last two decades of Spanish domination (1621-40). Philip IV's minister, Olivares, was central in attempts to absorb Portugal, on a variety of levels, into Spain. In a relatively bloodless coup in 1640, a group of Portuguese nationalists attacked the Palace in which the nominal governor of Portugal—Margaret of Savoy, the duchess of Mantua—was resident. After defeating the guard, they arrested the governor (or "vice-reine") and shot her secretary, Miguel de Vasconcelos, who "received his instructions directly from the count-duke [Olivares], whose creature he was" (Vertot 24); the subsequent period is known as the Restoration. Within days, the Duke of Bragança (1604-56) was crowned John IV of Portugal; Spain did not recognize Portugal's independence until 1668.

2 *"The Jesuits, being charged with fraudulent practices ... Franciscans"*: Innocent X (1574-1655) was Pope (1644-55) when the "Congregation for the Propagation of the Faith" (also known as the "Propaganda"), a body responsible for regularizing and coordinating missionary work and principles for the Roman Catholic Church, rejected Jesuit toleration of non-Christian beliefs; Innocent X also refused to recognize Portugal's

independence. Jesuits are members of a Catholic religious order, the Society of Jesus, founded by St. Ignatius of Loyola. Franciscans are members of another Catholic religious order, founded by St. Francis of Assisi. By "Brahminical ... doctrine" Owenson refers to Hindu beliefs; priests and scholars were traditionally drawn from the Brahmin "caste" (see note 29).

3 *"Alentejo ... Algarva"*: Alentejo (Alemtejo) and Algarva (Algarve) are both regions in southern Portugal. Alentejo borders Spain and was invaded by that country in 1801. It is also the birthplace of Vasco da Gama (c.1469-1524), a famous explorer who charted a route between Portugal and India around the Cape of Good Hope in southern Africa, and was thus instrumental in establishing Portugal's control in India.

4 *"Moorish castle"*: "Moor" is a European term of often loose usage; it can refer to any Muslim, but in the context of Spanish and Portuguese history refers more specifically to those Muslims of Spanish, Arab, and Berber descent who ruled much of the Iberian peninsula (that is, modern Spain and Portugal) for centuries. Owenson, like many of her contemporaries, uses the term "Mussulman" to refer to Muslims from other regions.

5 *"a Roman fortress ... Coimbra"*: Coimbra, a city in north-central Portugal, is the site of some Roman ruins; it was also mentioned in reports of Wellesley's campaigns in Portugal (1808-10).

6 *"Carthage ... Hannibal ... Scipio Africanus"*: Carthage was a city on the northern coast of Africa (in present-day Tunisia), and was involved in a number of military conflicts with Rome known as the "Punic Wars." Hannibal (247-182? BC) was "A celebrated Carthaginian general" who "subdued all the nations of Spain" (Lemprière 262). He also fought in the Punic Wars and ruled Carthage for a time. Scipio Africanus (Publius Cornelius) (236-184/3 BC) was a Roman general who conquered Spain. He is best known for decisively defeating Hannibal in 202 BC.

7 *"d'Acugna ... the House of Braganza"*: Owenson brings together two of the leading families involved in the overthrow of Spanish power in seventeenth-century Portugal. The Duke of Bragança became King John IV of Portugal after the Revolution; two members of the Acugna family figured prominently in the revolutionary party. See the "Introduction" for more details.

8 *"that nothing is, but what is not"*: This phrase is uttered by Macbeth: "Present fears / Are less than humble imaginings: / My thought, whose murther yet is but fantastical, / Shakes so my single state of man, that function / Is smother'd in surmise, and nothing is / But what is not" (Shakespeare, *Macbeth* 1.3.137-42).

9 *"Hilarion"*: Saint Hilarion (c. 291-371), a Palestinian, converted to Christianity and lived for a time as a hermit in Egypt; according to traditional accounts, he was strongly influenced by the ascetic principles of Saint Anthony of Egypt (c. 251-356). Both saints are associated with the early development of monastic life.

10 *"Lisbon"*: Lisbon, on the west coast of Portugal, is the nation's capital.

11 "*vice-reine* ... *Vasconcellas* ... *Goa* ... *Hindostan*": On the vice-reine and Vasconcellas, see note 1. Goa, a port-city on the west coast of India, was successfully invaded by Portugal in 1510, and was still under Portugal's control in the early nineteenth century. "Hindostan" was a common term for India.

12 "*Francis Xaverius*": Francis Xavier (1506-52) was a missionary from the Basque region of Spain. Known as "Apostle to the Indies," he landed at Goa in 1542 and spent the next three years in southern India; he then travelled to other regions in Asia, but briefly returned to India in 1548. He was credited with many conversions and miracles, including the raising of the dead.

13 "*Cape Verd* ... *Guinea, and* ... *the line*": Cape Verd is a group of islands in the Atlantic, near the northwest coast of Africa, colonized by Portugal in the fifteenth century. Guinea is a coastal country in west Africa, south of Cape Verd, and used at the time by Portuguese traders. "The line" is a common term for the equator. Hilarion is following Vasco da Gama's route (see note 3), travelling southward down the west coast of Africa, then around the Cape of Good Hope at the southern point of the continent, and then northward through the Indian Ocean to India.

14 "*Tamerlane*": Tamerlane (or Timur or Timur-Lengue) (1336-1405) was a Mongol who served under Ghenghis Khan's son, but then seized power. His conquests included Persia, India, and Egypt. Bernier links him directly to the Mughals, Islamic rulers of India, who were especially powerful from the sixteenth to mid-eighteenth centuries: "Tamerlane, so renowned for his conquests; who married his near kinswoman, the only daughter of the Prince of the nations of Great Tartary, called Moguls, who have left and communicated their name to the strangers that now govern Indostan, the country of the Indians" ("Bernier's Voyage" 60). The Mughal Empire was established two hundred years after Timur, by Timur's descendant, Baber. English audiences would likely be most familiar with Timur via Nicholas Rowe's play, *Tamurlane* (1702); Fitzpatrick reports that it was while Owenson's father played the title role in Rowe's play with great success in England that he met and courted Jane Hill (6).

15 "*Imposter of Mecca*": This is a common European epithet in the period for Muhammad (570?-632), the Prophet of Islam.

16 "*the Pagoda of Brahma*," "*the temple* ... *in the deserts of Palmyra*," "*the Caaba of Mecca*," "*the tabernacle of Jerusalem*": By "Pagoda of Brahma," Owenson means a Hindu temple. The "deserts of Palmyra" are the site of Aramaean temples: "[Palmyra] is now in ruins, and the splendour and magnificence of its porticoes, temples, and palaces, are now frequently examined by the curious and the learned" (Lemprière 439). The "Caaba of Mecca" is a building sacred in Islam. The "tabernacle of Jerusalem" likely refers to that which housed the Ark of the Covenant within the Temple of Jerusalem.

17 "*the death of Cardinal Henry, uncle to the King Sebastian*": King Sebastian of Portugal (1554-78), who ruled from the age of three, died in defeat at "The Battle of the Three Kings," after trying to invade Morocco for political and religious purposes (Vertot 9-17). The only remaining legitimate male heir from the royal family was Cardinal Henry (1512-80); he ruled Portugal from 1578-80. When he died without an heir, Portugal's throne was left open to claims from Philip II of Spain, who became King of Portugal in 1580 (see note 1).

18 "*HAMILTON's New Account of the West Indies*": Hamilton spent time in the region between 1688 and 1723, and so Hamilton's reference here is to Portugal's Inquisition rather than Spain's. Owenson elides the distinction.

19 "*from Tatta to Lahore …*": The Indus river travels along the northwestern edge of the subcontinent, through modern-day Pakistan. Tatta (Thatta) is close to where the Indus meets the Arabian Sea; Lahore is just south of the Indus, but quite a distance inland. Cashmire (Kashmir), a mountainous region north of the Indus, is west of Tibet (or Thibet, as Owenson spells it). This journey, eastward from Tatta to Lahore and then north to Cashmire, is a trek of over 500 miles. The longest leg of Hilarion's journey, however, would be from Goa to Tatta, along the Indian coast.

20 "*came riding on an ass*": Owenson may be taking this phrase from the Bible: "behold, thy King cometh unto thee: he *is* just, and having salvation; lowly, and riding upon an ass" (Zech. 9.9). Saint Hilarion is often depicted riding on an ass.

21 "*bungalow of twelve oars*": The word "bungalow" is Hindi in origin and was, by 1800, used in English to refer to a one-storey house, but Owenson clearly means a ship.

22 "*Alexander*": Alexander the Great (356-323 BC), a Macedonian ruler and military leader, "conquered all the provinces of Asia Minor … and made himself master of Egypt, Media, Syria, and Persia.… His conquests were spread over India, where he fought with Porus, the powerful king of that country" (Lemprière 31).

23 "*Dara having advanced …*": Dara (1615-59) and Aurangzeb (1618-1707) were brothers who fought over who would succeed their father as emperor; Aurangzeb was victorious over Dara in 1658, imprisoned their father, Shah Jahan (1592-1666), and took the throne. Dara's eldest son, Solyman, played a prominent role as a military commander during part of the conflict; for Owenson's representation of Solyman, see Volume II. Both Bernier's travelogue and Dow's translation deal with this part of Indian history. Owenson's readers would likely be more familiar with John Dryden's representations of Aurangzeb and Solyman in the play, *Aureng-Zebe* (first published in 1676).

24 "*Gentiles*": "Gentile" and "Gentoo" are terms commonly used in orientalist discourse of the period to refer to an Indian of the Hindu faith.

25 "*Autre fois … de leurs fêtes*": "In the past, the Jesuits had an establishment in this city, and fulfilled their sacred functions, and presented the splendour of their festivals to the eyes of Mahometans and Gentiles."

26 *"pious sancassees"*: "Of all the numerous classes of devotees, none are so much respected as the Saniassees and Yogeys. They quit their relations, and every concern of this life, and wander about the country without any fixed abode" (Craufurd 121).

27 *"Pundit"*: "Pundit is a Sanskrit word, and an honorary title, signifying doctor or philosopher" (Craufurd 189*n*).

28 *"Gazettes de la cour ... dans toute l'empire"*: "The gazettes of the Delhi court, the public newspapers which noted, day by day, and not in the turgid style for which Orientals are blamed, what happens of importance in the court and in the provinces—these gazettes are circulated throughout the empire." Anquetil Duperron also provides excerpts from these gazettes.

29 *"The higher casts ... "*: Bernier defines four castes which his translator, like a number of others in Owenson's list of sources, terms "tribes"; "caste" (spelled "cast" by Owenson and her contemporaries) is a term of Portuguese origin. "The first is of Brahmans, men of the law; the second, of Quetterys, men of arms; the third, men of Bescue, or traffick, commonly called Banians; and the fourth, men of Scydra, that is, handycraftsmen and labourers" ("Bernier's Voyage" 183).

30 *"Camdeo, the god of 'mystic love'"*: This deity was commonly identified with the Roman god of love, Cupid, by Romantic-era orientalists and writers.

31 *"Indian jama"*: Craufurd describes the "Jama" as a "long muslin robe" (284).

32 *"the Gayatras, or text of the Shaster"*: Owenson uses a signification of "Shaster" decried by Dow: "Shaster, literally signifies Knowledge: but is commonly understood to mean a book which treats of divinity and the sciences. There are many Shasters among the Hindoos; so that those writers who affirmed, that there was but one Shaster in India, which, like the Bible of the Christians, or Koran of the followers of Mahommed, contained the first principles of the Brahmin faith, have deceived themselves and the public" ("Dissertation" 1: xxxv*n*).

33 *"the small consecrated mark of the tallertum"*: Owenson provides a definition of the term in a footnote in Chapter XIV. Kindersley writes, "The *tellertum* is a paste worn by some casts on the forehead"; it "is at once an ornament, and an indication of their tribe and religious profession" ("History" 156*n*).

34 *"Bhudda ... faquirs"*: Jones suggests that "there were *two* Buddhas, the younger of whom established the new religion, which gave so great offence in *India*, and was introduced into *China*"; the other was an avatar of Vishnu ("On the Chronology" 292-93). In *Luxima*, Owenson added an extensive note on Buddhism, writing, in part, that "It was perfected from the idea of a simple abstraction of the soul from all earthly care, to that of the threefold Intelligence, Creator, and Ruler" and that the faith "denounced" "him who shall strike a woman, even with the leaf of a rose" (43*n*). Faquirs are usually described as religious mendicants in the orientalist scholarship used by Owenson.

35 *"Avaratas, or incarnations"*: I.e., avatars.

36 *"zenanas ... sacred privacy"*: A zenana is a room reserved for women and understood, by many of Owenson's contemporaries, to function as the architectural equivalent of a veil, isolating women from society for reasons of strictly defined modesty.

37 *" 'Duties of a faithful Widow'"*: Owenson here cites the title of a chapter in Colebrooke's four-volume translation, *Digest of Hindu Law* (2: 567-80). Colebrooke also contributed an essay to *Asiatick Researches* under a similar title, "On the Duties of a Faithful Hindu Widow." "Shanscrit" (Sanskrit) is the classical literary language of the Hindus, often serving as a common tongue for written works.

38 *"Caves of Elora ... Temple of Jaggarnauth ... Ganges"*: The Caves are temples carved out of solid rock in Elora, in western India; the Temple of Jaggarnauth is on the east coast of India; the Ganges is a major river and sacred in Hinduism.

39 *"The riches of her opulent family ... "*: Owenson alters her source. According to the translation of the Laws of Menu which Owenson cites, a woman could only inherit if her sonless father "appointed" her to bear a son for him; the grandson would then inherit the wealth, and responsibilities, that would otherwise have fallen to sons (Jones, *Institutes* 3: 352-53). Luxima, as a vestal (and so under a vow of chastity), could clearly not fulfil such a commitment and thus could not, according to the *Institutes*, play a role in the inheritance of her family's property.

40 *"says De Bernier"*: It is unclear which edition Owenson is quoting here, but the passage appears in his letter on Cashmire—a letter regularly included in editions of Bernier's travelogue.

41 *"The Women are so sacred in India ... "*: The quotation is taken from Dow's "Dissertation on the Origin of Despotism in Indostan" (3: x, not 3: 10). In *Luxima*, Owenson also notes Buddhism's opposition to violence against women (see note 34). The same regard for women's physical safety was often imputed to pre-colonial Ireland. See, for instance, Thomas Moore's lyric, "Rich and Rare were the Gems She Wore," as well as Moore's note to the poem.

42 *"the biographer of Xavier"*: A number of biographies of the saint were in print by the early 1800s, and these miracles are regularly mentioned in such texts.

43 *"Cet excès de chaleur ... brulante"*: See "Voyage de Bernier." "This excessive heat results from the position of the high mountains which are found to the north of the road, stopping the cool winds, reflecting the rays of the sun onto travellers, and leaving a burning heat in the country."

44 *"Il (Bernier) ... des Indes en Europe"*: "He (Bernier) had no sooner climbed what he calls the hideous wall of the world (because he considers Cashmire a terrestrial paradise)—that is to say, a high mountain, black and barren—when, descending on the other side, he sensed air that was more fresh and temperate. Nothing surprised him more, in these mountains, than finding himself, all of a sudden, transported from India to Europe."

(Bernier's travelogue was originally written in the first person, but, in the *Histoire Générale*, Bernier's text is rewritten in the third person.)

45 *"Indian Caucasus"*: A chain of mountains, also known as Hindu Kush, west of Cashmire; it is the setting for P. B. Shelley's *Prometheus Unbound*.

46 *"Sirinigar"*: Owenson subsequently refers to Sirinigar (Srinigar) as the capital of Cashmire.

47 *"L'Eternel ... et de sa beatitude"*: "The Eternal, absorbed in the contemplation of his essence, resolved in the fullness of time to create beings of his essence and his beatitude."

48 *"expiate a crime"*: See note 73 regarding the significance of expiation.

49 *"Rajahs ... Ryots"*: Craufurd divides "Rajahs" into two groups, "kings or great Rajahs" and "inferior Rajahs, or nobles" (90), and characterizes "Ryots" as "peasants" (91) and "cultivators of the ground" (333).

50 *"Il ne faut ... couverte de riz"*: "Refreshing foods are not needed in these nations, and mother nature prodigiously provides them with forests of lemons, of oranges, of figs, of palm trees, of coconut palms, and of fields covered with rice."

51 *"Sweet as from blest voices uttering joy"*: This line is taken from John Milton's *Paradise Lost* (1667): "The multitude of Angels with a shout / Loud as from numbers without number, sweet / As from blest voices, uttering joy, Heav'n rung / With Jubilee" (3.345-48). For a discussion of Owenson's use of Milton in *The Missionary*, see Rajan (130-31; 134-36).

52 *"hymn to Camdeo"*: Jones' translation of the "Hymn to Camdeo" was well known in the early nineteenth century. On Owenson's debts to Jones, see Drew (241-54).

53 *"Feed on thoughts ..."*: These lines are taken from a passage in *Paradise Lost* in which the poet speaks of "wander[ing] where the Muses haunt / Cleer Spring, or shadie Grove, or Sunnie Hill, / Smit with the love of sacred Song" (3.27-29): "Then feed on thoughts, that voluntarie move / Harmonious numbers; as the wakeful Bird / Sings darkling" (3.37-39).

54 *"quietism ... Archbishop of Cambray"*: François de Salignac de la Mothe Fénelon (1651-1715) became Archbishop of Cambray in 1695; he publicly defended a leading advocate of quietism, Madame Guyon (Jeanne-Marie Bouvier de La Motte, or Madame Du Chesnoy, 1648-1717), in his *Explication des Maximes des Saints Sur la Vie Intérieure* (1697). Pope Innocent XII was critical of their beliefs, and of Fénelon's *Explication*. In *Luxima*, Owenson expands on this early reference to quietism by adding Guyon's name to the note and including a second: "The mystic sect which Fénélon, A. B. of Cambrai, and the celebrated Mme. Guyon founded in Paris, was limited in its doctrines, and called 'The Religion of Love'" (33n).

As Owenson indicates in both texts, the doctrine was "well-known." A number of her sources for *The Missionary* include references to the doctrine, including Voltaire's *Essai* and Stockdale's *History*. Hilarion's comparison of Luxima's beliefs to European "doctrines of mystic love" would find support in some comparative religious studies of the eighteenth century: Craufurd notes, in the 1792 *Sketches*, "Some are of [the] opinion, that the extravagant notions of *the illuminated* and *quietists*, that have figured among the Christians, and that still exist in different parts of Europe, came originally from the devotees of Hindostan" (1: 249).

55 *"pariah"*: "Beside the four *casts* ..., there is an adventitious tribe, or race of people, called in the Sanskreet, Chandalas; and on the coast of Coromandel, Pariars; who are employed in the meanest offices.... Their number, compared with that of any other cast, is inconsiderable, and seems evidently to consist of those persons that have been expelled [from] their *casts*" (Craufurd 108*n*).

56 *"one who should descend from heaven"*: Owenson uses a common figure here, and it is not clear if she has a specific source in mind.

57 *"The rose withers ..."*: Owenson ascribes this passage to Sadi (1184-1291), author of the *Garden of Roses* (1258), but the quotation is untraced. She may, however, be misremembering Jones' translation of an ode by Hafiz (c. 1320-89), published as "Ode III" in Jones' essay, "Traité sur la poësie orientale": "Si le rose se fane, dis gaiement, apporte du vin du couleur de rose. / Si la mélodie du rossignol ne se fait plus entendre, écoutons la mélodie des coupes passant à la ronde" (5: 466). (If the rose fades, cheerfully say, bring wine the colour of the rose. / If the melody of the nightingale can no longer be heard, listen to the melody of the winecups passing around.) But similar imagery abounds in Persian poetry of this period. Jones ranks Sadi and Hafiz among the best Persian poets ("On the Mystical Poetry" 1: 460).

58 *"The new Emperor ... at Lahore"*: This passage appears in Volume 3 of Dow's translation.

59 *"the pomp and circumstance of war"*: See Shakespeare's *Othello*: "Farewell the neighing steed and the shrill trump, / The spirit-stirring drum, th' ear-piercing fife, / The royal banner, and all quality, / Pride, pomp, and circumstance of glorious war!" (3.3.351-54).

60 *"performing poojah"*: "Pooja, is properly worship" (Craufurd 170*n*).

61 *"a wretched Chancalas"*: See note 55.

62 *"while looks intervened, or smiles"*: This loose quotation of Milton is taken from Eve's argument that she and Adam should work separately because they distract each other from work: "For while so near each other thus all day / Our task we choose, what wonder if so near / Looks intervene and smiles, or object new / Casual discourse draw on, which intermits / Our dayes work brought to little, though begun / Early" (*PL* 9.220-25). While they work apart, Eve is tempted and eats the fruit of the forbidden tree, leading to their expulsion from Eden.

63 *"Saint Catherine de Gênes"*: Saint Catherine of Genoa (1447-1510); she is supposed to have written *Dialogues of the Soul and Body* and *Treatise on Purgatory*, first published in 1551.

64 *"urged a sweet return"*: This reference is taken from the same section of *Paradise Lost* as the lines in note 62, but here Adam concedes to Eve, agreeing to work apart: "But if much converse perhaps / Thee satiate, to

short absence I could yeild. / For solitude somtimes is best societie, / And short retirement urges sweet returne" (9.247-50).

65 *"fourteen Indras reign"*: Indra is a Hindu deity, but the reference is probably an erroneous one; Romantic-era orientalists understood the reigns of fourteen Menus, not Indras, to constitute a significant period of time. According to Maurice, "the reigns of fourteen ... Menus are only a single day of Brahma," and each day of Brahma represents a single era of many millions of years (1: 140).

66 *"Peruvian quipas"*: A "quipas" (quipos) is a set of cords in which colours and knots are used to record information. This comparison might seem offhand, but it is a suggestive one. Alan Richardson argues that Helen Maria Williams, in *Peru* (1784), "suggests an association between Spanish conquest in the Americas and the consolidation of British control in Bengal" in India (267).

67 *"steeped it in forgetfulness"*: This is a variation on a phrase in Shakespeare's *Henry IV Part 2*: "O sleep! O gentle sleep! / Nature's soft nurse, how have I frighted thee, / That thou no more wilt weigh my eyelids down / And steep my senses in forgetfulness?" (3.1.5-8).

68 *"hidden 'man of the heart'"*: See the biblical passage, "But *let it be* the hidden man of the heart, in that which is not corruptible, *even the ornament* of a meek and quiet spirit, which is in the sight of God of great price" (1 Peter 3.4).

69 *"Christian Magdalene"*: Mary Magdalene was a follower of Jesus, and was at both his crucifixion and resurrection. According to the Bible, Jesus "had cast seven devils" "out of" her (Mark 16.9; see also Luke 8.2), and she is sometimes denominated "the penitent."

70 *"Laws of Menu"*: Owenson is referring to Jones' *Institutes of Hindu Law*.

71 *"He who talks to the wife ... "*: Owenson conflates a number of items in the *Institutes of Hindu Law*. According to Jones' translation ("Chapter the Eighth. On Judicature; and on Law, Private and Criminal"),

352. Men, who commit overt acts of adulterous inclinations for the wives of others, let the king banish from his realm, having punished them with such bodily marks, as excite aversion. (3: 324)

356. He, who talks with the wife of another man at a place of pilgrimage, in a forest or a grove, or at the confluence of rivers, incurs the guilt of an adulterous inclination. (3: 325)

374. A mechanick or servile man, having an adulterous connexion with a woman of a twiceborn class, whether guarded at home or unguarded, *shall thus be punished*: if she was unguarded, *he* shall lose the part *offending*, and his whole substance; if guarded, *and a priestess*, every thing, *even his life*.

375. *For adultery with a guarded priestess*, a merchant shall forfeit all his wealth after imprisonment for a year; a soldier shall be fined a thousand *panas*, and be shaved with *the urine of an ass*. (3: 327)

377. Both of them, however, if they commit that offence with a priestess *not only* guarded *but eminent for good qualities*, shall be punished

like men of the servile class, or be burned in a fire of dry grass or reeds. (3: 328)

72 "*Yogis*": See note 26.

73 "*Indian excommunication*": Owenson again revises Jones' *Institutes* to suit her literary purposes. What she, perhaps following Dow's example (1: xxix), terms "excommunication" is arguably better described as a form of exile and stigmatization for those who commit the most serious crimes but fail to show contrition. According to Jones' translation ("Chapter the Ninth. On the Same; and on the Commercial and Servile Classes"),

235. The slayer of a priest, a soldier or merchant drinking arak, or a priest drinking arak, mead, or rum, he, who steals the gold of a priest, and he, who violates the bed of his *natural or spiritual* father, are all to be considered respectively as offenders in the highest degree, *except those, whose crimes are not fit to be named*:

236. On such of those four, as have not actually performed an expiation, let the king legally inflict corporal punishment, together with a fine.

237. For violating the paternal bed, let *the mark of* a female part be impressed *on the forehead with hot iron*; for drinking spirits, a vintner's flag; for stealing sacred gold, a dog's foot; for murdering a priest, *the figure of* a headless corpse:

238. With none to eat with them, with none to sacrifice with them, with none to read with them, with none to be allied by marriage to them, abject and excluded from all social duties, let them wander over this earth:

239. Branded with *indelible* marks, they shall be deserted by their paternal and maternal relations, treated by none with affection, received by none with respect: such is the ordinance of Menu.

240. *Criminals of* all the classes, having performed an expiation, as ordained by law, shall not be marked on the forehead, but condemned to pay the highest fine. (3: 368-69)

While sacrilege is associated here with the crimes of murder and incest, apostasy is not mentioned and the emphasis is on social rather than sacred forms of exclusion; moreover, expiation reduces the penalty. Owenson seems to be eliding these laws with the contemporary European understanding of loss of caste, a penalty brought to public attention by the 1806 Vellore Mutiny (see note 97).

74 "*sacrament of baptism*": Baptism marks a person's entrance into the Catholic church as well as rebirth as a person purged of any past sins. In ritual terms, Luxima has decisively left the Hindu religious community through excommunication and joined the Catholic religion through baptism, becoming a new person in the process. Owenson questions the force of such rituals by representing Luxima's beliefs and affections as unchanged.

75 "*would not be comforted*": The phrase is taken from the fulfillment of a prophecy from Jeremiah (31.15) in Matthew. In Matthew, the reference is

to a parent's grief at losing her children: "Rachel weeping for her children, and would not be comforted, because they are not" (Matt. 2.18). In Jeremiah, exile is also implied: "there is hope ... that thy children shall come again to their own border" (Jer. 31.17).

76 "*Selon les témoignages ... plusieurs caravans*": "According to the testimony of all Cashmirians, each year one sees many caravans leaving their country."

77 "*highways and public places*": Owenson alludes to Biblical passages in which Christ speaks of gathering people, passages pertinent to the missionary project referred to here. See, for instance, Matthew (22.9-10) and Luke (14.23).

78 "*Il faut ... la nature du climat*": "It is especially important to keep in mind the possibility that abstinence from the flesh of animals is a consequence of the climate."

79 "*Une laine ... de Cashmire*": "A wool, or rather a hair, which is called 'touz,' is taken from the chests of the wild goats of the mountains of Cashmire."

80 "*God in all, and all in God*": This is a common phrase, related to "God may be all in all" (1 Cor. 15.28).

81 "*Kindersley's History of the Hindu Mythology*": Owenson here cites Kindersley's "Introductory Remarks"; many of Owenson's mythological identifications in *The Missionary* are taken, almost word for word, from this text.

82 "*C'est dans ... Chûte des Anges*": "It is in the Shaster that one finds the story of the Fall of the Angels."

83 "*which chilled his which increased*": In *Luxima*, Owenson excises this garbled passage. The revised passage reads, "It was by words like these, timidly and tenderly pronounced, that the feelings of the spiritual guide were put to the most severe test; it was words like these, which cherished and fed his passion, while they awakened his self-distrust" (235).

84 "*Carnatic ... the Ghauts*": The Carnatic is a region in southeastern India. "Ghaut" was understood to denote a range of hills or mountain pass.

85 " *... one extended blaze...* ": Many of the details in this scene, as well as much of the footnote on bamboo fires, are taken directly from Kindersley's translation, "The History of the Nella-Rajah" (224-25).

86 "*vocal aid*": This is probably an allusion to Milton's "vocal Air" (*PL* 9.530), a phrase used to describe the serpent's speech as, having just approached Eve's ear, he begins his "fraudulent temptation" (9.531). The reference reinforces the parallel between Cashmire and Eden, as well as Luxima and Eve, while emphasizing Luxima's innocence—the serpent is tempted away from Luxima's ear before it can harm her.

87 "*with darkness compassed round*": This quotation is taken from Milton's invocation to his muse, Urania, in which he represents her as his solace in a corrupt world: "fall'n on evil dayes, / On evil dayes though fall'n, and evil tongues; / In darkness, and with dangers compast round, / And

solitude; yet not alone, while thou / Visit'st my slumbers Nightly" (*PL* 7.25-29).

88 *"female seik"*: "Seik" was a variant spelling of "Sikh" in British orientalist scholarship at the turn of the century. The Sikh religion was founded in the sixteenth century, and its followers were frequently from the Punjab region in northern India, just south of Cashmire.

89 *"sound of tinkling brass"*: Owenson alludes to the biblical passage, "Though I speak with the tongues of men and of angels, and have not charity, I am become *as* sounding brass, or a tinkling cymbal" (1 Cor. 13.1).

90 *"Sketches of the History of the Religion ... "*: The *Sketches* are attributed to Quintin Craufurd.

91 *"sword of Mahmoud and arms of Timur"*: There are a number of rulers named Mahmoud (Mahmood), but Owenson is probably referring to Mahmood I. According to Dow's translation, his rule began in 997 and ended with his death in 1028, and he invaded Hindostan no less than twelve times, often to suppress uprisings against his rule. Dow's translation emphasizes his mercenary motives and forced conversions: "Mahmood plundered Cashmire of all its great wealth, and having forced the inhabitants to acknowledge the Prophet, returned with the spoil to his capital of Ghizni" (1: 59). On Timur, see note 14.

92 *"Scindi"*: Scindi (Sind) is a region in the northwestern part of the Indian subcontinent; Tatta is one of its cities.

93 *"when one cheek was smitten ... "*: Owenson's narrator here cites a common Christian precept derived from the Bible (see Matt. 5.39).

94 *"Awe from above ... nought else dismayed"*: In Milton's poem, Satan's rebel angels confront Gabriel's forces and Satan realizes the greater strength of the other side: "to strive or flie / He held it vain; awe from above had quelld / His heart, not else dismai'd" (*PL* 4.859-61).

95 *"bought golden opinions ... "* and *"Dominicans"*: Macbeth uses this phrase: "We will proceed no further in this business: / He hath honor'd me of late, and I have bought / Golden opinions from all sorts of people, / Which would be worn now in their newest gloss, / Not cast aside so soon" (Shakespeare, *Macbeth* 1.7.31-35). The Dominicans are a Catholic religious order; the order was founded by St. Dominic and was closely associated with the Inquisition (the first Grand Inquisitor, Torquemada, was a Dominican).

96 *"thoughts of lost happiness ... "* and *"equal ruin"*: These are both allusions to Milton's epic: "his doom / Reserv'd him to more wrath; for now the thought / Both of lost happiness and lasting pain / Torments him" (*PL* 1.53-56); "If he whom mutual league, / United thoughts and counsels, equal hope / And hazard in the Glorious Enterprize, / Joynd with me once, now misery hath joynd / In equal ruin" (*PL* 1.87-91).

97 *"not all lost in loss itself"* and *"archangel ruined"*: Owenson takes both of these references from Milton's description of Satan and his fallen legions: "with looks / Down cast and damp, yet such wherein appear'd / Obscure som glimps of joy, to have found thir chief / Not in despair, to

have found themselves not lost / In loss it self" (*PL* 1.522-26) (the "chief" is Satan; Satan rallies his troops, so to speak, in subsequent lines); "his form had yet not lost / All her Original brightness, nor appear'd / Less then Arch Angel ruind" (*PL* 1.591-93).

98 "*insurrection of fatal consequence*": The "Vellore Mutiny" took place on 9 July 1806, and involved an uprising of Indian troops (called "Sepoys") in the British garrison at Vellore; one of the primary reasons for the uprising, according to contemporary accounts, was the forced anglicization of the soldiers' dress and appearance. Such anglicization was deemed to pose the threat of loss of caste. See the "Introduction" for more details. In his *Memoir* of the uprising, the former Governor of Vellore, Bentinck, also mentions Nundydroog and Bangalore: in October 1806, British officers in both locations, nervous after Vellore, took steps to quash feared uprisings (barricading themselves in buildings, calling for reinforcements, and so forth), but Bentinck insists that no meaningful evidence emerged to suggest that any uprisings were indeed imminent (36).

99 "*eve of St. Jago de Compostello*": St. Jago de Compostello is better known as St. James the Greater, one of the apostles. This form of his name alludes to a tradition in which, after his execution by Herod Agrippa I (see Acts 12 in the Bible), the apostle's body was miraculously transported to Spain, finally resting in Compostela.

100 "*delirious fever*": Owenson sanitizes and somewhat distorts details from Stockdale's *History*; delirium appears only in a later stage of what is represented as a serious gastrointestinal disorder. In the *History*, the "place where exercise is impossible" is a prison cell of the Inquisition, the only preventative is a diet designed to avoid the indigestion that leads to the condition, and the predominant symptom is "a violent fever, accompanied by trembling, anxiety, and vomiting" (239).

101 "*nought value he or shunned*": This quotation is taken from Milton's description of Satan's disregard: "The Monster moving onward came as fast / With horrid strides, Hell trembled as he strode. / Th'undaunted Fiend what this might be admir'd, / Admir'd, not fear'd; God and his Son except, / Created thing naught vallu'd he nor shun'd; / And with disdainful look thus first began" (*PL* 2.675-80).

102 "*dark spotted flower in the garden of love*": As Rajan notes, Hegel uses this phrase in his chapter on India in *The Philosophy of History*; Rajan suggests that Hegel "may well have been aware of *The Missionary* and could be alluding to it in this passage" (247*n*).

103 "*Historical*": Owenson here draws on Bernier's account of this expedition and so terms her details "historical."

104 "*an European Philosopher*": François de Bernier.

Appendix A: Imperial Administration and Religious Difference

1. From François Bernier, *Bernier's Voyage to the East Indies* (first English translation published 1671-72), 170-71, 184.

I very much applaud the missions, and pious and learned missionaries—they are absolutely necessary: it is the honour and prerogative of Christianity to have every where through the world substitutes of the apostles. But after all that I have seen, and after all the converse and discourse I have so often had with those obstinate infidels, I may take leave to say, that I almost despair to see struck such great strokes as the apostles did, who converted two or three thousand people in one sermon; finding by experience, and knowing very well upon other accounts, after I have travelled through all the places of the missions in the East, that all the missionaries together, not only in the Indies, but in all the Mahometan dominions, do indeed by their instructions, accompanied with charity and alms, make some progress among the Gentiles, but do in ten years not make one Christian of a Mahometan.... Our Christians of Europe ought to wish, and even to employ their power, care, and charity, that missionaries may be sent over all, such as may be no charge to the people of the country, and whom want may not induce to do mean things, as well for the reasons already alledged, as for this cause, that they may be ever ready to lay hold on all occasions, always to bear witness to the truth, and to labour in the vineyard when it shall please God to give them an overture. But for the rest we ought to be disabused, and not to suffer ourselves to be so easily persuaded of so many stories, and not to believe the thing to be so facile as some make it. The sect is much too libertine, and too attractive to quit it.... [Hindus] are also bound to wash their whole body thrice, or at least before they eat; and they believe, that it is more meritorious to wash themselves in running water than in any other. And it may be, that the legislators in this point also have had a respect to what is proper and convenient for this country, where nothing is more desirable than washing and bathing. And they find it troublesome enough to observe this law, when they are in cold countries: I have seen some of them that were like to die, because they would there also observe their law of washing their body by plunging themselves into rivers or ponds, when they found any near; or by throwing whole buckets of water over their heads, when they were remote from them. When I told them, upon occasion, that in cold countries it would not be possible to observe that law of theirs in winter (which was a sign of its being a mere human invention) they gave this pleasant answer: that they pretended not their law was universal; that God had only made it for them, and it was therefore that they could not receive a stranger into their religion; that they thought not our religion was therefore false, but that perhaps it was good for us, and that God might have appointed several differing ways to go to heaven; but they will not hear that our religion should be the general religion for the whole earth; and theirs a fable and pure device.

2. **From Alexander Dow, "A Dissertation concerning the Customs, Manners, Language, Religion, and Philosophy of the Hindoos," in Vol. 1 of *The History of Hindostan* (first published in 1768), xix–xx.**

The learned of modern Europe have, with reason, complained that the writers of Greece and Rome did not extend their enquiries to the religion and philosophy of the Druids. Posterity will perhaps, in the same manner, find fault with the British for not investigating the learning and religious opinions, which prevail in those countries in Asia, into which either their commerce or their arms have penetrated. The Brahmins of the East possessed in ancient times, some reputation for knowledge, but we have never had the curiosity to examine whether there was any truth in the reports of antiquity upon that head.

Excuses, however, may be formed for our ignorance concerning the learning, religion and philosophy of the Brahmins. Literary inquiries are by no means a capital object to many of our adventurers in Asia. The few who have a turn for researches of that kind, are discouraged by the very great difficulty in acquiring that language, in which the learning of the Hindoos is contained; or by that impenetrable veil of mystery with which the Brahmins industriously cover their religious tenets and philosophy. These circumstances combining together, have opened an ample field for fiction. Modern travellers have accordingly indulged their talent for fable, upon the mysterious religion of Hindostan. Whether the ridiculous tales they relate, proceed from that common partiality which Europeans, as well as less enlightened nations, entertain for the religion and philosophy of their own country, or from a judgment formed upon some external ceremonies of the Hindoos, is very difficult to determine; but they have prejudiced Europe against the Brahmins, and by a very unfair account, have thrown disgrace upon a system of religion and philosophy, which they did by no means investigate.

The author of this dissertation must own, that he for a long time, suffered himself to be carried down in this stream of popular prejudice. The present decline of literature in Hindostan, served to confirm him in his belief of those legends which he read in Europe, concerning the Brahmins. But conversing by accident, one day, with a noble and learned Brahmin, he was not a little surprized to find him perfectly acquainted with those opinions, which, both in ancient and modern Europe, have employed the pens of the most celebrated moralists. This circumstance did not fail to excite his curiosity, and in the course of many subsequent conversations, he found that philosophy and the sciences had, in former ages, made a very considerable progress in the East.

3. From Alexander Dow, "Dissertation on the Origin of Despotism in Indostan," in Vol. 3 of *The History of Hindostan* (first published in 1772), xc-xci.

Men who submit to bodily servitude, have been known to revolt against the slavery imposed on their minds. We may use the Indians for our benefit in this world, but let them serve themselves as they can in the next. All religions must be tolerated in Bengal, except in the practice of some inhuman customs, which the Mahommedans have already, in a great measure, destroyed. We must not permit young widows, in their virtuous enthusiasm, to throw themselves on the funeral pile, with their dead husbands; nor the sick and aged to be drowned, when their friends despair of their lives.

The Hindoo religion, in other respects, inspires the purest morals. Productive, from its principles, of the greatest degree of subordination to authority, it prepares mankind for the government of foreign lords. It supplies, by its well-followed precepts, the place of penal laws; and it renders crime almost unknown in the land. The peaceable sentiments which it breath[e]s, will check the more warlike doctrines promulgated by the Coran. The prudent successors of Timur saw that the Hindoo religion was favourable to their power; and they sheathed the sword, which the other princes of the Mahommedan persuasion employed in establishing their own faith, in all their conquests. Freedom of conscience was always enjoyed in India in the absence of political freedom.

Attention must be paid to the usages and very prejudices of the people, as well as a regard for their religion. Though many things of that kind may appear absurd and trivial among Europeans, they are of the utmost importance among the Indians. The least breach of them may be productive of an expulsion from the society, a more dreadful punishment Draco himself could not devise. But the caution about religion is superfluous: these are no converting days. Among the list of crimes committed in Bengal, persecution for religion is not to be found; and he that will consent to part with his property, may carry his opinions away with freedom.

4. From [Quintin Craufurd], *Sketches Chiefly Relating to the History, Religion, Learning, and Manners of the Hindoos* (1790), 131–33.

Whatever opinion may be formed of the Hindoo religion itself, we cannot deny its professors the merit of having adhered to it with a constancy unequalled in the history of any other. The number of those who have been induced or compelled to quit their doctrines, notwithstanding the long period of their subjection, and the persecutions they have undergone, is too inconsiderable to bear any proportion to the number of those who have adhered to them.

It is a circumstance very singular, and merits particular attention, that, contrary to the practice of every other religious society, the Hindoos, far from disturbing those who are of a different faith, by endeavours to convert them, cannot even admit any proselytes; and that, not withstanding the exclusion of others, and though tenacious of their own doctrines, they neither hate nor despise, nor pity, such as are of a different belief, nor do they think them less favoured by the Supreme Being than themselves. They say, that if the Author of the universe preferred one religion to another, *that only* could prevail which he approved; because to suppose such preference, while we see so many different religions, would be the height of impiety, as it would be supposing injustice towards those that he left ignorant of his will; and they therefore conclude, that every religion is peculiarly adapted to the country and people where it is practiced, and that all, in their original purity, are equally acceptable to God.

The Brahmans, who translated from the Sanskrit language the laws and customs of the Hindoos, say, in the preliminary discourse prefixed to their work;

"From men of enlightened understandings and sound judgment, who, in their researches after truth, have swept away from their hearts malice and opposition, it is not concealed that the diversities of belief, which are causes of enmity and envy to the ignorant, are in fact a demonstration of the power of the Supreme Being."

5. From Sir William Jones, Preface to *Institutes of Hindu Law: Or, the Ordinances of Menu* (first published in 1796), 3: 53-54, 62-63.

It is a maxim in the science of legislation and government, that *Laws are of no avail without manners*, or, to explain the sentence more fully, that the best intended legislative provisions would have no beneficial effect even at first, and none at all in a short course of time, unless they were congenial to the disposition and habits, to the religious prejudices, and approved immemorial usages, of the people, for whom they were enacted; especially if that people universally and sincerely believed, that all their ancient usages and established rules of conduct had the sanction of an actual revelation from heaven: the legislature of *Britain* having shown, in compliance with this maxim, an intention to leave the natives of these *Indian* provinces in possession of their own Laws, at least on the titles of *contracts* and *inheritances*, we may humbly presume, that all future provisions, for the administration of justice and government in *India*, will be conformable, as far as the natives are affected by them, to the manners and opinions of the natives themselves; an object, which cannot possibly be attained, until those manners and opinions can be fully and accurately known. These considerations, and a few others more immediately within my province, were my principal motives for wishing to know, and have induced me at length to publish, that system of duties, religious and civil, and of law in all its branches, which the *Hindus* firmly believe to have been promulged in the beginning of time by Menu, son or grandson of Brahmá, or, in plain language, the first of created beings, and not the oldest only, but the holiest, of legislators; a system so comprehensive and so minutely exact, that it may be considered as the *Institutes* of

Hindu Law, preparatory to the copious *Digest*, which has lately been compiled by *Pandits* of eminent learning, and introductory perhaps to a *Code*, which may supply the many natural defects in the old jurisprudence of this country, and, without any deviation from its principles, accommodate it justly to the improvements of a commercial age....

It is a system of depotism and priestcraft, both indeed limited by law, but artfully conspiring to give mutual support, though with mutual checks; it is filled with strange conceits in metaphysicks and natural philosophy, with idle superstitions, and with a scheme of theology most obscurely figurative, and consequently liable to dangerous misconception; it abounds with minute and childish formalities, with ceremonies generally absurd and often ridiculous; the punishments are partial and fanciful, for some crimes dreadfully cruel, for others reprehensibly slight; and the very morals, though rigid enough on the whole, are in one or two instances (as in the case of light oaths and of pious perjury) unaccountably relaxed: nevertheless, a spirit of sublime devotion, of benevolence to mankind, and of amiable tenderness to all sentient creatures, pervades the whole work; the style of it has a certain austere majesty, that sounds like the language of legislation and extorts a respectful awe; the sentiments of independence on all beings but God, and the harsh admonitions even to kings are truly noble; and the many panegyricks on the *Gáyatrì*, the *Mother*, as it is called, of the *Véda*, prove the author to have *adored* (not the visible and material *sun*, but) that *divine and incomparably greater light*, to use the words of the most venerable text in the *Indian* scripture, *which illumines all, delights all, from which all proceed, to which all must return, and which alone can irradiate* (not our visual organs merely, but our souls and) *our intellects.* Whatever opinion in short may be formed of Menu and his laws, in a country happily enlightened by sound philosophy and the only true revelation, it must be remembered, that those laws are actually revered, as the word of the Most High, by nations of great importance to the political and commercial interests of *Europe*, and particularly by many millions of *Hindu* subjects, whose well directed industry would add largely to the wealth of *Britain*, and who ask no more in return than protection for their persons and places of abode, justice in their temporal concerns, indulgence to the prejudices of their own religion, and the benefit of those laws, which they have been taught to believe sacred, and which alone they can possibly comprehend.

6. From Sydney Owenson, *Patriotic Sketches of Ireland* (1807), 1: 65-72.

The odium of bigotry is generally thrown upon the subordinate sect of every country. Bigotry, however, is in fact the cosmopolite of religion, and adheres with more or less influence to every mode of faith. Of the countless sects into which the christian church is divided,[1] it appears that each, "dark with excessive light," arrogates to itself an infallible spirit, which shuts the gates of mercy on the rest of mankind, while it condemns or opposes to the utmost stretch[2] of its ability, all whose faith is not measured by the standard of its own peculiar creed. All perhaps are alike zealots; the difference is, that the zeal of some is their privilege, and of others their crime.[3] The Irish, nationally considered with respect to their prevailing religion, never were a bigotted people, though the

---

1   "Les Chrétiens (says Helvetius) qui donnaient avec justice le nom de barbarie et de crime aux cruautés qu'exerçaient sur eux les payens, ne donnèrent-ils pas le nom de zelé aux cruautés qu'ils exerçaient à leur tour sur ces mêmes payens?"—"Did not the Christians, who justly gave the epithets of *barbarity* and *crime* to the cruelties inflicted on them by the pagans, dignify with the name of *zeal* those cruelties which they retaliated in their turn?"

2   "Je considerais cette diversité des sectes qui regnent sur la terre, et s'accusent mutuellement de mensonge et d'erreur; je demandais, quelle est la bonne? chacune me repondait, '*c'est la mienne;*' chacune me disait, '*moi seule*, et mes partisans pensent juste; tous les autres sont dans l'erreur.' Et comment savez-vous que votre secte est la bonne? 'Parceque Dieu l'a dit.' Et qui vous dit que Dieu l'a dit? 'Mon pasteur, qui le sait bien; mon pasteur me dit, et ainsi croire, *et ainsi je crois*: il m'assure que tous ceux qui disent autrement que lui *mentent*, et je ne les écoute pas.'"—*Emile,* t. 9 l. 4.——"While I surveyed this diversity of sects prevailing on the face of the earth, and accusing one another of error and falsehood, I inquired, 'Which is the right?' Each replied: 'It is ours: we alone possess the truth, and all others are in mistake.'—'And how do you know this?'—'Because God himself has declared it.'—'Who told you so?'—'Our minister, who is well acquainted with the divine will: he has ordered us to believe this, and accordingly we do believe it. He assures us that all who contradict him speak false and therefore we do not listen to them.'"

3   "Hélas! si l'homme est aveugle, ce qui fait son tourment, fera-t-il encore son crime?" *De Volney,* ch. iv. p. 24.——"Alas! if man is blind, shall this blindness, which constitutes his misery, be also imputed to him as a crime?"

vivacity of their imagination has sometimes devoted them to superstitious illusion. When christianity took the lead of druidism in Ireland, it was preserved and nurtured by the same mild principle of toleration, as suffered its admission; and though the druidical tenets flourished for two centuries after the arrival of the first christian missionary in the island, yet neither historical record, nor oral tradition, advances any detail of religious persecution adopted on either side. The tenets preached by the christian missionary, or the arguments opposed by the heathen controvertist, awakened no further interest in the public consideration, than a desire to embrace that mode of faith, which came home with most force to reason, and to truth. If the arguments held out were not always attended with conviction, the doubtful superiority was never decided at the sword's point; if the cross was sometimes unavailingly raised, the arm[1] which supported it was protected from injury by the egis of toleration; nor were tortures invented, persecutions enforced, or oppressions exercised, to obtain the abjuration of a long-cherished tenet, to prove the orthodoxy of a doctrinal point, or to establish the infallibility of a speculative theory.[2] As yet free from that fanatic spirit which strews the earth with human victims, and still "opposes man against the murderer man," the Irish would have rejected with horror and incredulity that prophecy, which should have foretold such a series of religious barbarities as attended the expulsion of the Moors from Spain, the *conversion* of the Mexicans in America, the revocation of the edict of Nantz, and the establishment of the popery laws in their own country.

---

1 "Can that church be the church of Christ," says the tolerant bishop of Novogorod, "whose arm is red to the shoulder with human gore?"

2 "César et Pompée," says Voltaire in his English Letters, "ne se sont pas fait la guerre pour savoir si les *poulets sacrées* doivent *manger* et *boir*, ou bien manger seulement; ni pour savoir si les prêtres devaient sacrifier avec leur chemise sur leur habit, ou leur habit sur leur chemise. Non! ces horreurs étaient réservés pour *la réligion de la charité*."—"Cesar and Pompey did not fight to determine whether the consecrated fowl ought to eat and drink, or to eat only; nor whether the priests should officiate with their surplice over their gown, or their gown over their surplice. No: these horrors were reserved for the religion of charity."

7. "Extract from the Minutes of the Court of Directors, 25th July, 1809," in Bentinck's *Memorial ... Containing an Account of the Mutiny at Vellore* (1810), 53-54.

[After the "Vellore Mutiny," the local Governor, Lord William Cavendish Bentinck, was summarily dismissed; this extract gives the Directors' reasons for rejecting Bentinck's appeal of that decision.]

Resolved, That under the impressions universally entertained, both in India and Europe, at the breaking out of the Vellore Mutiny, that it was occasioned by the wanton or needless violations of the religious usages of the Natives—an opinion considerably sanctioned by the Supreme Government of Bengal, and even countenanced by the first dispatches of the Fort St. George Presidency; and under the impressions, then also general, of the dangers to which the Company's interests were exposed, and of the necessity of a change in the chief offices of the Civil and Military Command, as well to vindicate the national respect for the religious usages of our Native subjects, as to make a sacrifice to their violated rights, to restore public confidence, and to relieve the Executive Body of the Company, with whom so much responsibility rested, from the anxiety and apprehensions occasioned by so unexampled and alarming a calamity, it became natural and expedient for them to remove Lord William Bentinck from the Government, and Sir John Cradock from the Command of the Army of Fort St. George. And although from the explanations that have since been given by those personages respectively, and from the further evidences which have come before the Court, it appears that the Orders in question were far from being intended by the Members of the Madras Government, to trench in the least upon the religious tenets of the Natives, and did not in reality infringe them, although the uninformed Sepoys were led at length to believe that they did; yet the effects produced have been so disastrous, and associated in the Native mind with the administration of the then Governor and Commander-in-Chief, and those Officers besides having in the judgment of the Court been defective, in not examining with greater caution and care into the real sentiments and dispositions of the Sepoys, before they proceeded to inforce the Orders for the Turban; the Court must still lament, that as, in proceeding to a change in the Madras Government, they yielded with regret to imperious circumstances, so, though they have the pleasure to find the charges originally

advanced against the conduct of the Governor and the Commander-in-Chief, respecting the violation of Cast, to have been, in the
sense then attached to them, misapplied and defective, also in general vigilance and intelligence; yet that, as the misfortunes which
happened in their Administration, placed their fate under the government of public events and opinions, which the Court could not
controul, so it is not now in their power to alter the effects of
them.

8. From J. J. Stockdale, Preface to *The History of the Inqui-sitions* (1810), xvi.

The page of history, antient and modern, even of these our days,
now open for our inspection and our improvement, clearly proves,
that the Roman Catholic religion was, is, and will continue, in
principle and in practice, unchanged and unchangeable. Oh
Protestants, observe then, as you have done hitherto, towards your
Catholic brethren, perfect tolerance, perfect charity:—but, always
bear in mind the fable of the wolves and the sheep. *Remember never
to give up your vigilance. Remember the massacre of St. Bartholemew;* and
remember, that Popery, having been driven out of Rome, has taken
refuge amongst us, and is, with unceasing activity, daily gaining
proselytes to its cause, especially among our highest and lowest
classes. Read the following pages with more than serious—with
solemn attention, for Popery is making rapid advances against your
religion: and
THE EMBRYO OF THE INQUISITION
(*may I never find it necessary to be more explicit on this subject*)
IS ACTUALLY ESTABLISHED IN EVERY PART OF
THE UNITED KINGDOM.

9. From Charles Grant, *Observations, On the State of Society Among the Asiatic Subjects of Great Britain, particularly with respect to Morals; and on the means of improving it.—Written chiefly in the Year 1792* (1813), 76, 77, 79-80.

Are we bound for ever to preserve all the enormities in the Hindoo system? Have we become the guardians of every monstrous
principle and practice which it contains? Are we pledged to support, for all generations, by the authority of our government and

the power of our arms, the miseries which ignorance and knavery have so long entailed upon a large portion of the human race? Is this the part which a free, a humane, and an enlightened nation, a nation itself professing principles diametrically opposite to those in question, has engaged to act towards its own subjects? It would be too absurd and extravagant to maintain, that any engagement of this kind exists; that Great Britain is under any obligation, direct or implied, to uphold errors and usages, gross and fundamental, subversive of the first principles of reason, morality, and religion....

We proceed to observe, that it is perfectly in the power of this country, by degrees, to impart to the Hindoos our language; afterwards through that medium, to make them acquainted with our easy literary compositions, upon a variety of subjects; and, let not the idea hastily excite derision, *progressively* with the simple elements of our arts, our philosophy and religion. These acquisitions would silently undermine, and at length subvert, the fabric of error; and all the objections that may be apprehended against such a charge, are, it is confidently believed, capable of solid answer.

The first communication, and the instrument of introducing the rest, must be the English language; this is a key which will open to them a world of new ideas, and policy alone might have impelled us, long since, to put it into their hands.

To introduce the language of the conquerors, seems to be an obvious means of assimilating the conquered people to them. The Mahomedans, from the beginning of their power, employed the Persian language in the affairs of government, and in the public departments. This practice aided them in maintaining their superiority, and enabled them, instead of depending blindly on native agents, to look into the conduct and details of public business, as well as to keep intelligible registers of the income and expenditure of the state. Natives readily learnt the language of government, finding that it was necessary in every concern of revenue and of justice....

But undoubtedly the most important communication which the Hindoos could receive through the medium of our language, would be the knowledge of our religion, the principles of which are explained in a clear, easy way, in various tracts circulating among us, and are completely contained in the inestimable volume of Scripture. Thence they would be instructed in the nature and perfections of the one true God, and in the real history of man; his creation, lapsed state, and the means of his recovery, on all which points they hold false and extravagant opinions; they would see a pure, complete, and perfect system of morals and of duty, enforced by the most awful sanctions, and recommended by the most interesting motives; they would learn the accountableness of man, the final judgment he is to undergo, and the eternal state which is to follow. Wherever this knowledge should be received, idolatry, with all the rabble of its impure deities, its monsters of wood and stone, its false principles and corrupt practices, its delusive hopes and vain fears, its ridiculous ceremonies and degrading superstitions, its lying legends and fraudulent impositions, would fall. The reasonable service of the only, and the infinitely perfect God, would be established: love to him, peace and good-will towards men, would be felt as obligatory principles.

10. From James Mill, *History of British India* (1817), 1: 429, 431.

To ascertain the true state of the Hindus in the scale of civilization, is not only an object of curiosity in the history of human nature; but to the people of Great Britain, charged as they are with the government of that great portion of the human species, it is an object of the highest practical importance. No scheme of government can happily conduce to the ends of government, unless it is adapted to the state of the people for whose use it is intended. In those diversities in the state of civilization, which approach the extremes, this truth is universally acknowledged. Should any one propose, for a band of roving Tartars, the regulations adapted to the happiness of a regular and polished society, he would meet with neglect or derision. The inconveniences are only more concealed, and more or less diminished, when the error relates to states of society which more nearly resemble one another. If the mistake in regard to Hindu society, committed by the British nation, and the British government, be very great; if they have conceived the Hindus to be a people of high civilization, while they have in reality made but a few of the earliest steps in the progress to civilization, it is impossible that in many of the measures pursued for the government of that people, the mark aimed at should not have been wrong....

It was unfortunate that a man so pure and warm in the pursuit of truth, and so devoted to oriental learning, as Sir William Jones, took up, with that ardour which belonged to him, the theory of a high state of civilization in the principal countries of Asia. This theory he supported with all the advantages of an imposing manner, and a brilliant reputation; and gained for it so much fame and credit, that for a time it would have been very difficult to obtain a hearing against it.

Beside the illusions with which the fancy magnifies the importance of a favourite pursuit, Sir William was actuated by the virtuous design of exalting the Hindus in the eyes of their European masters; and thence ameliorating the temper of the government; while his mind had scope for error in the vague and indeterminate notions which it still retained of the signs of social improvement. The term civilization was by him, as by most men, attached to no fixed and definite assemblage of ideas. With the exception of some of the lowest states of society in which human beings have been found, it was applied to all nations in all the stages of social advancement.

11. From Rev. of Lady Morgan's *Dramatic Scenes from Real Life* and "Illustrations of the State of Ireland" (1833), 95–97.

We concur with Lady Morgan in thinking that Ireland greatly needs repose; but we cannot hope that the gift of knowledge will be alone sufficient to ensure that blessing. In saying that Ireland needs repose, we mean not that of indolent supineness, not the sleep of forgetfulness and stupefaction, but that healthful rest which comes from the absence of pain and disease. To say that Ireland requires repose, is but to say that it requires the removal of those grievances which have hitherto been productive of irritation and disquiet....

Foremost amongst the causes which impede the attainment of tranquillity in Ireland may be placed the tithe system. Need we wonder that it should be so fruitful a source of discontent, if we consider who are the payers of tithe, and who the receivers? If tithe is unpopular even in England, where the parishioner and the incumbent are Protestants alike, what must it be in Ireland, where its obnoxiousness is not softened by any such identity of creed? where, on the contrary, the pecuniary grievance is aggravated by sectarian antipathies? where it is paid by the impoverished Catholic occupant to the minister of that which he regards as a hostile church? ...

[O]n whatever footing the temporalities of the Protestant

Church in Ireland are placed, it is advisable in that country that the land-tax which might succeed to tithe, should be raised not exclusively for that church.... We would especially wish to see a general tax of this kind employed in the good work of conciliation, in removing the marks of partiality, in mitigating the jealousy of rival sects. We would wish that out of this general fund, payment should be made, not only to the Established Church, but to the Presbyterian and the Catholic. At present the Catholic is less favourably treated than the Presbyterian. The State pays an annual sum to the Presbyterians of the North of Ireland, (a very deserving body of men,) and has recently granted them an increased supply. While the Established Church and the Presbyterians are thus acknowledged and paid, six millions of Catholics, forming three-fourths of the population of Ireland, are exposed to the irritating spirit of discontent and hatred which such partiality engenders. They regard the exception as a stigma—and can we say that they so regard it without reason?

12. **From George Salmon, *The Indian Mutiny and Missions: A Sermon, Preached on Behalf of the Church Missionary Society, on Sunday, September 5, 1857* (1857), 12-15.**

Now although many heathen lands have been won to the Gospel, because devoted bands of missionaries have not hesitated to tread where their predecessors have been martyred, and undeterred by the falling of those around them, have closed up their ranks, and pressed forward; yet if our friends who have perished in India can with any truth be described as martyrs to missionary zeal, I shall not urge you to persevere in the work. But I have no hesitation in expressing my belief that missionary exertion has not been to any appreciable degree the cause of the recent outbreak, and that there is reason to think that these events would equally have occurred, if missionaries had not been in the country. And it is creditable to this country how very generally this has been acknowledged. For it shows that the nation is now, on the whole, superior to that cowardly weakness, which when surprised by unexpected disaster, thinks of nothing but looking out for some convenient scapegoat on which to lay the blame. Some fifty years ago the Vellore Mutiny gave rise to a complete panic on the subject of the missions in India, although there was not a Protestant missionary within several hundred miles of the place at the time, nor were they even then permitted to enter the Company's territories. On that occasion, men, on other subjects enlightened beyond the age, were heard to denounce all toleration of missions in India, and some were even base enough to protest against all attempts for the enlightenment of India, on the ground that if the natives were raised to a level with ourselves, it would be impossible to retain our dominion over them. Now, however, even in quarters least favourable to missionary enterprise, it has been freely acknowledged how little it is chargeable with the recent events. The most successful scenes of missionary labour are in the South, which has remained perfectly tranquil. In no place where mutinies have taken place has any peculiar hostility been shown to the missionaries, and where missionaries have lost their lives, they have perished as Europeans, not as missionaries; and have only shared the fate of all the other Europeans who fell into the enemy's hands. It is notorious too, that no conversion of Sepoys had taken place, or even been attempted by the missionaries, that class being, for obvious reasons, most inaccessible to missionary exertions. It is true that the cry of interference with their religion has been raised as a ground for mutiny both on this and on the former occasion. But what kind of interference? Not the attempt to make voluntary converts, but the fear that the Government would deprive them by force of their religion. For we must bear in mind this peculiarity of the Hindoo tenets, that they *could* be deprived of their religion by force. None of you *can* be compelled to abandon his faith; not even by threats of martyrdom, if you choose to despise them. But a Hindoo might lose his caste by acts quite beyond his control, and one of their tenets has been that such loss of caste was absolutely irrecoverable.... And the means by which a celebrated Mahometan prince was said to have made extensive conversions, was the forcible pollution of his Hindoo subjects by hundreds at a time. They had lost their caste, they could no longer be Hindoos; they might as well then be Mahometans. Thus you see that the cry about the cartridges with which this mutiny commenced, was not altogether without plausibility. To a Hindoo mind it was conceivable that the Government might some day announce to its soldiers that they had all polluted themselves by touching the unclean thing; that they had irretrievably lost their caste, and therefore might as well become Christians. But though the more credulous may have believed in this asserted project of the Indian Government, it is certain that it was but a pretext, (those very cartridges have been used without scruple against us,) and that though danger to their faith was alleged as a ground for mutiny, the hope of plunder was in most cases the moving cause. And in fact it would seem now as if the chief instigators and contrivers of the outbreak were not Hindoos but Mahometans. But what need is there to search for causes for an attempt, the motives of which lie on the surface. How can we forget that in India some one hundred and fifty or one hundred and eighty millions of natives are governed by a mere handful of Europeans, the proportion of European soldiers who have held India to the whole population being, as I have heard it stated, somewhat the same as the proportion of Hindoos in England to the whole population. Is it possible that the inhabitants can quite voluntarily submit to be governed by aliens in blood, in language, and religion? I say, *religion*, because I see no reason to doubt that the attachment of natives to their religion has helped to swell the ranks of the mutineers. But while I believe that this alone would never have caused a rebellion, I believe also that their attachment to their religion would make them impatient of English rule, if there were not a missionary in India. We may make no attempt to press our religion on them, we may be quite indifferent about our religion, but this will not make them indifferent about *theirs*; and whether they regard us as professors of a false religion, or as destitute of religion altogether, in either case the element of religious animosity will be added to heighten whatever other sense of grievances they may feel. And grievances no doubt they must feel. We may feel satisfaction in comparing our rule with the state of anarchy and intestine war from which we have delivered them, but we have ruled there so long, that the present generation cannot be expected to retain any such lively remembrance of those former evils, as to induce them patiently to submit to present ones. The higher rank of natives, who find themselves necessarily shut out from the highest civil and military posts, may not unreasonably think that a bad Government (or what we would think a bad Government) administered by native hands, is preferable to good Government administered by Europeans. And without imputing any misconduct to the Europeans employed in the government of India, (although among so many it is quite credible that there may be some who fall short of the high character deserved by that great body) yet among the large number of natives necessarily employed officially under our rule, and imperfectly restrained by the European rulers, who are compelled often to rely on the representations of these native officials, there is ample room for many instances of oppression and injustice which the inhabitants could only be expected to bear from the feeling that strength was on our side. But the whole foundation of the mutiny, was the conviction which spread itself among the native soldiers that the strength was with them. It is so easy to point out errors after the event that I do not like to use any strong language; but we can now see that those soldiers were relied on to an extent fatally unwise. They saw the great arsenal of Northern India left in their power without a European regiment to guard it. In station after station they saw tempting heaps of treasure to be had for the robbing; and can we wonder that the temptation should have been too great for them, or search for causes of such an event? Let us rather thank God that it did not take place sooner. When our hands were full with the Russian war for instance, or before the establishment of that system of telegraphs, which by the timely notice it gave of the disturbances, has proved the safety of so many of our posts.

Appendix B: Reviews of and Responses to Owenson's Writing

1. From Rev. of *Woman: Or, Ida of Athens*, by Sydney Owenson, *Quarterly Review* 1 (1809): 50–52.

"Bacchantes, animated with Orphean fury, slinging their serpents in the air, striking their cymbals, and uttering dithyrambics, appeared to surround him on every side." p. 5.

"That modesty which is of soul, seemed to diffuse itself over a form, whose exquisite symmetry was at once betrayed and concealed by the apparent tissue of woven air, which fell like a vapour around her." p. 23.

"Like Aurora, the extremities of her delicate limbs were rosed with flowing hues, and her little foot, as it pressed its naked beauty on a scarlet cushion, resembled that of a youthful Thetis from its blushing tints, or that of a fugitive Atalanta from its height." &c. &c. p. 53.

After repeated attempts to comprehend the meaning of these, and a hundred similar conundrums, in the compass of half as many pages, we gave them up in despair; and were carelessly turning the leaves of the volume backward and forward, when the following passage, in a short note "to the Reader," caught our eye. "My little works have been always printed from *illegible* manuscripts in one country, while their author was resident in another." p. vi. We have been accustomed to overlook these introductory gossipings: in future, however, we shall be more circumspect; since it is evident that if we had read straight forward from the title-page, we should have escaped a very severe head-ach.

The matter now seems sufficiently clear. The printing having to produce four volumes from a manuscript, of which he could not read a word, performed his task to the best of his power; and fabricated the requisite number of lines, by shaking the types out of his boxes at a venture. The work must, therefore, be considered as a kind of overgrown *amphigouri*, a heterogeneous combination of events, which, pretending to no meaning, may be innocently permitted to surprize for a moment, and then dropt for ever.

If, however, which is possible, the author like Caliban (we beg Miss Owenson's pardon) "cannot endue her purpose with words that make it known;" but by *illegible* means *what may be read*, and is, consequently, in earnest; the case is somewhat altered, and we must endeavour to make out the story.

Ida of Athens, a Greek girl, half ancient and half modern, falls desperately in love with a young slave; and, when he is defeated and taken prisoner, in a fray more ridiculously begun and ended than the wars of Tom Thumb the Great, marries a "Disdar-aga," to save his life. This simple personage, instead of taking possession of his fair bride, whom he has "placed on an ottoman of down," *couleur de rose*, rushes from the apartment "to see a noise which he heard:" and has scarcely thrust his head out of the street door, when, to his inexpressible amazement, it is dexterously sliced off by "an agent of the Porte;"[1] and Ida, without waiting for her thirds, runs joyfully home to her father. Meanwhile the Greek slave, who had, somewhat unpolitely, looked through the Disdar-aga's "casement," and seen Ida in his arms, very naturally takes it in dudgeon, and enrols himself among the Janissaries. Ida, on her side, having no engagement on her hands, falls in love with an English traveller, who offers her a settlement, which she very modestly rejects. A long train of woe succeeds. Her father is stripped of his property, and thrown into a dungeon; from which he is delivered by the Janissary on duty, (the prying lover of Ida) who, without making himself known, assists them to quit the country, and embark for England. "They launch into the Archipelago, that interesting sea, so precious to the soul of genius;" iv. p. 45, and after many hair-breadth scapes, arrive in London. Here they are cheated, robbed, and insulted by every body; and the father, after being several days without food, is dragged to a spunging house, where he expires! Ida runs frantically through the streets, and falls into the arms of the English traveller, who is now become a lord, and very gallantly renews his offers, which are again rejected. In consequence of an advertisement in the public papers, Ida discovers a rich uncle, who dies very opportunely, and leaves her "the most opulent heiress of Great Britain."

The fair Greek abuses her prosperity; but before her fortune and reputation are quite gone, the slave makes his appearance once

---

1 Wrong:—he turns sick as he is running after the "Capadilger Keayassa," and dies in a ditch.—See vol. iii. p. 143. *Printer's Devil.*

more,—not as a Janissary, but as a General Officer in the Russian service; and being now convinced that the familiarity of the Disdar-aga led to no unseemly consequences, marries his quondam mistress *for good and all*, and carries her to Russia, "a country *congenial by its climate* to her delicate constitution and luxurious habits; and *by its character*, to her tender, sensitive and fanciful disposition!" iv. p. 286.

Such is the story; which may be dismissed as merely foolish; but the sentiments and language must not escape quite so easily. The latter is an inflated jargon, composed of terms picked up in all countries, and wholly irreducible to any ordinary rules of grammar or sense. The former are mischievous in tendency, and profligate in principle; licentious and irreverent in the highest degree. To revelation, Miss Owenson manifests a singular antipathy. It is the subject of many profound diatribes, which want nothing but meaning to be decisive. Yet Miss Owenson is not without an object of worship. She makes no account indeed of the Creator of the universe, unless to swear by his name; but, in return, she manifests a prodigious respect for something that she dignifies with the name of Nature, which, it seems, governs the world, and, as we gather from her creed, is to be honoured by libertinism in the women, disloyalty in the men, and atheism in both.

This young lady, as we conclude from her Introduction, is the *enfant gâté* of a particular circle, who see, in her constitutional sprightliness, marks of genius, and encourage her dangerous propensity to publication. She has evidently written more than she has read, and read more than she has thought. But this is beginning at the wrong end. If we were happy enough to be in her confidence, we should advise the immediate purchase of a spelling book, of which she stands in great need; to this, in due process of time, might be added a pocket dictionary; she might then take a few easy lessons in "joined-hand," in order to become *legible*: if, after this, she could be persuaded to exchange her idle raptures for common sense, practise a little self-denial, and gather a few precepts of humility, from an old-fashioned book, which, although it does not seem to have lately fallen in her way, may yet, we think, be found in some corner of her study; she might then hope to prove, not indeed a good writer of novels, but a useful friend, a faithful wife, a tender mother, and a respectable and happy mistress of a family.

2. From Rev. of *The Daughters of Isenberg: A Bavarian Romance*, by Alicia Tindal Palmer, *Quarterly Review* 4 (1810): 66-67.

To remark on the traits of nature, probability, common sense, &c. which distinguish this publication is superfluous, after the analysis into which we have entered. The author speaks with some confidence of her own powers, and not unjustly, for she is a giantess among the pigmies. She spells somewhat more correctly than Miss Owenson, whom she at once imitates and ridicules, and she appears to know the meaning of most of her words. She has also a pretty taste for literature, and translates, with no better aid than a pocket dictionary, several English nouns into French, with very commendable accuracy: thus landlady is rendered *la hôtesse*, castle, *chateau*, artifice, *ruse*, &c. There is moreover an attempt at Italian, which only fails because the wicked vocabularies do not teach the art of putting *two* words together.

With all this, we cannot conscientiously encourage the fair author to proceed in her present course of study; we see in it little prospect of profit, and less of reputation: if, however, she determines to persevere, we must then strenuously and imperiously insist on her checking her odious propensity to profane and blasphemous ejaculations. Miss Palmer is not, like Miss Owenson, a pupil of nature, and perhaps is scarcely conscious of her own impiety; yet can habit so far overcome all reverential awe for a positive precept! In some cases she manifests a degree of humility which might almost be spared. "I like," says an ancient writer, "I like such tempers well, as stand before their critics with fear and trembling, and before their Maker like impudent mountains."

3. Rev. of *The Missionary: An Indian Tale*, by Sydney Owenson, *British Critic* 37 (1811): 651.

No one will deny Miss Owenson the praise of a lively fancy, and most prolific invention, but surely every reader must agree, that this lady has still to cultivate the sober qualities of judgment, without which, alas! her productions will pass in rapid succession from the shelves of the circulating library, to far less agreeable places and purposes. The story of this novel is so outrageously romantic, so beyond all bounds of consistency and probability, so very absurd and preposterous, as almost to excite commiseration for the mind that could combine, or the hand which could write such a complication of extravagance. What does the reader think of a Cadet of a noble Portuguese family, preferring first the gloom of a convent to the splendour of his rank, thence emerging as a volunteer missionary to the extreme parts of India, to convert the Hindus to Christianity. What again does he think of this missionary, who becoming enamoured of a female priestess, educated in all the subtle and mysterious dogmas of her religion, inspires her with the tender passion to such an extreme, that he bears her from her friends, her idols and her country, that both narrowly escape the flames of the inquisition at Goa; and finally——But, gentle reader, we are tired, as we think that thou must [be] also.—To refer thee for more to the book itself, we cannot in honesty attempt; but we still hope that time and reflection may mature and correct the abilities of this lively lady, and that she may still produce works which we may peruse with satisfaction, and consistently with our duty recommend.

4. From Rev. of *The Missionary: An Indian Tale*, by Sydney Owenson, *Critical Review* 23 (1811): 182-83, 195.

We shall make but few remarks on the present production, but give the heads of the tale in as concise a manner as the subject will permit. The taste for this kind of reading is so various, that, what pleases one, another will throw away in disgust. The lady, who would delight in the description of a masked ball, given by the Lady Ann, *so* and *so*, or the elegant and fashionable attentions of my Lord ——, will find but little interest in the account of traversing a dreary waste where the dry and hot air parches the lip and the feet tread, as in a channel of burning lava, or in perusing the horrors of an auto da fè. Miss Owenson's former heroine figured away on the classical soil of Athens: her present favourite is a native of Upper India. Instead, therefore, of descriptions of scenery, with which an English mind is familiar, Miss Owenson makes us acquainted with the Black Rock of Bimbhar, leads us from Tatta to Lahore, by the course of the Indus, and from Lahore, she repays us for our fatiguing journey, by setting us down in the delicious Garden of Eden, the vale of Cashmire. She gives us a fine view of the vast chain of the Indian Caucasus, and introduces us to no less a personage than the Brachmachira, the beautiful Priestess of Cashmire. And, what is more, she makes us as familiar and as sociable with those gay gentlemen, Brahma, Vishnu, and Co. as if we had been brought up under the same firm all our lives, as well as with Monsieur Camdeo, the god of mystic love, and a long *et cetera* of personages which make up the Indian mythology. [The reviewer then provides a twelve-page plot summary, with extensive quotations.] ...

We forbear to make many remarks on this performance of Miss Owenson, after having given the heads of the story so amply. But we must in justice say that in painting the missionary's feelings, his virtuous struggles, his remorse, his love, and the delicacy of his conduct and behaviour to the beloved object of his affections, Miss Owenson has displayed great force of expression, and a strong glow of rich colouring. At the same time we cannot but condemn her numerous conceits, and her frequently affected phraseology. Miss Owenson should learn to divest her style of its luxuriant redundancies, and to write in a more simple and natural manner. She would then have more, and more permanent admirers.

5. From Rev. of *France*, by Lady Morgan, *Quarterly Review* 17 (1817): 260–62, 264, 276–77, 281–86.

FRANCE! Lady Morgan appears to have gone to Paris by the high road of Calais and returned by that of Dieppe. In that capital she seems to have resided about four months, and thence to have made one or two short excursions; and with this extent of ocular inspection of that immense country, she returns and boldly affixes to her travelling memoranda diluted into a quarto volume, the title of France! One merit, however, the title has—it is appropriate to the volume which it introduces, for to falsehood it adds the other qualities of the work,—vagueness, bombast, and affectation. This does not surprize us, and will not surprize our readers when they are told that Lady Morgan is no other than the ci-devant Miss Owenson, the author of those tomes of absurdity—those puzzles in three volumes, called Ida of Athens, the Missionary, the Wild Irish Girl, and that still wilder rhapsody of nonsense, O'Donnell—which served Miss Plumptre, kindred soul! in her famous tour through Ireland,[1] as an introduction to society, a history of the country, and a book of the post-roads.

---

1 *Quarterly Review*, No. XXXII. Art. III.

Lady Morgan remembers—with more anger than profit—the advice which we gave her in our first Number on the occasion of Ida of Athens; and, in the Preface to her present publication, treats us with the most lofty indignation—she informs us, that we made "one of the most hastily composed and insignificant of her early works, a vehicle for accusing her of licentiousness, profligacy, irreverence, blasphemy, libertinism, disloyalty, and atheism. To cure her (she adds) of these vices, we presented a nostrum of universal efficacy; and prescribed (by the way Lady Morgan's language smells vilely of the shop since her marriage) a simple remedy, a spelling-book and a pocket-dictionary, which, superadded to a little common sense, was to render her that epitome of female excellence, whose price Solomon has declared above riches."—p. viii.

There is an inveterate obliquity in Lady Morgan's mind, which prevents her from perceiving, or stating a fact as it really exists. In copying our *recipe* (to accommodate our language to her ear) she has omitted the principal ingredient. We were not so lightly impressed with the danger of her case, as to suppose that it might be alleviated by a spelling-book and a vocabulary only: there was, *as she well knows*, another book, which we recommended her to add to the list; and it was on the humble and serious study of this, (need we add that we spoke of the Bible?) that we mainly relied for that amendment in her head and heart, which her deplorable state seemed to render so desirable.

In the wantonness of folly she tells us, that, in "pursuance of our advice, she set forth 'like Cœlebs in search of a wife,'"—not quite, as we shall prove to Lady Morgan before we have done with her— "and with her Entick in one hand, and her Mavor in the other, obtained the reward of her improvements, in the person of a Doctor Morgan; and, in spite of the 'seven deadly sins,' which the Quarterly Review had laid to her charge, is become, she *trusts*, a respectable, and, she is *sure*, a happy mistress of a family." Lady Morgan does well to speak thus modestly of the former part of her position:—of the latter, she may be as positive as she pleases. Happiness is a relative term, or, as it is more correctly explained by Slender to his cousin Shallow, *thereafter as it may be.* We have no reason to believe that all the captives of Circe were unhappy. But to proceed—

"The slander thus hurled at her happily fell hurtless; the enlightened public," as she informs us, "by its countenance and favour, acquitted her of all the charges; placed her in a *definite* rank among authors, and in no undistinguished circle of society." As the climax of her triumph over us, she boasts that O'Donnell has been translated into three languages. *What* three languages she does not state; but if the *English* be one of them, we humbly beg to be informed where the work is to be had, that, by the help of the said translation, we may have the pleasure of opening its treasures to our readers.

Lady Morgan, in the passages just quoted, seems strangely anxious to persuade the world that we accused her of *personal* licentiousness, profligacy, &c. but she does both us and herself injustice. We spoke then, as we shall do now, only of her works. We disclaim all personal acquaintance with Lady Morgan—we never saw her; and, except as a book manufacturer, know absolutely nothing about her—and it is not without sincere pain that we feel ourselves obliged to repeat, on the occasion of her *latest and most important* work, the same charges, (but with increased severity and earnestness,) which were forced from us by her *earliest and most insignificant.*

Before we proceed to show how little Lady Morgan is mended of Miss Owenson's graver faults, and how very like FRANCE is to *Ida of Athens*, we must notice a more venial error which we formerly recommended for correction, and which we lament to find as bad as ever [i.e., errors in the text]....

Our charges (to omit minor faults) fall readily under the heads of—Bad taste—Bombast and Nonsense—Blunders—Ignorance of the French Language and Manners—General Ignorance—Jacobinism—Falsehood—Licentiousness, and Impiety.—These, we admit, are no light accusations of the work; but we undertake, as we have said, to prove them from Lady Morgan's own mouth....

JACOBINISM.—Lady Morgan, though a knight's *Lady*, is, we are afraid, somewhat of a democrat, and we strongly suspect that her present rank does not sit naturally upon her; she certainly takes all the opportunities she can find, and liberally makes them when she cannot find them, to sneer at and depreciate the legitimate government, the royal family, and nobility of France, and to extol the enemies of France, of her own country and of the civilized world.

—"The horrors of the revolution" are, it seems, "bug-bears dressed to frighten children," (i.91) and, what is still more surprizing, the legitimate monarchy of France, and not the revolution, is answerable for all those enormities, because

"the generation which perpetrated these atrocities were the legitimate subjects of legitimate monarchs, and were *stamped*

with the character of the government which produced them, and the
Marats, Dantons, Robespierres belong *equally* to the order of
things which preceded the revolution, and to that which filled
up its most frightful epochs."—i.92.

If this, which we take to be the greatest discovery of modern
times, be true; if the monarchy be really guilty of the crimes of the
republic; if Louis and not Marat, if Maleherbes and not Danton; if
the Princesse de Lamballe and not Theroigne de Mericourt are the
real perpetrators of the regicide and the massacres of September
because the regicides and the *massacreurs* were born under the
legitimate monarchy, we appeal to Lady Morgan's impartiality
whether the same rule must not be further extended, and whether
all the glories in arms and arts, all the private virtues and public
bounties of her idol Napoleon ought not to be attributed to the
ancient government, under which he was not only born but carefully educated both in arts and arms? Our readers smile at this
argument, and at the virtues of Napoleon. We assure them that
there is hardly any virtue, and no kind of merit which Lady Morgan's blind devotion does not attribute to "the child and champi-
on of jacobinism." In addition to being "the *greatest captain* of the
age," (i.97.) (she does not except the *greater* who conquered him,)
Lady Morgan assures us that "his manners were kind and gracious,"
and "his feelings generous" (ii.181.)—that he was "popular for
many little acts of generosity and bonhommie," (i.97.) and that "his
personal bravery" rendered him "worthy the devotion of his soldiers." (i.151.) ... Such are a few of the topics of Lady Morgan's
loyal and judicious admiration of Buonaparte; we trust them, without a comment, to the execration of every lover of truth.

—In the same way she heaps her jacobinical admiration upon
every person and thing which belongs to the revolution, and vili-
fies and libels all that is connected with the legitimate government.

"How true Frenchwomen can be in feeling and sympathy to
their husbands has been painfully evinced during the horrors of
the revolution, the struggles of twenty-five years of emigration,
and *above* all, during the political vicissitudes and conflicts in
France which have occurred *since the return of the Bourbons*."—
i.179.

Thus Lady Morgan asserts that the trials to which domestic
feeling has been subjected have been more numerous and more

cruel since the restoration, than during the revolution;—a restoration which has exhibited the execution of two traitors taken with arms in their hands, and convicted in due course of law; and a revolution in which (to omit the *noyades* and *fusillades* which tainted the rivers, and drenched the soil of France with innocent blood) 5000 persons were massacred, in the streets of Paris alone, within six and thirty hours, and fifty or sixty a day sent to the guillotine, without the forms of a trial, for ten or twelve successive months.

For the devoted wives of the royalists she has only a cold and general phrase; for the heroic attachment of the injured queen to all the duties of a wife and mother, she has not a word....

LICENTIOUSNESS.—Lady Morgan *quizzes* (to borrow her own phraseology) with great taste, the respect which a catholic people pays to the Holy Virgin; but she grows particularly facetious, or, as they say in Ireland, *roguish*, in relating that, on a procession at Boulogne-sur-mer, in honour of the Mother of our Saviour,

> "The priests, to their horror, could not find a single *virgin* in that maritime city, and were at last obliged to send to a neighbouring village for the *loan of a virgin*—A *virgin* was at last procured; *a little indeed the worse for wear;* but this was not a moment for fastidiousness, and the Madonna was paraded through the streets."—i. p. 59.

We say nothing of the staleness of this joke, borrowed from the loose tales of Boccacio and La Fontaine, nor of the ignorance that travesties a French Notre Dame into an Italian Madonna: we only request our readers to consider what manner of woman she must be that revives and displays such false and detestable grossness of which even a modern jest book would be ashamed....

—Some of our readers may have heard the title of a most profligate French novel called "Les Liaisons Dangereuses." We had hoped that no British female had ever seen this detestable book; it seems we were mistaken. Lady Morgan sneers at the Court of Louis XVIII. "because all '*Liaisons Dangereuses*' are banished from it." p. 132. And, lest her meaning should be mistaken, she distinguishes "Liaisons Dangereuses" by marks of quotation, and goes on to say that when *piety* usurps *their* place, (i.e. the place of deliberate seduction and debauchery, or, as she delicately words it, of "gallantry and the graces,") it is as if chimney sweepers were to usurp the place of Cupids. *ibid*....

IMPIETY.—Madame de Maintenon declares that some of the gay men of the court were "pleins de grandes impiétés, et de sentimens d'ingratitude envers le roi." To us, who have been taught to "fear God and honour the King," this does not seem a very extraordinary, nor a very hazardous remark; but Lady Morgan is of a different mind, and parodies Scripture for the purpose of turning it into ridicule.—"It was the *fashion* of that *pious* day to *confound the sovereign and the Deity, and to consider the King both 'as the law and prophets'* within the *purlieus* of his own court."—p. 47....

—When she would describe the streets of Paris, it is by a profane allusion—their narrowness is "an original sin without redemption."

—On the occasion of the homage paid to the King, she takes the favourable opportunity of uttering another horror. She laments that he is obliged to hear so much flattery, because, "as the Chevalier de Boufflers says, with more levity than becomes the subject, Il n'y a que DIEU qui ait un assez grand fond de gaieté pour ne pas s'ennuyer de tous les hommages qu'on lui rend."

Levity!—"more levity than becomes the occasion!"—and, with this gentle observation, she registers and disseminates a blasphemy which we dare not translate, and which, if any of our readers has patience to read a second time, he will find to be as silly as it is impious....

Some of these expressions would have led us to suppose that this Lady Morgan was an atheist; she seems to intimate, however, towards the conclusion of her work, that she is only a deist, and that she has as much and the same kind of religion as the American savages. She says that at a certain fête made for *her*, the manuscripts of the atheist Voltaire were displayed, and the *sublime* ode of the atheist Chenier, in praise of the said Voltaire, was recited with an emotion on the part of the audience

> "only to be felt and understood by this ardent people to whom *genius* is but another word for *divinity*, and who, next to the great spirit, venerate those whom he has *most informed with the rays of his own intelligence*."—p. 243.

That is to say, *Voltaire* and *Chenier* are worshipped by Lady Morgan's ardent friends next to what she calls, in imitation of the Iroquois, the *Great Spirit*! and lest anyone should mistake her distinct meaning, she distinguishes the words *Great Spirit* by a peculiar type. On the daring blasphemy of the concluding line, which represents the God of all purity as illuminating, with the brightest rays of his own intelligence, the minds of such monsters of vice and infidelity, we almost tremble to think again....

We must now have done:—to confess the truth we have long since been weary of Lady Morgan, and shall not therefore offend our readers by any further exposure of the wickedness and folly of her book; of both of which we have given an idea less perfect, we readily admit, than we had materials for, but one which will, we hope, prevent, in some degree, the circulation of trash which under the name of a *Lady* author might otherwise find its way into the hands of young persons of both sexes, for whose perusal it is utterly, on the score both of morals and politics, unfit.

6. "Glorvina's Warning," *Blackwood's Edinburgh Magazine* 4 (1819): 720-22.

Glorvina's Warning
Sir Charles—Glorvina

Sir C. Glorvina! Glorvina, beware of the day,
When the Quarterly meets thee in battle array!—
For thy volumes, all damned, rush unread on my sight,
Glorvina! Glorvina, ah! think ere you write!
See! see, where the witty and wise about town
Are struggling, who foremost shall trample thee down!
Proud Gifford before hath insulted the slain!—
And Croker, in spleen, may pursue thee again!
But hark, in this dread preparation for war,
What lady to Paris flies frantic and far!—   10
'Tis mine, Doctor Morgan's, my bride may not wait,
So heavy are hissing the arrows of fate!—
In vain, for the Quarterly visits thee there,
And its pages are read with a sigh of despair!
Weep, lady! thy prospects are faded—undone—
Oh, weep! but thy tears only add to their fun!
For their black ink is poison—a dagger their pen,—
And the book they once stab, may not waken again!
  Glor. Go preach to thy patients, thou death-telling seer,
Or if Gifford and Croker so dreadful appear,   20
Go, crouch from the war, like a recreant knight,
Or, draw my silk shawl o'er thy organs of sight!
  Sir C. Ha! laughest thou, old lady, thy husband to scorn?

White bird of the common, thy plume shall be torn!
Shall the goose on the wing of the eagle go forth?
Let her dread the fierce spoilers who watch in the north!—
Let her fly from the anger of Jeffrey's sure eye,
Ah! home let her speed—for the havoc is nigh!—
But lonely and wild is my lady's abode!
And cursed by a spell that will force her abroad!—   30
Ah, why, when her mansion is desert and cold,
Is Dublin too hot this fair lady to hold?
While carriages roll thro' the street of Kildare,
Due south to the Green, and due north to the SQUARE,
Will none check their steeds, as in triumph they prance,
At the door of the travelling lady from France?—
Woe! lady! *bad* ever is followed by *worse*,
And the demon was with thee, whose blessing is curse!
For evil hath scandal been arming thy tongue;—
Glorvina! the dirge of thy glory is sung!   40
Ah! fashion beholds thee—to scoff and to spurn!
Return to thy dwelling—all lonely return!—
  Glor. False wizard, avaunt!—I have marshalled my clan,
Their pens are a thousand—their genius is one!
They mock thy prescriptions!—they laugh at thy breath,
Go! preach to thy patients of danger and death!—
Then welcome be Croker—his smile or his frown,
And welcome be Crawley—we'll trample them down!
Their colour shall vary from yellow to blue,
Like the cover of Constable's famous Review!   50
When my heroes impassioned for victory strain,
Sir Richard the learned!—and Ensor the vain!
All active, all armed, in their author's array!—[1]

---

1   The text here is certainly incorrect, nor can I, from any manuscript, sup-
    ply a reading on which we can rely with any certainty—"All armed in
    their author's array."—What can this mean? it implies a direct contradic-
    tion, which has, however, led me to the true reading—"unarmed"—
    though I have not ventured to give it a place in the text—the lady says,
    her heroes are "unarmed," i.e. (as she proceeds to explain) "in their
    author's array"—in the peculiar dress of their profession as authors,
    "cedant arma togæ."—*Theobald.*
      This passage was first suspected by Mr Theobald, who proposed an
    alteration, which, while it furnishes an intelligible meaning, loses sight
    altogether of the poetry, as is too often the case with verbal critics. By

Sir C. Glorvina, Glorvina, beware of the day!
'Twas my studies in youth gave me mystical lore,
And the womb of the Future in fear I explore!
Time trembles in pain, as his pulses I feel,
But fate must be known tho' I may not reveal!
I tell thee, that London with laughter will ring,
When the blood-hounds of Murray at Florence shall spring!— 60
Ho! Colburn! arouse thee, arouse thee with speed,
And arm thy gazette—'tis a moment of need!—
Ho! Maga!—green Maga!—awaken each sprite!
Raise—raise your oak-crutches to cover her flight!
Oh! would that thy book went to sleep of itself,
Like pamphlets unbound on a dust-covered shelf!
But mourn! for a darker departure is near—
The wise shall condemn, and the witty shall sneer!
And she, that fair lady whose home is the Lake,[1]

---

looking to the work, which it is evident our immortal poet had in his
eye during the whole of this prophecy, we may perhaps be led to the
true reading.

"All plaided and plumed in their tartan army," is the original line;
while comparing this with the line which stands in the text, it occurred
to me that our poet wrote,

"Ill-paid, 'tis presumed—in their author's array." From their appearing
"in their author's array," she not unnaturally infers, that the auxiliaries on
whose aid she relies, are ill-paid. The Oxford Editor has silently printed—"instinctive alarm."—*Warburton.*

This is one of those passages where we do not know which to admire
most, the imagination of the author, or the ingenuity of the critic; but
after the best consideration I could give the passage, the emendation
appears to me rather acute than true; the heroine of our dialogue means
to say, the activity of her champions is such, that they proceed at once to
the field, without changing their ordinary dress—once thought that we
might perhaps read, "All armed, though in authors array"—meaning that
her defendants were not, as the phrase is, out of elbows; but it is more
easy to suggest plausible corrections, than to interpret the words which
maintain stubbornly their place in the text: and the critic should not forget, that deviation from the language of the author, more frequently indicates ignorance than ingenuity.—*Johnson.*

1 "That fair lady, whose home is the Lake."

The heroine, who, as she says, is "placed in a definite rank among
authors, and in no undistinguished circle of society," appears rather
provoked at this passage, as may be gathered from her reply. The allusion

With sworded Sir Arthur, thy doom shall partake,   70
In vain shall she combat for Morgan le Fay.[1]
  Glor. Down, soothless insulter, I scorn what you say!
What ages of rapture roll fair to my sight!
What glories to come swim before me in light!—
Behold thro' the curtains of fate as I look,
O'Donnel!—and flirting with young Lalla Rookh!—
With Bertram is waltzing Glorvina the fair!
And Ida is wrestling with Lady Clancare![2]
Near apostate Hemeya see Imogen's face!
Oh never a ball such a galliard did grace!—   80
In the beauty of fame they return to my sight!—
Be they saved—be they damned—I will write—I will write!

7. From Rev. of *The Life and Times of Salvator Rosa*, by Lady Morgan, *Edinburgh Review* (1824): 316.

We are not among the devoted admirers of Lady Morgan. She is a clever and lively writer—but not very judicious, and not very natural. Since she has given up making novels, we do not think she has added much to her reputation—and indeed is rather more liable than before to the charge of tediousness and presumption. There is no want, however, either of amusement or instruction in

---

appears to be to the chapter in the Mort d'Arthur, that relates Sir Arthur's adventures with the Lady of the Lake. See also "A Treatise on Bathing," by Sir A. Clarke, Knight of the Bath Temple at Dublin, sold by the author—half price to bathers.

1   "Morgan le Fay."
    "And the other sister, Morgan le Fay, was put to school in a nunnery; and there she learned so much, that she was a great clerk of necromancy; and after that she was wedded to King Urience, of the land of *Gore*."— *King Arthur*, &c. page 4.

2   Ida of Athens—from the robust frame, and out-of-door habits of Lady Clancare, the reader may be apprehensive of Ida's not being a match for her—this ethereal creature, however, had the advantage most probably of much practice. The reader cannot forget how often she is described as retiring to the gymnasium—sometimes she is painted to us as engaged there at her toilette!—from this circumstance, we supposed the gynaceum might have been intended by the learned authoress, but this line appears to prove that we were mistaken, and we are anxious to acknowledge our error in the most public manner.

her late performances—and we have no doubt she would write very agreeably, if she was only a little less ambitious of being always fine and striking. But though we are thus clear-sighted to her defects, we must say, that we have never seen anything more utterly unjust, or more disgusting and disgraceful, than the abuse she has had to encounter from some of our Tory journals—abuse, of which we shall say no more at present, than that it is incomparably less humiliating to the object than to the author.

8. From Rev. of *Dramatic Scenes from Real Life*, by Lady Morgan, and "Illustrations of the State of Ireland," *Edinburgh Review* 58 (1833): 86–87.

Perhaps few, if any, writers of ability have, without serious dereliction on their part, incurred a larger share of ridicule and censure than Lady Morgan. Criticism has rarely been friendly to her, and frequently unjust. Her blunders have been magnified into gross instances of ignorance—her flippancies into scandalous violations of propriety. Even misprints and errata have been adduced as proofs of her insufficient acquaintance with French and Italian. We have witnessed with regret this spirit of acrimony and unfairness; odious even if a man had been the subject, and still more odious when manifested against a woman. But these attacks have afforded cause for disapprobation rather than for surprise. Lady Morgan as a writer had many qualities which invited assailants. She had sufficient cleverness to be worthy of notice—sufficient vehemence in the expression of her political opinions to render her obnoxious to the opposite party—and a sufficient display of crude reasonings, and inaccurate statements, to afford opportunities for a malicious critic, by dexterous selection, to reduce the value of her works greatly below their real amount. While we deprecate the severity with which she has been treated, we cannot wholly defend her. The public ought to be put on their guard against the faults of attractive writers, more than against those whose dulness is an effectual antidote. Lady Morgan was justly amenable to much of the censure which she received; but the censure ought to have been mixed with commendation. Her critics were blameable in withholding the due award of praise, and in treating some of her best performances as if they were a mere tissue of error and conceit. There are, perhaps, nowhere in Lady Morgan's writings, ten consecutive pages of which we wholly approve—but at the same time, perhaps, any ten pages of hers would be found to contain more graphic expressions, more original ideas, more pointed specimens of sparkling truth, than a fourfold number in many a work which scarcely merited a single censure. Impartial treatment of Lady Morgan requires a full estimate both of her merits and defects. Each are so numerous and so prominent, that an exclusive notice of either would raise her much higher, or depress her much lower, than what we conceive to be her true position. Her faults are chiefly those of her sex and country. She is apt to be guided by the impulse of feeling, where calm judgment is chiefly required. She is frequently incorrect in her reasonings, and unsound in her conclusions. Her style is overlaid with excess of ornament and quotation. She is fond of elaborate turns and foreign phrases, and loves to say common things, in an uncommon manner;—clothing her ideas in a garb which no more resembles that which would be selected by a chastened taste, than the gaudy dress of a fancy ball resembles the common costume of society. These are her prevailing faults; but she has many merits to counterbalance them. A lively imagination—a good deal of humour—a fervid flow of animated language, sometimes swelling into eloquence—much epigrammatic point and felicity of language—no slight share of dramatic talent—and the faculty of characteristic delineation. These are the agreeable qualities which her writings exhibit, and which, after the largest admissible deductions for her defects, leave an ample balance in her favour.

9. From Henry F. Chorley, "Lady Morgan," *The Authors of England* (1838), 51, 52-53, 54-55.

It is no holiday feat for a woman, self-educated, to have won by her own unassisted hand, in defiance of the ceaseless outpouring of malice and evil report, an European reputation.... Miss Owenson's early novels, "St. Clair," "The Novice of St. Dominick," "The Wild Irish Girl," "Patriotic Sketches," "Ida," and "The Missionary,"—though they may be said to belong to a past dynasty of fiction, when the story was all in all, and the manner of telling it but little heeded; when tears to any measure could be drawn by tenderly wrought love-scenes, and heroines and heroes were absolved from the necessity of possessing the individualities of human character, so but they "protested enough," and acted up to their protestations,—have still something of their own which distinguishes them among their contemporaries. Their scenery, their passion, their enthusiasm is eminently national; and, being dashed off with all the fervour and self-confidence of youth, it is not wonderful that they speedily made their way to distinguished success.... Ere we conclude, however, we must once again advert to the fate they [Owenson's writings] have encountered, to their reception, not by the public of Europe, but by the critical few. And we do this to record our protest against the dishonest and personal acrimony with which for some twenty years they have been indiscriminately attacked, and attacked by those, too, whose registered attachment to ancient institutions and principles, ought, we think, for consistency's sake, to have enjoined upon them at least a slight degree of courtesy and forebearance towards a writer of the gentler sex. If to have endured "the pitiless pelting storm" of vituperation and misconstruction in fighting the hard fight of unpopular against popular opinions; if, in short, to be zealous and consistent in the support of an adopted creed, is a thing worthy of recognition, then never did honour fall upon a fitter object than the recent pension, granted, at the instance of a liberal minister, to the authoress of "Italy."

10. Rev. of *Luxima, the Prophetess: A Tale of India*, by Lady Morgan, *Literary Gazette* (1859): 636.

Accidental circumstances, independent entirely of its intrinsic merit, invest the republication of this work with no ordinary interest. That it has been very recently remodelled by its authoress, and that she was engaged on it "only a few days before her decease," as the preface tells us, would in itself be sufficient to recommend it in no ordinary manner; but coming on us as it does just at the close of that terrific convulsion which has set us all thinking so seriously about the character, religion, and prejudices of the Hindoo, and presenting us as it does in a most engaging form with the reflections and conclusions of a lady of no ordinary powers of discernment half a century since, the book asserts claims to our attention which it is impossible not to recognise. To our mind it is as fitting a monument as could have been devised to the memory of one whose excellent gifts and fascinating character have been almost as much ours as our fathers'.

Appendix C: A Selection of Owenson's Poetry from Poems *(1801)* and The Lay of an Irish Harp *(1807)*

1. "The Lyre," from *Poems.*

The Lyre

"Thine was the meaning music of the heart." Thompson.

> I.
> Dear Lyre, I hail thee! for I owe thee much,
>   Melodious soother of my weary hours;
> Obedient ever to thy mistress' touch,
>   That wakes to sympathy thy passive powers!
>
> II.
> I come;—o'er thy elastic chords to fling
>   The essence of each flow'ret's rich perfume;
> And fondly twine around thee as I sing,
>   A wreath of fragrance, wove in fancy's loom!
>
> III.
> Oft as the star of eve unveil'd her light,
>   To bathe its glories in the lucid streams;   10
> Or twilight sunk upon the breast of night,
>   So oft thou'st wrapt me in elysian dreams!
>
> IV.
> Oft as the trembling moon-beam stoop'd to sip
>   The od'rous drops, of rose-embosom'd dew;
> Or quaff'd the nectar of the lily's lip,
>   So oft I've softly sung, and sigh'd to you!
>
> V.
> Then o'er thy chords I pour'd a strain of woe,
>   O'er thy responsive lays enraptur'd hung;
> Thy lays in melting sympathy would flow,
>   Thy chords give back the woes to thee I sung!   20

VI.

As true vibrative to the frolic lay,
To every careless touch of laughing pleasure,
As wildly playful, and as sweetly gay,
As madly sportive was thy jocund measure!

VII.

Still, still responsive to thy mistress' soul,
Thy trembling chords my trembling tones return'd;
Amidst my sighs thy sighing accents stole,
With pathos melted, or with fervor burn'd!

VIII.

And tho' Apollo's beam ne'er warmed thy strain,
Nor o'er thy chords love swept his purple wing,   30
Thou'st rapture raised to an extatic pain,
When genuine feeling only touch'd the string!

IX.

Rais'd the quick throb within the sensate heart,
Awoke each dormant extacy of soul,
Seduc'd the sigh to heave,—the tear to start,
And o'er each finer nerve, her magic stole!

X.

Oh, thou to feeling's touch be sacred still,
Still may she steal vibrations from thy string;
Still to her witching powers sweetly thrill,
And o'er each sense her soft enchantment fling!   40

2. "Sonnet," from *Poems*.

Sonnet

On seeing a sprig of the Sensitive Plant dead in a lady's bosom.

    Ah! timid, trembling thing, no more
Shalt thou beneath each rude breath sink,
    Thy virgin attribute is o'er,
From ev'n the gentlest touch to shrink!
    No more the zephyr's balmy kiss,
Shall find thy chaste reluctance such,

Still shrinking from the fragrant bliss,
Still vibrating to every touch:
  Proud of thy feeling power, the breast
Of Adila with rival pride   10
  You sought,—and drooping there confest,
That feeling power surpass'd, and died!
  There to thy keen sensations peace be given,
And there from earth remov'd, enjoy thy heaven!

3. "The Sigh," from *Poems*.

The Sigh

I.
Ah! trembling vagrant, say why would'st thou
  From thy guardian bosom rove,
Or say, soft fugitive, how could'st thou
  Trait'rous to that bosom prove?

II.
For when thou'rt heard, incautious rover,
  As love's true denizen thou'rt known;
And those fond secrets oft discover
  The timid heart would guard—its own!

III.
Dan Cupid too with thee advances,
  Commander of his motley troop;   10
Of downcast look, and timid glances,
  And all Love's witching, various group!

IV.
Of throbbing pulses, glowing blushes,
  Smother'd groans, "cross-threaded arms,"
Paley looks, and sudden flushes,
  Trembling fears, and fond alarms!

V.
Thou Love's aerial vassal art too,
  Then tell-tale from my lips away;
Steal back into my beating heart too,
  Lest thou its confidence betray!   20

4. "Retrospection," from *Poems*.

Retrospection

Written on the Author's visiting the home of her childhood after an absence of eight years.

I.
Ye golden hours which softly fled away,
  Like aerial Gossamer on vernal breeze;
Rapid as thought, or bright electric flash,
  Soothing as zephyr's murmur 'midst the trees.

II.
Bless'd halcyon hours beyond recov'ry fled,
  Sportive to Time's eternal goal ye danc'd,
Crown'd by the blooming wreaths which Fancy wove,
  And led by Hope ye smilingly advanc'd!

III.
For ye Contentment cull'd her choicest sweets,
  Fair Innocence illum'd ye with her beams;   10
Imagination each wish realiz'd,
  And on life's vista shed her orient gleams!

IV.
When o'er my senses steals the sweet, sad gloom
  The mingled thrill of pleasure and of pain;
Nor can the gaiety of youthful mind,
  The dark intrusion of felt cares restrain!

V.
Then Fancy wanders thro' remembrance paths,
  Culls each sweet flower to scatter o'er the waste
Which grief has made, and seeks in mem'ry's page
  To lose the present ills in joy long past!   20

VI.
Then ye dear scenes, (perhaps devoid of charm,
  Save what my fond ideas round ye twine,)
Where first my dawn of life so blissful gleam'd,
  Then, then in memory only are you mine!

VII.

Ah! Why ye scenes, has time's sharp, ruthless fang
  In eight short years such cruel havoc made,
Each fond memento of past bliss destroy'd,
    Destroy'd each charm, and on each beauty prey'd!

VIII.

I sought the hawthorn tree, beneath whose shade,
  Full oft I pass'd my truant hours gay,   30
The spot where once it bloom'd I quickly found,
    The tree itself had droop'd into decay!

IX.

I sought the cot, near my parental home,
  Where oft I stole the warlock tale to hear,
To feast on oaten cake or new laid egg,
    I found the place;—alas! no cot was there;

X.

And you, ye treasur'd objects of my heart!
  Dear, loved companions of my early days
With whom I ran my life's first frolic course,
    Mingled my smiles, and sung my untaught lays!   40

XI.

Oft on a stream that wound its trickling way,
  I will remember, near our lov'd abode,
We venturous launch'd our barks of paper built,
    Freighted with currant red, (delicious load,)

XII.

And as (true emblem of our careless days,
  Gliding life's stream) we eager bent our eyes,
On passing ship, for theirs who swiftest sail'd,
    Claim'd both the fleet and fruit, a glorious prize!

XIII.

Full various were our sports, yet not in sports
  Alone, pass'd on the tenor of our days;   50
So romps succeeded oft th'instructive page,
    And even wisdom mingled with our plays!

XIV.

And you my some-time brother,[1] o'er whose birth
  Genius presided! wit new strung his lyre;
The muse her future bard to slumbers sung
  And e'en his lisping numbers did inspire!

XV.

Thus form'd my infant taste, and from thy lips,
  My mind imbib'd th'enthusiastic glow;
The love of literature, which thro' my life
  Heightened each bliss, and soften'd every woe!   60

XVI.

My sainted mother too, methinks I view
  Thy endearing smile, my ever sweet reward;
For each unfolding talent ever gain'd
  Thy fond approvings, and thy dear regard.

XVII.

Even still methinks, soft vibrate in mine ear,
  Thy well remember'd tones, and still I trace
In thy dear eyes, thy fond maternal love,
  Catch thy last look, and feel thy last embrace.

XVIII.

The dying wish that hover'd o'er thy lips,
  Thy last, last words, soft, trembling, broken, faint,   70
That my sad breaking heart received of thine,
  And spoke the woman's conquest o'er the saint!

XIX.

Were these, "dear child of all my tenderest care,
  Transfer that duteous love to me you pay'd,
To thy dear sire;—live but for him," and died;—
  Say blessed spirit, have I disobey'd?

---

1 Thomas Dermody, a youth whose wonderful and precose talents were
  acknowledged and patronized by the first characters of rank and taste in
  the kingdom.

XX.

Oft does my mem'ry sketch the social group,
  At closing eve, that circled round the fire;
Sweet hour that fondly knit each human tie,
  Unites the children, mother, friend, and sire!   80

XXI.

Full oft the legendary tale went round,
  Historic truth, or Car'lan's heart-felt song;[1]
For though but little understood, I ween
  We lov'd the music of our native tongue!

XXII.

And oft went round the puzzling, forfeit game,
  Play'd with nice art, and many a sportive jest;
Repeated oft—yet sure to win a laugh,
  For those we longest know, we lov'd the best!

XXIII.

Dear happy group, and e'en as happy good,
  Why guileless spirits from each other torn!   90
Why has the world unclasp'd thy social bond,
  And left my fond heart its fond hopes wreck to mourn?

XXIV.

Thus calmly flows some pure, expansive stream,
  Pellucid, clear, while o'er its surface plays
The soften'd shade of each o'er-drooping plant,
  The moon's pale beam, or sun's meridian rays!

XXV.

But lo! should earth's convulsive struggles throw
  Th'impending rock in scatter'd masses o'er,
'Tis forced to disunite in sep'rate streams,
  Dwindles to viewless rills, and 's seen no more!   100

---

1 Carolan, the celebrated Irish bard.

5. "Fragment I: The Irish Harp," from *Lay of an Irish Harp*.

The Irish Harp.[1]

"Voice of the days of old, let me hear you.—
Awake the soul of song." OSSIAN.

I.
WHY sleeps the Harp of Erin's pride?
Why with'ring droops its Shamrock wreath?
Why has that song of sweetness died
Which Erin's Harp alone can breathe?

II.
Oh! 'twas the simplest, wildest thing!
The sighs of *Eve* that faintest flow
O'er airy lyres, did never fling
So sweet, so sad, a song of wo.

III.
And yet its sadness seem'd to borrow
From love, or joy, a mystic spell;   10
'Twas doubtful still if *bliss* or *sorrow*
From its melting lapses fell.

---

1 With an enthusiasm incidental to my natural and national character, I visited the western part of the province of Connaught in the autumn of
1805, full of many an evident expectation that promised to my feelings,
and my taste, a *festival* of national enjoyment. The result of this interesting little pilgrimage has already been given to the world in the story of
the "Wild Irish Girl," and in a collection of *Irish Melodies*, learned among
those who still "*hum'd the Song of other times*." But the hope I had long
cherished of hearing the *Irish Harp* played in perfection was not only far
from being realized, but infinitely disappointed. That encouragement so
nutritive to genius, so indispensably necessary to perseverance, no longer
stimulates the Irish bard to excellence, nor rewards him when it is
attained; and the decline of that tender and impressive instrument, once
so dear to Irish enthusiasm, is as visibly rapid, as it is obviously unimped-
ed by any effort of national pride or national affection.

IV.

For if amidst its tone's soft languish
A note of love or joy e'er stream'd,
'Twas the plaint of love-sick anguish,
And still the "joy of grief" it seem'd.

V.

'Tis said *oppression* taught the lay
To him—(of all the "sons of song"
That bask'd in Erin's brighter day)
The *last* of the inspir'd throng;   20

VI.

That not in sumptuous hall, or bow'r,
To victor chiefs, on tented plain,
To festive souls, in festal hour,
Did he (sad bard!) pour forth the strain.

VII.

Oh no! for he, opprest, pursued,[1]
Wild, wand'ring, doubtful of his course,
With tears his silent heart bedew'd,
That drew from *Erin's* woes their source.

VIII.

It was beneath th' impervious gloom
Of some dark forest's deepest dell,   30
'Twas at some *patriot hero's tomb*,
Or on the drear heath where *he* fell.

IX.

It was beneath the loneliest cave
That roofs the brow of misery,
Or stems the ocean's wildest wave,
Or mocks the sea-blast's keenest sigh.

---

1 The persecution begun by the Danes against the Irish bards finished in
   almost the total extirpation of that sacred order in the reign of
   Elizabeth.

X.

It was through night's most spectral hours,
When reigns the spirit of *dismay*,
And *terror* views demoniac pow'rs
Flit ghastly round in dread array.   40

XI.

Such was the time, and such the place,
The bard respir'd *his* song of wo,
To those, who had of Erin's race
Surviv'd their freedom's vital blow.

XII.

Oh, what a lay the minstrel breath'd!
How many bleeding hearts around,
In suff'ring sympathy enwreath'd,
Hung desponding o'er the sound!

XIII.

For still his Harp's wild plaintive tones
Gave back their sorrows keener still,   50
Breath'd *sadder* sighs, heav'd *deeper* moans,
And wilder wak'd *despair's* wild thrill.

XIV.

For still he sung the ills that flow
From dire oppression's ruthless fang,
And deepen'd every patriot wo,
And sharpen'd every patriot pang.

XV.

Yet, ere he ceas'd, a prophet's fire
Sublim'd his lay, and louder rung
The deep-ton'd music of his lyre,
And *Erin go brach*[1] he boldly sung.   60

---

1   Ireland for ever!—a national exclamation, and, in less felicitous times, the
rallying point to which many an Irish heart revolted from the influence
of despair.

6. "Fragment III: To Mrs. Lefanue," from *Lay of an Irish Harp*.

To Mrs. Lefanue.[1]

"Hélas, en l'amitié—les talents, la vertu
Pourront-ils trouver ton égale." VOLTAIRE.

I.
Oh why are not all those close *ties* which enfold
Each human connexion like those which unite us!
Why should *interest* or *pride*, or feelings so cold,
Alone to sweet *amity's* bondage invite us?

II.
Thou wert just in that age when the soul's brightest ray
Illumines each mellowing charm of the face,
And the graces of youth still delightedly play
O'er each *mind-beaming* beauty which Time *cannot* chase.

III.
I was young, inexperienc'd, *unknowing, unknown,*
Wild, ardent, romantic, a *stranger* to *thee*;   10
But I'd heard worth, wit, genius, were all, all thine own;
And forgetting that thou wert a *stranger* to *me.*

IV.
My heart overflowing, and new to each form
Of the world, I sought thee, nor fear'd to offend
By unconscious presumption: oh sure 'twas some charm
That *thus* led me to seek in a *stranger,* a *friend*!

---

1 Grand-daughter to the friend of *Swift*—daughter to the celebrated
Thomas Sheridan—to the *Author* of *Sidney Biddulph*—and sister to the
Right Hon. *Richard Brinsley Sheridan*—claiming a connexion equally intimate with many other characters scarcely less eminent; yet by a unity in
her own of the most *unblemished virtue* and the most *brilliant talents,*
reflecting back upon her distinguished kindred a lustre pure and permanent as that she has received from it.

V.
Yes, yes, 'twas a charm of such magical force
As *Reason* herself never wish'd to repel,
For it drew its sweet magic from Sympathy's source,
And *Reason herself* bows to *Sympathy's* spell.   20

VI.
Yet fearful of failing, and wishful of pleasing,
How *timidly anxious* thy notice I woo'd!
But oh! thy first warm glance each wild doubt appeasing,
With courage, with fondness, my faint heart endu'd.

VII.
No never (till mem'ry by death shall be blighted)
Can our first touching interview fade from my mind,
When *thou*, all delighting, and I *all* delighted,
I, more than confiding; thou *much more* than kind.

VIII.
Forgetful, scarce germ'd was our friendship's young flower,
My heart o'er my lips unrestrain'd seem'd to rove,   30
Whilst *thou* sweetly veiling thy MIND'S BRIGHTER power
Left me much to *admire*, yet still *more to love*.

IX.
Till warm'd by a kindness *endearing*, as *dear*,
A wild, artless song was respir'd for thee;
'Twas a national lay![1] and oh! when shall the tear
Which was shed o'er *that* song, be forgotten by me.

X.
And now since that sweet day some years have flown by,
And some golden hours of those years have been mine;
But each year as it fled never twisted *one tie*
Round my heart, like *that* tie which first bound it to thine.   40

---

1   "*Eamunh a Cnuic*," or, "Edmund of the Hill."

7. "Fragment X: The Boudoir," from *Lay of an Irish Harp*.

The Boudoir.

To ★★★★★★★★★★

"Là, vers la *fin du jour* la simple vérité
Honteuse de paroitre nue
Pour cacher sa rougeur, cherche l'obscurité.
Là, sa confidence légitime rapproche deux amis."
              De Mouslier.

I.
What need'st *thou* ask, or *I* reply?
Mere words are for the stupid *many*;
I've ever thought a speaking look
The sweetest eloquence of any!

II.
Yes, thou may'st come, and at the hour
We consecrate to pensive pleasures,
When feeling, fancy, music, taste,
Profusely shed their dearest treasures.

III.
Yet come not ere the sun's last beam
Sleeps on the west wave's purple breast,   10
Nor wait thee till the full-orb'd moon
Resplendent lifts her silver crest.

IV.
But steal the *softer* hour between,
When *Twilight* drops her mystic veil,
And brings the anxious *mind repose*,
And leaves the sensient *heart* to *feel*.

V.
Yet turn not towards the flaunting bow'r
That echoes to the joyless laugh
Of gossip dames, nor seek the hall
Where Riot's sons her goblet quaff.   20

VI.

But with a still and noiseless step
Glide to the well-known fairy room,
Where *fond Affection* visits oft,
And never finds the heart from home.

VII.

Fear not to meet intruders there,
Thou 'lt only find my harp and me,
Breathing perhaps some pensive song,
And waiting anxiously for thee.

VIII.

And I will wear the vestal robe
Thou lov'st, I know, to see me wear;   30
And with that sweet wreath form'd by thee
(Though faded now) I'll bind my hair.

IX.

And round my harp fresh buds I'll twine,
O'er which departing day has wept;
And wildly soft its chords I'll touch
As though a *sigh* its chords had swept.

X.

And I will *hum* the *song* thou lov'st,
Or thou each bosom-chord shall thrill
With thine *own* soul-dissolving strain,
Or *silent*,[1] we'll be happier still.   40

XI.

Well now, thou know'st the *time*, the *place*,
And—but I merely meant to tell thee,
That thou might'st come! yet still I write
As though some witchcraft charm befel me.

---

1 "Le secret *d'ennuyer*—est celui de *tout dire*."

8. "Fragment XXIV: To him who said, 'You live only for the World,'" from *Lay of an Irish Harp.*

To him who said, "You live only for the World."
   "Vivons pour nous....
   Que l'amitie qui nous unie
   Nous tiens lieu du monde."
            Voltaire.

            I.
            Oh! no—I live not for the throng
            Thou seest me mingle oft among,
               By fashion driven.
            Yet one *may* snatch in this same world
            Of noise and din, where one is hurl'd,
               Some glimpse of heaven!

            II.
            When *gossip* murmurs rise around,
            And all is empty show and sound,
               Or *vulgar* folly,
            How sweet! to give wild fancy play,   10
            Or bend to thy dissolving sway,
               Soft melancholy.[1]

            III.
            When silly beaux around one flutter;[2]
            And silly belles gay nonsense utter,
               How sweet to steal
            To some lone corner (*quite perdue*)
            And with the dear elected *few*
               Converse and *feel!*

---

1 "Our ideas," says *Zimmerman,* "never flow more copiously than in those
   moments which we rescue from an uninteresting and fashionable visit."
2 "Ces enfans dont la folie recrue, dans les
   Sociétés vient tomber tous les ans." Moliere.

IV.

When forced for tasteless crowds to sing,
Or listless sweep the trembling string,
   Say, when we meet
The eye whose beam alone inspires,
And wakes the warm soul's latent fires,
   Is it not sweet?   20

V.

Yes, yes, the dearest bliss of any
Is that which midst the blissless many
   So oft *we* stole:
Thou know'st 'twas midst such cold parade
And idle crowds, we each betray'd
   To each—a soul.   30

9. "Fragment XXX: The Minstrel Boy," from *Lay of an Irish Harp.*

The Minstrel Boy.

I.

Thy silent wing, oh Time! hath chased away
Some feathery hours of youth's fleet frolic joy,
Since first I hung upon the simple lay,
And shared the raptures of a minstrel boy.

II.

Since first I caught the ray's reflected light
Which genius emanated o'er his soul,
Or *distant* follow'd the enthusiast's flight,
Or from his fairy dreams a vision stole.

III.

His bud of life was then but in its spring,
Mine scarce a *germ* in nature's bloomy wreath,   10
He taught my infant *muse* t' expand her wing,
I taught his youthful heart's first sigh to breathe.

IV.

In sooth he was not one of *common* mould,
His fervid soul on *thought's* fleet pinions borne,

Now sought its kindred heaven sublimely bold,
Now stoop'd the woes of kindred man to mourn.

V.

For in his *dark* eye beams of genius shone
Through the pure crystal of a feeling tear,
And still pale Sorrow claim'd him as her own,
By the sad *shade* she taught his smile to wear.   20

VI.

Though from his birth the *Muses'* matchless boy,
Though still *she* taught his wild strain's melting flow,
And proudly own'd him with a mother's joy,
He only call'd himself "the Child of Wo."

VII.

For still the world each finer transport chill'd
That stole o'er feeling's nerve or fancy's dream,
And when each pulse to *Hope's* warm pressure thrill'd,
Experience chased *Hope's* illusory beam.

VIII.

Too oft indeed, by *Passion's* whirlwind driven,
Far from cold Prudence' level path to stray,   30
Too oft he deem'd that light "*a light from heaven*"
That lured him on to Pleasure's flow'ry way.

IX.

To bliss abandon'd; now pursued by wo;
The world's sad outcast; now the world's proud gaze;
The *vine* and yew alternate wreath'd his brow,
The *soldier's* laurel, and the poet's bays.

X.

Example's baleful force, temptation's wile,
Guided the wanderings of his pilgrim years;
Fancy's warm child, deceiv'd by *Fortune's* smile,
That steep'd th' expecting glance in mis'ry's tears.   40

XI.

The sport of destiny, "*Creation's heir*,"
From realm to realm, from clime to clime he rov'd,

Check'd by no guardian tie, *no parent* care,
For oh! a parent's love his heart ne'er prov'd.

XII.

Yet vain did absence wave the oblivious wand,
One spark still glim'ring in his breast to chill,
Illum'd by Sympathy's unerring hand,
That still awaked his *lyre's responsive* thrill.

XIII.

Though o'er eternity's unbounded space
The *knell* of many a fleeting year had toll'd,   50
And weeping mem'ry many a change could trace
That made affection's vital stream run cold;

XIV.

Yet still those laws *immutable* and true
To nature's void, *attraction's* sacred laws,
Each *spirit* to its *kindred spirit drew*,
Of *sweet effects*, the fond *and final cause*.

XV.

But oh! when cherish'd *Hope* reposed its soul
Upon a new-born *certainty* of joy,
Death from the arms of pending pleasures stole,
And *years* of promis'd bliss, the *Minstrel Boy*.   60

Select Bibliography

A List of Orientalist Sources Cited in *The Missionary*:

[Many of these works appeared in a variety of editions; editions marked with an asterisk have pagination which corresponds to the few page references that Owenson provides.]

Anquetil Duperron, Abraham Hyacinthe. *Législation Orientale*. Amsterdam: Marc–Michel Rey, 1778.

Bernier, François. *Bernier's Voyage to the East Indies. A General Collection of the Best and Most Interesting Voyages and Travels in All Parts of the World, Digested on a New Plan*. Ed. John Pinkerton. London: Longman, Hurst, Rees, Orme, and Brown, 1808-1814. 8: 57-234.

Colebrooke, H. T. *A Digest of Hindu Law on Contracts and Successions; with a Commentary by Jagannát'ha Tercapanchánana*. Translated from the Original Sanscrit by H. T. Colebrooke. 4 vols. Calcutta: The Honourable Company's Press, 1798.

*Craufurd, Quintin. *Sketches Chiefly Relating to the History, Religion, Learning, and Manners of the Hindoos*. London: T. Cadell, 1790.

*Dow, Alexander. *The History of Hindostan, Translated from the Persian*. 3 vols. Dublin: Luke White, 1792.

Forster, George. *A Journey from Bengal to England, Through the Northern Part of India, Kashmire, Afghanistan, and Persia, and into Russia, by the Caspian-Sea*. 2 vols. London: R. Faulder, 1798.

*Grose, John Henry. *A Voyage to the East Indies*. New ed. 2 vols. London: S. Hooper, 1772.

Guyon, Abbé [Claude-Marie]. *Histoires des Indes Orientales, anciennes et modernes*. Paris: Jean Desaint & Charles Saillant, 1744.

Hamilton, Alexander. *A New Account of the East Indies. A General Collection of the Best and Most Interesting Voyages and Travels in All Parts of the World, Digested on a New Plan*. Ed. John Pinkerton. London: Longman, Hurst, Rees, Orme, and Brown, 1808-1814. 8: 258-522.

"Voyage de Bernier au Royaume de Kachemire." *Histoire Générale des Voyages; Ou, Nouvelle Collection de toutes les Relations de Voyages par Mer et par Terre*. By Prevost d'Exiles. 20 vols. Paris: Didot, 1746-1770. 10.2: 92-121.

Institutes of Hindu Law: Or, The Ordinances of Menu, According to the Gloss of Cullúca. Comprising the Indian System of Duties, Religious and Civil. Verbally translated from the Original Sanscrit. With a Preface, by Sir William Jones. The Works of Sir William Jones. [Ed. Anna Maria Jones.] 6 vols. London: G. G. & J. Robinson and R. H. Evans, 1799. 3: 51-470.

Kindersley, N. E. "Introductory Remarks on the Mythology, Literature, &c. of the Hindoos." *Specimens of Hindoo Literature*. London: W. Bulmer, 1794. 1-49.

Shastar, traduit en Français. Untraced.

*Sonnerat, Pierre. *Voyage aux Indes Orientales et à la Chine, fait par ordre du Roi, depuis 1774 jusqu'en 1781.* 2 vols. Paris, 1782.

*[Stockdale, J. J]. *The History of the Inquisitions, Including the Secret Transactions of those Horrific Tribunals.* London: J. J. Stockdale, 1810.

Thévenot, Jean de. *The Travels of Monsieur de Thevenot into the Levant.* "Newly done out of French." London: H. Clark, 1687.

Voltaire, François Marie Arouet de. *Essai sur l'Histoire Générale, et sur les Moeurs et l'Esprit des Nations.* 7 vols. Geneva: [n.p.], 1756.

Other materials:

Arbuckle, Elisabeth Sanders, ed. *Harriet Martineau's Letters to Fanny Wedgwood.* Stanford CA: Stanford UP, 1983.

Atkinson, Colin B., and Jo Atkinson. "Sydney Owenson, Lady Morgan: Irish Patriot and First Professional Woman Writer." *Éire-Ireland* 15 (1980): 60-90.

Bentinck, William Cavendish. *Memorial Addressed to the Honourable Court of Directors by Lord William Cavendish Bentinck, Containing an Account of the Mutiny at Vellore, with the Causes and Consequences of that Event, February 1809.* London: John Booth, 1810.

Berlatsky, Joel. "Roots of Conflict in Ireland: Colonial Attitudes in the Age of the Penal Laws." *Éire-Ireland* 18 (1983): 40-56.

Boylan, Henry. *A Dictionary of Irish Biography.* Dublin: Gill and Macmillan, 1978.

Brewer, William D. "Unnationalized Englishmen in Mary Shelley's Fiction." *Romanticism On the Net* 11 (August 1998): n.pag. Online. Internet. http://users.ox.ac.uk/~scat0385/mwsfiction.html

Byron, Lord (George Gordon). *Byron's Letters and Journals.* Ed. Leslie A. Marchand. London: John Murray, 1978.

—. *Poetical Works.* Ed. Frederick Page. Corr. John Jump. Oxford: Oxford UP, 1970.

Campbell, Mary. *Lady Morgan: The Life and Times of Sydney Owenson.* London: Pandora Press, 1988.

Chatterjee, Amal. *Representations of India, 1740-1840: The Creation of India in the Colonial Imagination.* New York: St. Martin's Press, 1998.

Chorley, Henry F. "Lady Morgan." *The Authors of England.* London: Charles Tilt, 1838. 51-55.

Colebrooke, Henry. "On the Duties of a Faithful Hindu Widow." *Asiatick Researches* 4 (1795): 209-19.

"The Company's Raj." *Blackwood's Edinburgh Magazine* 82 (Nov. 1857): 615-42.

"Copy of a Letter from the Governor General in Council, to the Secret Committee of the Court of Directors, dated 2 November 1807; relating to THE MISSIONARIES." *Papers Relating to East India Affairs.* Ordered, by the House of Commons, to be printed, 14 April 1813. 41-47.

Craufurd, Quintin. *Sketches Chiefly Relating to the History, Religion, Learning, and Manners, of the Hindoos*. 2nd ed., enlarged. 2 vols. London: T. Cadell, 1792.

Curtin, Nancy J. *The United Irishmen: Popular Politics in Ulster and Dublin, 1791-1798*. Oxford: Clarendon Press, 1994.

Dean, Dennis R. Introduction. *The Missionary (1811)*. By Sydney Owenson. Delmar NY: Scholars' Facsimiles and Reprints, 1981. v-x.

Deane, Seamus, gen. ed. *The Field Day Anthology of Irish Writing*. 3 vols. Derry: Field Day Publications, 1991.

Dennis, Ian. *Nationalism and Desire in Early Historical Fiction*. New York: St. Martin's Press, 1997.

Dixon, W. H., ed. *Lady Morgan's Memoirs: Autobiography, Diaries and Correspondence*. 2 vols. London: Allen, 1862.

Drennan, William. *Fugitive Pieces in Verse and Prose*. Belfast: F. D. Finlay, 1815.

Drew, John. *India and the Romantic Imagination*. Delhi: Oxford UP, 1987.

Dunne, Tom. "Fiction as 'The Best History of Nations': Lady Morgan's Irish Novels." *The Writer as Witness: Literature as Historical Evidence*. Ed. Tom Dunne. Cork: Cork UP, 1987. 133-59.

—. "Haunted by History: Irish Romantic Writing 1800-50." *Romanticism in National Context*. Ed. Roy Porter and Mikuláš Teich. New York: Cambridge UP, 1988. 68-91.

Ferris, Ina. *The Achievement of Literary Authority: Gender, History, and the Waverley Novels*. Ithaca: Cornell UP, 1991.

—. "Writing on the Border: The National Tale, Female Writing, and the Public Sphere." *Romanticism, History and the Possibilities of Genre*. Ed. Tilottama Rajan and Julia M. Wright. Cambridge: Cambridge UP, 1998. 86-106.

Fitzpatrick, William John. *The Friends, Foes, and Adventures of Lady Morgan*. Dublin: W. B. Kelly, 1859.

Flanagan, Thomas. *The Irish Novelists, 1800-1850*. New York: Columbia UP, 1959.

Foster, R. F. *Modern Ireland, 1600-1972*. Markham: Penguin, 1989.

Fox, Henry Edward. *The Journal of the Hon. Henry Edward Fox*. Ed. Earl of Ilchester. London: Thornton Butterworth, 1923.

"Glorvina's Warning." *Blackwood's Edinburgh Magazine* 4 (1819): 720-22.

Grant, Charles. *Observations, On the State of Society Among the Asiatic Subjects of Great Britain, particularly with respect to Morals; and on the means of improving it.—Written chiefly in the Year 1792*. Ordered, by The House of Commons, to be printed, 15 June 1813.

Grattan, Henry. "Declaration of Irish Rights (Speech in the House of Commons, April, 1780)." *Irish Literature*. Ed. Justin McCarthy et al. New York: Bigelow, 1904; New York: Johnson Reprint, 1970.

Hegel, Georg Wilhelm Friedrich. *The Philosophy of History*. Trans. J. Sibree. New York: Dover, 1956.

Holy Bible. King James Version. Toronto: Collins, 1975.

Home, Henry (Lord Kames). *Sketches of the History of Man*. 1774. 4 vols. Hildesheim: Georg Olms Verlagsbuchhandlung, 1968.

Hume, David. *An Inquiry Concerning the Principles of Morals.* 1751. Ed. Charles W. Hendel. New York: Bobbs-Merrill, 1957.

Jones, Sir William. "On the Chronology of the Hindus." *The Works of Sir William Jones.* [Ed. Anna Maria Jones.] 6 vols. London: G. G. & J. Robinson and R. H. Evans, 1799. 1: 281-313.

—. "On the Mystical Poetry of the Persians and Hindus." *The Works of Sir William Jones.* [Ed. Anna Maria Jones.] 6 vols. London: G. G. & J. Robinson and R. H. Evans, 1799. 1: 445-62.

—. "Traité sur la Poësie Orientale." *The Works of Sir William Jones.* [Ed. Anna Maria Jones.] 6 vols. London: G. G. & J. Robinson and R. H. Evans, 1799. 5: 433-503.

Kindersley, N. E., trans. "The History of the Nella-Rajah; a Hindoo Romance." *Specimens of Hindoo Literature.* London: W. Bulmer, 1794. 83-328.

Kirkpatrick, Kathryn, ed. *The Wild Irish Girl: A National Tale.* By Sydney Owenson. Oxford: Oxford UP, 1999.

"Lady Morgan." *New Monthly Magazine* 119 (1860): 354-57.

Leask, Nigel. *British Romantic Writers and the East: Anxieties of Empire.* Cambridge: Cambridge UP, 1992.

Leerssen, J. Th. "How *The Wild Irish Girl* Made Ireland Romantic." *Dutch Quarterly Review* 18 (1988): 209-227.

—. "Fiction Poetics and Cultural Stereotype: Local Colour in Scott, Morgan, and Maturin." *Modern Language Review* 86 (1991): 273-284.

—. "On the Treatment of Irishness in Romantic Anglo-Irish Fiction." *Irish University Review* 20 (1990): 251-63.

Lemprière, John. *Lemprière's Classical Dictionary of Proper Names mentioned in Ancient Authors.* 1788. New York: Routledge and Kegan Paul, 1984.

Lew, Joseph. "Sydney Owenson and the Fate of Empire." *Keats-Shelley Journal* 39 (1990): 39-65.

Livermore, H. V. *A New History of Portugal.* New York: Cambridge UP, 1976.

Lloyd, David. *Anomalous States: Irish Writing and the Post-Colonial Moment.* Durham NC: Duke UP, 1993.

Majeed, Javed. *Ungoverned Imaginings: James Mill's History of British India and Orientalism.* Oxford: Clarendon Press, 1992.

"Marriages." *Gentleman's Magazine* 82 (1812): 87.

The Matron of Erin: A National Tale. 3 vols. London: Simpkin and Marshall, 1816.

Maurice, Thomas. *The History of Hindostan; Its Arts and Sciences, as Connected with the History of the Other Great Empires of Asia.* 3 vols. London: W. Bulmer, 1795. Rpt. New York: Garland, 1984.

McLoughlin, Thomas. *Contesting Ireland: Irish Voices against England in the Eighteenth Century.* Dublin: Four Courts Press, 1999.

Mill, James. *The History of British India.* 3 vols. London: Baldwin, Cradock, and Joy, 1817.

Milton, John. *Paradise Lost. The Complete Poetry of John Milton.* Ed. John T. Shawcross. Rev. ed. Garden City, NY: Doubleday, 1971. 249-517.

McGann, Jerome J. *The Poetics of Sensibility: A Revolution in Poetic Style.* Oxford: Clarendon Press, 1996.

Moore, Thomas. *The Letters of Thomas Moore.* Ed. Wilfred S. Dowden. 2 vols. Oxford: Clarendon Press, 1964.

—. *Memoirs of Captain Rock.* 1824. New York: AMS Press, 1978.

Morgan, T. Charles. *Sketches of the Philosophy of Life.* London: Colburn, 1818.

Moskal, Jeanne. "Gender, Nationality, and Textual Authority in Lady Morgan's Travel Books." *Romantic Women Writers: Voices and Countervoices.* Ed. Paula R. Feldman and Theresa M. Kelley. Hanover: UP of New England, 1995. 171-93.

Mullan, John. *Sentiment and Sociability: The Language of Feeling in the Eighteenth Century.* Oxford: Clarendon Press, 1988.

Nairn, Tom. *Faces of Nationalism: Janus Revisited.* New York: Verso, 1997.

Neff, D. S. "Hostages to Empire: The Anglo-Indian Problem in *Frankenstein, The Curse of Kehama,* and *The Missionary.*" *European Romantic Review* 8 (1997): 386-408.

Nussbaum, Felicity. *Torrid Zones: Maternity, Sexuality, and Empire in Eighteenth-Century English Narratives.* Baltimore: Johns Hopkins UP, 1995.

"Obituary: Lady Sydney Morgan." *Gentleman's Magazine* 206 (1859): 537-38.

"Obituary; with Anecdotes of Remarkable Persons." *Gentleman's Magazine* 82 (1812): 594-606.

Owenson, Sydney (Lady Morgan). *The Book of the Boudoir.* 2 vols. London: Henry Colburn, 1829.

—. *The Lay of an Irish Harp.* Philadelphia: Manning, 1807.

—. *The Life and Times of Salvator Rosa.* 2 vols. London: Henry Colburn, 1824.

—. *Luxima, the Prophetess: A Tale of India.* London: Charles Westerton, 1859.

—. *The Missionary: An Indian Tale.* London: J. J. Stockdale, 1811.

—. *The Novice of Saint Dominick.* 1805. 4 vols. 2nd ed. London: Phillips, 1806.

—. *The O'Briens and the O'Flahertys.* 1827. London: Pandora Press, 1988.

—. *Patriotic Sketches of Ireland, Written in Connaught.* 2 vols. London: Phillips, 1807.

—. *Poems, Dedicated by Permission, to the Right Honourable The Countess of Moira.* Dublin: Alex Stewart, 1801.

—. *St. Clair; Or, the Heiress of Desmond.* London: E. Harding, S. Highley, and J. Archer, 1803.

—. *Woman; Or, Ida of Athens.* 4 vols. London: Longman, Hurst, Rees, and Orme, 1809.

Perkins, Pamela, and Shannon Russell. Introduction. *Translation of the Letters of a Hindoo Rajah.* 1796. By Elizabeth Hamilton. Peterborough: Broadview Press, 1998. 7-48.

Pratt, Mary Louise. *Imperial Eyes: Travel Writing and Transculturation.* New York: Routledge, 1992.

Ragussis, Michael. *Figures of Conversion: "The Jewish Question" and English National Identity.* Durham, NC: Duke UP, 1995.

Rajan, Balachandra. *Under Western Eyes: India from Milton to Macaulay.* Durham, NC: Duke UP, 1999.

Redding, Cyrus. "Indian Affairs—Vellore Massacre—Lord Canning." *New Monthly Magazine* 111 (1857): 489-500.

—. "Lady Morgan." *New Monthly Magazine* 116 (1859): 206-16.

"Report of the Commission." 9 August 1806. Bentinck 67-71.

Rev. of *The Daughters of Isenberg: A Bavarian Romance*, by Alicia Tindal Palmer. *Quarterly Review* 4 (1810): 61-67.

Rev. of *Dramatic Scenes from Real Life*, by Lady Morgan, and "Illustrations of the State of Ireland." *Edinburgh Review* 58 (1833): 86-113.

Rev. of *France*, by Lady Morgan. *Quarterly Review* 17 (1817): 260-86.

Rev. of *The Life and Times of Salvator Rosa*, by Lady Morgan. *Edinburgh Review* 40 (1824): 316-49.

Rev. of *Luxima, the Prophetess: A Tale of India*, by Lady Morgan. *Literary Gazette* 2.48 (28 May 1859): 636.

Rev. of *The Missionary: An Indian Tale*, by Sydney Owenson. *British Critic* 37 (1811): 651.

Rev. of *The Missionary: An Indian Tale*, by Sydney Owenson. *Critical Review* 23 (1811): 182-95.

Rev. of *Woman: Or, Ida of Athens*, by Sydney Owenson. *Quarterly Review* 1 (1809): 50-52.

Richardson, Alan. "Epic Ambivalence: Imperial Politics and Romantic Deflection in Williams's *Peru* and Landor's *Gebir*." *Romanticism, Race, and Imperial Culture, 1780-1834*. Ed. Alan Richardson and Sonia Hofkosh. Bloomington, IN: Indiana UP, 1996. 265-82.

Roberts, Nancy. *Schools of Sympathy: Gender and Identification Through the Novel*. Montreal-Kingston: McGill-Queen's UP, 1997.

Said, Edward. *Orientalism*. New York: Vintage Books, 1979.

Salmon, George. *The Indian Mutiny and Missions: A Sermon, Preached on Behalf of the Church Missionary Society, on Sunday, September 5, 1857, by the Rev. George Salmon, F.T.C.D.* With an appendix. Dublin: Madden and Oldham; London: Wertheim and MacIntosh, 1857.

Sha, Richard C. "Expanding the Limits of Feminine Writing: The Prose Sketches of Sydney Owenson (Lady Morgan) and Helen Maria Williams." *Romantic Women Writers: Voices and Countervoices*. Ed. Paula R. Feldman and Theresa M. Kelley. Hanover: UP of New England, 1995. 194-206.

Shakespeare, William. *The Riverside Shakespeare*. Ed. G. Blakemore Evans. 2 vols. Boston: Houghton Mifflin, 1974.

Sharafuddin, Mohammed. *Islam and Romantic Orientalism: Literary Encounters with the Orient*. New York: I. B. Tauris, 1994.

Shelley, Mary Wollstonecraft. *The Letters of Mary Wollstonecraft Shelley*. 3 vols. Ed. Betty T. Bennett. Baltimore: Johns Hopkins UP, 1980.

Shelley, Percy Bysshe. *Letters of Percy Bysshe Shelley*. 2 vols. Ed. Frederick L. Jones. Oxford: Clarendon Press, 1964.

—. "A Defence of Poetry." *Shelley's Poetry and Prose*. Ed. Donald H. Reiman and Sharon B. Powers. New York: Norton, 1977. 480-508.

Sked, Alan. *Decline and Fall of the Habsburg Empire, 1815-1918*. New York: Longman, 1989.

Smith, Adam. *The Theory of Moral Sentiments.* 1759. London: Bohn, 1853; rpt. New York: Kelley, 1966.

Spear, Percival. *India: A Modern History.* Ann Arbor: U of Michigan P, 1961.

Starke, Mariana. *The Widow of Malabar, A Tragedy.* London: Minerva, 1791.

Stevenson, Lionel. *The Wild Irish Girl: The Life of Sydney Owenson, Lady Morgan (1776-1859).* New York: Russell & Russell, 1936, 1969.

Suleri, Sara. *The Rhetoric of English India.* Chicago: U of Chicago P, 1992.

Teeling, Charles Hamilton. History of the Irish Rebellion of 1798 *and* Sequel to the History of the Irish Rebellion of 1798. Shannon: Irish UP, 1972.

Todd, Janet. *Sensibility: An Introduction.* New York: Methuen, 1986.

Tracy, Robert. "Maria Edgeworth and Lady Morgan: Legality versus Legitimacy." *Nineteenth-Century Fiction* 40 (1985): 1-22.

Trumpener, Katie. *Bardic Nationalism: The Romantic Novel and the British Empire.* Princeton: Princeton UP, 1997.

Vertot, Abbé [René Aubert de]. *The History of the Revolutions of Portugal.* London: Longman, Hurst, Rees and Orme, 1809.

Viswanathan, Gauri. *Outside the Fold: Conversion, Modernity, and Belief.* Princeton: Princeton UP, 1998.

Watson, Nicola J. *Revolution and the Form of the British Novel, 1790-1825: Intercepted Letters, Interrupted Seductions.* Oxford: Clarendon Press, 1994.

Whelan, Kevin. *The Tree of Liberty: Radicalism, Catholicism and the Construction of Irish Identity, 1760-1830.* Notre Dame IN: Notre Dame UP, 1996.

Wright, Julia M. "'The Nation Begins to Form': Competing Nationalisms in Morgan's *The O'Briens and the O'Flahertys.*" *ELH* 66 (1999): 939-63.